His Lorship's
True Lady

GRACE BURROWES

Published by Grace Burrowes Publishing, 21 Summit Avenue, Hagerstown, MD
21740.

Cover design by Wax Creative, Inc.

ISBN: 1-941419-55-0
ISBN-13: 978-1-941419-55-7

CHAPTER ONE

"Children, much less three children and one of them a *female*, will not do."
More strongly than that, Hessian Kettering could not put his sentiments, not in
the presence of his niece. "I have no patience with noise, drama, or dirt, while
children delight in all of the foregoing."

Worth Kettering passed Hessian the baby, whose charming attributes
included a penchant for batting at the noses of unsuspecting uncles.

"Lord Evers's will names you as guardian of all three of his minor offspring,"
Worth said, pouring himself a fresh glass of lemonade. "Unless you want to
tangle with Chancery—at considerable expense—then you have become the
legal authority over three children. The boys will remain at school for the rest
of the term, and for the girl, you simply hire a governess or two."

Hessian did not attempt to sip from his own drink with an infant in his arms.
The child was a solid little bundle with her papa's dark hair and brilliant blue
eyes—also a piercing shriek when she was unhappy.

Hessian and Worth were enjoying the morning air on the back terrace of
Worth's London town house, Worth's Alsatian hound panting at their feet. The
breeze was mild, the sun warm, and the plane maples providing just the right
amount of shade.

That Lord and Lady Evers had gone to their reward seemed impossible.
They'd been Hessian's closest neighbors in Cumberland, and Lady Evers had
been a friend.

More than a friend, for a very brief time.

"You raise another issue," Hessian said, nuzzling the baby's crown. Why were babies so wonderfully soft? "Children are expensive, and my coin is limited. I'm spending more than I should on this wife-hunting ordeal. I must have been daft to let you talk me into it. Ah, my niece knows a handsome fellow when she sees one."

The baby was beaming at him, as only a baby could. Angels might exude as rich a benevolence as did one contented infant, though angels didn't grin half so winningly.

"My daughter likes you because you resemble me," Worth said, "and I didn't convince you to come to London. That feat lies squarely at Jacaranda's feet."

Jacaranda being Worth's wife and the mother of the little cherub in Hessian's arms. "Why can't they stay this sweet?"

"Children?"

"The ladies. I can muster a scintilla of patience for an innocent child, but the matchmakers will drive me straight to Bedlam."

Hessian was the current Earl of Grampion, and however impoverished the title and distant the family seat—Cumberland was quite distant—earls were rare prizes, sought after by bankers' daughters, American heiresses, and barons' sisters.

Bachelor earls were also sought after by merry widows and straying wives, about which, some helpful brother might have warned a fellow.

The baby sighed a mighty sigh as if to echo her uncle's sentiments, and Hessian tucked the child against his shoulder, the better to rub her little back.

"Your finances are healthy enough," Worth said, draining his glass. "Especially considering where you were a few years ago. You have a talent for economizing."

Worth was being kind, a tendency more in evidence since his marriage. "Three children will set me back considerably. Do you know how much it costs to launch a young lady in proper society?"

Hessian didn't know exactly, but he'd seen the finery those young ladies sported, the carriages they drove, the millinery they delighted in. He saw their accoutrements at one social event after another, and in his nightmares.

"As it happens, I do know, because that's my daughter you're cuddling so shamelessly, and I've already set aside funds for her dowry."

Babies were made for cuddling, brothers were apparently made for causing problems. "Lady Evers had a sister. Did the will mention her in any regard? Mention any family at all?"

Everybody had family, though Hessian's family was limited to a younger sister, a niece, Worth, Jacaranda, and this darling child. So far. Given the mutual devotion of the baby's parents, she'd have siblings by the score.

Worth scratched the hound's ears. "Lord Evers was the last of his line, save for his sons. The boy Lucas is Lord Evers now, and if you coax my daughter to sleep, I will never forgive you. It's too early for her nap."

"She's tired of listening to your prattling." Hessian rose to take the baby on a tour of the garden, for, like her uncle, she delighted in the out of doors.

The dog looked to Worth, who got to his feet rather than allow Hessian to take the child anywhere unsupervised. Who would have thought Worth Kettering, former prodigal son, would be such a doting papa?

"Lady Evers does have a sister," Worth said. "Mrs. Roberta Braithwaite, wife of the late Colonel Hilary Braithwaite. She's something of a hostess, but being a widow, she's hardly a suitable legal guardian for the next Lord Evers."

Hessian recalled meeting the colonel and Mrs. Braithwaite several years ago at one of the Everses' dinner parties.

"Mrs. Braithwaite won't serve," he said. "All I can remember of her is a tittering laugh and suspiciously orange hair." And that Lady Evers had barely tolerated her older sister.

No help there, for Hessian would not inflict on a small child the company of a woman he'd taken into dislike within five minutes of bowing over her hand.

The dog gamboled ahead to have a drink from a fountain in the back corner of the garden. Hess's own canine had remained in Cumberland, and though he'd had the beast five years and more, he couldn't muster any longing for its company.

"Not only will Mrs. Braithwaite not serve," Worth said, picking up a stick and tossing it over the dog's head, "but the will awards you guardianship of these children. They can visit wherever you please, and the boys will doubtless spend much of the year at public school, but you have sole authority over them and their funds."

Hessian raised his niece above his head for the sheer pleasure of seeing her smile.

"Drop her and I will kill you, Hessian, assuming Jacaranda doesn't beat me to it."

Hessian gently lowered the baby, who was grinning and waving her arms madly. "Your papa is a grouch. When he won't let you have a pony, you tell your dear Uncle Hessian, and I'll buy you an entire team and a puppy."

"Casriel already promised her a pony," Worth said.

Casriel, as in the Earl of, was Jacaranda's oldest brother. Hessian occasionally played cards with him when they were both of a mind to dodge the matchmakers.

"Then Casriel will have to un-promise her. I'm her godfather, and that means—Worth Kettering, you have become positively possessive."

Worth had plucked the baby from Hessian's arms. "Need I remind you, Jacaranda has seven brothers, and at least half of them come around at regular intervals and appropriate my daughter's company without any heed for the child's papa. Hadn't you better run along, Hess?"

"You're my man of business, and that means you have to put up with me. Why should I run along?"

The dog was *in* the fountain now, happily splashing about and creating a great ruckus.

"You should run along because your youngest ward is soon to arrive at your town house, and it's only fair that you give your staff some notice."

Worth's sense of humor was unique—very unique. "The Evers estate is in Cumberland. Why should a small child be dragged the length of the realm for the pleasure of being sent right back north where she belongs?"

"You're her guardian, and thus she belongs in your care. That's what the Evers solicitors said, in any case, but I suspect the staff in Cumberland simply wanted to be free of the little dear at the earliest opportunity. Andromeda, come!"

Hessian stepped back, because only an idiot failed to take into account that wet dogs—

"Damn and blast," Worth bellowed as the dog shook violently, sending water in all directions. The baby began to cry, the dog whined, and for those reasons—not because of a poor jest about a small child invading the Grampion town house—Hessian made his exit through the garden's back gate.

* * *

Lily Ferguson's finishing governess had warned her that a young lady must appear pleasantly fascinated with scandals and engagement announcements, no matter that they bored her silly. Lily was rumored to be an heiress and her late mama had married into a ducal family—albeit an *Irish* ducal family—and thus Lily was doomed to make up the numbers when prettier, more vivacious women were unavailable.

"Aspic and small talk," Lily muttered.

They were equally disagreeable. Fortunately, the Earl of Grampion's dinner party was lively and the general conversation loud enough to hide Lily's grousing.

"I beg your pardon, my dear?" Neville, Lord Stemberger, asked. Because his lordship apparently longed for an early death, he leaned closer to Lily's bosom to pose his question.

At the head of the table, a footman whispered in Lord Grampion's ear. The earl was a titled bachelor with vast estates in the north. Thus, his invitations were coveted by the matchmakers.

Then too, he was attractive. On the tall side, with blond hair that had a tendency to wave, blue eyes worthy of a Yorkshire summer sky, and features reminiscent of a plundering Norseman. Strikingly masculine, rather than handsome.

Perhaps he had bad teeth, for the man never smiled. Lily would ask Tippy for details regarding the Kettering family, for Tippy studied both Debrett's and the tattlers religiously.

Lily had found Grampion a trifle disappointing when they'd been introduced. His bow had been correct, his civilities just that—not a spark of mischief, not a hint of warmth in his expression. Many handsome men were dull company, their looks excusing them from the effort to be interesting, much less charming.

Lily's musings were interrupted by the sensation of a bug crawling on her flesh. Lord Stemberger's pudgy fingers rested on her forearm, and he remained bent close to her as if entirely unaware of his own presumption.

At the head of the table, Grampion rose and bowed to the guests on either side of him, then withdrew.

Excellent suggestion.

Lily draped her serviette on the table. "If you'll excuse me, my lord. I'll return in a moment." Thirty minutes ought to suffice to fascinate Lord Stemberger with some other pair of breasts.

She pushed her chair back, and Lord Stemberger, as well as the fellow on her right, half rose as she departed. So polite of them, when they weren't ogling the nearest young lady or her settlements. Across the table and up several seats, Uncle Walter appeared engrossed in an anecdote told by the woman to his right.

Lily made her way down the corridor, intent on seeking refuge in the ladies' retiring room, but she must have taken a wrong turning, for a raised male voice stopped her.

"Where the devil can she have got off to?" a man asked.

A quieter voice, also male, replied briefly.

"Then search again and keep searching until—Miss Ferguson." The Earl of Grampion came around the corner and stopped one instant before knocking Lily off her feet. "I beg your pardon."

A footman hovered at his lordship's elbow—a worried footman.

"My lord," Lily said, dipping a curtsey. "Has somebody gone missing?"

"Excuse us," Grampion said to the footman, who scampered off as if he'd heard a rumor about free drinks at the nearest pub.

"No need for concern, Miss Ferguson, this has been a regular occurrence over the past week. My ward has decided to play hide-and-seek all on her own initiative, well past her bedtime, after promising me faithfully that she'd never, ever, not for any reason—I'm babbling." He ran a hand through his hair. "I beg your pardon. The child will be found, I've no doubt of it."

This was the polite, chilly host to whom Lily had been introduced two hours ago? "How old is she?"

"Almost seven, though she's clever beyond her years, perhaps due to the corrupting influence of two older brothers. I found her in the hayloft last time, and we'd been searching for hours. The nursery maids don't think she'd leave the house at night."

No wonder he was worried. Even Mayfair was no place for a lone six-year-old at night. "How long has she been missing?"

His lordship produced a gold pocket watch and opened it with a flick of his wrist. "Seventeen minutes, at least. The senior nursery maid tucked the girl in at nine of the clock—for the third time—and was certain the child had fallen asleep. She went back into the bedroom to retrieve her cap at ten, and the little imp wasn't in the bed."

"You could set the guests to searching."

Grampion snapped the watch closed. "No, I could not. Do you know what sort of talk that would start? I'm supposed to be attracting a suitable match, and unless I want to go to the bother and expense of presenting my bachelor self in London for the next five Seasons, I cannot allow my tendency to misplace small children to become common knowledge."

Lily smoothed back the hair he'd mussed, then tidied the folds of his cravat, lest some gossip speculate that he'd been trysting rather than searching for his ward. He was genuinely distraught—why else would he be baldly reciting his marital aspirations?—and Lily approved of him for that.

For resenting the burden and expense of a London Season, she sympathized with him, and for his honesty, she was at risk for liking him.

And that he'd blame himself for misplacing the child… Lily peered up at him, for Grampion was a tall specimen.

"Where is your favorite place in the house?" she asked.

"I don't have a favorite place. I prefer to be in the stables, if you must know, or the garden. When the weather is inclement, or I have the luxury of idleness, I read or tend to correspondence in my library."

His complexion was a touch on the ruddy side, the contours of his features a trifle weathered now that Lily could study him at close range. As a result, his eyes were a brilliant blue and, at present, full of concern.

"Come with me," Lily said, taking him by the hand. "That you found your ward in the stable is no coincidence. You say she's been in your home for only a week?"

Grampion came along peacefully. "She's an orphan, her parents having died earlier this year. The will named me as guardian, and so she was left almost literally upon my doorstep. The poor child was quite close to her mother and barely knows me from among a dozen other neighbors."

"What's her name?"

"Beelzebub, on her bad days. Her parents named her Amy Marguerite, her mother called her Daisy."

Lily dropped his lordship's hand outside the library, which was across the corridor from a formal parlor. "What do you call her?"

He focused on a spot above and to the left of Lily's left shoulder. "Sweetheart, poppet, my dear, or, when I can muster an iota of sternness, young lady."

"Refer to the child as Daisy, but do not acknowledge that she's in the room."

"You believe she's in the study?"

"I'm almost certain of it, my lord, if you frequent the study late at night. You will lament her absence, worry aloud at great length, and confirm to me that losing the child would devastate you."

He considered the door latch. "Devastate might be doing it a bit brown. With practice, I could endure to lose her for ten minutes here and there."

He'd be devastated if the child wasn't soon found. Lily was more than a little worried, and she hadn't even met the girl.

His lordship pushed open the door and gestured for Lily to precede him.

No wonder he preferred this chamber. Books rose to a height of two stories on shelves lining two sides of the room. The windows on the outside wall would look over the garden, and the furnishings were of the well-padded, sturdy variety that invited reading in unusual positions for long periods.

The wall sconces had been turned down, throwing soft shadows across thick carpets, and the hearth blazed with a merry warmth.

A pleasure dome, compared to small talk and aspic.

"We simply can't find her," Lord Grampion announced. "Daisy is very clever at choosing hiding places, and I despair of locating her when she doesn't want to be found."

"Where have you looked?" Lily asked as a curtain twitched in the absence of any breeze.

"We're searching the house from top to bottom, the maids are starting in the cellars, the footmen in the attics. Nobody will sleep a wink until Daisy is once again tucked safely in her bed."

Lily pointed to the curtain, and Grampion nodded.

"She must matter to you very much, my lord, for you to leave your guests and set your entire staff to searching."

"Of course she matters to me. She's the dearest child, and I'm responsible for her happiness and well-being."

His lordship was clearly not playacting. In the space of a week, Daisy had captured his heart, or at least his sense of duty. Many daughters commanded less loyalty from their blood relatives, and nieces were fortunate to have a roof over their heads.

As Uncle Walter so kindly reminded Lily at every opportunity.

"Do you think she might be lost?" Lily asked as his lordship silently stalked across the room. "It's so very dark out tonight. Not a sliver of a moon in the sky."

"Daisy is too clever to be lost," Grampion said, pushing back the curtain. "But she's not too clever to be found."

A small blond child sat hunched on a window seat. She peered up at the earl, saying nothing. Most parents would have launched into a vociferous scold. Grampion instead sat beside the child and tucked her braid over her shoulder.

"I couldn't sleep," the girl said, ducking her head. "I miss home."

"So do I," the earl replied. "Are your feet cold?"

Bare toes peeked out from beneath the hem of a linen nightgown. "Yes."

The earl scooped her up and settled her in his lap. "You gave me a fright, Daisy. Another fright, and you promised not to do this again."

She sat stiffly in his arms, like a cat who had pressing business to be about in the pantry. "Will you beat me?"

"Never."

He should probably not have admitted that, and Lily should not be witnessing a moment both awkward and intimate. She took a step back, and the child's gaze swung to her.

"Who's she?"

Grampion rose with the girl in his arms. "Miss Lily Ferguson, may I make known to you Miss Amy Marguerite Evers, my ward. Daisy, this is Miss Lily."

He'd chosen informal address, which made sense. "Hello, Daisy. The earl was beside himself with anxiety for you."

"Worried," Grampion said. "I was worried, and now I'm taking you up to bed, young lady."

"May I have a story, please?"

Grampion should refuse this request, because naughty behavior should be punished rather than rewarded.

"His lordship has many guests who will all remark his absence," Lily said, holding the door open. "I know a few good stories, though, and will stay with you until you fall asleep."

Grampion led the way up two flights of stairs, pausing only to ask a footman to call off the search. The nursery was lavishly comfortable, but all the furnishings looked new, the toys spotless and overly organized on the shelves.

Where were the girl's brothers, when her toys wanted a few dings and dents?

"You will behave for Miss Lily," his lordship said. "Do not interrupt to ask why nobody has ever seen a dragon, or how dragons breathe fire without getting burned."

"Yes, sir."

"Try to go to sleep," Grampion went on, laying the child on her bed and brushing a hand over her brow. "Miss Ferguson, a word with you, please."

"I'll be right back," Lily told the girl.

His lordship plucked a paisley shawl from the back of a rocking chair and led Lily into the corridor.

"One story," he said, draping the shawl around Lily's shoulders. "No more, or you'll still be reading when the sun comes up. And you may slap me for asking, but are you enamored of Lord Stemberger?"

The shawl was silk, the feel of it lovely against Lily's skin. What sort of bachelor earl kept silk shawls for the nursery maids?

"I am in no fashion enamored of Lord Stemberger. Why?"

"He…" Grampion appeared to become fascinated with the gilt scrollery framing a pier-glass across the corridor. "He did not conduct himself as a gentleman ought at table. Sitting beside him, you might not have noticed where his gaze strayed, but I will not invite him back. He lacks couth."

Lily approved of Grampion very much for speaking up when many other men would have looked the other way or, more likely, guffawed in their clubs over Stemberger's coarse behavior.

Grampion lacked warmth, but he was honorable, and to an orphaned child, he'd been kind.

"See to your guests, my lord," Lily said. "I'll tend to the dragons and be down shortly."

"Miss Lily?" came a soft question from the child's bedroom. "Are you coming?"

Grampion bowed over Lily's hand, his grasp warm in the chilly corridor. "One story. Promise me. The child needs to know I mean what I say."

"One story," Lily said. "One happily ever after complete with a tamed dragon. I promise. Now be off with you."

CHAPTER TWO

Hessian rode along, resentful of the advanced morning hour, resentful of the odd looks from nursery maids and dairymaids alike, resentful of *everything*.

Except the child. He could never be resentful of Daisy. He did resent worrying about her though.

Daisy said not a word, despite having begged for this outing. She'd earned a boon by going for an entire day without running off, destroying a fragile heirloom, or spilling a drink "by accident."

Hessian nodded to a vis-à-vis full of young ladies, all of whom he'd probably danced with, none of whom he recognized. He resented that too—why must London be so full of marriageable young women and so devoid of interesting company?

Daisy sighed, an enormous, unhappy expression in which Hessian mentally joined.

"Shall we return to the house, poppet?" At the plodding walk necessitated by having a child up before him, the day would be half gone before they were home, and yet, this was one way to spend time with Daisy that both she and Hessian seemed to enjoy.

"I like it here. I like the trees."

If Hessian set her down, she'd likely be up one of those trees, thoroughly stuck, before he'd even dismounted.

"When we come again, we can feed the ducks." Every self-respecting earl longed to stand about among quacking, honking, greedy ducks, risking his boots and his dignity at the same time. For her, he'd do it though. In the damned rain if necessary.

His generous offer earned him no reply, but what had he expected? Daisy was becoming a withdrawn child, and that had him close to panic. Her mother had been pragmatic and good-humored. She'd loved Daisy madly, of that Hessian had no doubt.

Daisy sat up so abruptly, the horse halted. "It's the dragon lady!"

A woman in an elegant blue riding habit sat a chestnut mare, a groom trailing her by several yards. Her hair was looped in two braids over her left shoulder, and those braids—glossy auburn, nearly matching the color of the horse's coat—confirmed her identity.

"Miss Ferguson," Hessian said as she halted her mare. "Good day."

Long ago, as a boy quivering to begin his studies at university, Hessian had occasionally accompanied his father to London. He'd known Lily Ferguson then because her uncle and Papa had been acquainted, but the girl Lily Ferguson and this grown version had little in common.

In Hessian's unerring adolescent opinion, little Lily had been a brat; and in her estimation, he'd doubtless been a rotten, self-important prig. The passage of time had wrought substantial improvements on her side of the balance sheet. For all she was petite, Miss Ferguson made an elegant picture on her mare.

She inclined her head. "My lord, and Miss Daisy. What a pleasant surprise. Shall we enjoy the park together?"

The lady's greeting to Hessian was cordial, but upon Daisy she bestowed a beaming, conspiratorial smile. To a small child, that smile would hint of tea parties in the nursery, spying from balconies, and cakes smuggled up from the kitchen.

"Daisy, can you greet Miss Ferguson?" For the child who'd nearly leaped from the saddle at the sight of the lady had remained silent.

"Good day, Miss Lily."

"What is your horse's name, Daisy?"

The girl squirmed about to peer up at Hessian, but he busied himself with turning the gelding to walk beside Miss Ferguson's mare.

"Hammurabi."

"Ah, the lawgiver," Miss Lily said. "What is his favorite treat?"

After several minutes, Hessian realized that Miss Ferguson was asking questions that required answers other than yes or no, and by virtue of patient silences, she was getting those answers. Daisy's replies gradually lengthened, until she was explaining to Miss Lily that the tree branches outside her bedroom window made patterns on the curtains in the shape of the dreaded Hydra from her storybooks.

"That cannot be pleasant when you are trying to fall asleep," Miss Ferguson said. "When next this Hydra tries to prevent your slumbers, you must banish him."

"But the shadows are there, every night. Even if there isn't any moon, the torches in the garden make shadows on my curtains. How do I banish shadows?"

Interesting question.

"You open the curtains of course," Miss Lily replied, "and then you can see that the same old boring trees are in their same old boring places in the garden, night after night. No wonder they delight in dancing when the breeze comes along."

Daisy looked around at the plane maples towering overhead. "They dance?"

"A minuet, I think, unless a storm is coming, and then it's more a gigue. Grampion, do the trees dance up in Cumberland?"

"Oh, routinely. They're almost as lively as debutantes during the first reel of the evening." And ever so much more soothing to a man's nerves.

"My mama danced."

Hessian fumbled about for a response to Daisy's first mention of either parent.

"My mama loved to dance," Miss Lily observed. "I'm an indifferent dancer, though a dear, departed friend once told me that dancing improves if a lady stands up with the right fellow."

"My papa is dead. That means he's in heaven, except he was put in a box when he died. Does the box go to heaven? Like a package?"

Why did this topic have to come up now, without warning, in public, in conversation with a young lady whose company Hessian found a good deal more bearable than most of her kind?

"Perhaps now is not the time—" Hessian began.

"Daisy, do you remember the story about Moses?" Miss Ferguson asked. "He made the sea step aside so he could take his people to safety?"

"I remember."

"Well, the sea doesn't normally have such accommodating manners, does it? Something unexplainable and wonderful was involved, like dragons breathing fire without scorching their tongues. Getting to heaven is something like that. You needn't drag along the part of you that got sick, and had megrims, and suffered nightmares. The forever part of you slips into heaven like Moses dashing right across the sea."

"Wonderful, but we can't explain it," Daisy said, petting Ham's withers. "Only good people go to heaven."

Miss Lily guided her mare around a puddle, and just as the trees overhead were mirrored on the puddle's surface, insight reflected off of Daisy's comment.

Good people went to heaven; therefore, bad little girls did *not* go to heaven, and they thus avoided ending up in a wooden box beneath the churchyard.

No wonder Daisy saw monsters in the night shadows. Quite logical, from a child's point of view.

"Daisy, have you ever had a good dream?" Miss Ferguson asked. "One where you could fly, or glide up the steps without your feet touching the carpet?"

"Yes. I dreamed I was a kite, and I could see all of Cumberland like a bird. It was very beautiful, and I wasn't afraid at all."

"You're an astute little girl," Miss Ferguson said. "You know that was a dream. When you were dreaming it, did you know it was a dream?"

This was all tiresomely abstract—Hess couldn't recall when last he'd dreamed of anything more interesting than a well done roast of beef—but as the horses clip-clopped along, Daisy appeared to consider Miss Ferguson's question.

"I thought I was a kite. I didn't know it was a dream when I was in the sky. When I woke up, I was sorry it was over."

"That is what heaven is like," Miss Ferguson said, "but it's real. When you dreamed, you forgot all about the part of you that was kicking at the covers, or a little chilly for want of an extra blanket. In heaven, you get to keep the good parts—the love, the joy, and the laughter—but you don't have to carry along any of the hard parts."

No vicar would explain death and heaven to the child thus, and Hessian wouldn't either. The words sounded right to him, though, and he appreciated that Miss Lily was making the effort.

Appreciated it greatly.

"Does my mama still love me?"

Hessian could answer that. "Your mother loved you and loves you still, the way Ham loves his carrots. Even when the carrots are stored away in the saddle room, Ham loves them. Even this minute, far from his stall, he's enthralled with the notion of his next carrot. Your parents love you, always, ten times more than that."

Carrots. Not his most inspired analogy. Miss Ferguson hid a smile under the guise of adjusting the drape of her habit over her boots.

"My mare adores a big, crunchy carrot too," Miss Ferguson said. "I'm not that fond of them myself. What about you, Daisy? What is your opinion regarding carrots?"

The ladies chattered back and forth about vegetables, rabbits, and dragons who ate toasted rabbits, and all the while, Hessian wondered how long it would have taken Daisy to ask him about heaven. They ambled beneath the maples, until the horses approached the gate onto Park Lane.

"I have very much enjoyed today's outing," Miss Ferguson said. "My thanks to you, Lord Grampion, and to you, Miss Daisy. You will remember to pull the curtains back, won't you?"

The reminder was for him, though directed at the child.

"We will remember," Hessian said, "and thank you, Miss Ferguson, for bearing us company."

He inclined his head and nearly steered Hammurabi across the street, except he could feel Daisy lapsing back into a silence too brooding for one of her years. With Miss Ferguson, the girl had actually chattered, and if ever Hessian longed to hear a female chatter, it was Daisy.

"Miss Ferguson," he said, "might you pay a call on us Tuesday? I would not want to impose, and I know the Season is demanding of a lady's time, but—"

"Please say you'll come," Daisy said. "Please?"

The smile came again, the soft, sweet, slightly mischievous smile. "I would love to see you on Tuesday, Daisy. I will count the hours until we meet, and I'll want to hear about your dreams then, so be sure they are grand."

"I'll be a kite again," Daisy said. "Is Tuesday soon?"

Well, no. Tuesday was four entire, long, dreary days and nights away. "Soon enough," Hessian said. "My thanks again for your company, Miss Ferguson."

And for aiming just a bit of that dazzling smile at him too.

* * *

"What sort of sister dies as the Season is about to begin?" Roberta Braithwaite asked as she paced the confines of her private parlor. "Most inconsiderate of dear Belinda, but then, she was a trifle on the self-centered side."

Belinda had been the pretty, younger sister. Her death was unfortunate, of course, but then, Belinda would never have to grow old—another injustice.

"The timing of your bereavement is lamentable, ma'am," Penelope Smythe said.

Dealing with Penelope's soft voice, bland opinions, and mousy ways took an endless toll on Roberta's patience, and yet, a widow who lived alone risked talk. Penelope was the companion hired to prevent talk and boredom, though she fulfilled the first office more effectively than the second.

"You have been working on that nightgown since Yuletide, Penelope. What does it matter how many flowers you wear to bed?"

Penelope blushed, which on such a pale creature was sadly unbecoming. "The needlework soothes my nerves, Mrs. Braithwaite. If you'd rather I start on a pillowcase, I'll happily—"

Roberta swiped her finger over the center of the mantel and revealed a thin layer of gray dust. Time to threaten doom to the housekeeper again.

"Spare me your pillowcases. I'll not become one of those pathetic creatures whose parlor is overrun with framed cutwork, lace table runners, and scriptural samplers. The weather is lovely. Isn't it time for your constitutional?"

Time for Roberta to enjoy a solitary tea tray. If Penelope noticed that her walk coincided with the afternoon tea tray, she never mentioned it. Perhaps she met a beau in the park and created her flowery nightgowns with him in mind.

Doubtless, he'd have spots and only one set of decent clothes. His name would be Herman, and at best, he'd clerk for a tea warehouse in the City.

"I've already taken my walk today, ma'am. I happened to see Lord Grampion, and he had a small child up before him."

"Grampion rode out with a child?" The Earl of Grampion was a widower whom polite society claimed had spent too many years rusticating in Cumberland.

"I had no idea he'd remarried."

On one of Roberta's duty visits to Belinda, she'd met Grampion. He'd been a complete waste of good looks on a fellow with about as much warmth as a Cumbrian winter night. He'd put Roberta in mind of the proverbial bishop in a bordello.

And he was guardian of all three of Belinda's children now. Such a pity.

Penelope bent closer to her hoop. "The child bore a resemblance to you, ma'am, though her hair was fair. She was very quiet, from what I could see."

"She bore a resemblance to me? Do you think he hauled my poor Amy Marguerite the length of the realm? Tore an orphaned child from her home with her parents barely cold in the ground?"

"I couldn't say, ma'am."

Then Roberta would consult with somebody who could say, for Grampion turning up in the company of a child was a very great coincidence.

"I have neglected dear Lady Humplewit for too long," Roberta said, moving a candlestick and revealing more dust. "Mourning for my sister has made a complete wreck of my social life, but Dorie Humplewit is an old acquaintance. She'll understand that one needs the occasional breath of fresh air and a cup of tea shared with a good friend."

"You're very fortunate in your friends, ma'am."

Dorie was a hopeless gossip. If Grampion was in Town—how did Penelope know an earl by sight, anyway?—and if his lordship had brought the children south, Dorie would know. She also wasn't stingy with the teacakes or the cordial, and as constrained as Roberta's finances were, both were appreciated.

"You needn't wait dinner for me," Roberta said. "A cold tray in your room will do. I might be going out tonight, and I wouldn't want you to have to dine alone in that drafty dining room."

"Very thoughtful of you, ma'am."

Roberta considered for a moment that Penelope was being sarcastic, but decided that the girl was simply trying to hide her pleasure at being given an evening to herself.

To embroider more flowers on a nightgown nobody would ever see. "Do you know anything about raising children, Penelope?"

The needle paused over the fabric. "I'm the oldest of eight, ma'am, six of them boys."

"You poor thing. One can hardly imagine a worse fate. No wonder your nerves need soothing. Write a letter to your mama and tell her you recall her nightly in your prayers."

"Yes, ma'am, and my papa and my brothers and sister too."

Roberta swept from the parlor, lest Penelope regale her with a list of their very names.

"Come along," Roberta snapped at the maid of all work, who was as usual lingering in the vicinity of the footmen's stairs. "I must change into suitable attire for a discreet call on a friend. Lady Humplewit has sent a note that her spirits are very low, else she would never impose on me so soon after the loss of a dear family member. We must bear up at such times as best we can and think of our friends rather than our own needs."

The maid followed Roberta up the steps a respectful three paces behind, and she did a creditable job of assisting Roberta into a subdued, gray outfit.

"You're excused," Roberta said, choosing a bonnet with a gray silk veil. "Mind you, don't let me catch you ogling the footmen. I will be forced to turn you off without character. A widow can't be too careful, and neither can her staff."

The girl looked suitably horrified, bobbed a deferential curtsey, and fled the room.

Roberta managed not to laugh until the door was closed, though the pleasure of intimidating the help was short-lived. The maid was probably doing a dratted sight more than ogling the footmen, and that was yet another injustice when a widow already had enough tribulations to bear.

* * *

"Grampion is practically your neighbor up in Yorkshire," Lily said. "One ought to be acquainted with one's neighbors."

Devlin St. Just, Colonel Lord Rosecroft, and husband to the most stubborn woman in the realm, sent up a prayer for patience. Emmie had insisted that Lily Ferguson have his escort for this outing, and thus here he was, strolling the boulevards of Mayfair, when he might have been on horseback in the park.

"My dear Miss Ferguson, when next we are in the library at Moreland House, I will find a map of England and instruct you on the geography of the north. York is as much as a week's ride from parts of Cumberland, and that's if the weather's cooperating."

One didn't instruct Lily Ferguson lightly. She was what St. Just's countess called sensible to a fault. Coming from Emmie, who was a monument to pragmatism, that bespoke a prodigious amount of sense. Lily had befriended Emmie several years ago, when the countess was enduring her first London Season, overwhelmed by in-laws, and much in need of confidence.

And thus, Lily Ferguson commanded Rosecroft's loyalty—and his occasional escort. "My lord, would you honestly rather be lounging about, scratching and making rude noises with your brothers while you play your ten thousandth hand of cards? It's a fine day for a visit."

Rosecroft had two extant brothers, or half-brothers, technically. "We no longer make rude noises. Sets a bad example for the children." And the children were a fiercely competitive lot. "Have you taken an interest in Grampion? I'll keep your confidences if you have."

Lily was right about the weather. Spring was at her tantalizing best today, the air mild, the breeze scented with new foliage and possibilities. By tonight, the grass might sport a dusting of snow.

Such were the dubious charms of London at the beginning of the Season, and matters generally went downhill as the year progressed.

"The Earl of Grampion is an acquaintance," Lily said. "His ward is new to London and in need of reliable friends. I think you'll enjoy her company."

In her way, Lily Ferguson was kind. She kept most people at arm's length, though Emmie claimed that was purely self-defense when an unmarried woman was the sole heir to both her mother's and her father's fortunes.

"Madam, I do not befriend sweet young ladies." Rosecroft had sounded like His Grace of Moreland. Maybe that was a good thing?

"You don't befriend much of anybody unless they have four legs, a mane, and a tail. This is Grampion's town house."

The neighborhood was lovely, and the steps had recently been swept and scrubbed, though Grampion's front door lacked even a pot of heartsease. Rosecroft didn't account himself the heartsease-noticing sort, but his countess would have remarked the lack of flowers.

He rapped the brass lion's head knocker, and the door was opened by a liveried footman. "Good day, madam, my lord. Won't you please come in?"

The fellow's wig sat perfectly centered on his head, his buttons shone as brightly as the nearby mirror, and his gloves were spotless.

Rosecroft handed over a card. "If the earl is receiving, Miss Lily Ferguson has come to call."

The footman bowed to a deferential depth and took his leave.

"That chandelier rope would make a fine swing, don't you think?" Lily asked, handing Rosecroft her bonnet. Her cloak and gloves came next, revealing a dress of such drab brown, Rosecroft had seen mud puddles of a more attractive hue.

"My older daughter would be up that rope the instant she had this foyer to herself." Bronwyn was a much-beloved bad influence on her younger cousins, much as Rosecroft had been on their parents. "My countess would notice that the carpets are either new or very freshly beaten, the pier-glass positively sparkles, and the wainscoting has a fresh coat of polish. You notice the nearest means of causing mayhem."

"I was a child once, Rosecroft, several eons ago. Your countess would notice that you're nervous." Lily appeared to be assessing the weight of the chandelier when any other woman would have been stealing a glance at herself in the mirror. "You and Grampion will get on famously, which is to say, you'll nod, exchange the minimum of civilities, and take each other's measure with a glance. Ask him about his stables and I won't be able to get a word in edgewise."

"He has stables?"

Lily smirked and used the toe of her slipper to straighten the carpet fringe.

Rosecroft's countess fretted that Lily needed a bit more airs and graces. Rosecroft was of the opinion that Lily needed a bit more joy. She didn't go through life so much as she perused it from a skeptically amused distance. He himself might once have been said to suffer from the same affliction.

The footman emerged from the corridor. "His lordship invites you to join him in the library. If you'd follow me, please?"

"One doesn't receive callers in the library," Rosecroft muttered.

"One receives friends there. You'd receive callers in your saddle room, if your countess allowed it."

Rosecroft would receive friends in his saddle room. Mere callers wouldn't qualify for such a privilege.

The Grampion library was an inviting space, with more than the usual complement of bound books. The standard appointments were in evidence—globe, ornate fireplace, comfortable chairs, reading table, writing desk—as was a suitably attired earl, though his lordship looked to have gone short of sleep.

"Grampion, good day," Lily said, sweeping a curtsey. "My friend, Devlin, Lord Rosecroft, was good enough to provide me an escort today. Rosecroft, Hessian Kettering, Earl of Grampion. I hope we find you well?"

Rosecroft exchanged bows with his host, all the while evaluating the earl for any spark of interest in Lily, and Lily for any interest in the earl. Grampion was a reasonably good-looking fellow on the settled side of thirty—the most marriageable age in Emmie's opinion—and his manners were correct if not quite gracious.

He and Lily would make a fine pair, all proper decorum. Rosecroft was relieved to form that opinion, but he was disappointed too.

Lily was an orphan who'd been taken in as a girl by her uncle. Life had apparently taught her early that sentiment was a quagmire for the unwary. A union between Lily and Grampion would be based on common sense and, upon that most tepid of consolations, mutual esteem.

Rosecroft could not approve of such an earthly purgatory, but Lily would likely settle for it and not even realize how much the compromise had cost her.

CHAPTER THREE

Lily had seen Grampion at the Duchess of Quimbey's musicale on Saturday night. She'd not approached him for two reasons. First, Uncle Walter had been in attendance, thus ensuring Lily's every move had been discreetly monitored. Second, Grampion had enjoyed a surfeit of female attention. He'd been honest about attempting to attract a good match, which occasioned an irrational spike of disappointment regarding the rest of Lily's social Season.

And yet, this visit had been at his instigation.

"Shall we repair to the garden, my lord?" Lily suggested when the introductions were behind her. "The pleasant weather won't last, so we should enjoy the fresh air while we can."

In the garden, Rosecroft might wander off to sniff hyacinths, the better to spy on Lily from behind the hedges. When choosing her escort for the day, she'd had to weigh benefits and burdens, and Rosecroft's protectiveness—a word used by men to excuse both nosiness and high-handedness—fell into the burden category.

The other option, bringing along dear cousin Oscar, would have been more sensible.

Lily was heartily sick of being sensible.

"The garden?" Grampion's brows drew down. "My roses are many weeks from putting on a display, Miss Ferguson, and the crumbs from the tea tray might attract pigeons."

"The very point, my lord. Where is my dear friend, Miss Daisy?"

Grampion pointed straight up, to the balcony above his head. "I fear Daisy has abandoned me. I'm far too boring a fellow to keep the fancy of such a lively young lady. I would offer to read to her, but she—"

A small blond head appeared over the railing above. "You would read to me? In the daytime? Truly?"

"If you can go for the rest of today without hiding," Grampion replied, "or breaking any valuables, or—"

"Spilling anything," Daisy finished. "Miss Lily is here."

A child ought never to interrupt an adult or be caught eavesdropping. Across the library, Rosecroft pretended to study the globe, but he was doubtless attending every word.

"I promised I would visit today," Lily said, "and I've brought my friend, Lord Rosecroft, with me. Can you come down and make your bow to us?"

Daisy was slow to respond—deliberate, rather, like the earl—and Rosecroft, having the instincts of a veteran papa, knew better than to indicate he sensed the girl was studying him. After a reluctant descent, she scampered across the library to Grampion's side.

"Miss Daisy Evers," Lily began, lest Grampion reprove the girl for dashing about, "may I make known to you my friend, Devlin St. Just, Lord Rosecroft. Daisy is more properly called Miss Amy Marguerite, though that's rather a lot of name for such a little girl. My lord, make your bow."

He did better than that. He bowed over Daisy's hand and offered her a black Irish smile that had doubtless left hearts fluttering across the entire Iberian Peninsula.

"Miss Daisy," Rosecroft said. "You were tempted to slide down that spiral banister, weren't you?"

She peered at Grampion, as if to determine whether such a thing were possible.

"My Daisy would never be so indecorous before company," Grampion replied, smoothing a hand over the girl's crown. "Miss Ferguson suggests we should repair to the garden. I saw a pair of butterflies there earlier, though I'm sure they're gone now."

Daisy towed him toward the French doors, and the sight tugged at Lily's heart. Grampion was trying, making an effort to cheer his little ward, and many men—many adults—would not have bothered.

"What color were they?" Lily asked.

"Blue."

"Blue is my favorite color," Rosecroft observed. "The same shade of blue as Miss Daisy's eyes."

Lily was always surprised when Rosecroft bestirred himself to flirt. His wife had confided that before buying his colors, he'd been an awful rascal, always in demand as an escort, and the best of big brothers to his nine siblings. War had changed him, and not for the better.

Peace, a happy marriage, and the green dales of Yorkshire were working their magic though.

"The earl has blue eyes," Daisy said. "I had a cat that had blue eyes, but Alba fell in love and had kittens in the stable."

Grampion let the child lead him out to the terrace, a space that put Lily in mind of the earl himself.

Not a single leaf lay on the flagstones, the balustrade was in excellent repair, and below the terrace, the garden was divided into tidy symmetric beds arranged around a dry fountain. The whole was pleasing, but… lacking something. Dull, unremarkable, and… uninviting.

Though safe. Daisy would come to no harm playing in this garden, and play she must.

"I have a cat," Lily said. "A more contrary fellow than Hannibal, you never met. When I was younger, I never knew if he was about to scratch me or curl in my lap. Now he mostly sleeps."

Grampion led his guests to the wrought-iron grouping in the sun. "Daisy, if you'd like to return to the nursery, I will look in on you later."

Lily nearly stomped on the earl's toes. "I'm sure Daisy needn't return indoors quite yet."

"Do the mews lie across the alley?" Rosecroft asked.

Thank you, my lord.

"They do," Grampion replied.

"I am a great admirer of the equine. Perhaps Miss Daisy might introduce me to the horses?"

"Hammurabi likes carrots," Daisy said. "I don't like carrots, but I like Ham."

"Then you must introduce his lordship to Hammurabi," Lily said. "Grampion can remain here and enjoy the pleasant air with me."

And also endure a lecture or two.

"One carrot," Grampion said, "and mind you don't get your pinafore dirty."

Rosecroft left with the girl at his side, and Grampion watched them make their way across the garden. The earl had blue eyes, as Daisy had said, and those eyes were worried.

"Rosecroft has a daughter about Daisy's age," Lily said, "and another younger daughter. The novelty of a child participating in an informal social call won't bother him in the least. I had hoped that Daisy and Bronwyn might become friends."

Grampion's gaze remained on the girl even as Rosecroft took her hand and led her into the alley. "Would that be wise, Miss Ferguson? When my objective in London has been accomplished, I'll return to the north, and Daisy will come with me."

Lily wasn't unduly plagued by romantic sentiments—she could not afford to be—but finding a mate should be more than an objective.

"Is Daisy to have no friends because you're determined to rusticate into great old age? Determined to never vote your seat? Never to visit family in

Town as the rest of society does? Should she have been denied even a pet because animals seldom outlive their owners?"

When she'd been not much older than Daisy, Lily had been denied pets, friends, and so much more.

Grampion held a chair for her. "You're very fierce, Miss Ferguson."

And he was very polite. His eyes, an unusual sapphire blue, held nothing but respect. A respectful man was a treasure, if the respect was sincere.

"My parents are both gone, and I have no siblings, my lord." How that half-lie hurt. "If I could have friendship for an afternoon, I'd be grateful. The company of even one friend made a very great difference to me when life became challenging."

Tippy, though a finishing governess, had been an ally when Lily had been without other sources of support.

Grampion lacked friends. This insight came to Lily as she smoothed her skirts and took the proffered seat. Grampion didn't understand the loneliness Daisy was enduring, the way a fish didn't understand water. The earl also lacked extended family, or his dealings with the child wouldn't have been so... tentative, so careful.

"I note you refer to having friends in the past tense," Grampion said, taking the seat beside Lily. "Have you no longer any need of these friends?"

Drat all perceptive men to the mews. "My closest friends are mostly married." And they were all acquired in the past few years, chosen in part for their own recent arrivals in London.

Grampion patted her hand. "You'll marry. We all marry eventually. If we're lucky, we marry one of these friends you esteem so highly, or so I'm told."

Lily wanted to swat him with her reticule, when he was merely offering well-intended reassurance.

"You said you'd come to Town to find a wife." He'd plainly admitted as much, and being a man, his search for a spouse was a commendable attention to duty. When a young woman sought a partner in holy matrimony, she was forward, fast, pathetic, or scheming.

"One comes to London when seeking a spouse," Grampion said. "How long do you suppose it takes to perform introductions to a horse?"

"Rosecroft loves all horses, and he's fond of cats too. I suspect he's allowing us a private moment on purpose."

The rascal. Lily was out of doors with Grampion, and the neighboring houses would have a view of this terrace, in theory. In fact, trees shaded that view, and the servants in the house were not adequate chaperones.

"How do you endure it?" Grampion asked as a green leaf had the effrontery to twirl down from the towering oaks. "How do you endure the relentless matchmaking, speculation, and innuendo? I was married as a younger man, but the situation was..."

He flattened the oak leaf against the table, tracing its veins with a single finger. "The lady and I had known each other for some time, our families were neighbors, and there was none of this... this traveling hundreds of miles for a glorified livestock auction. The young women appraise me as a suitable husband, and the widows have a less honorable end for me in mind."

He was genuinely bewildered by polite society's reception of a titled bachelor. That he'd not mince words—the widows in Mayfair could be more rapacious than Corsairs—pleased Lily.

"Some men enjoy being lionized as a marriage prize," she said. "Some women do too, but never for very long. A man may have many bachelor Seasons, and his value as a husband only increases. A woman can have more than one Season, but she does so at her peril."

Lily's unmarried state caused more talk by the year, all of it unkind. She was too particular, too fussy, too rich, according to the gossips.

Grampion brushed his fingers over a pot of lavender in the center of the table. "You must be very brave, then, to have withstood those perils for more than a Season or two."

What graceful hands he had. "Was that an insult?"

"More of a compliment, I hope. I dread my evenings in polite society, Miss Ferguson. You will think that the boy who once upon a time knew everything has become quite the coward."

A coward did not take a bereaved child under his roof and trouble over her moods and upsets, though Grampion's comment was somewhat unusual. "Do you miss your first wife?"

"Sadly, no. I do not. I daresay if death had befallen me, she'd give the same reply."

Grampion was being honest again, though this honesty was dreadful. For him too. "Perhaps your first experience of marriage will inform your second attempt."

"In such event, may heaven defend the young lady involved. Shall we see what's keeping your cousin in the mews?"

He rose, and Lily accepted his arm. "Will you hare off to the Lakes as soon as you've found a bride?"

"That depends on the bride. If she wants to linger in London, planning a wedding with all the trimmings, she should be indulged. The family seat is in Cumberland, and we'll raise our children there."

Cumberland was more remote than parts of Scotland. Lily envied Grampion the distance from London and the prospect of raising children. He would be a conscientious and involved papa, and he missed his home.

Then too, there were his startlingly blue eyes and his graceful hands. The debutantes were considering his title, while the widows were likely inspecting the man.

Lily could be concerned with neither, though she was determined to do what she could for the girl.

"You must not settle," Lily said, halting their progress at the top of the steps. "You must not offer for a lady simply because you think she'll say yes. Most of them will say yes to the prospect of being your countess. They'll smile and flirt and speak of the honor you do them, while they secretly plan to leave you to your ruralizing after they present you with a son or two. Few of them will take any interest in Daisy at all."

He led Lily down the steps at a decorous pace, as if she'd remarked on the robins flitting about overhead, rather than betrayed her entire gender.

Did Grampion never shout? Run? Curse? Would he be decorous even when consummating his nuptial vows?

"I know why Daisy trusts you," he said. "You are forthright. I admire honesty above all other virtues, Miss Ferguson, and you must promise, as a fellow wayfarer among the perils of polite society, that you will not settle either."

He squeezed Lily's hand, as a cousin or brother might have, or a particularly fond friend.

"My mother married very well," she said, "and my uncle is known to be quite well fixed. He prevents the fortune hunters from bothering me." Uncle Walter prevented the charming, eligible bachelors from bothering Lily as well.

"Then your uncle came too late to his responsibilities," Grampion said. "Some fellow left you disenchanted with the lot of us. I'm sorry for that. Will you promise me that only a man worthy of your regard will have your hand in marriage?"

Nobody else had bothered to apologize for Lily's disillusionment, least of all the transgressor himself. "We will promise each other."

Grampion paused by the dry fountain, which would need a good cleaning before it could be filled.

"Daisy has made my search for a wife more difficult," he said. "The first time I married, I was inebriated on a young man's version of familial duty, honor, and the not incidental pleasures resulting from attending to same."

"Your wife was pretty, your father approved the match." And Grampion had had at least a young man's usual complement of lust. Where had that passion gone, and did he miss it?

"My wife was very pretty, to appearances, and entirely acceptable as a spouse to the young fool who married her. She would not do, though, as Daisy's mama. That realization colors my willingness to propose to the young ladies I've been introduced to so far."

"Good for you, my lord. Daisy will ensure you find a wife worthy of you both."

Grampion studied the fountain, which was a simple three-tiered tower of successively wider bowls. Birds would enjoy it, and the sound would be soothing. Now it held dead leaves and twigs.

"Who will safeguard your choice, Miss Lily?"

He posed the question with a quiet sincerity that called for a humorous response. Lily hadn't any to offer—she was responsible for her own choices, thank you, kind sir—so Daisy's return to the garden was fortunately timed.

"My lord!" Daisy called. "Lord Rosecroft taught Ham a trick! He says yes when I ask if he loves me. He says yes for a carrot, and I can make him do it again!"

Daisy barreled straight for the earl, arms upraised. Not until the last moment did Grampion seem to grasp that the child expected to be lifted into his embrace. He caught her up and perched her on his hip.

"Well done, Daisy. Teaching a fellow to mind the ladies is always a fine notion."

Daisy beamed at this praise, while Grampion's smile provided an answer to a question Lily had mused upon earlier.

The earl avoid smiling to hide crooked teeth. He had beautiful, white teeth and a gorgeous smile. The first debutante to catch sight of that smile would get herself compromised as quickly as she could, and Grampion wouldn't have a clue what he'd done to earn such a fate.

* * *

Lying to anybody did not sit well with Hessian, but lying to a lady was particularly uncomfortable—and Hessian had dissembled with Lily Ferguson, even if he hadn't told outright untruths.

"Why in the name of all that's dear can't the damned Frenchie chef cook a decent beefsteak?" Worth Kettering set his plate aside and took a swallow of wine.

"Try mine," Hessian said, switching plates with his brother. "You never used to be pernickety about your nourishment."

The club's dining room was nearly empty, the Season having only begun. As more families poured in from the shires, the clubs would fill up with temporary residents, and at every hour, the members would be socializing, reading, dining, and avoiding mixed company.

"I'm not pernickety," Worth said, slicing off a bite of Hessian's steak. "This one's at least cooked. I'll take the other home to Andromeda if you don't care for it."

Hessian was too preoccupied to be hungry. "How is Jacaranda?"

"My dearest lady wife is in a taking. She had her heart set on presenting Yolanda to polite society this spring, and Lannie has decided next year will suit better. Lannie said to give you her regards."

Yolanda was their younger half-sister, and she'd dwelled at Grampion Hall with Hessian over the autumn and winter. By agreement among the siblings, she was enjoying the spring and summer with Worth and Jacaranda, and at present taking a respite at Trysting, Worth's country retreat.

"You will convey to Yolanda my approval of her decision," Hessian said. "Polite society is a trial when one has twice her years."

Across the room, laughter erupted at a table of young bucks who'd been drinking since Hessian had sat down to read a newspaper nearly two hours ago.

"You might consider conveying that sentiment to her in a letter," Worth said around another mouthful of steak. "Quaint custom, sibling correspondence. Yolanda didn't want to distract you from your wife hunt."

Letters to Yolanda invariably descended into near accusations of abandonment, which was ridiculous. "Yolanda didn't want to overtax Jacaranda with an infant in the house."

Very likely, Yolanda was being considerate of all and sundry. She was a sweet young lady, and Hessian would miss her when she married.

Another prevarication. He missed her already.

"You will endeavor to find a bride sooner rather than later," Worth said. "I'd like to depart for Trysting early this year. Town will be hot and crowded before too many more weeks go by, and my ladies will fare better in the country."

"You must do as you please, Worth." The wine was barely adequate, the potato as unappealing as the steak. "I cannot promise to find a bride any time soon." In truth, Hessian couldn't promise to find a bride ever.

Worth sat back as the swells at the table by the window went off into whoops about somebody's attempt to serenade a young lady by the full moon and instead waking her widowed mama.

"You have to try, Hess." Worth kept his voice down. "You can't dismiss every woman on the first dance. Many a young widow wouldn't mind winters in the north when there's a title involved. We fellows all look the same in the dark."

Worth was a financial genius, seeing opportunities where others saw only risk and sniffing out risk where others saw certain reward. He'd grown enormously wealthy on the strength of his commercial instincts, and he'd put the earldom's finances on the path to good health as well.

In other regards, dear Worth could be a nincompoop.

"Marriage involves more than groping about in the dark, Worth. In fact, the groping part ceases to hold much interest all too quickly, and then you're left trying to think up ways to avoid meals together."

"I'm sorry. I hadn't any idea your first marriage was so bleak."

Neither had Hessian, until recently. The prospect of remarrying had occasioned some reflection, as had a certain conversation with Miss Lily Ferguson.

The need to find a step-mama for Daisy made taking a bride more urgent, but discussions with Lily Ferguson made Hess less willing to offer for just any good-natured young lady. Daisy's needs were important, and more complicated than he'd first realized.

As were his own needs.

"My first marriage was bearable. Unlike Lily Ferguson, her ladyship never outgrew a penchant for dramatics and mischief. I'll choose more wisely this time, and then you—"

One of the young men had detached himself from the rest of the raucous group doing justice to the club's selection of spirits.

"Grampion, Sir Worth. Good evening."

"Islington." Worth spared the fellow a nod.

Islington had come down from university five or six years ago and thus considered himself quite the rake about Town. His blond hair was done in an elaborate Brutus, and his cravat had likely taken half the afternoon to tie. Neither affectation hid the fact that his waistcoat strained at every button, and his breath would have felled an elephant at forty paces.

"Noticed Grampion riding out with the Ferguson chit the other morning."

Lily Ferguson was not a chit. "The park is lovely this time of year, and Miss Ferguson is excellent company."

Islington remained by the table.

Hess sent Worth a look. Invite him to sit, and I shall kill you slowly and without remorse. Worth busied himself pouring exactly the same measure of wine into both glasses.

Islington grasped his lapels. "Excellent company, yes. Well. Others have thought the same. You're new to Town, and Lily Ferguson isn't. New to Town. You see." He winked, or perhaps an insect had flown into his eye.

Worth cleared his throat.

"I'm not sure I take your meaning," Hessian said, "me being new to Town and all."

Islington leaned closer, bringing with him the stench of prolonged overimbibing. "The damned girl looks well enough, and she's bound to have decent settlements and all, but she's much too outspoken. Much. One of them unnatural daughters of Sappho, if you take my meaning. You'll want to look elsewhere, whether you're thinking to marry or otherwise keep company with the lady."

He winked again.

Lily was honest and sensible, and among people suffering a paucity of useful ambitions, this was the thanks she got. Gossip from fools, probably years after she'd offered some buffoon a set-down for leering at her bodice.

Hessian rose, and Worth set the wine bottle on the opposite side of the table.

"Islington, you accurately perceive that I am the veriest bumpkin of an earl. I do so love my acres up in Cumberland."

"Pretty place, Cumberland, so I'm told. Don't think I'd care for it."

The group across the room had fallen silent, as had the several other tables of diners in the room. That was fine. Good, in fact, for what Hessian had to say was not private.

"The benefit of all the ruralizing I've done is that I spend many a morning tramping about with my fowling piece, and I feel it only fair to warn you, I am a dead shot."

"Dead shot," Worth echoed. "I've never seen Grampion miss a target when sober, and his lordship is always sober."

In fact, Worth hadn't seen Hessian so much as lift a firearm in the past ten years, much less take aim at a hapless pheasant going about its avian business.

"I'm sober now too," Hessian said, "while you must be given the benefit of gentlemanly tolerance, considering how assiduously you've been at the spirits."

"Doesn't do to remain sober after sundown." Islington's confreres hooted their agreement with that profundity.

"Doesn't do to malign a lady's good name either," Hessian said. "Particularly when she's not on hand to defend herself against the charges."

The hooting stopped, but Hessian wasn't finished. "In fact, Islington, were you not half seas over, I'd offer you a demonstration of my accuracy with a firearm on the field of honor. Lily Ferguson is a lady, and if dunderheaded young men speak out of turn within her hearing, then I applaud her for calling such specimens to account. How else will they mend their ungentlemanly ways before more serious harm is done?"

"Serious harm?"

The last word had come out on a gratifying, if malodorous, squeak.

"I'm glad you take my point. Perhaps a bit of fresh air will help clear your head. We wouldn't want your drunken maunderings to give anybody reason to take offense."

Hessian remained on his feet, several inches taller than Islington and years more willing to put his fists where his honor lay.

Worth made a little shooing motion with his hand.

Islington backed away from the table, until he bumped into the next table, which was empty. He turned and strode from the room, his friends watching his departure in silence.

"Well done." Worth saluted with his wineglass. "The boy needed a talking-to."

Hessian resumed his seat. "He's not a boy, and if he gossips about decent young women, he's not a gentleman either."

"So," Worth said, placing the wine bottle by Hess's elbow. "Tell me about Lily Ferguson and this little ride in the park."

To discuss the situation with Worth was a curious relief. "Lily Ferguson is kind, honest, and practical. She's taken an interest in Daisy, and I account Miss Ferguson a friend."

Worth frowned at the remains of his brother's steak. "Papa knew her Uncle, as I recall, and I have vague memories of teasing her in the park as a boy. Is she pretty?"

She was beautiful, when she was peering up at Hessian in the midday sunshine, exhorting him to choose wisely or not at all. Her hair was all dark fire and soft embers, her hands both competent and elegant. Her eyes changed color with her moods and attire, going from agate to smoky gray.

Those eyes bore the steady regard of a woman who knew who she was and what she wanted in life.

So why did that woman dress in the most unprepossessing ensembles ever sewn by a Mayfair modiste? As a girl, Lily Ferguson had been vain and fussy. As a woman, she aspired to out-nun the most devout Papists for drab attire.

"Miss Lily is comely," Hessian said, "though she doesn't trouble over her appearance inordinately. Do we endure the apple torte here, or cast ourselves on the mercy of your cook?"

Worth tossed his serviette on the table. "Walk me home, and I'll introduce you to a raspberry trifle that will make you glad you're old enough to spoil your dinner at will."

"I do not approve of gluttony, Worth."

Worth signaled the waiter to wrap up the uneaten meat for Andromeda.

Worth was collecting females, while Hessian had Daisy, and the prospect of bringing her up under his roof was such an unlooked-for boon, Hessian couldn't muster any envy toward his brother.

Toward anybody.

On the walk to Worth's town house, Hessian wondered what color Miss Lily Ferguson's eyes would be if she decided that what she wanted out of life was to become the Countess of Grampion. When her husband made love to her for the first time, would she allow him to leave enough candles lit that he could discern the passion in her gaze?

Had he been a betting man, Hessian would have said yes. Lily Ferguson would not have allowed her husband to settle for groping in the dark. Married to her, a man would be required to make love and to acquit himself to the lady's complete satisfaction.

Lucky fellow.

CHAPTER FOUR

"Only a brave hostess holds a garden party this early in the Season," Emmaline, Countess of Rosecroft, said.

"Or a foolish one," Lily replied. She was attending the Chuzzleton gathering because Uncle Walter had insisted. Somebody had to show the Ferguson flag, or Mrs. Chuzzleton—who had both eligible sons and a widow's interest in Uncle Walter's fortune—would issue invitations until the Thames froze over.

Somewhere on the premises, Oscar was doubtless swilling punch at a great rate, pausing only to flirt with young ladies or dally with a straying wife. Sensible people lingered near the tents in case the clouds that had been threatening all morning decided to water Mrs. Chuzzleton's flowers.

"A pity the Holland bulbs did not accommodate Mrs. Chuzzleton's social schedule," her ladyship said, twirling her parasol.

The countess—who insisted Lily call her Emmie when they were private—had married very much above her station when she'd spoken her vows with Rosecroft. She was thus well outside the circle of ladies who might have known Lily as a girl. Her ladyship was also unlikely to note minor lapses of deportment in a woman all of society thought headed for life on the shelf.

The shelf loomed in Lily's awareness like a patch of the Promised Land, and she prayed nightly that Uncle Walter's plans for her included decades of peace and relative independence in obscure spinsterdom.

"The tulips must have been spectacular," Lily said, though now, past their prime, they looked... pathetic. Stems without flowers, petals rotting on the dirt, leaves soon to follow.

"Shall we see if the buffet has anything to offer?" her ladyship suggested. "I'm not that hungry, but this breeze has become too refreshing."

The buffet sat beneath a tent at the foot of the garden. "God forbid we should suffer rosy cheeks from an abundance of fresh air."

The tent would be as stuffy as the garden was chilly, with everybody packed in too closely, speaking too loudly, and discreetly spilling their punch on one another's slippers when they realized how liberal Mrs. Chuzzleton had been with the sugar.

"Is something amiss, Lily?"

Well, yes. As Rosecroft had handed Lily out of the coach, he'd quietly conveyed that Werther Islington would be taking a repairing lease for the foreseeable future. Lily had no idea what his lordship had been going on about. Islington was a bachelor from a decent family, so he showed up in the predictable locations looking overfed and acting under-couth.

"Do you know a Mr. Werther Islington?"

Her ladyship's parasol stilled. "He's friends with Rupert Sharp."

That explained it. Rupert, who was anything but sharp, had got the benefit of Lily's insight regarding his marital prospects two years ago, and what young men lacked in brains, they made up for in wounded pride. Uncle had been wroth with her, though Uncle was equally disapproving of Lily's rare friendly impulses toward the bachelors.

And there was Rupert's mama, hovering over the sandwich table just inside the tent.

"I'm off to find the ladies' retiring room," Lily said. "You needn't join me. It's too early for the rakes to be out of bed, and the fortune hunters are all swarming about the free food and drink."

"True enough. I'll find Rosecroft, and we can tear ourselves away from this bacchanal despite its endless blandishments."

"I'll meet you in the mews. Give me five minutes."

Five minutes to sit in peace and quiet, while the throbbing in Lily's head eased and her sense of impatience with a wasted day ebbed. Tomorrow, she would take Bronwyn to meet Daisy, and that—turning a pair of little girls loose in a nursery full of dolls—held far more appeal than any of polite society's gatherings.

Retiring rooms were usually on the first floor, so inside and up the main stairs Lily went. The staff was doubtless busy with the guests in the garden, and the quiet in the house was welcome.

Seeing neither maid nor footman from whom to ask directions, Lily took the first turning and ran smack into the Earl of Grampion.

"She's after me," he said, glancing over his shoulder. "Thank God you found me."

"Who's after you?"

"The Humplewit creature," he said, taking Lily by the hand and leading her along the corridor. "She has eighteen hands, her teeth are filed to sharp points, and her prehensile tongue could reach right into a man's exchequer, there to secure the contents into her permanent possession."

Footsteps sounded from the opposite direction.

Grampion pulled Lily into an alcove, where the scent of hyacinths blended with fresh greenery. A replica of the Apollo Belvedere wore a garland of ivy around his shoulders as he peered out into the gardens, the stone embodiment of male perfection.

Grampion was a good deal more interesting.

"Dorie Humplewit is a known flirt," Lily whispered as the footsteps came closer. "You mustn't think anything of it."

"I am a known unwed, titled bachelor. Do you know how easily—?"

"Oh, Gram-pee-un! Gram-peeeeeee-un!" a woman called. "Mustn't be coy, my lord!"

The earl tugged loose a velvet drape so it shielded one side of the alcove, then wrapped his arms about Lily and turned, putting his back to the corridor.

"I'm sorry," he whispered. "She mustn't see you." His hand cradled the back of Lily's head, and though he'd taken her by surprise, Lily had sense enough to remain in his arms.

Heavenly choruses, he knew how to hold a woman. Everything lined up as nature intended, and Lily nearly screeched with the frustration of not embracing the earl in return. She kept her arms at her sides, lest any part of her be visible from the corridor.

"I know you're here somewhere," Lady Humplewit cooed. "No need to be shy, my lord. We're both adults and know what we're about."

Grampion had wrapped one arm about Lily's waist. The other held her so her forehead rested against his chest. She was entirely supported, entirely hidden from view, and entirely undone.

He pressed closer, so they were both shielded behind the loose drape. Lily breathed in the scent of him—shaving soap that hinted of cedar, lavender from a freshly laundered shirt, a whiff of starch from his cravat, and mint from his toothpowder.

He was particular about his hygiene, and his height came with a good deal of muscle. He was warm too, a lovely pleasure after the chilly garden. Lily relaxed against that warmth as the footsteps faded.

"Thank God," Grampion muttered.

And still, he did not let Lily go, and neither did she try to leave his embrace.

* * *

Lily Ferguson was lovely to hold. The male part of Hessian's brain, which he'd ceased paying attention to within a year of his marriage, didn't notice Lily's curves and softness so much as it consumed them like a beggar devours a feast.

Her shape—diminutive, but unmistakably an adult female in great good health—made a general impression while Hessian reacquainted himself with details of female anatomy long forgotten. The nape of a woman's neck was exquisitely soft beneath the pad of his thumb, and the back of her head fit his palm as if his hand were made for that purpose.

She could turn slightly and allow a more snug fit of his body to hers, and where his chest was flat, hers was… not.

Soft, full, feminine… Hessian had wrapped the lady close lest his hands wander where they must not.

Lily's lack of height was a revelation. The first Countess of Grampion had been tall and willowy, exuding an aura of frailty, for all her determination to wed him. Hessian had feared mishandling her and then lost any interest in handling her at all.

He had lost interest in turning Lily Ferguson loose. Small but mighty came to mind, for her shape was quintessentially feminine. She remained quiescent in his embrace as the threat of discovery faded and silence returned.

Hunger was a problem solved with a meal. The feelings plaguing Hessian spoke of deprivation so long entrenched as to wrench normal reactions from his grasp. He wanted to swive Lily Ferguson, and he wanted to hide her away at Grampion Hall through a succession of long, passionate winters.

Which would not do.

Just as he might have let go of her, she hugged him. "You've had a fright. Perhaps I underestimate Lady Humplewit's intentions where you are concerned."

Lily couldn't step back because of the wall. Hessian let her go, and rather than drop his gaze to locations a gentleman didn't study, he put his hands in his pockets and admired Apollo's toes.

"Lady Humplewit claimed to be in search of diversion, though I suspect becoming my countess would fit that description for her."

Lily moved away from the wall. "You are not in search of diversion. I like that about you. I'm prone to the same shortcoming."

Hessian wanted to wrap his arms around her again. "To regard life as a gift to be cherished rather than an endless, privileged boredom to be endured is a shortcoming?"

Lily twined her arm with his. "I suspect we have more than those two options, and we might be able to cherish the gift while occasionally indulging in a morning on a pirate ship."

Arousal never did much to improve a man's intelligence, though it could certainly sharpen his senses. "I beg your pardon?"

"Had you forgotten I'm bringing Bronwyn to play with Daisy tomorrow?"

Holding Lily, Hessian had forgotten where Cumberland was. "I will look forward to your visit." He'd count the hours. "Shall we return to the garden?"

"Yes, for I must take my leave of our hostess, and you must attach yourself to some old fellow who needs a sympathetic ear regarding his gout. Colonel Dingle is reliably infirm. The widows will avoid his company, and thus you'll be safe."

Hessian promenaded along, when he wanted instead to stick his head out the window and shout, I cannot play this role!

Could not dodge widows, dance with debutantes, and deal with society's expectations for three more months.

Neither, however, could he continue to neglect the earldom's succession. Worth had put the Kettering finances to rights, more or less, but as Worth had pointed out, even with both brothers applying themselves to the challenge, nothing guaranteed a son would be born.

With only one brother married, the odds of a legitimate heir were halved.

"I must apologize for imposing on your person," Hessian said as they reached the bottom of the stairs. "Had we been found conversing alone, gossip would have ensued."

His capacity for mendacity was growing apace, for he was not in the least sorry to have held Lily Ferguson in his arms.

"Lady Humplewit needs a credible reason to be wandering the corridors of the house alone if she's to spread gossip about you accosting me. I gather the ladies' retiring room is not on the first floor?"

"The gentlemen's retiring room is upstairs, suggesting the ladies' would be on the ground floor. Lady Humplewit was plainly lying in wait to ambush me."

She'd nearly succeeded. Hessian had asked if he could be of assistance, and she'd latched on to his arm like a rowan tree sinking roots into the face of a precipice. He'd shaken loose and trotted off ostensibly in search of a housemaid.

And his freedom, of course.

"Too bad you haven't a sister here to guard your back," Lily said. "You do have a brother in Town, though."

"We were estranged for many years, but yes, I have a brother. Worth is disgustingly happy with his lady wife, besotted with his daughter, and I suspect more fond of his dog than he is of me. He's directed me to find a countess so he might repair to his country estate posthaste. I'm whining."

Also being honest, because Worth's leap into the joys of holy matrimony had come just as Hessian had made the effort to repair a familial breach of many years' standing. That breach was healed—or at least repaired—in part because Worth no longer clung to his status as an earl's disenchanted younger brother.

Worth had become entirely the creature of his womenfolk, and made it appear like a damned happy fate too.

"You look so severe when you're lost in thought," Lily said as they approached the door to the garden. "And yet, I've seen you smile."

"I will smile when I recall the moments spent with you and Apollo in that alcove. You are a good friend, Lily Ferguson. I again apologize for embroiling you in my troubles."

"No apologies necessary. Prepare to weigh anchor and repel boarders tomorrow at two of the clock, my lord."

She sailed off in the direction of the tent at the foot of the garden, a small craft of a female sturdy enough to navigate any storm, even as the wind whipped at her skirts and a fine mist began to fall from the sky.

* * *

"Why didn't I kiss him?" Lily could pose that question because Emmaline was a reliable confidante, and Bronwyn had insisted on riding up on the box. With Rosecroft as her de facto papa, Bronwyn had probably charmed the reins away from John Coachman before the carriage had left the mews.

Emmaline drew the shade down on her side of the bench, even though the sun was on Lily's side. "Maybe you didn't kiss the earl because you are a lady?"

"Don't be obtuse. I am the niece of the Honorable Walter Leggett, a woman of mature years. I am not prone to missishness or dithering." To be held by Grampion had been so... sweet. And frustrating. "I have a normal complement of curiosity, though, and would prefer not to die without having even once kissed a man whom I esteem."

And desire, of all the inconvenient realizations.

"You're prone to common sense, Lily. You can't go around kissing stray earls and have any sort of reputation left."

Grampion wasn't stray, or dashing, or flirtatious. He was the least sentimentally romantic man Lily had encountered in years, and yet, she regretted not sampling his charms.

"The right earls don't kiss and gossip," Lily said as the coach rattled around a corner. "I do believe Winnie's at the ribbons."

"Her hair will be a fright before we arrive."

Though Emmaline would have brought a comb and spare hair ribbons. She was so unassuming, so unconcerned with impressing anybody but her husband, that her preparedness for any situation was easy to overlook. She would not have missed an opportunity to share a stolen kiss with a man she fancied though. The countess was as determined as she was quiet.

"Didn't you ever long to have somebody muss your hair, Emmie? Long for somebody to tempt you from the path of propriety?"

"Yes. That's why I married Rosecroft."

The horses slowed to a walk.

"Yes? He mussed your hair, so you gave him your hand?"

"More or less, but if you'd asked me prior to my marriage, I'd have said the view when one strays is so often disappointing."

Emmaline had been immured in rural Yorkshire prior to her marriage.

"Then one isn't straying properly."

"You've done a deal of straying, Lily, to offer that opinion? Perhaps conducted a survey on the topic?" her ladyship asked as the coach rocked to a halt.

"I have been a pattern card of probity." *As far as anybody knows.*

The groom opened the door, and Bronwyn peered inside. Though she wasn't related to Rosecroft, she bore a resemblance to him: swooping brows, snapping eyes, and an air of brisk command, though she was barely of age for the school room.

"We're here," she said. "I drove almost all the way, and John Coachman says I'm ready to put the Four-In-Hand Club to shame."

"Do you suppose you'd hurt their feelings?" the countess asked as the footman handed her down.

"I might hurt their horses' feelings, if I won all the races," Bronwyn replied. "I'd be sure to win by only inches."

"Very thoughtful of you," Lily said, climbing out and taking the girl's hand. "Miss Daisy hasn't a pony, so you must not boast of your skill at the ribbons or in the saddle. You wouldn't want to provoke her to envy."

Though a little childish jealousy might be a relief from grief and homesickness.

Bronwyn took Emmaline's hand and tugged both ladies toward the door. "I will be kind to the less fortunate. Her Grace says all ladies are kind to the less fortunate. Miss Daisy hasn't got a papa or a mama or a pony, and I don't know what could be less fortunate than that."

She hasn't a cat either, though she does command the devotion of at least one earl.

Grampion met them in his library, apparently his favorite place to receive callers. When introductions had been made all around, and Emmaline had ushered the little girls into the garden, Lily was once again left alone with the earl.

Emmaline was something of a strategist too, thank the heavenly powers.

"You're smiling," Lily said, though it was the most subdued version of Grampion's smile she'd seen. "Does that mean you're recalling a moment shared with me and the Apollo Belvedere?"

The smile became more complicated. "And if I am?"

Lily had done little else besides recall that moment and regret that she'd not made more of it, despite all common sense to the contrary. She drew Grampion away from the French doors, went up on her toes, and kissed him.

* * *

Hessian had slept badly. The incident with Lady Humplewit had tempted him to pack up Daisy, his belongings, and his correspondence, and head north at a brisk gallop. Cumberland was breathtaking in any season, but Cumbrian summers were beyond description.

Two thoughts had stopped him from fleeing London, the first being duty.

Always duty. In this case, the duty to notify Worth of his departure meant enduring lectures such as only a happily married younger brother could deliver on the subjects of connubial bliss and the joys of fatherhood.

The second factor discouraging Hessian from tucking tail and decamping for parts north was now kissing him witless.

Lily Ferguson was a puzzle. She marched about, exuding pragmatism and self-possession when, in fact, she was full of passion and contradictions. In the silence of the library, her kiss shouted her desire for him. She melded her body to his—all the best curves in all the best places—and fisted her fingers in his hair.

As if he'd be able to resist her overtures? The last person with whom Hessian had attempted more than a fleeting encounter had been Daisy's mama, and that had been friendly, a little awkward, and ultimately bewildering.

Lily Ferguson was not bewildered. She was a woman intent on plundering Hess's self-restraint. She was making excellent progress toward her goal too.

Lily knew what she was about—almost. Her kisses were bold, her grip on Hessian bolder, and yet, he tasted a hint of rage in her ardor. Her kiss communicated desire, but also the loneliness and self-doubt that went with years of not being desired by anybody. Years of making up the numbers, being invited for the sake of courtesy, and being danced with out of politeness.

Hessian well knew the tribulations endured on the margins of polite society, and Lily deserved so much more. He gathered her close, reveling in the abundance of womanliness in his arms. The particular rustle of fabric when she pressed nearer and her soft sigh when she was unapologetically embraced told him she wanted to be not only desired, but also cherished.

Hessian longed to give her that and more. He started with a soft swipe of his tongue, and Lily startled, then settled in to investigate, reciprocate, and explore.

He stroked his fingers over her nape, and some of her desperation eased. Her first forays into a deeper kiss were tentative, and in his response, Hessian assured her that she could take her time and linger over her discoveries.

As he lingered over his.

Lily used no padding, no excesses of corsetry. She might be wearing a double chemise or jumps instead of stays, her shape was so genuinely evident beneath his hands. Her shoulders, back and arms were sturdy, and the thought of her legs wrapped around Hessian's flanks…

He eased out of the kiss, but not out of the embrace.

"Why did you stop?" Lily's question was adorably disgruntled.

"I don't pretend to know much about children, but I have younger siblings. Worth's greatest talent growing up was coming upon me when I was most in need of solitude. The children would not abandon us here for long, and I was growing…"

He shifted his hips, enough that Lily would feel the results of their intimacies—a rousing salute to pleasures too long ignored.

"You're...? From kissing me?"

Lily was delighted with herself, and Hessian was delighted with her too. "I hope you are similarly carried away, else I shall have to reconsider my technique."

She patted his lapel and stepped aside, studying the shelves to the right. According to Hessian's organizational scheme, she'd become fascinated with etymological treatises.

"I wanted to kiss you," she said, taking down a slender red volume.

Hess wanted to nuzzle the place where her neck and shoulder joined. She'd smell good there—good there too—like flowers and mischief. He stared hard at the molding, except smirking Cupids were not the stuff of regained self-control.

"I account myself singularly well favored to have been the recipient of your overtures."

Lily opened the book, which was written in French. "Does that mean you liked kissing me?"

In the garden, somebody shrieked, a happy noise that suggested happy relationships were blossoming all over the property. And yet, Lily's question had been genuine rather than coy.

"I like you, Lily Ferguson. For a first effort, I liked our kiss. You needn't fret that I'll take you to task for a pleasure about which we both grew enthusiastic."

"This book on insects is easier to translate than your lordly pronouncements. What do you mean for a first effort you liked our kiss?"

In bed, Lily would be fearless. She wouldn't ask for what she wanted, she'd demand it and give as good as she got.

Hessian risked repositioning a curl that lay against her neck. "I mean, I'm out of practice. I suspect you are too."

She paced off, book in hand. "I'm not in the habit of accosting men to kiss them, or for any other purpose. Yesterday surprised me."

He wanted to chase after her, to get his hands on her, touch her hair, her clothes, her bare skin, and put her hands on him. In defense of his ability to hold a conversation, he withdrew to the hearth and propped an elbow on the mantel.

"You aren't fond of surprises. Neither am I." And yet, as the sharp edge of desire faded, heat lingered. Hessian was awake in a way he hadn't been before Lily had kissed him. His senses were keener, his imagination focused on matters other than correspondence, social invitations, and Daisy's concerns.

"Surprises can be good," Lily said, running her finger down a page of French. "You took me in your arms yesterday, so Lady Humplewit wouldn't see me. You smell of goodness. I can't think when you put your arms around me."

Hessian could think—of beds, pillows, naked limbs, and pleasure. "Sometimes, to abandon reason for a moment is a relief. I'd forgotten that.

You never used to be able to stand even the sight of a bug, and now the subject appears to fascinate you."

He'd forgotten so much that was good and sweet.

Lily snapped the book closed. Her stillness vibrated with more unpredictable, interesting questions—and with anxiety?

"I wasn't able to abide the sight of a bug?"

"I was raised with only one sister, but I suspect few girls enjoy insects. I'm glad you kissed me." Hessian hoped that was what she needed to hear, because it was the truth. "I enjoyed kissing you. I've grown duller than I realized, which was dull indeed, and content in my dullness. Lily, I thank you for… for your interest. You needn't worry that I'll develop expectations or spread tales. For a moment, a butterfly lit on my windowsill, and she must be allowed to flutter off and be about her business, if that's what she wishes. A gentleman never presumes on a lady's favor."

Good God, he was making a hash out of what was meant to be a compliment.

Lily clutched the book with a curious desperation. "A butterfly, my lord?"

My lord was not good, but if Hessian took her in his arms again, then the sofa before the hearth would become the scene of a debauch. If Lily were to lie back against the pillows, then Hessian could brace himself—

He studied the spiral staircase, but even those curves were fraught. "My point, madam, is that a stolen moment needn't become the basis for any worries on your part. I'm not Lady Humplewit, to take advantage of another's trust."

Lily turned her back to him, which was no damned help at all. Some of her hair was in a soft, twisty bun, and some of it curled over her shoulder, a perfect metaphor for Hessian's emotional state. He was half pleased and half embarrassed to have taken liberties with a lady's person.

Though she'd taken liberties with his person too, and about that he was delighted. He resisted the temptation to adjust his falls, though the nape of Lily's neck was stirring him in exactly the wrong direction.

He'd taken two steps closer to her when voices on the terrace stopped him.

Lily tossed him the book. He sat and opened it to a random page, the rising evidence of his wayward thoughts hidden behind a chapter titled "Common Butterflies Native to Southern Britain."

Lily sank into a chair two yards away and folded her hands in her lap just as Daisy, her guest, and Lady Rosecroft came through the French doors.

"The upper side of the male's wings are the same blue as hyacinths in bloom," Hessian said. "The underside is a grayish-brown, and red spots adorn his hind wings." He stared at the book as if reading, though the topic on the page was a biographical sketch of some French lepidopterist. "The markings on the female are less uniform across individuals, but are no less attractive for being more subtle and unique."

"Thank you," Lily said. "Your translations are quite enlightening. Bronwyn, is that a grass stain on your pinafore?"

The children chattered, the countess fussed, and Lily did a creditable imitation of a woman slightly bored with a visit that was more charitable than social. Hessian pretended to turn the pages of the book and occasionally volunteered an answer to a childish inquiry. When it was time for the guests to take their leave, he saw them to the door and thanked them cordially for paying a call.

He even invited Miss Bronwyn to come again at the earliest opportunity, and the countess allowed as how that would suit agreeably on Monday next. He bowed them on their way and managed to not kiss Miss Ferguson farewell or even stare at her mouth.

He did, however, admire her retreating form, until Bronwyn turned around and waved farewell to him.

CHAPTER FIVE

"I had not taken Dorie Humplewit for a hoyden," Roberta said.

She and Penelope were returning from donating to the poor box at St. George's on Hanover Square. The outing was timed to coincide with the carriage parade in Hyde Park a half-dozen streets to the west.

Conspicuous charity was the only kind Roberta could justify, not that a widow needed to justify good stewardship of her limited resources.

The biweekly trek to St. George's allowed Roberta to see and be seen without going to the expense of maintaining a team. She hadn't sold the colonel's town carriage yet, but she was considering it.

The dratted thing still stank of his pipes and probably always would.

"I'm sorry Lady Humplewit disappointed you," Penelope said.

"For God's sake, we're not in a footrace. How am I to greet friends passing by if you insist on subjecting me to a forced march?"

"Sorry, ma'am."

"You can't help it, I know. A long meg doesn't realize how much harder she must work to exude womanly grace. Having some height myself, I do sympathize, but you must—"

As they crossed Bond Street, the traitor herself, Lady Dorothy Humplewit, tooled past in a red-wheeled vis-à-vis, one of her daughters at her side. The unfortunate young lady had buck teeth, which she tried to hide by affecting a serious demeanor. Difficult to do when she hadn't a brain in her pretty head.

Roberta smiled gaily and gave a small, ladylike wave. Dorie waved back more boisterously than she ought, but then, Dorie had to affect good spirits. Her plans for Grampion had failed utterly.

"To think I call that brazen creature my friend. I barely mentioned to her that my only niece has been given into the keeping of a bachelor earl, and the next thing I know, Lady Dremel conveys the most shocking confidences. Mrs. Chuzzleton had best review the guest list for her future garden parties more carefully."

Two years ago, Roberta would have been invited to that garden party.

"I thought Lord Grampion was a widower, ma'am."

"And thus he's a bachelor. Don't be tedious, Penelope."

"My apologies, ma'am."

Penelope had to apologize frequently, for she had no sense of guile, no ability to anticipate the subtler currents in a conversation. She would have made a good solicitor, taking satisfaction in a life of tedium and routine.

"We shall find a bench and enjoy the fresh spring air for one-quarter of an hour." Grosvenor Square lay across the next street, a lovely green expanse where the less socially ambitious could spend some time out of doors. "I must consider how to go on with Lady Humplewit. She is a friend of long standing, and one doesn't discard friends lightly."

Roberta needed to have a stern word with her dressmaker, for today's walking dress was too snug about the bodice. One could not march across Mayfair in such ill-constructed attire without becoming quite winded.

Two young men vacated a bench at the approach of the ladies. The handsomer of the two tipped his hat and swept a bow in the direction of the bench.

"Such nonsense," Roberta muttered. "I'm a woman of mature years and have no time for flirting dandies."

"Of course not, ma'am."

The bench was hard, the sunshine bright enough to give a widow in first mourning freckles despite her veil, and the day a disappointment from every perspective.

Dorie Humplewit was known for enjoying her widowhood, but according to Lady Dremel, that enjoyment had become a business venture. Dorie would accost single gentlemen of means in private locations and arrange for friends to come upon the couple at the wrong moment. The gentleman would face a choice of offering marriage or purchasing silence—from the very woman who'd drawn him into the interlude.

"The most vexing part," Roberta muttered, "is that she needn't even... well, you know. She simply endures a few kisses from a man she, herself, has chosen."

"I beg your pardon?"

"Don't interrupt me when I'm thinking." Dorie's scheme was disgraceful and undeniably clever. The worst that might happen was she'd end up married to a man of her own choosing. If the fellow took umbrage at being kissed, well, a gentleman ought to have known better. That he ended up married to a woman more clever and daring than he was his own fault.

The fellows who'd given up the bench lounged beneath the shade of a nearby maple, showing off their tailoring and trying to catch Roberta's eye.

Her finances had grown perilous, and she didn't have time for foolish young men and their silly behavior. Something about Dorie's scheme begged for further examination, though Roberta herself had no interest in being kissed.

Fourteen years of marriage to the colonel had been penance enough. For a lifetime of financial security, she might endure some groping, but then, marriage should have provided her that security—and in exchange for a great deal more than mere groping.

Alas, the colonel had not enjoyed much business acumen.

"Grampion's brother is excessively wealthy." And dear little Amy Marguerite was in Grampion's care, without the comfort of even a female member of the earl's household to take the girl in hand.

A devoted auntie—and Roberta was entirely prepared to fulfill that office— ought to shower the child with boundless affection, becoming the next thing to a fixture in Grampion's household.

Roberta considered that prospect and considered inveigling Grampion into marriage.

He was a widower. He'd know how to deal with his base urges without overly troubling his wife, or Roberta would soon provide him instruction on the matter.

He was titled—never a bad thing.

He danced well enough and did justice to his evening finery, which would make all the other widows jealous—also not a bad thing.

He was very likely wealthy, and the family wealth was vulgarly abundant— the best kind.

"I'm still very much in my prime."

Penelope was too busy admiring the foliage to comment, or she accepted that statement as so obvious, it required no assent.

Then too, Roberta was dear Amy Marguerite's only living female relation. Grampion, being dull as a discarded boot, would see a certain economy in marriage to the person who by rights ought to have responsibility for the child's moral development.

And yet… any earl would expect his wife to produce an heir, a spare, and who knew how many little insurance policies against the crown's greedy ambitions.

Marriage to Grampion was out of the question. "Come along," Roberta said, rising. "You have enough burdens in the appearance department that you ought not to risk freckles, my dear."

"Very true, ma'am."

One of the dandies blew Roberta a kiss.

"Wretched beasts," Roberta said, hastening her step. "A woman is never free from the admiration of such as those when she has decent looks and a fine figure. I hope you grasp that in your very plainness, the Almighty has spared you much tribulation."

"I'm most grateful for heaven's mercies."

Roberta was too, especially when heaven gave a lady a brain to equal her other endowments. Dorie Humplewit's scheme was clever, as far as it went. More clever still would be a scheme that assured that Amy Marguerite's doting auntie became a fixture not in the earl's household—what an excruciating fate that would be—but in his expense ledger.

And if Roberta had to put up with a child underfoot to achieve that goal, well… nursery maids and governesses could be had for coin, and coin was something Grampion would be happy to provide to the woman who took the brat off his hands.

The poor, bereaved child, rather.

* * *

"Mama said if ever I'm in trouble, and she or Papa couldn't come to me, I was to write to the Earl of Grampion and he'd help me."

Daisy tucked a pink tulip into her boat. The boat was paper, so it could carry only one blossom at a time around the fountain.

Bronwyn waited for the boat to bob across to her side. "My papa would help me, and so would my mama. Then would come Grandpapa and Grandmama and the uncles and aunties. The earl seems nice."

Daisy was nice too, even though she was an orphan without a pony, puppy, or cat.

"I knew the earl before," Daisy said, watching the little boat. "At home, we're neighbors. Mama sometimes went to visit him, and I came along."

"You miss your mama," Bronwyn said as the boat came closer. The tulip weighed it down, and in another few passes, the little boat would sink. "Do you miss your papa too?" Daisy never mentioned her papa.

"My papa was old. He liked my brothers a lot, even though he said they made too much noise. Papa wasn't mean. He smelled like his pipe."

The boat arrived at Bronwyn's side of the fountain. "Why did you choose a pink tulip?"

"They were my mama's favorite."

Making friends with somebody who was sad was hard, because if she was your friend, you felt sad too.

Bronwyn sent the boat back toward Daisy. "What is your favorite flower?"

"A daisy, of course. What's yours?"

"I don't know. I like delphiniums because Grandmama says they are the color of Grandpapa's eyes. I like honeysuckle because it's sweet."

"I thought it only smelled good."

The boat was sinking lower and lower. "We should make our next boat out of sticks. Paper boats don't work very well. When the honeysuckle blooms, I'll show you how to get the nectar from it. We can pretend we're bees."

The tulip now floated on the surface of the water without benefit of a boat. "By the time the honeysuckle blooms, I might be sent away."

What was the point of making a new friend if she was just going to be sent away? "Have you been bad?"

"Yes, but the earl says I'm making progress."

Bronwyn rose and dusted off her pinafore. "If you're making progress, he shouldn't send you away. That's not fair."

Daisy popped to her feet. "I'll tell you what's not fair, making us wear white pinafores then sending us outside to play. A brown pinafore would be better for the garden."

"Or green. Have you climbed that tree yet?" A big maple grew next to the garden wall, and a bench sat beneath it. "We could climb from the bench to the wall to the tree."

"Is it bad to climb on things like that?"

"Daisy, we're supposed to be playing. Climbing a tree is playing, and then we can pretend the tree is our pirate ship, or our long boat, or our royal barge."

"One of the nursery maids is named Sykes. She says if I'm bad, I'll be sent away."

"I didn't have a nursery maid until Mama married Papa. Heavers is jolly and stout and loves me and my sister the best."

Bronwyn climbed the bench and scrambled onto the wall and into the tree while Daisy stood below, casting glances at the house.

"Come on, Daisy. Unless you want to be in charge of the hold on the royal barge. Even a royal barge probably has rats in the hold. You could be the Royal Ratter and use a great stick to beat all the imaginary rats."

Daisy stood on the bench. "I don't understand something. If your papa wasn't your papa from the day you were born, then how is he your papa?"

"Because he loves me and he loves my mama, and he's the only papa I know."

Daisy was an awkward climber, but she made it up onto the wall and sat, her feet kicking against the stones.

"So you can get another papa after your first one dies?"

At this rate, Daisy would never be fit for duty in the crow's nest. Bronwyn plopped down beside her. "Yes, if he loves you and you love him. I expect you can get another mama too."

"I don't want another mama."

"Neither do I. I don't want you to be sent away either."

They pondered that possibility in silence. Bronwyn suspected if they talked it over, Daisy might begin to cry. Daisy cried a lot, which made sense. If Bronwyn had lost both of her parents, she'd cry forever.

"Do you know how you are called Daisy, even though your name is Amy

Marguerite?" Bronwyn asked, getting to her feet.

Daisy managed to get herself to a standing position on the wall. "Yes, and my other name is Samantha."

"Well, my family calls me Winnie, from Bronwyn. You can call me Winnie too. I'll be Captain Winnie, and you can be First Mate Daisy. Let's go up to the poop deck and look for pirates."

"I thought we were the pirates."

"We'll be in Lord Nelson's fleet for now. They got to win all the battles."

"Lord Nelson was killed in one of those battles."

Bronwyn swung up into the maple, which was at the lovely, soft stage of growing new leaves. "Everybody dies, Daisy, and then we go to heaven. You can't worry about that. Lord Nelson got to be a hero because he died fighting for King George. Are you coming?"

Daisy took a moment to choose her route into the tree—she had probably been cautious even before her parents had died—and then she followed Bronwyn into the hold of their seventy-four gunner.

Bronwyn grabbed a sturdy branch and began to climb. "Why do you suppose they called it the poop deck? Why not the pee deck, or the manure deck?"

Daisy started to giggle, and the branch she hung on to shook with her laughter, and that made Bronwyn laugh, and they decided they'd name their ship the HMS Poop Deck.

* * *

Uncle Walter sat at the end of the breakfast table, a cup of coffee in one hand, the financial pages in the other. He was a lean, white-haired gentleman with twinkling blue eyes and a black heart.

Lily stirred a lump of sugar into her tea and waited, for if she'd learned nothing else in the past ten years, she'd learned to deal with Uncle carefully.

He finished his coffee and set the cup on its saucer. "So what have you planned for this glorious spring day, dearest niece?"

He kept despotic control of her social schedule, and when he wasn't dictating to her outright, he was spying on her through the servants or Oscar.

"I was hoping for some time to speak with you, Uncle. I've encountered an unforeseen challenge."

He poured himself more coffee, the acrid scent reaching Lily, though she sat eight feet down the table. "You excel at dealing with challenges. I've every confidence you'll manage this one, whatever it might be."

"My challenge is the Earl of Grampion." And his tender, passionate kisses. His devotion to an orphan, his relentless decency. Lily was capable of admiring men, even of liking them—she liked the Earl of Rosecroft—but Grampion had the power to destroy her.

"He's a challenge to many," Uncle said, heaping sugar into his coffee. "He's about as warm as a Methodist spinster in her shroud. All the charm in that family went to the wealthy younger brother, and he's my objective. Pass the milk."

Lily brought her uncle the milk. The command was a reminder: Do as I say. Do everything just as I say.

"I knew you were acquainted with the previous earl, Uncle. I did not realize that he'd brought his heir to Town with him years ago."

Uncle poured a dollop of milk into his coffee, then another. "And how did you come across that revelation?"

"As a girl, the Lily Ferguson whom Grampion knew detested bugs. I made the mistake of taking an interest in butterflies."

The milk pitcher was a porcelain rendition of a Greek urn in miniature, wreathed in a gold, pink, and green garland of glazed roses. The parlor was snug thanks to a blazing fire, and the sideboard held fluffy eggs, golden toast, jam, butter, and scones—a veritable feast.

Lily had sold her soul for this feast, and for many others like it.

"I do recall the previous earl dragging his sons around Town on one or two occasions. I first met the heir hacking in the park, as I recall, or possibly at some fencing exhibition. Grampion was a dull boy, never said much, not the sort to cause his pater difficulties. You'll manage him."

"Then I have your permission to cut him?" For this was Lily's technique of last resort. Anybody who might have known "Lily Ferguson as a girl" was shown either impatient indifference or—how she hated what her life had become—frigid stares.

She dwelled on a double-sided precipice. On one side were accusations of extreme eccentricity, on the other was the dangerous truth.

Uncle folded the newspaper and laid it on the table so he could sip coffee and read at the same time.

"You may not cut him, you daft girl. Remind him that you took a bad fall while at that expensive finishing school in Switzerland, and thus many of your earliest memories are hazy. God knows, most of mine are. Pass the butter."

Once again, Lily rose and complied. "I can dis-remember all day long, Uncle, and have on many occasions, but Grampion notices details. In some small particular, I might falter, and then he'll ask questions."

Uncle studied her over the top of his cup of coffee. He threatened gently, he managed invisibly, he insinuated and implied until Lily dared not thwart him. To anybody else, he was a doting relation who'd generously taken in an orphaned niece and showered her with every advantage.

To Lily, he was the devil's man of business, though he'd never raised a hand to her, never even raised his voice to her.

"You have managed well all these years, Lily. I forget to tell you that, but considering your antecedents—perhaps because of them—you have taken excellent advantage of the opportunities before you. I do appreciate it.

Nonetheless, I plan to coax Sir Worth Kettering into inviting me to join him in a particularly lucrative investment scheme, and thus his brother's favor matters. Deal cordially with Grampion, and we'll all benefit."

All meant Uncle and Oscar, though Lily benefitted as well. She was alive, wasn't she?

"And if his lordship should become curious, or note some inconsistency between the Lily he knew and the Lily I am now?"

Uncle beamed at her. "You are a clever young lady, and your active mind will appeal to a dry stick like Grampion. Why else do you think I put you in his path? I'm not suggesting you engage in outright folly, but a lonely bachelor and a difficult spinster have common ground while passing a Season in London. You do so love children, and Grampion is clearly unprepared to raise a child."

Damn Uncle to the Pit. "I am better able to serve your ends if I know what they are, sir. Grampion hasn't taken a liking to me, but the girl—Amy Marguerite—has."

As much as Lily hated to lie, she did not trust Uncle except to operate consistently in his own self-interest. If Uncle believed Lily and Grampion enjoyed each other's company, then he'd use that to his advantage.

"The girl likes you," Uncle said, turning the newspaper over, "in a matter of days, you've recruited the poor little mite a playmate and brought along your countess friend for a social call on the earl's household. Neatly done, Lily. If I know you, there's another outing of the same nature planned. You'll take the children on a picnic in the park and do doting-auntie things with them. Grampion will be relieved and charmed, and Worth Kettering will look with favor upon my household. All comes right if you do your part."

No, all did not come right. All unrolled in a progression of years where Lily was told what to wear, with whom to waltz, when to plead a headache, and when to ruin a young man of whom Uncle disapproved.

"I'm taking Bronwyn to visit Amy Marguerite on Monday," Lily said. "I cannot promise to earn anybody's favor for you, Uncle, but I will do my best."

"You always do, dearest niece. I so admire that about you."

He went back to the mistress who'd held him in thrall since Lily had first met him—the financial pages—while Lily sipped tea and waited for her stomach to settle.

It never did, not entirely. Fear circled her life like a raptor. When she couldn't spot its shadow on the path before her, she knew it would reappear at the worst moment and threaten every kind of safety a woman held dear.

"I'm off to pay a call on Tippy," Lily said. "She might remember some details of Grampion's boyhood visits to London."

"The very recollections I pay her for. I'm told Grampion likes to hack out on Tuesdays, Thursdays, and Saturdays. The usual predawn lunacy in Hyde Park. Never saw much sense in it, myself."

"The fresh air is invigorating, and the horses are happier for stretching their legs."

Lily had given the right answer, the answer that assured Uncle she'd drag herself out of bed at the ungodly hour preferred by London gentlemen for their morning rides. She'd drag herself to whatever balls, routs, Venetian breakfasts, soirees, musicales, and at-homes Uncle put on her schedule. She'd drag herself to the card parties and charity auctions too.

He'd never asked her to compromise her virtue, never asked her to do more than relay gossip word for word, and yet Uncle was her gaoler as surely as if he chained her to the cart's tail and whipped her through London daily.

Next month, on her twenty-eighth birthday, Lily would gain nominal control of an inherited fortune. Uncle would doubtless continue to manage all of the money and most of Lily's time.

If she remained under his roof.

With no money in hand, few friends, and a history of felony wrongdoing, Lily's escape would present many challenges.

She'd faced many challenges and survived. Spending time with Grampion was simply one more torment added to a list that was as long as Lily's memory, and as near as her own name.

CHAPTER SIX

Hessian left the library door ajar, not to let the spring breezes waft through his house, but because with the door open, he could hear activity in the foyer and thus avoid an ambush if callers disrupted his day. In Cumberland, one visited back and forth with the neighbors, and that was all very pleasant, but in London, socializing was a more portentous undertaking.

Politicians' wives held dinner parties that decided every bit as much legislation as did parliamentary committee meetings.

A conversation over cards might put a complicated investment scheme in motion.

Ladies sharing a cabriolet for the Fashionable Hour could plan a match between their grown children.

If Worth came sauntering by, or one of Jacaranda's host of brothers dropped around, Hessian wanted even the few minutes' notice that he gained by leaving the library door open.

Monday arrived, and well before the appointed hour for Lily Ferguson's visit, somebody gave the front door knocker a stout rap. Hessian rose from his desk and donned his jacket. Perhaps the lady was as eager as the children—and Hessian—for this call to begin.

"When last Miss Ferguson called, I did not quite make a cake of myself," he informed his reflection in the mirror over the library's sideboard. "Neither did I inspire the lady into rapturous enthusiasms."

Butterflies were shy creatures and so were certain northern earls. Hessian was rehearsing a gracious smile—charming was beyond him—when a feminine voice came from the direction of the foyer.

Not Miss Ferguson. Whoever had presumed on Hessian's morning was unknown to him and lacked Lily's gracious, ladylike tone. Hessian was back at his desk—for he'd got halfway across the room at the tap of the knocker—no smile in evidence, when the butler brought in a card on a silver tray.

"Mrs. Braithwaite has come to call, with her companion Miss Smythe." Hochman's tone—utterly correct—suggested the caller hadn't impressed him.

Hessian took the card, plain black script on vellum. Daisy's aunt… Drat the luck. "Show the ladies to the guest parlor and let the kitchen know we'll need a tea tray, please."

"Very good, my lord. Should I notify the nursery as well?"

God, no. "No, thank you. If anybody asks, the child is resting from a trying weekend." Daisy had tried the patience of every member of the household, waking three times each night in some peculiar state of somnolent terror.

"Let's use the good silver, Hochman, and if Miss Ferguson arrives while I'm entertaining Mrs. Braithwaite, please put the library to use. Miss Ferguson might entertain herself and the children by reading them a story on the mezzanine."

"I understand, my lord." Hochman bowed and withdrew, the silver tray winking in his gloved hand.

Mrs. Braithwaite was much as Hessian recalled her. Her figure was fuller and her use of henna more in evidence. She was handsome rather than pretty, and her gray walking dress sported a dizzying abundance of lace.

Mourning garb, this was not.

At her side was a lovely, willowy blonde in sprigged muslin, one of those pale, quiet creatures who belonged in some enchanted forest with a book of spells rather than swilling tea in Mayfair.

When the bowing and curtseying had been dispensed with, Hessian led the ladies to the formal parlor and ploughed onward to the civilities.

"Mrs. Braithwaite, please accept my sincere condolences on the loss of your sister. Lady Evers was much loved by all the neighbors, and we will miss her dearly."

Had Hessian loved Belinda, Lady Evers? He'd made love with her on three slightly awkward, mostly forgettable occasions. She'd affectionately pronounced him a failure at dalliance—which he absolutely had been—but he'd liked her and had never questioned her devotion to her children.

"You are so kind to say so, my lord," Mrs. Braithwaite replied. "I know Belinda could be headstrong, which often happens when a pretty child is overindulged. She was fortunate to find an older husband, because mature men can be so tolerant. This is a lovely town house."

One did not speak ill of the dead, and yet, Mrs. Braithwaite had just called her own departed sister headstrong and spoiled.

"My brother found this property for me," Hessian said. "I'm quite comfortable here." He had been quite comfortable here, before Daisy had arrived.

"So much room for one man," Mrs. Braithwaite said, taking a seat on the sofa. "Though I adore French silk on the walls. So elegant, but not the least fussy."

Hessian was not prepared to discourse on the topic of French silk wallpaper—if that's what it was. "The premises are near my brother's residence and allow me to entertain modestly. I do hope the weather continues mild."

He also hoped Mrs. Braithwaite had no plans to overstay the thirty minutes prescribed for most social calls. Miss Smythe had settled beside her on the sofa, so Hessian allowed himself to take a wing chair.

"We can never be certain about the weather," Mrs. Braithwaite replied, "and I came here to discuss with you another topic entirely. I'm told my dearest niece Amy Marguerite is in your keeping."

Oh, that was subtle, but then, Hessian preferred honesty to innuendo if the lady was intent on verbal pugilism.

"Lord and Lady Evers did me the honor of appointing me guardian of their children," Hessian said. "Had I known you bided in Town, I would have paid a call on you in due course to appraise you of that fact."

Whatever due course was.

Mrs. Braithwaite pulled off her gloves and laid them on the low table before the sofa. "My lord, I'm sure you did mean to pay me that courtesy, but my concern for the child will not allow me to wait upon your convenience. Her brothers will bide mostly at school, I'm sure, but she is the youngest and the only girl. I must know when you will allow her to join my household."

Kendall, the first footman, appeared in the parlor door holding a laden silver tray.

"Kendall, if you'd set the tea before me?" Hessian gestured to the low table flanking the sofa.

"Nonsense," Mrs. Braithwaite said. "Penelope will pour out. Set the tray before her."

Kendall, who hailed from Martinique by way of Lisbon, maintained an impassive expression— and possession of the tray.

"I shall pour for my guests," Hessian said, "and please get the door on the way out, Kendall."

The footman bowed and withdrew, closing the door silently. Pray God that Bronwyn and Daisy didn't shriek the house down upon catching sight of each other.

Hessian made a good, long production out of serving the ladies tea, while he wrestled with the question of what role Mrs. Braithwaite ought to play in Daisy's life. He'd been preoccupied with managing Daisy herself and had frankly put off the question of what to do about the girl's aunt.

He was a widower with little experience with children, but then, Mrs. Braithwaite apparently had no experience with children.

She watched Hessian maneuver around the silver service as if China black, sugar, and milk were some arcane test of social acceptability, and she the judge qualified to eliminate those who failed the examination.

"You may speak freely before Miss Smythe," Mrs. Braithwaite said. "She is entirely in my confidence."

She is not in mine. "That is good to know, Mrs. Braithwaite. However, your visit today takes me by surprise. Had you written, I might have been better prepared to discuss Amy Marguerite's situation with you, but your suggestion will require considerable thought. Amy Marguerite has endured a great loss, and I take seriously my responsibility to provide her with a safe, stable home where she can recover from the blow grief has dealt her. Do have some cake. Cook prides herself on a light hand with the sweets."

Miss Smythe sat through this balderdash, gaze fixed on the window as if she were posing for a cameo.

Mrs. Braithwaite set her cup and saucer on the tray. "My household would be a perfect haven for a grieving child. Surely you must see that, my lord. I live the quiet life of a widow, barely socializing, while you maintain a peer's bachelor establishment. I can raise Amy Marguerite in gentility and propriety, surrounding her with the love of a blood relation and sparing you the bother of a small child underfoot."

Hessian for the most part ignored his title. When the Earl of Grampion was announced, part of him still expected his father to strut forth, though Papa hadn't been much for pomp and ceremony either.

Hessian also rarely went to the bother of voting his seat, avoided London, and, for cards and socializing, preferred a humble club favored by Border families.

But sometimes, being the earl was necessary and useful.

He topped up Miss Smythe's tea cup—leaving Mrs. Braithwaite's empty—and set the silver pot on the tray.

"Mrs. Braithwaite, forgive my lack of delicacy, but do you imply that I, Lord and Lady Evers's closest neighbor, who am in fact Amy Marguerite's godfather, who has known her since birth, and was a frequent guest in her parents' home, am somehow less capable of providing a haven for the girl than is an aunt whom she might not even recall?"

Mrs. Braithwaite sat very tall. "I am her only adult relation, my lord. Of course, she'll recall me."

"You visited your sister about four years ago, if I remember aright. Amy Marguerite would have been three. How often have you written to her since then?"

"One does not write to an illiterate child."

"Perhaps you sent a gift on her birthday or at Yuletide?"

Mrs. Braithwaite maintained an affronted silence.

"Do you even know when her birthday falls?"

"What matters the date of a child's birth, my lord, when she can't be with family to celebrate the occasion?"

Lily Ferguson would know what to say to that. Hessian's responses begged for a dusting of profanity, lest this presuming creature mistake his meaning.

"Your devotion to your niece does you credit, Mrs. Braithwaite," Hessian said, rising. "I will consider your request, but Amy Marguerite was entrusted to my care, and Lord and Lady Evers's final arrangements made no provision for turning the child over to you for rearing. You are asking me disregard the wishes of the child's parents and shirk my duty, and that I am unlikely to do. For the present, the girl needs stability, not upheaval, so I will thank you to respect my wishes."

Miss Smythe scooted to the edge of the sofa, but did not rise until Mrs. Braithwaite was on her feet.

"My lord, Amy Marguerite is a female. Surely when Lady Evers assented to naming you as guardian, she did so anticipating that your household would include your own lady wife. Until such time as you can offer at least that much female guidance to the child, my household is the more appropriate home for her."

Hessian opened the door and stood by it. "I was widowed by the time Amy Marguerite was born, and her parents well knew my circumstances. I'll wish you good day, Mrs. Braithwaite, and thank you for your interest in your niece. Feel free to send her a note of condolence, or some small token of her mother's memory, if any you have. Miss Smythe, a pleasure to meet you."

Mrs. Braithwaite drew in such a long breath, Hessian thought she might pop a nacre button off her bodice. She tried subjecting him to a sniffy, up-and-down perusal, but he was a northern earl, and her indignation was nothing compared to the tempers and feuds his tenants and neighbors could get up to over imagined slights.

He accompanied the ladies to the foyer, mostly to ensure they did in fact leave the premises, and waited until the butler had closed the front door behind them.

"Hochman, I am not at home to Mrs. Braithwaite in future, unless I specifically tell you otherwise."

"I'll inform the footmen, my lord. Miss Ferguson and Miss Bronwyn have arrived, and Miss Daisy has joined them in the library."

"Well done. The young ladies might want a tea tray in the garden."

"With plenty of biscuits?"

"Hochman, you are a man of discernment."

While Hessian was a man much in need of sensible conversation and a strategy for dealing with Mrs. Braithwaite.

* * *

No more embracing, no more yearning, no more kissing.

Lily's strategy where Lord Grampion was concerned was simple, also painful. She resigned herself to cordiality—he deserved at least that—and to as much truthfulness as she could afford. She had stolen a memorable kiss, and must content herself with that treasure.

"Greetings, ladies," the earl said, bowing over Lily's hand and then over Bronwyn's. "I am delighted to see you."

"So am I," Daisy said. She aimed a smile at Bronwyn, who grinned back, and for reasons known only to little girls, this occasioned a cascade of giggles.

Once upon a time, long, long ago, Lily had giggled like that with Annie, and the sound still had the power to make her smile.

"What will you be today?" his lordship asked. "Corsairs, Wellington at Waterloo, Good Queen Bess presiding over her court? Perhaps you'll put the fountain to use re-enacting the Battle of Trafalgar, though the weather's a bit cool for that entertainment."

He aimed the question at the girls, and Lily was assailed by the realization that at some point, this rather serious, titled fellow had been a boy. He had climbed trees, dammed up streams, likely built campfires in the home wood, and gone swimming without benefit of clothing or adult supervision.

Despite the typical self-absorption of an adolescent, he'd also noticed at least one difficult, younger female child taking the air in Hyde Park.

"What's Trafalgar?" Daisy asked.

"That's where Lord Nelson died." Bronwyn said. "Heroes can be dead and still be heroes, but I prefer the ones like my papa and Wellington, who are still alive. Wellington's horse is Copenhagen. He was sometimes naughty, but a fine battle mount."

Daisy looked fascinated. "Your papa is a hero?"

"Perhaps you ladies might finish that discussion in the garden?" his lordship suggested.

"Or in the nursery," Lily said. "The weather is becoming threatening."

"So it is," the earl said. "We'll send a tea tray up to the nursery, then. Be off with you, and mind the breakables."

Daisy shot him a curious look as Bronwyn snatched her hand and dragged her toward the door.

Leaving Lily alone with a man whom she must neither encourage nor alienate.

"I had thought to leave Bronwyn with you for a short time," she said. "My cousin Oscar was to have accompanied us here, but woke with a megrim. I can return for Bronwyn later, or you can send her home with a nursery maid or footman."

Lily should have marched smartly for the door, but his lordship put a hand on her arm. "You walked here, did you not? With rain threatening, I insist on having the coach brought around. Allow me that small courtesy, for I've a favor to ask of you."

His blue eyes held no guile, no subtle, improper meaning. Had he leered at her, Lily's decision would have been so much easier.

"I like to stretch my legs." In truth, Lily had learned not to take Uncle Walter's coach when Oscar's gentlemanly excesses rendered him incapable of moving about on foot during daylight hours.

"Then perhaps you'll agree to walk in the park with me and Daisy on Wednesday?"

Say no... feign another obligation, fabricate some appointment you must keep. Except, feigning and fabrication were the genteel relations of deceit, and Lily had promised herself to be as honest with Grampion as possible.

"Your lordship's invitation extends to Bronwyn too, I presume?"

"I have the sense that every expedition benefits from Captain Bronwyn's leadership. Shall we sit?"

No, no, no. He hadn't yet ordered his team put to. A tea tray was doubtless being prepared for the library in addition to one for the nursery, and Grampion had mentioned a favor. Nobody asked Lily for favors, and she preferred it that way.

"I cannot stay long, my lord. My companion should have accompanied me in Oscar's absence, but she is inclined to colds when the weather is changeable." Miss Fotheringham also detested small children, hence Lily's choice of Rosecroft for her earlier call on Grampion.

Grampion patted the back of a wing chair. "You see before you a man wrestling with a dilemma, Miss Ferguson, and you are uniquely positioned to aid me in resolving it. Please, won't you tarry a moment?"

He invited, he flattered, he honestly requested. Lily had no defenses against these tactics. Had Grampion been imperious or improper, her arsenal would have been adequate to repel his advances, but he was simply gentlemanly.

She took a seat in a chair so comfortable, it practically begged her to toe off her slippers and curl up with a book. The faint scent of cedar came to her, suggesting this was his lordship's preferred reading perch.

"I was ambushed earlier today," Grampion said, taking the near end of the sofa. "Daisy's aunt presented herself on my doorstep, bold as you please, demanding that I hand Daisy over to her."

Oh dear. "You were tempted to comply?"

"I am a bachelor and a peer. In Mrs. Braithwaite's opinion, both sad attributes disqualify me from supervising the upbringing of one little girl. She is Daisy's only female relation, and thus I must uproot the child and surrender her posthaste, for I lack a wife, auntie, or other handy female to protect Daisy from my male ineptitude."

He was angry at the aunt's presumption, but Lily suspected he also felt honor-bound to consider the woman's request. "What was Daisy's reaction to her aunt?"

Grampion crossed his legs, a Continental pose most Englishmen eschewed, and twitched a seam straight on his breeches.

"Mrs. Braithwaite did not ask to see the child, did not seem to know that Daisy was under this very roof."

Or she had not cared. "Where else might Daisy be, if not here with you?"

"In Cumberland, in the care of the staff she's known her entire life. I've made arrangements for the remaining nursery maids from the Evers household to join my household at Grampion Hall when I return north."

When his wife-hunting was successfully concluded. "In the weeks since Lady Evers's death, Mrs. Braithwaite hasn't troubled to find out where Daisy is?"

A lordly nose wrinkled. "Either she hasn't troubled to find out where Daisy is, or she knew Daisy was here and anticipated that I'd refuse a request to meet with the girl."

"Would you have?"

"You should have been a barrister." He rose and used the cast-iron poker to move coals about on the hearth. "I took Mrs. Braithwaite into dislike when I met her several years ago at one of Lady Evers's dinner parties. I could not tell if Mrs. Braithwaite was flirting with me, or if she was nervous to be in titled company. Some people are. Or perhaps she'd had too much wine. She tittered and batted her lashes and found rather too many opportunities to lay her hand on my arm, which behavior I expect from nervous debutantes."

Lily expected the equivalent from presuming lords and knew exactly why Grampion had formed such a bad impression of Mrs. Braithwaite. The widow was Lord Stemberger in a dress, regarding everybody in her ambit as either an opportunity or an obstacle.

The earl stared at the flames, then added half a scoop of coal and dusted his hands. "I ought not to judge people on scant evidence, but ladies who are too fond of cosmetics provoke me to caution. This is not rational or fair, I know, but why alter one's appearance beyond the endowments conferred by the Almighty? Society should be accepting of an honest appearance, and to present oneself as something one is not... I'm maundering. My brother says I excel at maundering."

He resumed his seat. "She uses henna and rice powder in obvious quantities when there's no need. She's well-enough looking, not victimized by small pox. And her clothing is loud."

This last was offered quietly, like a confession. "Her clothing is loud?"

"All fussy and frilly to the eye, and she cannot lift a hand without rustling and swishing. My late wife used the same tactic. She could rivet a man's attention by virtue of adjusting her skirts, straightening a cuff, or merely crossing a room.

After she died, I thought I heard the rustle of her clothing rather than her voice."

He scrubbed a hand over his face. "I am daft. You will forget I said that. I spend much time reading poetry in duck blinds, or napping. My mind tends to run about like a march hare on the moor. What shall I do with Mrs. Braithwaite?"

Lily had the oddest urge to take his hand. "You must do what is best for Daisy, and I cannot think more upheaval and change fits that description."

"Precisely what I told Mrs. Braithwaite. I did my lordly best to crush her presumptions, but she'll be back. Scheming women have to be persistent, else their plans never come to fruition. One can't blame them, but neither can one afford them any sympathy."

His words were no less measured than any other comment he'd made, and yet, they cut Lily to the soul.

"Then you must crush her presumptions again," Lily said, rising, "and I really must be going." Before she began to cry, which would be stupid and useless.

"I haven't ordered the coach yet," Grampion said, standing as gentlemen must when a lady leaves her seat, "and I have yet to puzzle out exactly how I'll crush Mrs. Braithwaite's presumptions. She is Daisy's aunt, and I am…"

"You are an uncle," Lily said. "You have nieces too and thus have some familiarity with how a household accommodates a little girl. You mentioned a sister who bided with you in the north."

Grampion peered down at her, and Lily realized she'd made a mistake. The earl's brother had recently come into a minor title, a knighthood, or a baronetcy—Lily forgot which—but Worth Kettering was not of such a social stature that Lily should know the configuration of his household.

When Uncle Walter had revealed that he sought to partner with Kettering on some investments, Lily had done the usual research, else she would not have learned that Grampion's brother had married the current Earl of Casriel's sister, much less that they had one girl child and half-grown niece under their roof.

"I am an uncle, you're right, and I do have a half-sister, whom few know of. Yolanda was born on the wrong side of the blanket, though I'll call out anyone who mentions that fact, and Worth will gladly serve as second. Shall I ring for a tray? When I hosted Mrs. Braithwaite's call, I barely partook, and Cook will be wroth with me unless I do justice to her next offering."

You haven't ordered the coach for me. Except Lily was back in her chair, once again felled by Grampion's casual honesty. He had a bastard half-sister, of whom he and his brother were ferociously protective.

"I've upset you with all this family linen flung so casually out to dry," Grampion said, resuming his place on the sofa. "I apologize. Mrs. Braithwaite discommoded me."

"She apparently delights in discommoding others." She and Uncle would suit famously. "How do you suppose Daisy would fare in a household run by such a woman?"

"Daisy would fade into perfect, miserable obedience. I doubt Mrs. Braithwaite's companion said two words during the entire visit. Miss Smythe took not one tea cake and didn't so much as move from her seat without her employer's leave."

He fell silent, giving Lily a moment to study his profile.

"You have made up my mind, Miss Ferguson. Mrs. Braithwaite can be a doting auntie, but no more. I doubt she knows how to dote, but I suggested she start with a note of condolence to the child and some token in remembrance of Belinda."

"Belinda?"

Now Grampion was back on his feet. "Lady Evers."

Was he embarrassed by that slip? Neighbors of long standing grew familiar with each other, particularly in the remote countryside, and yet, Grampion looked uncomfortable.

"You cared for Lady Evers."

"Yes. Perhaps more than I ought, but when my wife died, Lady Evers took an interest in my welfare. She did not allow me to brood, at which I excel, particularly in winter." He tugged a bell-pull twice. "I suspect she had an agenda where I was concerned, but I was too grateful for her concern to take much notice of it."

Lily had no idea what he was going on about, but now she was compelled by manners to share a damned tea tray with him.

"You should order the coach brought around, my lord."

"When we've had our tea. I'm not in the habit of lengthy conversations and must fortify myself accordingly. Are you often burdened with the confidence of others?"

When Uncle Walter told Lily to elicit confidences, she did her best to accomplish that goal. "Sometimes. Young men tend to see me as safe, because Uncle won't allow them to develop presumptions. I'm not above their touch, but the family fortune means I'm beyond reach all the same. Most young ladies see me as plain and elderly, which makes my fortune less of an injustice in their eyes."

"If you are elderly, what am I—a fossil? I cannot call to mind any more ridiculous, irrational, tedious organization of creatures than polite society. What do you suppose the girls are up to?"

"Likely delivering old Boney a drubbing." Lily's composure was certainly taking a drubbing.

Rapid footsteps thundered overhead.

"The French are doubtless retreating," Grampion said as a footman brought in a tray. The service was porcelain and pretty. "Will you pour out, Miss

Ferguson?"

Lily wanted to leave, not deal with the tedium of the tea tray. And yet, Uncle had told her to curry Grampion's favor.

"I'm happy to serve," Lily said, which was half-true. "How goes the wife-hunting, my lord?"

"Wife-hunting?" He sat as well, while overhead, the British gave such enthusiastic chase that the chandelier swayed and bounced. "Oh yes... the infernal countess hunt. No progress, alas. I suppose if I were engaged, Mrs. Braithwaite might be more easily subdued. Scheming women tend to hover like midges until they've accomplished their ends."

Lily nearly dropped the teapot. "You've dealt with many women bent on intrigue?"

"My late wife dissembled her way into marriage, but that's a tale for another time. I'll take mine plain."

Lily passed him a full cup. "One woman does not represent the entire gender." Though one duplicitous wife would be hard to forget.

Grampion waited until Lily had fixed her own tea before he took a sip. The blend was aromatic and rich and the comfort lovely. She troubled Uncle Walter's staff as little as possible, because every one of them answered to him, reporting when Lily rose, when she dined, where she shopped, and with whom she danced.

"My wife was quite young, and I was an idiot," Grampion said. "In the end, we both had much to regret. I don't intend to let Mrs. Braithwaite impose any regrets on me."

"For Daisy's sake, I'm relieved to hear it." Also for his.

"I've no doubt that Daisy's aunt merely wants my money. A woman intent on her own material security knows few scruples."

Sometimes, she knew no scruples at all. "Another lesson learned from your lady wife?"

Grampion held up the tray of cakes. "Yes, but as you say, that's no excuse for impugning a whole gender. I am in the company of a woman who neither deceives nor manipulates, and she takes a kindly interest in Daisy without having any ulterior motive at all. Have as many cakes as you please. The children are not on hand to supervise us, and I'll eat whatever you leave on the plate."

Lily took two cakes.

Grampion aimed a look at her. His expression was utterly serious, his blue eyes were dancing.

She took two more.

CHAPTER SEVEN

Hessian saw his guests to the door, and while the little girls were whispering and giggling like free traders who'd liberally partaken of contraband spirits, Hessian kissed Miss Ferguson's cheek. He awarded himself this boon for having been a cordial host who never once raised the topic of clandestine embraces or passionate interludes.

"I'll come by for you on Wednesday at eleven," he murmured.

Both children left off conspiring to stare at him.

"You needn't come by," Miss Ferguson said. "I'll collect Bronwyn, and we can meet you at the foot of the Serpentine. My companion can wait for us in the coach."

For a woman whose kisses embodied reckless abandon, Miss Ferguson certainly seemed concerned with propriety.

"That will suit. My thanks for calling on us today."

"Mine too," Daisy said. "On Wednesday, we can have a sea battle."

"On Wednesday, we will have a decorous stroll in the park," Hessian said. "Ladies, good day."

Miss Ferguson and her charge departed, whereupon Daisy darted to the window of the parlor. Much waving and smiling ensued, while Hessian considered options and smiled a bit as well.

"We're going out, Daisy."

She turned from the window. "Out?"

"To pay a call on my brother. Worth is forever dropping in on me unannounced. It's time to return fire."

"Like Napoleon and Wellington?"

"Similar, but with fewer casualties, one hopes."

Worth welcomed them graciously, though his brows rose when he spotted Daisy clinging to Hessian's hand.

Hessian went on the polite offensive. "Miss Daisy, may I make known to you my brother, Sir Worth Kettering. Worth, please make your bow to my ward, Miss Daisy."

Worth was a big, good-looking devil, with unruly dark hair and blue eyes his wife called impertinent. He offered a silly bow, Daisy dimpled, and then Andromeda insinuated her nose into the child's palm.

"Meda likes you," Worth said. "That means you must be a capital little girl, despite keeping company with Grampion. Let's find my wife and she can introduce you to my niece."

Worth held out a hand to the girl—he was ever a favorite with ladies of any age—and yet, Daisy hesitated.

"It's all right," Hessian said. "He's hopelessly friendly, and I won't leave without you."

"Do you promise?"

Hessian's heart did a queer little hop, for Daisy's question had been in complete earnest. "I give you my solemn word. I will not leave this house without you."

Daisy pelted to his side, gave him a tight squeeze about the middle, then grabbed Worth's hand.

Hessian was still pondering the child's first spontaneous display of affection when Worth returned to the study.

"We are forgotten," he said. "Avery took one look at Daisy and began rhapsodizing in French about the dolls and the tin soldiers, and then a fancy dress ball got underway. Daisy is a dear little thing."

Worth's observation held a question, which Hessian ignored. "She's troubled. Sits up in the dead of night moaning and crying, but doesn't even seem to be awake, and apparently has no recollection of the drama the next day."

"That is odd. Avery has nightmares and can often describe them to us in detail for a week afterward. Shall we enjoy the sun while it's out?"

Typical of English weather, the sky had gone from drizzling to sunshine in less than an hour. "So you've never heard of a child having a waking nightmare?"

Worth led the way to the back terrace. "Is that what you came to see me about?"

Well, no, but Daisy's distress seemed so real in the dead of night, and all Hessian knew to do was take her hand and wait for her fear to pass. The first time it had happened, he'd nigh had an apoplexy, but within minutes, she'd curled up and gone right back to sleep.

"What do you know about Walter Leggett?" Hessian asked.

Worth looked around at the terrace furniture. "The damned chairs are wet. Let's visit the mews."

He was off across the garden—which was also quite damp—showing his usual lack of prudence when any odd notion wafted into his head. Money and the Kettering womenfolk were the only topics that gave Worth pause, and in those arenas, he was brilliant.

Hessian followed more slowly, tempted to turn and wave in the direction of the nursery windows.

"About Leggett?" Hessian prompted when he caught up to his brother in the stable aisle.

"Walter Leggett," Worth said, stroking the nose of a big, black, raw-boned gelding. "Third spare to the late Earl of Dearborn. Wealthy, likable, widower, one son. Oscar Leggett is the typical university wastrel trying to cut a dash about Town now that his so-called studies are concluded. The niece is rumored to have handsome settlements, but other rumors attach to Miss Ferguson as well."

A swallow flitted about overhead, and Worth's horse spooked to the back of its stall.

"Miss Ferguson's inclinations are not Sapphic," Hessian said, "at least not exclusively so."

Worth moved down the barn aisle. "Hess, have you been naughty?"

"Don't sound so hopeful. Miss Ferguson has taken an interest in Daisy and found her a playmate. Daisy seems to be doing better for having a friend."

"Screeching in the dead of night is doing better?"

Hessian greeted a mare whose proportions rivaled those of the black gelding. "I think it is, though I know that must sound odd. Daisy would probably also benefit from having a maternal figure in the household."

The mare brushed velvety lips over Hessian's palm.

"Gefjon doesn't like anybody," Worth said. "Why does she like you?"

I smell good. "My charms are subtle but substantial. I'm thinking of offering for Lily Ferguson."

Hessian braced himself for the near-violent fraternal behavior that passed for teasing. He and Worth had been estranged at one point for several years, and they still weren't exactly close.

"You and she would suit," Worth said. "And not merely because a crooked pot needs a crooked lid. She's no featherbrain, and neither are you."

"I'm a boring old stick." *Who would slay dragons to win more of Lily Ferguson's kisses.* "Miss Ferguson seems to like Daisy, and Daisy her."

"Hess, at the risk of pointing out the obvious, ten years from now, Daisy will be making her bow, and it's you Miss Ferguson would be seeing over the tea and toast each morning. Do you like her?"

As a younger man, Hessian would have dismissed the question. Marriage, he would have said, was about esteem, respect, and duty. He was a widower now, and he'd been married to a woman who hadn't particularly liked him, even as she'd spoken her vows.

"I enjoy Miss Ferguson's company, and we share a common perspective."

The mare craned her neck, indicating that Hessian was to scratch her great, hairy ear. He obliged, though it would result in dirty fingernails.

"What perspective might that be?"

"That life isn't an endless exercise in frivolity, that a child's welfare matters, that polite society is mostly ridiculous." That kisses should be delightfully unrestrained.

"All people of sense can agree on that last, but if Miss Ferguson is such a paragon of breeding and wisdom, why hasn't she married previously? She's an heiress, she's not hard on the eye, and if nothing else, you'd think Leggett would select a husband for her from the advantageous-match category."

Wealthy and titled, in other words.

"I'm advantageous," Hessian said. "Or getting there."

The mare butted him in the chest. Had she been so inclined, she could have sent him sprawling on his arse in the dirt. Worth too could have dealt a few blows—ridicule, incredulity, dismay—but he was instead looking thoughtful.

"You are in every way an estimable fellow," Worth said, "and nothing would make me happier than to see you matched with a woman deserving of your esteem, but your first question is about Leggett, and it's regarding him that I must raise a reservation."

Hessian scratched the mare beneath her chin, which she also seemed to enjoy. "Miss Ferguson says he runs off the fortune hunters. All I know of the man is that he was a friend of our papa and is quite well fixed."

"Is he? I have my fingers in financial pots that involve everybody from King George to the seamstresses on Drury Lane, and never once have I crossed paths with Leggett. Now he's apparently sniffing around at my club, making discreet inquiries about a venture I'm putting together with some Americans. Why?"

"Because you are a genius at making money."

"Why is Leggett only now coming to need that genius?"

"Perhaps he's investigated all other possibilities, made a sufficient sum, and hopes by investing with Worth Kettering to make a more than sufficient sum. I have taken every bit of the investment advice you've offered, and in a very short time, my finances have come right."

More than come right. Over the next five years, Hessian would accumulate capital at an astonishing rate, thanks to his brother.

Worth approached the mare, who pinned her ears. "She honestly likes you. You walk in here and command the notice of the most finicky female I know."

"She recognizes a yeoman at heart when she sees one. I have never thanked you for dispensing that financial advice. I am deeply grateful."

Worth wandered back to his gelding, who was affecting the horsy version of a wounded look. "You follow my advice. So many ask for it, then ignore it. I owed you after the way I left Grampion Hall in high dudgeon as a young man. You looked after Lannie, you extended the olive branch, you manage the ancestral pile. Had it not been for Jacaranda's influence, I might still be sticking my figurative tongue out at you and ignoring your letters."

Hessian had never considered that Worth felt guilty over the rift between them, which had been a case of mutual youthful arrogance more than anything else.

"I'm the earl," Hessian said, giving the mare a final pat on her nose. "I'm supposed to extend olive branches and all that other. Might we regard the topic of past misunderstandings as adequately addressed and instead return to the issue of Walter Leggett?"

Worth was a jovial fellow, often gratingly so, but for a moment, in the shadows of the stable, he looked very much like their father. The late earl had been dutiful, stern, and nobody's fool, though kind too. He had loved his children, but he'd lacked a wife at his side as his boys had made the difficult transition to young manhood.

"You have a gift for understatement," Worth said, "and yes, we can discuss Leggett, except I know very little about his situation. Over the years, everybody's fortune get an occasional mention in the clubs. This fellow's stocks took a bad turn on 'Change. That one married his spare to an heiress. Some other man is mad for steam engines—as I am—and yet another just bought vineyards in Spain, of all the dodgy ventures. Leggett's name doesn't come up."

Hessian found a pitchfork and brought the mare a serving of hay from the pile at the end of the aisle. "So he's discreet. Not a bad quality in a fellow." The next forkful went to the gelding, and thus every other beast in the barn began nickering and shifting about in its stall like drovers trying to get the attention of the tavern maid.

"Discretion is a fine quality, but I'm nosy," Worth said. "Will you also sweep the aisle, fill up the water buckets, and muck the stalls for me?"

"I miss Cumberland."

Worth took up a second pitchfork. "I miss Trysting."

They worked in companionable silence until all the horses had been given their snacks. The effort, small though it was, resolved a question for Hessian.

"If I'm considering courting Miss Ferguson, learning as much as I can about her situation strikes me as prudent."

"Stealing a few kisses would be prudent too." Worth propped both pitchforks beside the barn door. "The wedding night is rather too late to discover that your bride likes your title better than your intimate company."

"You needn't instruct me on that point."

A pause ensued, a trifle righteous on Hessian's part—only a trifle—and doubtless awkward for Worth.

"Sorry." Worth stood in the beam of sunshine angling through the barn doors, his gaze on the rain-wet garden. "About Leggett?"

"I'd like to know more where he's concerned, if you're comfortable gathering that information. Some of the wealth he's managing is not his own, but rather, Lily Ferguson's. What has he done with her money?"

Hessian would rather have lingered in the stables, with the beasts and the good smells and honest labor, but he was promised to a card party come evening—a gathering of earls, of all things, courtesy of his recent acquaintance with Lord Rosecroft—and Daisy might be in need of a nap.

"Most settlement money is simply kept in the cent per cents," Worth said.

"And most young ladies of good breeding and ample fortune are married off within a year or two of their come out. Lily Ferguson is comely, intelligent, very well-dowered, and as far as I can tell, in every way a woman worthy of esteem."

"And yet, we heard her insulted at my very club."

"Precisely. Most doting uncles would be anxious to see a niece well settled in her own household, a devoted husband at her side. If that were Leggett's aim, he's had years to achieve it."

"And those Sapphic tendencies?"

"An exaggeration at best, a ridiculous fabrication more likely."

Worth was silent while swallows flitted in and out of the barn and horses munched an unlooked-for treat. "Do you recall Vicar Huxley?"

"To my sorrow." The ordained man of Christ had beat his wife and children, while preaching love, tolerance, and turning the other cheek.

"You deduced what was afoot long before anybody else did," Worth said. "Does Miss Ferguson's situation strike you as similar?"

When week after week a woman was too stiff to rise from her church pew unaided and her children were perfectly behaved regardless of all provocation, even a gormless lad knew something was amiss.

"I am not an expert on abused women, but Miss Ferguson moves with a deal of bodily confidence. Her caution seems to be more of words and emotions than deeds, so I'd say no. Gentlemen are to protect the ladies and ensure their well-being though. That can easily shade into stifling a woman's freedom and disrespecting her independence. I'm sure a female of spirit and wit would be hurt by such insults."

"Lannie taught you that."

Doubtless, Jacaranda, Avery, and Worth's infant daughter were teaching him the same lesson. "You'll see what you can learn regarding Leggett?"

"He's trying to curry my favor, so a few polite inquiries from me will flatter his ambitions. Shall we storm the nursery?"

Yes, please. "Daisy and I are walking in the park with Miss Ferguson and her young friend on Wednesday at eleven. Perhaps Avery would like to join us?"

Worth crossed to the garden and held the gate open. "How will you get to steal any kisses with an infantry square of small children underfoot?"

Hessian sauntered through the gate. "The children occupy one another, leaving many an opportunity for a stolen kiss between the adults. It isn't complicated, Worth."

Worth should have burst forth in whoops of fraternal disrespect, should have punched Hessian on the shoulder, should have quipped that Jacaranda had stumbled upon that strategy months ago.

Instead, Worth walked to the house without another word, suggesting to Hessian that the family financial genius could learn a thing or two from his dull stick of an older brother.

* * *

Tippy was aging, and the realization both saddened and unnerved Lily.

Miss Ephrata Tipton hadn't been young when Lily had met her more than twenty years ago, and she was the closest thing Lily had to an ally. She was a slight woman, with intelligent brown eyes and graying brown hair. She'd doubtless been pretty when Lily had been too young and frightened to notice.

"You're kind to pay a call on me, miss," Tippy said, "but you needn't bother. Mr. Leggett sends my funds regularly, and I have all I need."

An odd thought occurred to Lily. "Do you have friends, Tippy?" She always seemed so brisk, so confident and self-sufficient.

Tippy's little parlor was a riot of cabbage roses—even her porcelain tea service was adorned with cabbage roses—dried bouquets, cutwork, and other evidence of a woman's pastimes, but Lily had never once come upon another caller here.

"Chelsea is growing so fast these days," Tippy said. "I hardly know who my neighbors are anymore."

Chelsea had the dubious fortune to lie close to London, and in a direction the city seemed determined to sprawl. Beyond the village, fields and pastures clung to the rural past, but every year, more houses and streets sprang up, and the fields receded, acre by acre.

"Does the vicar look in on you?" Did anybody take notice of a woman who'd spent her life devoted to a family to whom she wasn't related?

"I don't always get to services," Tippy said, opening her workbasket. "The weather can be so nasty, and my hip does pain me."

She took out an embroidery hoop, one she'd likely owned since before Lily's birth. The needle moved more slowly now, but the stitches were as neat as ever.

"Tippy, if I asked you to, would you move back to Uncle Walter's house?"

Tippy bent very close to her hoop. "Himself wouldn't want an old woman like me about. Creates awkwardness among the help to have a pensioner at the table."

Something about Tippy's posture, hunched over, getting in her own light, sent a chill through Lily. "You're afraid of him."

"You are too," Tippy retorted, "because we're both sensible creatures who know what he's capable of. You be careful, Miss Lilith Ann."

"You're not to call me that." Though Lily was glad she had.

"He's not here to chide me for it, though you're right. I ought not. How's that Oscar getting on?"

Why ask about him? "He's harmless and bored, drunk more often than he's sober. If he's to take over the family fortune, he has much to learn, and he doesn't seem to be in any hurry to learn it."

Tippy's needle moved in a patient rhythm. "Or his father isn't in a hurry to teach him."

Walter spun a web of influence and money, money and influence. He'd never turn over control of the finances to Oscar willingly, but if Oscar made himself useful, he'd at least be prepared when the transition became inevitable.

"Tippy, do you recall meeting the Earl of Grampion's heir?"

Tippy gazed off into the middle distance, sunlight gleaming on her poised needle. "Tall boy, blond, quiet? Odd name, something German. He was named for where his mother's people came from."

Increasingly, Tippy's recollections were like this—a mosaic of useless detail, speculation, and the occasional relevant fact. She still gave off the vibrant intelligence she'd had earlier in life, suggesting to Lily that Tippy simply disliked the memories of Lily's childhood.

"His given name is Hessian," Lily said, "and he informed me that, as a girl, I detested bugs."

Tippy's hands fell to her lap, hoop, needle, and all. "Oh dear."

Lily waited while Tippy frowned at the cabbage rose carpet.

"Children are invisible," Tippy said, smoothing a finger over the French knots in her embroidery. "They don't attend social functions, often don't use courtesy titles, and are mostly relegated to nurseries and schoolrooms."

Daisy was not invisible to Grampion, which was good. Lily was not invisible to him either, which was not good, however useful it might be for Uncle Walter.

"Outings to the park were very frequent," Tippy said. "Headstrong little girls benefit from fresh air and a chance to move about. Other children played in the park, some with nannies, some at that awkward age, boys not quite ready for university, impossible to occupy with studies all day. You could have met him on any number of occasions, possibly met the spare as well."

Tippy scooted about on her cushions and produced a small flask from some hidden pocket. She tipped a dollop of amber liquid into her tea.

"For my hip."

"Tippy, Grampion says we did meet."

Another dollop. "Then you explain to him that you're not right in the brainbox, you took a bad fall in Switzerland, and you can't recollect as well as other people. It happens."

It had not happened to Lily. "He noticed that bit about the bugs, he might notice some other inconsistency. Lying doesn't solve all problems, and one grows weary of deception."

One grew weary of being a deception.

"One does not grow tired of eating, Miss Lily. One does not grow tired of having a safe place to sleep, or a warm cloak in winter. You've read all the diaries, you've learned all I have to teach you. You've spent years being accepted as Walter Leggett's niece, and he's a powerful man."

The problem in a nutshell. No one dared cross Uncle Walter, least of all a frightened, half-starved fourteen-year-old girl who had no other options and didn't own a set of stays.

"Would you care for a nip, miss? It's a patent remedy and works a treat."

"No, thank you." Oscar could dwell in a continuous state of inebriation, but Lily dared not return home with a "patent remedy" on her breath. "The boy who recalled my disgust of bugs is the earl now, and Uncle wants me to cultivate his friendship."

"I wish I could help, miss."

Tippy had helped. For years, she'd been Lily's sole companion, her guide and support. That support was slipping, and not only because Tippy had decided to grow forgetful. If women occupied a vulnerable position in society, older women with neither fortune nor family navigated a sea of risks daily.

Lily rose. "If you recall anything, please do send for me." Notes were not a prudent way to communicate information of substance.

Tippy set aside her embroidery and pushed to her feet, though she moved more slowly than she had even a year ago.

"Tippy, are you ever lonely?"

Lily was lonely. Amid other emotions—terror, resentment, anxiety—loneliness had lurked unnoticed until recently. The girl Daisy had awakened it, and Grampion had given the loneliness a bitter, hopeless edge.

"I like my own company," Tippy said, linking arms with Lily and walking her to the door. "And I'm always glad to see you, but it might be best if you didn't come around for a bit, Lily. You can send me a note if you think I might be able to recall a detail or two, but I've grown forgetful, and it's all very much in the past."

Tippy had begun making this suggestion that Lily keep her distance about a year ago.

"Has Uncle Walter threatened you?" Though, if anything, Uncle would threaten Tippy for a lack of recall.

"No, miss. What's he to threaten me with? I have more than a bit put by after all these years. I help you to the best of my ability whenever you ask it of me. I've never breathed a word to anybody, and I never will. I was governess to

Miss Lily Ferguson, and she will always be in my prayers."

And yet, something was changing, despite the tidy sameness of Tippy's cottage. Lavender sachets held back the curtains. A rose velvet footstool sat before the window-end of the sofa. Embroidered cabbage roses adorned pillows, table runners, and framed samplers. Tippy even smelled faintly of roses, not a scent she could have afforded while in service.

God Save Our Good King George. Lily's work, a dozen years old, but nearly indistinguishable from Tippy's accomplishments.

And on the mantel, beneath that sampler, sat a pipe.

Oh.

Oh.

Tippy had a gentleman caller. The knowledge stabbed at Lily from many directions. She should be happy for Tippy, but instead, she was resentful, of the man, of the deception. She hoped he was worth Tippy's time and attention, and she was terrified that he'd take Tippy away.

"I'd best be going," Lily said, bending to envelop her former governess in a careful hug. Tippy had always been diminutive, and now she seemed fragile. "Send for me if you need anything. Anything at all."

"You drop me a note if you have more questions about your earl."

He's not my earl—though I wish he could be. "Thank you."

Lily climbed into the coach, knowing the duration of her visit would be reported to Uncle Walter, though none of the servants could relay what had passed between Tippy and her former charge.

"She's leaving me," Lily informed the elegant comfort of the town coach. "My only ally." Though Tippy, too, was Uncle Walter's creature.

And yet, Tippy had been the one to advise Lily to stash what pence and quid she could in a location Uncle Walter knew nothing about. A lady needed to save against a rainy day, Tippy had said with a wink, because in England, rain fell frequently.

Lily did have some money saved, though not enough. Not nearly enough.

CHAPTER EIGHT

Hessian's invitation to take the children to the park had been extended in a weak moment. He much preferred a ride at dawn, when all was still and calm, and the most that might be expected of him socially was a tip of the hat or muttered greeting.

For Daisy's sake, he'd ridden later in the morning, amid the nursemaids and governesses and their noisy, shrieking charges.

Now, he must brave utter chaos on foot for the sake of another hour spent with Miss Ferguson—and for Daisy's sake too, of course. A rowdy gang of schoolboys was playing kickball down by the Serpentine, a toddler had erupted into tears beneath a plane maple sporting a stranded kite. Other children threw rocks into the water, while nannies and governesses read—books positioned immediately before their faces—despite all the noise.

"I've come armed for combat," Miss Ferguson said, patting a large reticule. "My companion refused to stir from the house when the sun was so strong, but I have a ball, blanket, storybook, a few purloined tea cakes, and a flask of lemonade. What of you?"

"A flask of brandy." Hessian was telling the God's honest truth, and earned himself a smile. "Shall I carry your provisions?"

"You'd carry my reticule?"

"Of course." Hessian slung the strap over his shoulder. "You're the commanding officer on this sortie. You must be free to maneuver. Daisy, if you climb that tree, you'll get no pudding for a week."

This admonition—also entirely in earnest—provoked a spate of laughter from both Daisy and Bronwyn. They raced off after a hapless rabbit, while Miss Ferguson surveyed the surrounds as if she were indeed scouting enemy terrain.

"We want to avoid any stray boys," she said. "They are loud, mischievous, and curious."

The reticule weighed more than Hessian's longest fowling piece. "Was I loud, mischievous, and curious?"

"Bronwyn, do not stomp in that puddle."

The girl contented herself with finding a pebble to toss into the puddle, and for a moment, both children watched the rings spread across the surface.

"I mean you no insult, my lord, when I say that I can barely recall you as a boy."

Not an insult, but lowering. "I was not particularly memorable. My younger brother made it his mission in life to make sport of me, while my father expected a miniature earl to toddle out of the nursery, complete with consequence and self-possession."

The rabbit reappeared from the hedge, and the children crouched as if to sneak up on the poor creature.

"You were doomed," Miss Ferguson said, regarding Hessian with more seriousness than the moment wanted. "Your brother wanted a playmate, your father wanted a peer."

Habit prompted Hessian to disagree with her, to brush off the contradiction she pointed out.

With Lily Ferguson, only honesty would do.

"You are not wrong."

Her gaze was commiserating more than pitying. When had anybody commiserated with Hessian, Earl of Grampion?

"We must find a place in the shade," Miss Ferguson said, "where we can keep a vigilant eye on the children without the general public keeping its vigilant eye on us."

"Miss Ferguson, dare I hope you have designs on my person?" Worth might have said something like that, but the words had come from Hessian's own mouth—more honesty.

The rabbit hopped off a few yards and resumed nibbling. Bronwyn and Daisy, hand in hand, crept along behind it.

"You dare not hope any such thing," she retorted. "We are in Hyde Park, in view of half of Mayfair, and if I had designs on your person—not that I'd admit to such an unladylike ambition lest it fuel your manly self-importance—they would be inappropriate except in the most private of settings. I have designs on that patch of grass there."

She marched off, and Hessian followed.

Not quite a set-down, but neither had she exactly flirted with him. Hessian chose to be encouraged, because if Lily Ferguson wanted to deliver a set-down, she'd do so without ambiguity.

She chose a spot in dappled shade, away from the busiest walkways without being secluded. The blanket was a thick patchwork quilt gone soft with age. Her storybook was Aesop's Fables.

A second rabbit ventured from the hedge, and the girls held a conference, likely deciding whether to stalk one hare or both. Hessian offered Miss Ferguson a hand as she settled to the blanket, then took the place two feet to her right.

He had told Worth the truth: He enjoyed Miss Ferguson's company. She was a cool, tart lemonade compared to the overly sweet, tepid tea of the typical debutante or designing widow. Hessian had sampled the wares of a few of those widows, and had his own wares sampled, and found the encounters physically enjoyable.

Also sad.

"I feel a compulsion to warn those rabbits," Miss Ferguson said. "They are entirely too entranced by their clover."

She made a pretty picture in a wide-brimmed straw hat and old-fashioned walking dress of faded chocolate. Her millinery was as plain as any goose-girl's, not a frill, feather, or extra ribbon to be seen, and that only set off the elegance of her profile.

"The breeze warns those rabbits of the peril behind them. Most wild creatures who graze will arrange themselves thus, with their backs to the prevailing wind. Their eyes guard them from what's downwind, their noses from what's upwind, and their ears from hazards unseen."

Rather like Hessian in the ballroom. He kept his back to the wall, potted palms on at least one side, and eyes alert for a hostess seeking to pair him with any women save the wallflowers.

He liked the wallflowers, and hoped they liked him as well.

Miss Ferguson opened her book of fables to a random page. "You notice a great deal, my lord."

He noticed that Miss Ferguson was in a less approachable mood than when they'd shared an alcove with Apollo.

"I've spent many an hour pursuing wild game on my estate. For the most part, I tramp about, making a great racket and taking the air, but I have learned a few things from the beasts of the field. I notice that your ear has healed quite nicely, for example."

He'd like to nuzzle that ear. Perhaps all that twaddle about fresh spring air and the mating urge had some basis in science.

"My ear?"

"This very ear here." He touched her earlobe with his thumb and forefinger. "You slipped in the middle of a game of tag and got quite the gash on your ear. Your concern was not for your hearing, not for the consequences of a blow to the head, but for the imperfection your misadventure would leave. For weeks, you wore your hair such that your ear was covered, because there was a scar."

That ear was perfectly nuzzle-able now, no sign of any childhood mishap.

"Children heal better than adults do, but you should know, my lord, that my propensity for bad spills followed me past my childhood."

Hessian half-reclined on an elbow, lest he get to caressing her earlobe again—or any other part of her.

"You seem unscathed." Not quite true. In childhood, Lily Ferguson had borne a sense of entitlement, as if she'd already known she'd become an heiress. The present Lily did not suffer fools, but claimed modesty, humility, and common sense among her possessions.

The childhood Lily, in the opinion of a youthful Hessian, had been a pest.

"I am physically hale," she said, "but while at finishing school, I suffered a bad fall from an ill-tempered mount and took a blow to the head. I slept for two days and seemed to awaken unharmed, but, in fact, my memory is not whole. I can recall anything that happened after the fall, but not the fall itself and not all of what happened to me prior to it."

Another fact added itself to her recitation: A blow to the head could change personality, just as an apoplexy could. Winters were long in Cumberland, and Hessian had passed more than one reading through the medical treatises in the Grampion library.

"I'm sorry," he said. "I did not enjoy much of my youth and childhood, but I'd enjoy less if it hopped off into the hedges of my memory and eluded my recall. One likes to know one's own history."

Her gaze passed over him as fleetingly as a breeze. "Even if that history is painful?"

Another lady would have offered a quip, a flirtation, a flattery. Lily offered a difficult question—she'd lost both parents, after all—and Hessian liked her for it.

"I hope my painful memories protect me from future harm. By God, that child has hidden depths of patience. Her mother was persistent when fixed on a goal too."

Daisy had come within a yard of her quarry.

"Hidden depths of stealth. Girls learn early how to not be noticed. Then they are told that being noticed by the right sort of fellow in the right way defines success for them. It's confusing." She passed him the book. "Did life as an earl deal you many painful memories, my lord?"

Her question was an effort to turn the conversation to him—another skill most women learned early and well—and yet, Hessian wanted to answer. Kissing was all quite fine, but this conversation was personal, and that met a need kisses could not fulfill.

"My late wife occasioned some pain, for me and for my brother, and in the end for herself. She was from a local family, and I'd known her for years. I thought my brother had taken an interest in her—Worth got all the charm, you see—but she began to confide in me. She claimed that Worth had treated her callously, toyed with her, even trifled with her, and then scorned her."

Miss Ferguson loosened the ribbons of her straw hat. "Young men can be scoundrels."

The insult she'd been dealt in Hessian's club came to mind. Perhaps Worth could be convinced to ruin Islington.

And all of his lordship's drunken little friends too.

"A young man can also be gullible as hell," Hessian said, "and competitive with his only brother. Increasingly, the young lady found comfort in my embrace—great, strapping, bastion of male thick-headedness that I was. She would cry and fret, which required that even a brute such as I stroke her hair, pat her back, and lend her my handkerchief, all the while battling such thoughts as a gallant knight never admits save to his confessor."

"You are not a brute."

Which left great, strapping, and thick-headed. "I was a self-important prig. Worth came upon the young lady and me in an embrace that was innocent on my part and entirely calculated on hers. She'd escalated her accusations, claiming that she was with child and Worth had refused to marry her. She was begging me to save her good name, and then Worth stumbled upon us."

"This qualifies as a painful memory all around."

"Also as melodrama, though I could not see that at the time. Worth marched off in high dudgeon, convinced I'd dangled my title before the love of his life. Papa said to marry the girl and leave Worth to sort out his temper on his own, and I said... I said, 'Of course, Papa.'"

"Your brother hadn't trifled with her?"

"He'd barely stolen a few kisses. Her falsehoods became obvious in due time, and Worth and I have put it behind us, but one has regrets."

Hessian regretted the tree root digging into his hip, so he sat up and found himself a mere foot from Miss Ferguson.

"What are they doing now?" she asked, shading her eyes. Both children were prone in the grass, the rabbits forgotten a few yards away.

"Probably looking for lucky clovers, or perhaps studying life from a rabbit's-eye view." The view from Hessian's half of the blanket was pretty and thoughtful.

"Your brother apparently came right eventually," she said. "He's reported to have done quite well for himself."

"Worth is arse over teakettle in love with his wife, if that's what you mean." Also with his daughter, his niece, his dog... his life.

"I meant..." Miss Ferguson glanced around. "Financially. Worth Kettering is a nabob. All London knows it. The rumor is, he's even done a good turn for King George, who spends money faster than it can be minted."

Worth had done several good turns for the sovereign, about which one was enjoined to remain silent. "My brother left Grampion Hall rich in injured pride. He was determined to make his own way, and having a full complement of Kettering determination, he achieved that end spectacularly."

Hessian was close enough to the lady to get a hint of her fragrance—daffodils, an innocent, happy scent.

"You are proud of your brother."

"Obnoxiously so."

She watched the children, who were doubtless exchanging girlish confidences while enjoying the fresh air.

"You should know that my Uncle Walter seeks to do business with your brother. He hopes to curry Worth Kettering's favor by offering agreeable companionship in the form of myself to the nabob's older brother."

Miss Ferguson's disclosure smacked of intrigue, guile, and deceit, which Hessian would sort out later. If Walter Leggett sought to manipulate either Kettering brother, he was doomed to disappointment.

"What do you seek, Lily Ferguson?"

Now, she faced him. "To spend time in the company of a man whom I esteem, while ensuring an orphaned little girl whom I care about—despite all sense to the contrary—also has a pleasant outing."

Hessian was growing to loathe the word esteem. Esteem was not liking, desire, passion, friendship… Esteem was a hedge into which shy rabbits dodged when they had no wish to be involved in drama, and yet, Hessian had used the word himself.

Miss Ferguson was on her feet without giving Hessian a chance to assist her. "Those girls will get grass stains all over their pinafores. If you'd hand me the ball, please?"

He retrieved the ball from her reticule and tossed it to her. She caught it with her left hand and marched off toward the children.

"Ladies, it's time to work on our athletic skills!" She fired the ball across the grass with as much skill and accuracy as Hessian had encountered on the cricket pitches at public school.

The girls were on their feet, shrieking and chasing after the ball, while Hessian puzzled over a detail, probably to spare himself pondering Miss Ferguson's revelation about Leggett's scheme.

As a girl, Lily Ferguson had once fired a ball at him, straight at a location highly vulnerable to injury. The memory was as fresh as when she'd first offered the insult, because Hessian had moved at the very last instant and got a handsome bruise to the thigh.

Lily doubtless forgot the incident, but Hessian never would, and thus he was plagued by a question: When had Lily Ferguson become left-handed?

* * *

The front door clicked quietly closed, and barely audible footsteps passed

Roberta Braithwaite's parlor. She waited until those footsteps had started up the stairs—the third stair creaked—before speaking.

"You have become positively devoted to your constitutionals, Penelope."

The truant appeared in the parlor doorway looking appropriately guilty. "Good day, Mrs. Braithwaite."

"Well, come in," Roberta said. "I've no objection to you enjoying a bit of the air, provided you took Thomas with you."

"I did, of course. Just for a turn in the park." Penelope hovered in the doorway, while Roberta made herself a sandwich from the offerings on a tray. "You hadn't come down for breakfast, ma'am, so I thought luncheon would be set back. I'm sorry if I've upset the household schedule."

Whoever Penelope was meeting in the park, he'd put some color in her otherwise pale cheeks.

"Your outing has left you flushed," Roberta said. "Have a seat and let's get some sustenance into you. You must help me plan my next assault on the citadel of Grampion's stubbornness. What sort of man keeps a grieving child from her only female relation?"

Penelope perched on the edge of an armchair. "I'm sure I wouldn't know, ma'am. His lordship was not exactly approachable, was he?"

"Earls. The only thing worse is a new viscount for being contrary and self-important. Marquesses and dukes tend to be secure enough in their stations that they needn't put on airs, and barons know their places."

Roberta took a bite of ham with watercress and mustard. The bread was yesterday's and would have done better as toast.

"His lordship was quite informal with the children in the park today," Penelope said. Her sandwich consisted of butter and watercress, not a slice of beef or even a nibble of cheese.

More for me, Roberta thought, finishing her sandwich. "Grampion was frolicking in the park?"

"He was in the company of Miss Lily Ferguson, and they were supervising two small girls. I assume one of the girls was Amy Marguerite."

Roberta washed down her sandwich with lemonade that could have used more sugar. "How do you know Miss Ferguson?"

"You've pointed out her uncle, ma'am. You said Mr. Leggett was the brother of an old friend, and I've noticed that he seldom appears socially without his niece. I adore fresh butter."

As if Roberta would allow the kitchen to send up any other kind. "Lily Ferguson is the closest thing Walter has to a hostess. Miss Ferguson's mother died years ago, left the poor girl orphaned and positively awash in money."

Lady Nadine Leggett had been excessively pretty, but also so friendly, Roberta hadn't been able to resent her. Then Lady Nadine had married a ducal spare and shortly ended up a wealthy, titled widow.

Any woman would have found those turns of fortune deserving of a bit of jealousy. "She had little time to be a merry widow, though, more's the pity."

And Lady Nadine had been merry. Exceedingly merry. Roberta had had a letter or two from her confessing as much.

"Would you like more lemonade, ma'am?"

Roberta would have liked a nice, cool glass of hock, but German wines were not cheap. No wine worth drinking was cheap, no cheese worth serving, no dresses worth wearing…

"The lemonade is too tart. I am quite vexed with Lord Grampion. How dare he be gamboling in the park like some schoolboy on holiday when Amy Marguerite has been dealt such a grievous blow?"

Penelope began assembling a second sandwich. "If I may say, Amy Marguerite looked to be having a capital time. She was laughing and racing about, if that was her."

"Blond hair, about seven years old—or six, I forget which—on the petite side?"

"That sounds like her. The other girl was either older or of sturdier conformation. They got on famously, from what little I saw."

"Did Grampion snatch my poor Amy Marguerite away from her friend?"

"Oh, no, ma'am, but I did not want to tarry in the park in case you awoke and had need of me."

What a parcel of lies. Whatever callow swain Penelope had met had likely spared the poor thing only a moment or two of his time. Men were like that.

"I wonder if Walter Leggett knows what a baggage his sister was."

Penelope helped herself to a glass of lemonade. "One shouldn't speak ill of the dead."

Nobody ever said why one shouldn't speak ill of the dead. The living were on hand to take offense and mete out retribution for impolite talk. The dead were too busy strumming their harps.

"Lady Nadine—then Lady Alfred, for she married Lord Alfred Ferguson— got to enjoying her widowhood, and little more than a year after losing her husband, she was off on an extended stay in Rome. You know what that means."

Penelope peered at Roberta over one of the last two crystal glasses in everyday use. "She needed to work on her Italian?"

Roberta helped herself to a tea cake, though she'd had several already. "Was that an attempt to be humorous? Lady Nadine was an earl's daughter. Her skill with languages was impeccable, while her common sense was never sufficiently in evidence. She'd got herself in trouble, and while a child appearing directly after a man's death might be considered his offspring, Nadine's problem presented itself too long after any claim of legitimacy might have been made."

Penelope set down her glass. "That must have been very difficult for all concerned."

"Very embarrassing. As an old and dear friend, Lady Nadine could of course rely on my discretion, though others would not have been so kind. I never learned what became of the girl, and either the Leggett money or a belated dose of discretion kept the situation from becoming common knowledge."

Roberta rose, because this recitation of ancient history was stirring her imagination, and an active mind could be aided by an active body.

"I suppose," Penelope said, "these things happen in the best families. My papa always says a title is no guarantee of sense."

And lack of one no guarantee of brains. "Dorie Humplewit would not have kept Lady Nadine's confidences as I have."

"You are a very loyal friend."

Dorie Humplewit would have turned the whole situation to coin somehow. She would have blackmailed Walter Leggett, compromised him, blackmailed him and compromised him…

"Walter is a cold fish, for all he smiles and nods at the right times."

"I beg your pardon?"

"Walter Leggett. He has pots of money."

Penelope finished her second sandwich and her lemonade while Roberta paced the parlor.

"I have no wish to become Mrs. Walter Leggett." She would not mind in the least having his money, though. "I'd have to entertain, put up with Walter's wastrel son, and share a household with Miss Lily Ferguson."

"Is Mr. Leggett attempting to court you?" Penelope asked around a mouthful of tea cake.

"He would be if I wanted him to be, but one shudders to contemplate fulfillment of one's wifely duties. The colonel, God rest his soul, was all the husband I could ever need or want."

Roberta took another turn around the parlor, mentally assessing relationships, assets, and what information she had.

"Did Grampion appear to favor Miss Ferguson?" For this was key to the plan taking shape in Roberta's mind.

"I would say that, well, in my opinion, he did. Nothing improper, of course, but they were on a picnic blanket, sitting rather close, and Miss Ferguson didn't seem to mind."

"Grampion is a widowed earl on the prowl for a countess. Lily Ferguson would not have minded if he'd ripped off his clothing and sat in her lap."

Penelope's pale brows drew down. "Whyever would he—?"

"Fetch your workbasket, before you drive me daft, please."

Penelope dutifully trotted off, and must have fetched her workbasket by way of King's Cross, for she was gone long enough that Roberta's thoughts could organize themselves. Grampion had the girl, Grampion had money. Roberta wanted the girl, because Roberta wanted Grampion's money.

Not a huge sum, a few hundred pounds a year would do. Maybe a thousand. Amy Marguerite must not want for anything.

Grampion also, apparently, had taken a liking to Miss Lily Ferguson, and she to him. Neither parti had caught the eye of any other marital prospect—the society pages would have mentioned an heiress or an earl paying notable attention to a prospective spouse.

So the plan became quite simple: Miss Lily Ferguson must convince Grampion that Amy Marguerite—and a portion of the earl's money—belonged with Roberta, or Roberta feared Lady Nadine's letters might fall into the wrong hands.

Not even Dorie Humplewit on her most bold, ingenious day could have come up with such an elegant, effective solution.

CHAPTER NINE

I will kill Walter Leggett.

Lily played endless rounds of catch while both girls stood between the adults and tried to snatch the ball, and the earl ensured they occasionally could.

While Lily smiled, laughed, and hid a growing sense of despair. Hessian Kettering had been sorely betrayed by a woman's deceptions before. Now Lily was inveigling herself into his good graces, and he probably thought her very brave and forthright for disclosing Uncle's agenda.

She was a lying coward, and that had never bothered her as much as it did now.

Daisy made a great leap for the ball, missed, and collapsed in a heap.

"You nearly got it!" Grampion called, though his good cheer had no effect.

Daisy sat in the grass sniffling, Bronwyn standing over her worriedly. "Did you break your ankle, Daze? Maybe you broke your leg, or your ankle and your leg."

Grampion knelt in the grass. "I doubt it's broken. Daisy is a robustly healthy young lady, with strong bones and nimble reflexes."

He passed Daisy a handkerchief and unlaced her little half boot. "There, you see? A perfectly whole, pretty little foot."

"And a stocking," Bronwyn said, crouching. "Does it hurt like blazes, Daisy?"

"Y-yes, and I fell."

"You took a graceful tumble," Grampion retorted. "Can you wiggle your toes?"

She wiggled them.

"Can you wiggle your foot?"

Another wiggle.

He held his palm near her sole. "Can you kick my hand?" He made a production out of flinging his hand back when Daisy kicked his palm. "We have a mere field injury, which should come right with rest and a little cosseting. As it happens, Miss Ferguson has brought lemonade and cakes, also a storybook." He scooped Daisy up and got her situated piggyback. "Shall we to the blanket, Miss Ferguson?"

Lily's middle felt funny, and her heart was thumping against her ribs. She'd once wrenched her ankle badly when bringing the milk in from the dairy. She'd spilled one bucket and saved the other. Her foot had hurt for days, but all she'd got for her trouble was a thrashing and a week without supper.

"You're sure Daisy doesn't need a physician?"

"My Daisy is made of stern stuff. She'll come right, you'll see."

"I'm made of stern stuff too," Bronwyn announced. "But I would like some tea cakes."

Lily took Bronwyn's hand, though tea cakes wouldn't help what ailed her. She liked Grampion, she respected him, she was attracted to him, and every time she told herself that such nonsense could go nowhere, he did something honorable or dear and wrecked her intentions all to flinders.

This would not do.

Grampion read the fable about the crow who was clever enough to raise the water level in a pitcher by dropping rocks into it, while the girls devoured tea cakes and tossed crumbs to presuming pigeons. All too soon, the outing came to an end, for it was the last outing Lily would permit herself with his lordship.

While the girls made a final inspection of the hedges for their rabbit friends, Grampion assisted Lily to fold up the blanket.

They started with a good shake, then stepped closer to match the corners. Grampion closed his fingers over Lily's.

"Might you ride with me in the park tomorrow? Early, when it's quiet and free of children."

"My lord, I've confessed my uncle's intention to turn your brother up sweet by inflicting my company upon you. You need not be gallant."

He brushed a thumb over Lily's knuckles, a small gesture that bespoke a great mistake in progress.

"Your uncle is an idiot, Lily Ferguson, if he thinks either Kettering brother can be swayed by a

pretty face and intelligent companionship. Won't you please come riding with me?"

"That isn't wise."

Another subtle caress. "Haven't you had enough of being unrelentingly wise and proper? I certainly have. Also enough of being lonely."

More than enough. "You must not say such things." But if he must say them, how delightful that he'd say them to Lily.

He tugged the blanket from her grasp and folded it in a few brisk moves. "I am not a callow swain, to be deterred by your uncle's pawing and snorting, and you are not a mere girl, incapable of forming your own opinions. Won't you please come riding with me?"

Had he insisted, commanded, or assumed, Lily might have stood a chance. He asked—sincerely and politely.

"A short hack only, and I'll bring my groom."

"Of course you will. Meet me at the gate at six o'clock, and we'll have the place to ourselves."

"I'll look forward to that, my lord."

All the way home, Lily contemplated the folly of accepting Grampion's invitation and decided that tomorrow's outing with his lordship could be her last as easily as today's.

What difference would one more gallop in the park make?

Lily returned Bronwyn to her parents and endured Miss Fotheringham's lamentations about spring air and megrims. All the while, Lily considered a question: Uncle's attempts to insinuate himself into the Kettering family's good graces were no longer a secret, and yet, Grampion had asked for this outing in the park.

What had motivated Grampion's invitation, and—novel, delicious, forbidden question—if he was intent on courting Lily, why shouldn't she encourage his suit? Uncle wanted cordial relations with the Ketterings, and if Lily married the earl, Uncle would have exactly what he wanted.

As would—for once—Lily herself.

* * *

"You and I both prefer a certain order in life, a certain predictable progression of events," Hessian said. "I've come to London to spend time with my family and to entertain the notion of remarrying, for example, as one does. Stop wringing your tail."

Hammurabi left off whisking his tail around his quarters and instead hopped about on the alley's cobbles. His idea of predictability was that a dawn ride meant a whacking great gallop. That he was still three streets away from Hyde Park, and might dash his rider's brains out with his foolishness, apparently hadn't penetrated his horsey awareness.

"Settle, you," Hessian murmured. "We will soon be in the presence of ladies, and we both know better than to leap about and carry on at the mere prospect of female companionship."

Ham's restraint in this regard had been surgically enhanced, while all Hessian could call upon was years of self-discipline.

He had hoped that his initial interest in Lily Ferguson would calm to a more mature regard—hoped that he and she might become cordially bored with each other, from which perspective, marriage might be rationally contemplated.

Hessian's dreams were full of contemplations so far from rational where Lily Ferguson was concerned, he might have again been a lad of fifteen lusting after the scullery maid.

"Though the present situation differs from my youthful longings in several particulars. We're not cantering, damn you." Though Hessian permitted his horse a brisk—very brisk—trot.

"I am not fifteen, Lily Ferguson is not a menial about whom I must banish any wayward thoughts, and even as I enjoy the lady's company—greatly enjoy the lady's company—I can also admit that I'm being ridiculous."

Ham gave an energetic double kick out behind, snorted at nothing, and subsided into a gentlemanly gait.

"Kicking in public. You should be ashamed, you naughty boy." Though fresh morning air generally made Ham frisky.

Flower-girls wrapped in thick cloaks yawned as they set up their stalls. Link-boys, lanterns extinguished, wearily searched for a quiet place to rest from the night's labors, and dairymaids paused to visit with one another in misty alleys.

All was not right with the world—the Braithwaite woman had to be dealt with, for example—but in Hessian's world, all was moving in the loveliest of directions.

"I am so inspired by the pleasure of my next appointment that I can admit—only to you, my trusted friend—that Worth was right to bludgeon me into coming to London for the Season. Jacaranda doubtless put him up to it."

The gates of Hyde Park emerged from the thin fog, and Hessian brought his horse to the walk. "One must cling to a modicum of dignity, horse."

Though with Lily, Hessian was increasingly unconcerned with dignity or posturing of any kind. He could be honest with Lily Ferguson—about his frustration and challenges, even his fears—and he loved that she was honest with him.

Esteemed her forthright nature, rather.

Respected her pragmatism.

Bollocks. He was mad for her.

The lady herself was waiting just inside the gate. Hessian's heart leaped— what a hopeless cliché. His heart hopped about like a March hare, he was so pleased.

Though he was equally displeased to see a weathered groom perched on a dappled cob five yards away. Hang the proprieties—Hessian's intentions toward Miss Ferguson could not have been more respectable.

He tipped his hat. "Miss Ferguson, good day."

She saluted with her whip. "Your lordship. I see I must add promptness to your list of virtues. Patience does not number among my mare's attributes. Shall we be on our way?"

Miss Ferguson's habit was several years out of date, but the color—a soft brown trimmed in red braid—flattered her, and she sat her chestnut mare well.

"Let's be off," Hessian said, turning Ham to the path along the Serpentine.

They cantered off the fidgets, and thank the kind powers, the park remained quiet. The mist was slow to lift, and thus sounds were muffled, the horses' hoofbeats a quiet tattoo on a quieter morning. The trees were only beginning to leaf out, the daffodils not yet finished with their display, and the whole park had an enchanted, secluded feel.

"Shall we let the horses blow?" Miss Ferguson asked. "I confess my outings are usually more sedate."

Hessian's whole life was usually more sedate. "Shall I check your girths? Wouldn't want the saddle to come loose."

He swung off Ham and looped the reins around his wrist. Miss Ferguson's girths were doubtless snug enough, but Hessian wanted to be useful... to be gallant, to use Miss Ferguson's words. She swept her skirts aside while he tightened the buckle one hole.

"We've outpaced my groom," Miss Ferguson said.

"Then you'd best kiss me now, lest I expire for want of same." Oh, that was subtle, about as subtle as Hammurabi in pursuit of his carrots, or—

Miss Ferguson bent down and cupped Hessian's cheek in a gloved hand, then kissed him with a lingering thoroughness. She tasted of peppermint, and the combination of soft lips on Hessian's mouth, leather against his jaw, and his hat tumbling to the grass made the moment perfect.

The kiss ended too soon, and not soon enough, for Hessian's self-restraint had gone tumbling as well. Desire stirred from one stolen kiss, and that would not do when the outing was to continue on horseback.

"We must talk," Hessian said, taking half a step back.

"I prefer kissing you," Miss Ferguson replied. "I like conversing with you too, particularly when we're not plagued with demands for stories, games of catch, or tales of pirate treasure."

Hessian assisted her to dismount, and when the groom came bouncing up on his cob, Hessian passed him the mare's reins and Hammurabi's.

"If you'd walk them both, please. A brisk canter works up a sweat when they've yet to lose all of their winter coats."

The groom apparently saw the logic of Hessian's request—or the threat of retribution in his eyes—for he collected the horses and wandered into the mist with them.

"Of what shall we talk?" Miss Ferguson asked.

Of passion, of intimacies beyond mere kisses, of vows spoken with joy and enthusiasm, and a wedding night that—

"The day looks as if it will remain overcast," Hessian said, retrieving his hat and dusting off the brim. "I like the occasional cloudy day."

"I should not have kissed you, but I'm glad I did."

"I like your honesty—and kissing you. Like both rather a lot. One might even say…" Hessian took the lady by the hand and escorted her—he did not drag her—behind a lilac hedge weeks away from blooming.

This time, he took the initiative, bolting into the kiss with all the longing of a man who'd spent his nights dreaming of naked bodies, heated embraces, and long, long Cumbrian winter nights.

"The fashionable crowd gets it all wrong," he murmured against Miss Ferguson's lips. "They come to the Lakes in summer."

She burrowed closer, gripping the lapel of Hessian's riding jacket with one hand. "What are you going on about?"

"The Lakes show to best advantage in winter, when the nights never end."

A riding habit had voluminous skirts that buttoned and stitched together in a complicated arrangement. The intention was to accommodate both modesty and freedom of movement, which features allowed Miss Ferguson to insinuate a leg between Hessian's thighs.

He accepted that invitation and gloried in the feel of her—as enthusiastic as she was feminine—snuggled against him.

"Is this all you want from me, Miss Ferguson? Passionate kisses on a spring morning? I'm overjoyed to comply, but I also hope for more."

"I hope you will one day call me Lily," she said.

"Lily." Holding her was delightful and improper, abundantly satisfying and inadequate. "You will call me Hessian. My maternal antecedents hailed from that corner of Germany. Worth calls me Hess."

A silly little detail, but one a wife should know about her husband.

She nuzzled his cravat—he'd worn blonde lace for her this morning. "I don't want to let you go, Hessian."

That sentiment was quite mutual. "Might I hope that longing is metaphorical rather than merely a statement of present intent? For on my part, the same sentiment could be said to be both."

She stepped back. "And you say I should be a barrister. We haven't much time, sir. I'd ask for a translation of that last flight of verbosity."

She asked for his heart or, at the least, for a display of courage. "I have come to London to seek a countess. I hope my search is over."

Lily—he was to call her Lily—fluffed the crushed folds of his cravat. "When you make up your mind, be sure to drop me a note. I will rejoice at the lady's good fortune."

Hessian hadn't spoken with her uncle yet, hadn't asked permission to pay his addresses, hadn't given Worth a chance to learn what was afoot with Leggett.

"Will the lady do me a similar courtesy when she's made up her mind?" he asked.

A drop of condensation landed on Lily's shoulder. Hessian brushed it away, then ran his thumb over the curve of her jaw.

"I am not young, my lord. I will be eight-and-twenty in less than a month, and my uncle's wishes regarding my future must be considered."

The conversation was not going as Hessian had planned, but then, he hadn't planned much more than hasty grappling beneath the maples. Lily was owed much more, and fortunately for Hessian, courtships also unfolded in certain predictable stages.

"In the very near future, I will make a private appointment with your uncle. Will that suit?"

Her smile was troubled—perhaps by impatience or self-consciousness. Hessian was certainly impatient. He was not a blushing youth, and whatever Walter Leggett's demands regarding Lily's settlements, Leggett could hardly dismiss an earl of means and sterling reputation.

But then Hessian recalled Lily's words about her uncle's attitude regarding fortune hunters.

"He won't run me off, Lily. My situation is sound and improving steadily. Worth has aided me in taking the earldom's finances in hand, and Grampion prospers well beyond the ambitions my father had for it."

Hoofbeats clip-clopped on the path.

Lily seized him in a brief, torrid kiss, and stepped back. "Don't let me keep you from your appointments, my lord. I've enjoyed this outing exceedingly, but you're right. The sun appears reluctant to grace us with his presence today." She affixed herself to Hessian's arm and tugged him back in the direction of the horses. "We'd best be getting home before the morning turns rainy."

"Sensible, as always," Hessian said as the groom reappeared, the mare and gelding toddling along behind him. "I do so value your forthright nature, Miss Ferguson. You say what's on your mind and have no use for polite dissembling."

Hessian tightened Ham's girth one hole, while Lily stroked the beast's nose and ears. Ham lowered his head and whuffled like a shameless beggar.

Hessian glowered at the witless beast. "Have some dignity, horse."

Lily kissed Ham's nose. "I like a fellow who's able to set aside his pretensions from time to time and enjoy a stolen kiss, but far be it from me to tell a belted earl how to conduct himself."

"You'll lead my horse astray with such talk," Hessian retorted. "Let's get you back into the saddle before the poor fellow attempts public indiscretions."

The groom was busy checking his own girth while remaining in the saddle. That undertaking required focus, so Hessian boosted Lily onto her horse and took meticulous care to arrange her skirts over her boots.

Hammurabi waited at Hessian's shoulder—right at his shoulder—as if longing for more kisses just as his owner was.

"My damned horse is smitten."

Lily took up her reins and arranged her whip. "Perhaps the condition is contagious, for I adore a day that starts amid the fresh air and good company to be found on a morning hack."

Hessian stroked her mare's shoulder. "As do I. Perhaps we might share the same pleasure on Saturday, weather permitting?"

Lily gazed down at him. "With you, I'd ride in the rain, my lord. I'd ride anywhere, at any hour." She urged her mare forward, and Hammurabi nudged Hessian's backside.

Right. To horse. Assuming Hessian could endure the saddle in his present state. He kept Ham alongside Lily's mare until they reached the gates of the park.

"Until Saturday?" he asked.

"I'm attending the Bascombes' musicale tomorrow night," Lily said. "You might catch a glimpse of me there."

"I have always enjoyed good music. Thank you for an exceedingly pleasant hour, Miss Ferguson."

She saluted with her whip and trotted off into streets that still had little traffic. Hessian admired her retreating form—she rode with a natural seat and had the true equestrienne's ability to communicate with her mount in ways subtle and effective.

Though when had Lily Ferguson taken a liking to horses? As a child, she'd claimed to hate them because they invariably provoked her to sneezing and itching.

CHAPTER TEN

Lily took her time riding home, mostly because she didn't want to deal with Uncle Walter at the breakfast table. As long as she remained on her mare, the assignation with Hessian Kettering wasn't entirely over.

Hessian was such an odd name, but then, the Hessian soldier was very different from his English counterpart. The English soldier fought because he was more afraid of his officers than his enemies, and starvation often counted among those potential foes. The German soldier fought for his comrades and relied on them to protect him, and thus improved morale in any unit he was associated with.

Blücher's troops had saved the day at Waterloo too.

And Hessian, Earl of Grampion, was saving Lily, did he but know it.

She turned her mare into the alley that led to the Leggett stables and pondered the extent to which she was attracted to the earl for himself, and how much she longed—if fate were merciful and Lily very careful—for Grampion to free her from Uncle Walter's household.

A bit of both, if she were honest. Which she only occasionally could be.

"Good morning, Lily." Oscar sat on the ladies' mounting block. He held a bottle, likely a final vestige of the previous night's revels. "You're looking fine today."

Oscar was not looking fine. He had a smear of pink across his right cheekbone, his cravat was knotted crookedly, and his cuff sported what looked like a wine stain. When he assisted Lily to dismount, his breath was a foul miasma and his smile lopsided.

"Oscar, you'd best not let Uncle see you in this condition."

He resumed his seat on the mounting block, while the groom led the horses away. "I'm adept at sneaking up the servants' stairs. Besides, once Papa gets his nose into the financial pages, Napoleon escaping again wouldn't get his attention. You must have gone for quite a gallop, judging from the state of your mare."

Lily took the place beside him, for she was not adept at sneaking up the servants' stairs, more's the pity.

"I've let my mare get out of condition, but then, she's no longer young." Lily had told his lordship she herself was approaching her twenty-eighth birthday, which advanced her age by two years.

Another lie, among the last she'd tell him.

"I get the same lecture from Papa," Oscar said. "I'm no longer a boy. Care for a nip?"

"No, thank you. You're barely down from university. Why would Uncle lecture you about your age?"

Oscar was physically maturing, now that Lily took the time to study him. He'd been a chubby boy, fond of his sweets, and good-natured. He'd always had a crowd of equally good-natured wastrel friends, who'd dutifully danced with Lily when prevailed upon to do so.

Harmless boys who'd turn into harmless club men. Oscar was emerging into manhood late, and the result was a blond fellow with decent manners and a nice smile. Doubtless, Uncle Walter had once been much the same sort.

"I'm to make something of myself," Oscar reported gloomily. "I'm to amount to something. I have no objection in theory, but when my education has been more about tarts than tutors, one does puzzle over the practical implementation of Papa's notions."

Oscar had never been an object of his father's criticism before, while Lily had never known Uncle's tolerance.

"Uncle grows fixed on his objectives. Can you set aside a portion of your allowance and invest it?"

Oscar tipped the wine to his mouth, shook out the last drops, and set the bottle aside. "My allowance has been late the past two quarters. The fellows are patient about IOUs or standing me to a pint, but my allowance was never late before."

Was it late, or was Uncle up to one of his stratagems?

Lily liked Oscar, to the extent she could afford to like anybody. They left each other alone, which was a form of kindness.

"How many cravat pins do you have, Oscar?"

"Scads."

"Lose one or two and take them to the pawnbrokers," Lily said. "Don't give them to your valet to pawn. You do it yourself, lest anybody question Lumley about his errand. Take your old boots to another pawnbroker in a different part of Town and claim you lost them as the result of a drunken wager. Try to put the funds where nobody will find them, but if a maid cleaning your room should come upon your money and bring it to Uncle's attention, say you won it at cards."

The sounds of a normal morning routine came from inside the stable. Horses munching hay, a groom whistling God Save the King while he swept the aisle. This conversation wasn't normal, though, not between Lily and her cousin.

"I'm sorry, Lily," Oscar said. "I know Papa keeps a close eye on you. I hadn't realized it was that bad."

Because Lily and Uncle Walter made sure nobody realized exactly how contentious their relationship was.

"I manage," Lily said. "Once you have a few pounds together, take them to Worth Kettering to invest. He's discreet and canny, and your small sum will soon grow."

Oscar burped, perfuming the morning air with stale wine and garlic. "Papa wants to invest with Kettering. I've wondered if the Ferguson side of your family does business through him. They have the paternal portion of your inheritance to manage."

Since leaving her finishing school, Lily hadn't seen the Ferguson side of the family. Mama's husband had been a younger son of an Irish ducal family, and they preferred their seat to anything resembling English soil. Once a year, the current duke wrote to her, and he wrote back. All very proper and hopeless.

"How do you know the Fergusons are minding my father's fortune?" Lily knew it, because Walter had explained the finances to her in detail more than ten years ago.

"I'm lazy," Oscar said, "I'm not stupid. Any hatpin will open the drawers to Papa's desk, and if he don't want me poking about in his study, then he shouldn't keep our best brandy on his sideboard. Though lately, even the best brandy hasn't been worth the bother."

The joy filling Lily as a result of her dawn ride was fading, like a creeping fog obliterates the sun.

"Is Uncle in financial difficulties?"

"How can he be in difficulties when he has the Leggett half of your fortune to bring him right? I'm not saying he'd steal from you, but he might make himself a small loan to weather a rough patch."

Walter Leggett would steal from Old Scratch himself.

"Get whatever money you can to Worth Kettering," Lily said. "Do it yourself, don't trust the servants."

"Not even Lumley," Oscar murmured, suggesting he was sober enough to grasp the import of the conversation. "I can be careful. You be careful too, Lily. I've heard you're spending time with Kettering's titled brother. Is that at Papa's behest?"

Well, yes. Initially. "I enjoy the earl's company. Grampion doesn't put on airs and he's sensible."

"And if you can bag that one," Oscar said, squinting down the neck of his empty bottle, "you'd dwell in Cumberland, far from Uncle's reach. He'll never let Grampion pay you his addresses though."

"You seem quite certain of your conclusion."

Oscar tossed the bottle into the bushes. "Lily, if Papa's in dun territory and dipping into your funds to cover his losses, the last thing he'll do is get into settlement negotiations with the Kettering family. Before a titled lord takes a bride, her family's finances and his family's finances are shared in detail. Your Ferguson relations will bestir themselves to get involved, and then you have an earl and a duke peering at Papa's ledger books. He won't like that."

Lily's hopes—so fragile and new—took a bludgeoning. Oscar, hen-witted bon vivant and fashion plate, had seen what she had not.

"I have been an idiot."

Oscar patted her arm. "You're pretty. You needn't be clever."

She rose and paced away from the mounting block. She liked Oscar well enough, but she didn't like him touching her even with tipsy affection. Then too, he needed a bath and a long session with his toothpowder.

"I have been too focused on missing earbobs when I should have seen the larger context."

"You're not wearing earbobs."

And Lily hadn't been thinking. She'd been dreaming of a serious, passionate earl who intended to make an appointment to speak with Uncle Walter next week. Good God, what a muddle.

"We never had this conversation, Oscar. If anybody asks, we talked about how to bring my mare back into condition."

"Regular work," Oscar said. "Fine for a horse, has no appeal for me. Where are you off to?"

"I must change out of my habit. Uncle would scold me into next year if I showed up at breakfast in riding attire." And Lily felt a desperate compulsion to make sure her small hoard of money was where she had hidden it.

She let herself through the garden gate and took the servants' stairs up to her room.

* * *

"We're off to see your Uncle Worth and Aunt Jacaranda," Hessian said, extending a hand to Daisy. "At the rate your social schedule is expanding, I shall soon have to find you a pony."

The nursery maid, a stout, gray-haired bastion of starch and bombazine named Sykes, folded her arms.

Daisy's grip on Hessian's hand tightened. "Even if I'm bad, you'd give me a pony?"

Oh, for God's sake. Hessian hefted the child to his hip. "You cannot be bad, Daisy. You might make a misstep, have a lapse, exercise poor judgment, or do something you regret, but you cannot be bad. And yes, if you're consistently making poor choices, I might limit your time in the saddle temporarily, but that would take extreme provocation."

At this, the nursery maid sniffed.

Daisy shrank against him. "I'm not bad on purpose."

Hessian had had a wonderful ride in the park with Miss Fer—with Lily—not three hours past, and a call on Worth had become pressing. He'd like nothing better than to ignore the nursemaid glowering down her nose at Daisy and ignore the desperation in Daisy's grip on his neck.

A mess was brewing in his nursery, though, and messes invariably grew worse when ignored.

"Sykes, have you something to say?"

Her glower expanded to include Hessian. "A child benefits from routine, my lord. This haring about all over London when Miss Amy Marguerite ought to be in the schoolroom is why she doesn't sleep well. If she can't sleep, of course she'll be fidgety and difficult come morning."

"Fidgety and difficult?"

Daisy was absolutely still in his arms.

"And disrespectful. She doesn't finish her eggs and toast some days, forgets to say grace other days, and spends far too much time staring out the window like a simpleton."

Hessian wanted to cover Daisy's ears—and his own. "A simpleton?"

"Mooning about, my lord. Hardly speaks above a whisper much of the time and takes her sweet time answering common questions. She needs routine, order, and discipline, and she'll soon be showing her elders proper respect."

Hessian walked to the window, Daisy affixed to him like a barnacle. Sykes sounded like the late Earl of Grampion, and a bit like the present earl too.

Sykes did not, however, speak with a northern accent. "You traveled with Daisy from Cumberland?"

"No, sir. The other nursery maid, Hancock, comes from the north. Your housekeeper hired me because Hancock must have some rest, and the child keeps the household up until all hours."

With nightmares of routine and discipline, no doubt. "You're aware that Daisy has recently lost both parents and been taken away from the only home she's known?"

"All the more reason not to cosset her, my lord. Children must learn to weather life's trials with stoic gratitude. All the ponies in the world or a trip to the park every day won't help the girl learn those lessons."

"Clearly, you have never had a pony." Though, what excuse could there be for a London-bred maid's failure to appreciate Hyde Park in spring? "Sykes, I thank you for your suggestions regarding Daisy's welfare, but find that your approach to child-rearing and my own are incompatible. You will be given generous severance, a decent character, and coach fare to any location in the realm. Take as long as you need to find another position, but remove yourself and your effects from the nursery before sundown. The other maids will make accommodation for you in their dormitory."

Her mouth fell open, and her eyebrows disappeared beneath her lacy cap.

Daisy peeked up, then tucked her face against Hessian's throat. The tension went out of her, and Hessian stifled the rest of his lecture.

Children needed routine and order, true—at least, some children did some of the time—but they also needed love, understanding, affection, and joy.

So did titled lords. "I'll have a word with the housekeeper regarding your wages when Daisy and I return from our call. Good day."

He left the nursery maid standing in the middle of the playroom and knew a moment of pride in the child, for she hadn't stuck her tongue out at Sykes, though Hessian could feel the impulse quivering through her.

"She meant well." He set Daisy on her feet. "She was simply misguided. The poor woman has never raised a child of her own, and her theories are uninformed by parental experience."

Daisy took his hand. "Was she bad?"

"She was not well suited to her position. We will provide her every assistance in finding a post more in keeping with her skills." Scrubbing privies in the Antipodes, for example.

Daisy studied the newel post at the top of the steps. The wood was carved in the shape of a gryphon with folded wings.

"She said if I was bad, I'd be sent away."

"She was wrong." Good girls went to heaven, bad girls got sent away. Hessian put that conundrum together while Daisy blinked hard at the gryphon. "And you made a small miscalculation too, Daisy."

"Will you send me away?"

"Never. We are family now. Family is forever." Though sometimes, family got into stupid, stubborn muddles that took a few years to sort out. "Your miscalculation is understandable, because becoming a family in a situation like ours doesn't happen in an instant."

"I made a mistake?"

"We both did. You should have told me that Sykes was spouting stupidities, and I should have asked you how you were getting on in the nursery when we had privacy to air our honest feelings. You will join me for breakfast starting tomorrow, and we won't make the same mistakes in future."

Children did dine at the family breakfast table, once they had some manners. At Daisy's age, Hessian had taken great pride in his breakfast privileges, while Worth had remained in the nursery of a morning.

"You want me to eat downstairs? My brothers ate downstairs."

"You have fine manners, and mine are in good repair as well. We'll manage breakfast, as long as you don't steal the newspaper or the preserves."

"I don't care for jam. I like cinnamon."

"A lady of refined tastes. Would you like to slide down that banister?" Hessian's good spirits were to blame for that suggestion. This was what came of kisses in the park and sacked nursery maids.

"Slide down the banister?"

"You must never undertake to use of the banister when an adult is about, or even a servant, for they might think you should be tattled upon. A good polishing never hurt a well-made banister, and I have only the sturdiest banisters in my houses."

Hessian deposited Daisy on the banister, and down she went, grinning the whole way. She scrambled unaided from the bottom newel post and spun around like a top.

"I shall tell Bronwyn and Avery! I shall come down to breakfast every morning on the banister!"

"Mind you, don't let anybody see you. Decorum has a place in an earl's household." What would Lily think of this morning's work? Hessian couldn't wait to ask her—he flipped open his pocket watch—in about nine hours. "Let's be off to visit your uncle."

Daisy studied Hessian's outstretched hand. "I don't have any uncles."

What could he say to that? "You haven't any official uncles, but I'm sure Worth would love to be an honorary uncle to such a lovely little girl. I'll thrash him to tiny bits if he says otherwise."

"Boys like to fight. Mama said that, and Papa agreed."

Daisy was mentioning her parents, and that was good. "I'm sure fisticuffs won't be necessary. Now shall we be on our way?"

Daisy skipped half the distance to Worth's house, and Hessian got a few odd looks for having a child clinging to his hand. He also saw a few smiles. She bolted from his side the instant she spotted Avery at the top of Worth's main staircase, and amid much squealing and hopping about, the little girls disappeared to the second floor.

"And to think you said she was a withdrawn child," Worth muttered as he led the way to his back terrace.

"We sacked a nursery maid this morning. The effect was invigorating."

Worth paused, hand on the door latch. "You sacked a maid?"

"She had no compassion, no flexibility. Went maundering on about order, discipline, and stoicism. I ask you, when did Greek philosophy ever comfort an orphaned child?"

Worth's expression was hard to read, as if he'd like to say something, but couldn't quite find the words. His skills lay more with numbers, and God be thanked for those skills.

"I'm here to discuss a matter of some delicacy," Hessian went on. "Consultation with a sensible family member might help me see the best way forward."

Worth preceded him onto the terrace, where the Alsatian crouched like a sphinx on a patch of sun-warmed bricks. "I am ever ready to lend my counsel to your situation."

"I seek the opinion of a sensible family member," Hessian retorted. "Yolanda insists on rusticating at Trysting, so I was hoping Jacaranda might spare me a few moments."

Worth propped a hip against the balustrade. "You just made a joke. A bad joke, but a joke nonetheless." He scanned the sky. "No airborne swine. Interesting."

They exchanged a smile, the like of which they hadn't exchanged for years, then Hessian knelt to pet the dog.

"I'm considering offering for Lily Ferguson."

The dog rolled to her back, tongue lolling, tail waving even in her undignified position. Hessian knew exactly how she felt. Life was sweet. What mattered dignity?

"You did mention this. I've barely started looking into Leggett's situation, Hessian. When do you intend to begin paying your addresses?"

"I see no reason to hesitate. The sooner I'm engaged, the sooner the merry widows and blushing debutantes will leave me in peace." And the sooner he and Lily could be married. No need to state the obvious.

"Andromeda Kettering, where are your manners?"

Worth's stern tone provoked the dog to cocking her head, which made her pose all the more ludicrous.

"I have begun a few inquiries," Worth said. "I've set my clerks to making others. They will gather the best intelligence, from other clerks, opera dancers, moneylenders, and pawnbrokers. If Leggett's rolled up, he's done a damned fine job of keeping it out of the clubs."

Hessian rose, for the dog would let him scratch her belly until Michaelmas. "If he's rolled up, won't that become apparent during the settlement negotiations? Thanks to my brilliant brother, I have no need to marry an heiress."

Worth took up tummy-scratching duty. "But you should marry wisely, Hess. If Lily is an heiress, where's her fortune? If her fortune is gone, where did it go? Does Leggett have a gambling problem? Does Lily have an aunt in the care of a very expensive, discreet institution in Northumbria? You've waited this long to take another wife, you can wait a few more weeks."

Hessian plucked a sprig of honeysuckle from below the balustrade. "I am torn between appreciation for your caution and impatience with what feels like needless dithering. I'm marrying Lily, not her dratted relations."

The scent of the flower was sweet and soothing and put Hessian in mind of his baby niece.

"Hessian, at the risk of provoking your considerable contrariness, you aren't marrying anybody yet. First, you must make an appointment with Leggett, then the appointment must go well, then the courtship ensues, and finally the lady—why are you looking at me like that?"

"Because you've grown up. I daresay you gave the protocol not a single thought when you courted Jacaranda, but God forbid my nieces encounter a suitor such as you were. You're saying the situation could become messy."

"Very. Leggett doesn't smell right."

Lily's fragrance was even sweeter than the honeysuckle. "Very well, take some time to turn over a few rocks and poke about beneath a few hedges. Why are we out here getting the stink of dog all over our hands when we could be in the nursery making my infant niece smile?"

Worth rose, and the dog, apparently sensing that the conversation was headed elsewhere, wiggled to her feet.

"Why, indeed? By all means, let's make a raid on the nursery, though I suspect it has been overrun by Vandals or Yahoos or the 95th Rifles."

With the dog panting at Worth's side, they returned to the house. Worth's manner was subdued, for him, though perhaps it was more the case that Hessian's mood was unsubdued. To begin every day kissing Lily, truly kissing her. To pour her tea, hold her chair…

Hold her babies.

Hessian contented himself with holding Worth's firstborn for the two minutes that her papa allowed him the privilege. The Queens of the Nile had taken over the schoolroom and used blankets and desks to put a canopy over their royal barge, beneath which they consumed exotic fig cakes.

The fig cakes bore a strong resemblance to crumpets, which Hessian knew better than to remark.

He also knew better than to fuss when Worth demanded possession of the baby. Papas could be jealous where their daughters were concerned.

And throughout all of the children's laughter and the baby's smiles, Worth remained oddly quiet.

"Something is troubling you," Hessian said as they closed the nursery door. Daisy had elected to spend the afternoon with Avery, which decision gave Hessian a pang.

"You didn't want to leave Daisy in your own brother's keeping, Hess. Not even for two hours."

And that was a dodge. "Even in Cumberland, I doubt Daisy had many friends. The neighborhood is sparsely populated and Daisy's station is above that of the daughters of the yeomanry."

Then too, Lady Evers had been enormously attached to the girl, her only daughter.

Worth paused at the top of the steps. "Who are Leggett's friends?"

"Good God, you're like a hound after a lame hare. How would I know who Leggett's friends are when I've spent the last ten years rusticating in Cumberland?"

Worth started down the steps. "You're playing cards with Rosecroft, Tresham, Kilkenney, and Hazelton?"

"I have played cards with them." Three earls and a ducal heir who squabbled over farthing points like biddy hens over their corn.

"Make a few inquiries, sniff at a few hedges yourself. Leggett will expect that. I have something for you."

"Did one of my investments take a turn for the worse?" Though with Worth minding the ledgers, that was unlikely.

"Don't be preposterous." He turned into the office from which he oversaw a financial empire that included projects on four continents—South America was doubtless soon to join the ranks—and investors from several royal houses as well as several opera houses.

A silver rattle sat atop a stack of opened correspondence. A leather leash was coiled in the pen tray. A bit of untidiness, and dear because it was Worth's untidiness.

"Lady Evers's solicitor sent this for you," Worth said, holding out a bound book. "Her ladyship instructed that you should have this journal only after you'd taken custody of Daisy."

A year was tooled into the book's leather binding—eight years past. "I have custody of all the children and have undertaken correspondence with the boys. They'll join me and Daisy at Grampion this summer."

And Lily would be with them too, God willing.

Worth shoved the journal at him. "You are to read this and pass it along to Daisy if and when you think it appropriate. There are others—her ladyship was apparently a conscientious diarist—and those are boxed up and waiting for your return to Grampion. Lady Evers wanted this specific volume passed to you personally."

Hessian had solved the first mess of the day by sacking a nursery maid. The mess that lay on the pages of her ladyship's diary would not be so easily dealt with.

"Have you read it?"

"Hess, I don't need to. Daisy has your eyes, your chin, and your penchant for hanging back and studying a situation until she's grasped every detail of the terrain. If you had any suspicions that she's your progeny, to me those suspicions have been confirmed."

"And your observations prove nothing, because Lord Evers was also tall, fair, and of good, northern stock." Hessian took the book and shoved it into a pocket.

There it remained until he stashed the journal in the drawer of his night table, and tried his best to forget he'd ever seen the damned thing.

CHAPTER ELEVEN

The music was wonderful. A violinist, a pianist, and a cellist, each performing solo, and then as a piano trio. Lily had spent the evening alternately wishing she'd had more years to study the pianoforte and wishing Lord Grampion weren't such an eligible parti.

Mrs. Bascombe affixed herself to his side and introduced him to every unmarried woman in her vast music parlor, while Uncle Walter remained equally attentive to Lily.

"Deuced inconvenient," Uncle said, "when only the older brother socializes. Worth Kettering used to be quite the charming rogue, and now we're left with the earl, who's hardly his brother's equal."

"Grampion's appeal lies in a different direction," Lily said. He played a patient game of catch, took better care of his ward than some men did of their nieces, and did fine justice to evening attire.

Only once this evening had his blue, blue eyes met Lily's gaze, and she'd seen humor, patience, and determination in that passing glance.

"A title is the only direction some women pursue," Uncle said, rising. "I'm parched. Behave yourself, and we should be able to slip away in the next half hour. If Mrs. Bascombe allows you the privilege, please do further your acquaintance with Grampion."

He was off in the direction of the men's punchbowl, so Lily sought the refuge of the ladies' punchbowl in the parlor across the corridor.

She'd no sooner accepted the glass of lemonade dipped out for her by a footman than an older woman Lily didn't recognize appeared at her elbow. The lady had brassy blond hair, and her gown was well made but several years out of date. A portion of lace across her ample décolletage would not have gone amiss.

When Lily took her drink out to the balcony, the same woman followed her, which was beyond presuming.

"Good evening, Miss Ferguson."

"Ma'am. You have me at a disadvantage." Lily loathed being at a disadvantage. Her first year in London had been one tense encounter after another. Every new face had been potential disaster, every introduction a chance to blunder.

"I am being forward, aren't I?" The woman slowly waved a painted fan. She held the fan too low to send a breeze over her face, low enough to call attention to her bodice. "But then, I knew your mother, and in all the years I've seen you out and about in London, I haven't taken the time to introduce myself."

Polite society frowned on people who introduced themselves, and yet... this woman had been Mama's friend.

"Should I recognize you?"

"Oh, my gracious, no. I was out several years after your dear mama made her bow, but we became friends and correspondents. I'm Roberta Braithwaite, widow of the late Colonel Hilary Braithwaite. Your mother wrote me of you often."

No, she had not. "Thank you for introducing yourself, Mrs. Braithwaite. I hope your memories of my mother are cheerful."

Lily allowed that observation to stand alone, for she'd learned that silence was her friend. Let others prose on, leaving hints and details for Lily to stash away in memory. She'd keep quiet and avoid mistakes. Then too, Hessian had taken Mrs. Braithwaite into dislike, for the widow had she'd attempted a sneak attack on him as well.

"Your mama was very dear," Mrs. Braithwaite said, setting her drink aside untouched. "She was also very lively. I note that you are not plagued with her sense of adventure, shall we say?"

The innuendo was unkind and the scent of Mrs. Braithwaite's neroli perfume overwhelming.

"We must not malign the departed," Lily said. "Particularly not the dearly departed. If you'll excuse me, Mrs. Braithwaite, I appreciate the introduction, but my uncle—"

A manacle in the form of Mrs. Braithwaite's gloved hand closed around Lily's wrist. "Walter Leggett was the bane of your mama's existence. In your grandparents' eyes, he could do no wrong, while your mother was judged for every witticism and glass of wine. Her marriage was an escape, and I do believe it was a happy one."

Lily had barely known her mother. Periodic visits that never lasted long enough, an hour or two while Lily was supposed to play with a sister she'd found more fascinating than likeable. A few letters written to a child that conveyed equal parts loving concern and self-indulgence. Lily kept Mama's letters with her money, and if she'd had to choose, she would have parted with the coins first.

"Uncle says little about his sister other than to remark her high spirits."

Mrs. Braithwaite's fan moved faster. "And he probably says they were her undoing, though I can tell you from experience, a widow goes slightly mad when the grief becomes too much." She leaned closer, using the fan to shield her words. "I know about your sister, my dear—your half-sister—but your secret is safe with me."

Nobody, not even Uncle Walter, had ever spoken the words *your sister* to Lily. They sent a prickling sensation over her skin, part dread, part rejoicing.

"I beg your pardon, Mrs. Braithwaite?"

"Maybe Walter thinks you're too delicate to hear the truth, but he's a man. What do they know of the strength women claim? You have a half-sister."

Lily heard Hessian's laughter, warm and relaxed, amid the chatter coming through the French doors.

"Mrs. Braithwaite, this is not the place to make such an allegation. My mother was the much-respected widow of Lord Alfred Ferguson. I will not hear her maligned by a supposed friend."

Mrs. Braithwaite closed her fan and tapped Lily's forearm with it. "I mean nobody any harm, Miss Ferguson, though you deliver a very convincing set-down. Your mother was merely lonely, and some handsome rascal sought to comfort her grief in the most intimate manner. These things happen."

Lily turned from the view of the garden below, which was lit with torches and occupied by strolling couples, any pair of whom might overhear the wrong words.

"You'll excuse me, please. My uncle does not like to keep late hours." She must put distance between herself and the temptation to learn more of her mother, for Mrs. Braithwaite had had years to make Lily's acquaintance.

This was a carefully planned ambush, and Lily should have known better than to remain anywhere private with this woman.

Mrs. Braithwaite snapped her fan open. "I have letters. From your dear mama, revealing the extent of her indiscretion. One cannot fault her for half measures. Your sister, if she survived, would be little more than two years your junior."

Oh, Mama. "That is preposterous." And very close to the truth. "Take your allegations to my uncle if you seek to gain by them."

Through a sheer curtain, Lily could see Hessian in earnest discussion with the evening's pianist, a ducal son turned composer. The pianist had his lordship's whole focus, as did any matter—or person—to whom Hessian gave his attention.

Daisy, for example, and on a few precious occasions, Lily.

She had never expected a fairy-tale future. Food, clothing, shelter, a measure of safety in exchange for hard, hard work had been her fondest dream. Then Walter Leggett had come along, making promises and threats, and more promises.

"You are a sensible creature," Mrs. Braithwaite said. "So am I. We women must manage as best we can, and your uncle has nothing I want. You, however, do."

"I haven't even pin money," Lily said, "and I refuse to discuss this situation where anybody might overhear."

Another tap to her arm. "Such dignity. Your mother would have been proud of you. The more public the venue, the greater the privacy. You'd know that, if you had a tenth of your mama's penchant for mischief. In any case, you have influence over Lord Grampion."

Lily's mother would not be proud of her. Her mother would be endlessly ashamed, as Lily was ashamed.

"Say what you have to say, then, and be done with it."

"Grampion has recently become guardian to my niece, a dear little creature by the name of Amy Marguerite. I want the rearing of her, and he's being contrary. I respect his sense of duty, but that girl belongs with me."

Mrs. Braithwaite spoke like an ambitious horse trainer: I want that filly. She'll fetch a pretty penny once she's schooled over fences.

Nothing about Roberta Braithwaite was remarkable, for London in spring abounded with pragmatic widows. Her eyes, though, struck Lily as her most honest feature. Calculation gleamed from their depths, and a coldness that would destroy a child like Daisy.

Hessian had taken Mrs. Braithwaite's measure better than he knew. "If you seek a role in your niece's life, you should approach Grampion. He's nothing if not reasonable."

Mrs. Braithwaite slapped her closed fan against her palm, like a testy headmaster with his birch rod.

"I've tried to reason with Grampion, and he was nearly rude. I'm to await his consideration while the little imp gets her hooks deeper into his sense of honor. My sister was the same way—had an instinct for how to wrap a man around her finger."

Bitterness lurked in Mrs. Braithwaite's words, perhaps the bitterness of a woman scorned.

"I have no influence with his lordship," Lily said. "He is a man of independent judgment."

Mrs. Braithwaite's smile would have been well complemented by a forked tongue sampling the evening air.

"Nonsense, Miss Ferguson. You are your mother's daughter, and she never wanted for male attention. You curry the earl's favor, grant him a few liberties, compromise him into marriage, and then insist he evict a troublesome child from your nursery before his heir arrives. I'll be loyally standing by, ready to dote myself silly over the girl."

The violinist, a willowy brunette with dark eyes and dramatic brows, had joined the conversation with Hessian and the pianist. She was a gorgeous woman, the daughter of some Italian count and an Englishwoman. Men had been giving her appreciative glances all evening, while Hessian, his profile to Lily, gave the violinist a respectful bow.

Mrs. Braithwaite had an asset Lily lacked. Why hadn't Mama bequeathed Lily even a dash of ruthlessness? A hint of a spine? Surely a woman who flouted convention so boldly could have passed on some courage to her daughter?

"You want money."

"I need money, vulgar though the admission is. Grampion has money, his brother has even more money, and they can spare a bit for Amy Marguerite's widowed aunt. In exchange, I'll take adequate care of the girl, and Grampion can send her flowers on her birthday. Your task is to convince him that Amy Marguerite is better off with me, which she will be."

"And if I cannot convince him to surrender the girl to you?"

Mrs. Braithwaite snapped open her fan again. The pattern painted on the panels was a knight serenading a damsel, thorny pink roses vining around the damsel's stone tower.

"Personal correspondence is so easy to mislay," Mrs. Braithwaite said. "Who knows what might happen to your mother's old letters, or to your sister, should those letters fall into the wrong hands? Your sister is the by-blow of a man with a respected title, you know. Your mother let that much slip, though she didn't name names. I have my suspicions, though."

And those suspicions would remain beyond Lily's reach, unless Daisy took up residence with Mrs. Braithwaite. Mama had never mentioned who Lily's papa might be, only that the law prevented a union between Lily's parents.

"I have no proof anything you say is true, Mrs. Braithwaite. Not a glimpse of a letter, not a shred of gossip ever to corroborate your wild stories. I very much doubt I would have gone my whole life with a younger sister about whom I know nothing."

She had gone her first five years without meeting Annie.

"You're wise to doubt my claims," Mrs. Braithwaite replied, picking up her drink. "Ask your uncle. Ask the elderly aunts gracing every family tree, the pensioned governesses and former tutors. They know all the best scandals. I'll pay a call on you next week and bring you a sample of your mother's correspondence. In the meanwhile, do your best to insinuate yourself into Grampion's good graces. He's reserved to the point of coldness, but I've yet to meet the man who couldn't be charmed by a pretty young lady with a fortune."

She swanned off, leaving Lily's world in tatters.

For more than a decade, Lily had succeeded in convincing the world she was Mama's legitimate eldest daughter. In five minutes, Roberta Braithwaite had traded on that fiction to threaten the rest of Lily's life.

"Thought the damned creature would never leave you alone," Uncle Walter said, wineglass in hand. "You're looking a bit pale, Lily. Too much galloping about in the park at all hours."

That was the first indication he'd given that her dawn ride had come to his attention. "My mare wants conditioning. You know Mrs. Braithwaite?"

He took a sip of his wine, keeping the lady in view over the rim of his glass. "She was an acquaintance of your mother's, and I do appreciate a healthy figure on a woman. Nonetheless, Nadine's taste in friends was no more refined than her other inclinations. Let's leave, before some fool begs an encore from the musicians."

Lily spared Hessian not so much as a wave—not when her every move was observed by both a fan-wielding tool of the fiend and Uncle Walter.

By dawn on Saturday, Lily needed a plan that would protect Mama's past from becoming public, protect Daisy from her aunt, preserve Grampion's respect for Lily, and keep Uncle from suspecting trouble was afoot.

For the first time, Lily understood why her older half-sister, at the age of seventeen, had turned up her nose at propriety and reason, and eloped with Uncle Walter's house steward.

* * *

Hessian had used his morning to meet with his solicitor, for updating a will was something best done sooner rather than later. On the walk back to his town house, he missed Daisy skipping at his side, missed her chatter, her questions.

Why do trees lose their leaves, but not their pine needles?

Where do different kinds of birds come from?

Does London always stink on rainy days?

Were you friends with my mama, or only neighbors?

That last question had required some delicacy. Lady Evers had been a woman frustrated by a cordial marriage to a much older man, and Hessian, at a loss for how to deter a female bent on seduction, had been lonely too.

Most peculiar of all, Lord Evers had more or less expressed gratitude for Hessian's friendship with Belinda.

Then her ladyship's interest in dallying had ceased—or she'd given up on dallying with Hessian—and in less than a year, Daisy had arrived. Hessian had never known—and still didn't know for sure—whether a casual affair had rekindled her ladyship's sense of marital loyalty, or whether...

His steps took him past a shop that sold items for babies and young children. Daisy would delight in such an emporium, so he changed course for purposes of reconnaissance. Then too, he had nieces, and Daisy had brothers.

And what waited for him at home, besides correspondence, ledgers, and the domestic upheaval of having sacked a drill sergeant from his staff?

The shop owner had arranged the inventory to resemble a marvelously well-stocked nursery, and the whole place bore the scent of lavender, much as a nursery might. Fanciful animals sewn of cloth, embroidered blankets just the size for swaddling an infant, rattles, storybooks, a pair of hobbyhorses, and art supplies of every description filled the place.

And in the middle of this cave of wonders stood Lily Ferguson, the most delightful treasure of all.

"Miss Ferguson."

She held a stuffed horse, a velvet bay with black yarn for its mane and tail. "My lord. This is a surprise."

The shop girl watched the exchange, so Hessian offered a proper bow. "A fortuitous encounter for me. Perhaps you'll advise me regarding suitable gifts for Daisy and her brothers?"

They left the shop thirty minutes later with God only knew what—a herd of stuffed horses, or stuffed bears, possibly some storybooks, and an armada of miniature sailing ships. Hessian sent Lily's maid and footman home with her purchases and appointed himself her escort.

"I was hoping to linger a while longer at the shop," Lily said. "Uncle is in a mood today."

"Perhaps he was frustrated with my attention to the musicians last night. I hope you didn't feel neglected." Maybe that explained Lily's less-than-pleased reception of Hessian this morning? He hadn't wanted to single her out before a half-dozen gossips, and then the damned musicians had gone off on some flight about Herr Beethoven, orchestration, and English music publishers.

The musicians had kept the debutantes at bay, and thus Hessian had taken shameless advantage of Herr Beethoven's acolytes.

"I did not expect your special notice, my lord. The musical entertainment was superb."

They paused at an intersection, and Hessian spoke without thinking. "Come back to my house, Lily. We'll have a late luncheon, and nobody will be the wiser."

His suggestion was most improper, but then, they would soon be engaged. That changed the rules, to the point where very few rules applied beyond don't get caught.

"I ought not. Uncle will inquire as to my whereabouts."

Uncle's version of an inquiry came close to an interrogation, based on Lily's tone. "Then we decided to go back to the shop because I forgot a purchase." The lie rankled even as Hessian spoke it. "Or not. I'll walk you home and look forward to riding with you later in the week."

She looked down one street, then the other. Both were lovely Mayfair thoroughfares, with plane maples leafing out over busy traffic. Gracious homes lined each street, and to a casual onlooker, one choice would have been much the same as the other.

"Forgive me for tempting you from the path of common sense," Hessian said. "I was troubled to note Mrs. Roberta Braithwaite among the guests last night. She did not approach me, but the mere sight of her sent my enjoyment of the evening into the ditch."

The intersection cleared, and Lily led Hessian into the street. "She upset you."

"A woman like that can start talk, and that talk will not make Daisy's life easier. Mrs. Braithwaite says she wants to provide a home for the child, but I suspect she wants money." Maybe Lady Evers's diary could shed light on the role Daisy's aunt should play in her life? Hessian would have to read the damned thing to find out.

"Would parting with some coin be that much of a hardship?"

Lily sounded impatient with Hessian, not with the grasping woman who'd use a child to further her own security.

"The issue isn't coin and isn't even entirely the principle," Hessian said. "My concern is pragmatic: If Mrs. Braithwaite will threaten scandal or litigation over fifty pounds per quarter, what would she do to gain a thousand? What mad schemes would she fabricate, what wild stories would she propound? Why would Daisy be better off in the care of such a woman than in my own, considering I was clearly the choice of the girl's parents?"

When Hessian wasn't contemplating the pleasant prospect of his next encounter with Lily, such questions increasingly filled his mind. Lady Evers's journal weighed on his conscience, much as a pistol carried in his pocket would have disturbed the line of a well-tailored jacket.

Hessian would have to investigate the contents of that damned journal, though not today. He was escorting Lily in the direction of his town house, and the choice of destination had been hers.

"You think Mrs. Braithwaite would stoop to creating scandal for her own niece?" Lily asked.

"What does she have to lose? She'll cast herself as the wounded widow, longing for the company of her departed sister's daughter, and I'll be the unbending aristocrat, keeping a child from her only family on the strength of my arrogant, nipfarthing whim."

To describe the situation thus made Hessian seem unreasonable even to himself. And yet, he could not fathom releasing Daisy into the custody of that woman.

"You are not arrogant."

"I'm not a pennypincher either, but until recently, I had to manage my coin carefully. That is no secret."

Hessian escorted Lily into his house, the lack of a maid, chaperone, or screeching children making the situation feel a trifle improper—or daring.

Worth had doubtless flouted convention far more adventurously, but then, Worth hadn't been the earl.

"We'll take luncheon in the conservatory," Hessian informed the butler, "and I'll drive Miss Ferguson home in the phaeton."

"Very good, my lord."

Hessian offered Lily his arm, which was silly when no hazard greater than a carpet fringe threatened their progress.

"We've yet to set the tender plants outside, so my conservatory is quite the jungle."

Lily accompanied him without comment, which was odd. She never hesitated to speak her mind, and her opinions were always well-thought-out. She had every air and grace claimed by a true lady, and yet, when conversation would have settled Hessian's nerves, she remained silent.

He held the conservatory door for her, and then they were enveloped in warmth and quiet. Potted palms and ferns lined walkways between lemon and orange trees. Near the windows, boxes of Holland bulbs were sporting a few precocious daffodils and tulips. The fragrance of hyacinths joined the scents of greenery and rich earth.

"Daisy and her friends will discover this place on the very next rainy day," Lily said. "It's lovely."

Lily made no move to touch Hessian, and neither did her expression, posture, or tone invite him to embrace her.

"I've kept the door locked for the most part, lest Daisy disappear up a tree." But then, Daisy hadn't played that game since the night she'd met Lily.

"Mrs. Braithwaite introduced herself to me," Lily said, brushing her hand over an airy fern. "She claimed to have been an acquaintance of my mother's."

So Roberta Braithwaite was the serpent in the garden. "Did you believe her claims?"

Lily tugged off her right glove, finger by finger, then her left. "I wish I hadn't mentioned her name, when at long, long last we have a few minutes' privacy. Perhaps we can speak of her later."

Luncheon would be at least thirty minutes in preparation, and the conservatory doors boasted stout locks.

"As always, you make great good sense. So why are we standing three yards apart when I'd rather be kissing you silly?"

CHAPTER TWELVE

Lily's emotions were like the conservatory—a crowded tangle of obscured paths and dim shadows shot through with sunbeams of hope and the sweet scent of temptation. She longed to be courted by Hessian Kettering, but deceiving a man she respected took vast reserves of selfishness.

Self-preservation instincts, Lily had, but selfishness? Enough selfishness and calculation to marry him and carry forward a deception already ten years in the making?

And then there was Mrs. Braithwaite adding her complications, and all Lily knew was that now—right now—she wanted whatever she could have with Hessian, because even tomorrow was not hers to promise.

"We stand three yards apart," Lily said, "because the door is not locked, and luncheon should be delivered any moment."

The earl held out his right hand, palm up. "My kitchen has learned not to wait a meal on me. I'd rather have my food fresh and hot, after a short wait, than warm and overdone, though promptly served. I'd like to show you something."

Lily wanted to show him many things: the truth of her upbringing and the rotten scheme Mrs. Braithwaite had hatched foremost among them. The latter she'd certainly divulge, while the former... maybe someday?

She took Grampion's hand. His grasp was comfortable and confident, much like his kisses. "Where are we going?"

"Daisy is not the only person in this family to have a hiding place," he said, leading Lily down a path between the ferns. "I come here when I want solitude, or the maids are busy above stairs and I'm in need of a nap."

He opened another door, to a small rectangular room that might once have been an antechamber, though like the conservatory, the outer wall was glass.

That glass was obscured by a smoky tint such as the imagination fashioned in dream worlds. Hazy greenery lay beyond the glass wall, and a pair of clerestory windows were open, scenting the little room with scythed grass and hyacinths.

"You read here," she said, picking up a copy of Guy Mannering.

Hessian took the book from her, closed it, and set it on a small table. "I dream here."

The room was barely furnished—a chair in the corner, wall sconces on either side. A table that apparently doubled as a writing desk in the opposite corner and, along the glass wall, a bed made up with worn quilts. No knickknacks or art cluttered any surface, all was orderly and spartan.

"Does something trouble you, Lily?"

Everything troubled her. Uncle Walter, Mrs. Braithwaite, Oscar... but they were not here, and this privacy with Hessian might never come again.

Lily twisted the lock above the door latch. "I've missed you. That has troubled me." She stepped close and put her arms around Hessian. His reciprocal embrace was balm to her tattered nerves. "I can see why you doubt Mrs. Braithwaite's fitness to raise a child. Her manner is presuming."

Threatening, more like.

Hessian's hold on Lily was careful, his thumb whispering across her nape. "Am I presuming?"

She rested her cheek against the soft wool of his jacket, wishing she could give him all of her burdens and all of her trust. Hessian was overstepping polite decorum terribly—by embracing her, by being alone with her—and yet Lily wanted even more from him.

Hessian Kettering was good. He hesitated over white lies, he treasured stolen kisses. He approached life with clear notions of right and wrong, honorable and shameful.

In terms of standing and integrity, he was well above her touch, even above the touch of Walter Leggett's legitimate niece, but for the money that young lady had inherited. Lily's conscience shrieked at her to step away, to use this privacy to inform Grampion that his judgment of Mrs. Braithwaite was all too accurate.

"You do not presume, my lord. I wish you would."

His embrace became subtly more intimate, more cherishing. He kissed her, a different sort of kiss that presaged a different sort of closeness. Long, long ago, Lily had seen tavern maids and grooms when they'd thought themselves unobserved. Their passion had intrigued and troubled her, but she understood now why they'd been so bold.

Make me forget. Let me pretend. Stop time for me.

In the conservatory, water trickled in a peaceful whisper. Hessian's kisses descended in a lazy cascade over Lily's cheeks, her lips, her throat, to the swell of her bosom. He drew back and freed a half-dozen buttons marching down the middle of Lily's bodice—not nearly enough.

I am my mother's daughter after all. The realization brought Lily relief rather than shame. Loneliness could be a shroud, propriety a grave for a woman's dreams. Mama had been grieving and alone. She'd failed to produce sons—a great disappointment to the ducal Fergusons, of course—and when she'd lost her husband, she'd faltered.

Lily had wondered why a woman who had so much to lose had misstepped so recklessly, but the answer was in her arms.

Pleasure bloomed everywhere Hessian touched, everywhere he kissed. His expressions of desire approached reverence, and everything neglected, judged, and uncertain in Lily reveled in his loving. Anger threaded through her too— at Walter, at years of deception, at parents who'd left her alone too young— though she knew bitterness for false courage by another name.

She had *now* and would make no apologies for allowing herself one impetuous hour.

"Everywhere," Hessian murmured, pressing kisses to the swell of her breasts. "Flowers. You. Soft."

Lily tugged his shirt from his waistband, and his kisses stopped.

The breeze teased at her in novel places. The trickling water became loud in the contrasting silence. Lily pressed her forehead against Hessian's shoulder, praying that his scruples weren't about to destroy her fantasies.

"I haven't yet spoken with your uncle," Hessian said, tracing a finger along Lily's eyebrows.

"That can all wait until later." Much, much later.

Such a smile illuminated his eyes—tender, joyous, and so very naughty. "Later, then."

Lily had thought that she and Hessian had been intimate. Their kisses had been so bold, their embraces leaving little to the imagination, but she'd known nothing. The touches themselves mattered not half so much as the passion behind them.

Hessian scooped Lily up and laid her down on the bed. His handling of her was possessive and unapologetic. The lover held her, not the titled gentleman. He sat at her hip and yanked off his boots, then hung his waistcoat on the back of the chair, took off her shoes, and unbuttoned his falls.

"Hurry," Lily said. "Please hurry." Before she lost her nerve, before she denied herself what might be the most glorious hour of her life.

Hessian's version of hurrying was maddeningly deliberate. He undid more of her buttons, while Lily lay on her back, the old quilt twisted in her fingers. Then he unlaced the drawstring on her chemise and, finally, the laces on her jumps.

"You are like a holiday gift," he said, leaning forward to press his mouth over her heart. "Layers of lace and loveliness, but the best part of all is simply you."

No, the best part was him, caressing her bare breasts, making her ache, using his mouth in diabolically sweet, wicked ways.

"You will drive me mad, Hessian."

"I certainly hope to," he said, sitting up. "You deserve madness."

Then he was above her, braced on his forearms, and Lily wished she'd taken the time to undress him. He hadn't so much as turned back his cuffs, hadn't undone his damned cravat. That made her wild, and she set about addressing her oversight.

"I should have—" She unfastened the gold pin holding the whole business together. "Better. Hold... don't go anywhere."

"As if I could."

* * *

Lily's gaze was distraught as she stabbed Hessian's cravat pin into the mattress near the top corner of the bed.

He hadn't the patience to wait for her to undo his linen, for he'd tarried too long admiring her breasts, wallowing in the taste and scent and feel of her. Soft, soft skin. Luscious, subtle fragrances. Curves and hollows and wonders beyond his imaginings.

He gathered her in his arms, thanking heaven for stolen moments, and cursing all the modistes in Mayfair for skirts, petticoats, chemises, and every other frustration made out of fabric.

Lily raised her knees, which got matters somewhat organized, then she bit Hessian's ear.

"I'm trying not to rush," he muttered. "Do that again, and I won't answer for the consequences."

She sucked the spot she'd bitten, and Hessian retaliated by sliding her skirts up, up, and up, which he might have thought to do—had he been able to think—before falling on her like a beast.

Lily lifted her hips, so male hardness met female heat, though fourteen thousand froths and billows prevented any actual touching.

Hessian's palm connected with a smooth, muscular thigh, and he nearly shouted with rejoicing. No drawers. I am saved.

And he'd managed not to say that out loud.

Lily got him by the hair and tilted his head so she could kiss him. Her kiss tasted of determination and passion, certainly, but Hessian detected desperation as well. He wanted to believe he sensed desperate desire, though the setting was wrong, the timing was wrong, the very bed was all wrong.

Clearly, he had no instinct for casting off the dictates of convention. What manner of romance could flourish in a bare, cramped—?

Lily kissed him again, softly. "I have dreamed of you like this." She smiled at him as if he'd laid her on a bower of rose petals, not a glorified cot in a gloomy corner of his conservatory.

"You dreamed of linen sheets, sunbeams, a long afternoon, surely." He'd give her that, many times over. Along with champagne, French chocolate drops, and erotic poetry.

"No, Hessian. I dreamed of you, close and soon to be closer. Only you."

He laid his cheek against hers, and bless her for all time, she tugged skirts and petticoats and all that other whatnot aside, until no barriers remained. She arched up, he settled in, and they were skin to skin where it mattered.

"Kiss me," she whispered. "Kiss me forever."

He positioned himself intimately, and as the kissing resumed, the joining began.

Lily was snug and ready and heavenly. "Tell me if—"

She moved, and heaven became an understatement. All the hesitation and doubts fell away, all the questions. This was right. This was perfect. This was what every man hoped to find waiting for him at the end of every journey.

"When you do that," she whispered as Hessian found a slow, deep rhythm. "It's exquisite. It's good. I feel…."

"As do I." Glorious, grateful, aroused as hell.

A bird fluttered in through the window and back out, and that was right too. Hessian found the self-restraint to love Lily gently, but another time—many other times—he'd let passion soar and show her more dramatic pleasures.

Lily's hands moved on his back, until she pushed her palm beneath the waistband of his breeches and anchored herself with a firm grip on his backside. Her breathing changed, and Hessian dared hope he might satisfy her, even their first time. He forced himself not to speed up, not to let go, not to allow passion to overtake self-restraint.

And his virtue was rewarded.

Lily fetched up hard against him, then harder still, and Hessian didn't breathe lest her pleasure steal his last ounce of self-discipline. She thrashed, she bucked, she likely pinched him black and blue, and then she sighed against his neck and subsided onto the pillow.

He freed his hand from her hair and found the handkerchief in his breeches pocket. Thank God for tidy habits.

In one move, he withdrew and sat back. Completion roared through him the instant he wrapped the linen around his cock, and the pleasure nearly rendered him unconscious.

He leaned forward enough to crouch over Lily, whose breathing was still rapid. They remained like that, body heat and breath mingling, while streams of glory faded through Hessian's soul.

Ye gods, ye thundering, happy gods. If he'd had any doubts before, he was certain now: He was meant to be Lily Ferguson's lover, and she was meant to be his lady.

He should say something romantic, something witty, but the only words that came to him were honest. "I find myself transcendently fascinated with the prospect of our wedding night."

After uttering that profundity, Hessian became fascinated with the prospect of a nap. He dozed off to the steady beat of his lover's heart, his cheek pillowed on her breast, her fingers playing with his hair.

Hessian would undertake the wedding night with a good deal more forethought than he had this tryst. Nonetheless, he conceded that yielding to passion, however untidy on a first attempt, had unforeseen and lovely charms.

* * *

Outside the window of Walter Leggett's office, Lily stepped down from the Earl of Grampion's phaeton, and by a trick of the afternoon sunshine, she appeared for one moment to resemble her late mother. Nadine had been blond, while her daughters had turned out red-haired, but the angle of the jaw, the figure, the way of moving had bred true.

Walter let the curtain fall and stepped away from the window, though he wasn't likely to be detected. Lord Grampion was playing the perfect gentleman, all courtesy and consideration.

Lily was playing the role Walter had spent two years and a goodly sum training her to play. The investment had paid off handsomely, though not handsomely enough.

By the time Lily joined Walter in his office, she'd dropped the smiling, friendly façade she'd shown the earl. She wore instead the demure expression and watchful gaze Walter had first seen on her more than a decade ago. Unlike her mother, Lily had good instincts.

Nadine, God rest her wanton soul, had been a featherbrain, albeit a pretty one.

"You wanted to see me, Uncle?"

In truth, every time Walter laid eyes on his younger niece, he felt an echo of uncomfortable questions: Is there a better way to proceed than as I am doing? What does Oscar know or suspect, and would he understand my motives? Had I any choice but to do as I did?

Of course, Walter had had no choice. None at all. "How was your outing with Grampion?"

Lily no longer cowered by the door when Walter summoned her. The expensive finishing school in Switzerland, along with Ephrata Tipton's tireless lecturing, had given Lily the poise of a well-bred heiress who knew her own worth.

"The earl is good company," Lily said, drawing open the curtains. "He isn't vain and silly, like most men of his station, and his manners are faultless."

Walter yanked the curtain closed. "You'll fade the carpets and the wallpaper with the damned sunshine."

Lily stepped back, her expression cool. If Walter hadn't known better, he'd have thought the true Ferguson heiress gazed at him with faint reproach.

"Have you a megrim, Uncle? I can have Cook brew you a tisane."

He had megrims aplenty. "Tell me about Grampion. Has he mentioned any particular investments or projects?"

Lily tidied a shelf of books that Oscar had doubtless left in disarray. "He invests with his brother, Sir Worth, and speaks highly of him. I gather most of their ventures involve shipping, though some are domestic, and both brothers own sizable estates."

Nothing Walter had not already heard in the clubs. "You are very poor at intrigue, though Grampion seems to honestly like you."

Lily faced him, and the faint reproach had become something else. Resentment? Pique? Whatever lurked in her eyes, Walter didn't care for it.

"I have not known the earl long, Uncle, and one can't exactly ask him about finances in the normal course of a conversation, much less a conversation likely to be overheard. I am a mere female, in case you'd forgotten, not one of His Royal Majesty's court spies."

"You are an expense, Lily Ferguson, and never forget that. I could have left you in that coaching inn, fending off the stable lads and fretting over the butter stains on your apron."

A year ago, that observation would have elicited some reaction. Tears blinked back, pursed lips, a hurt look. Now Lily fished Walter's penknife out of the tray on his desk and tested the blade against her thumb.

"I am well aware of the circumstances in which you found me, Uncle. This blade is dull."

Doubtless the blade was dull because Walter had been burning midnight oil calculating income and expenses and fretting over Oscar's various follies. The lad had a good heart, but no head for business.

"Then as the lady of the household, you will have the blade sharpened, I'm sure. When next you and I find ourselves in the same company with the Earl of Grampion, you will contrive to add me to your conversation. You paid him no mind at all last night."

Lily set the knife down and perused the office as if she'd lost something of value somewhere among Walter's business effects.

"I was accosted last night by Mrs. Braithwaite, you'll recall."

He did recall. Roberta was aging well, not letting herself go to pot the way some women did. "Don't think because your mother tolerated Mrs. Braithwaite that she's good ton. Widows contrive as best they can, and nobody blames them for it, but neither should you waste your time with her."

"So she wasn't Mama's friend?"

Now, Lily busied herself dusting the globe, rotating it slowly while holding a linen handkerchief against the countries spinning past. This restlessness was unlike her, but then, the London Season made the greatest demands on her thespian skills.

Also on Walter's bank account. "Mrs. Braithwaite was one of myriad casual acquaintances who courted your mother's favor because Nadine married into a ducal family."

Lily let the globe drift to a halt and tucked her handkerchief into a skirt pocket. "She has threatened to pay a call on me."

Women and their infernal socializing. "Then you dole out two polite cups of tea to her, ask her whatever questions about your mother you're quivering to ask, and send her on her way. I will be out when she calls, lest the damned creature think to set her cap for me."

"I've asked Tippy all the questions about Mama I want to ask."

Lily was a bad liar, which was odd, because her life was an exercise in being somebody she was not—a successful exercise. She'd wanted for nothing while her mother had lived, then ended up in circumstances many a bastard orphan would have envied. Walter had taken her in hand when she'd turned fourteen and her older sister had gone daft for a handsome Scot.

Since then, Lily had known nothing but luxury. Still, she pined for a mother she'd barely known and a sister who'd not given two figs for an illegitimate younger sibling.

"Miss Tipton has grown increasingly forgetful," Walter said. "She might consider it a mercy that you've stopped plaguing her with your curiosity."

"You spy on her, Uncle?"

"You're growing quite bold, Lily. Spying is a vulgar undertaking. I keep an eye on a valued family retainer who is enjoying a well-earned retirement. If Miss Tipton should grow dangerously senile, I'll make provisions for her care."

Surely a cottage on some Hebridean island would suit.

"She is the closest thing I have to a true friend. Perhaps I would like to be responsible for her care."

Walter occasionally regretted not having remarried, but then he'd recall his late wife's moods, sulks, and fits of pique. Women were a bother, plain and simple, witness Lily's latest odd notion.

"You rely on me to take care of your every frippery and bonnet. If you think I've invested a fortune turning you into a lady, just so you can finish your days sharing a spinster cottage with your former governess, you are sadly mistaken."

Lily crossed her arms, and the resemblance to her mother struck again. Nadine had had a stubborn jaw. Perhaps that feature on Lily was becoming more noticeable with age.

"Isn't it more the case that you depend on me for your every pair of gloves and pipe of tobacco, Uncle? Also to pay for Oscar's light-skirts and inane wagers? Besides, once I marry, my husband will decide which elderly friend I can and cannot care for."

Walter took up the seat behind his desk, leaving Lily on her feet. The rudeness was deliberate. "Leggett women have an independent streak, witness the behaviors of your mother and sister. I had hoped that your more humble upbringing had instilled in you a firm grip of good sense and gratitude. If I am wrong, Lily, then I can arrange a repairing lease for you far to the north, or even back in Switzerland. I will find a facility that excels in curing stubborn females of their wayward tendencies."

Ah, lovely. Now Lily was staring hard at the carpet, hands fisted at her sides. A gratifying loss of composure, to be sure, and yet, she did not retreat.

"And if Grampion is thinking of offering for me, what would your explanation to him be for my sudden disappearance?"

Walter laughed. On this dreary damned day, encountering a cause for merriment felt especially good.

"Grampion is an earl, a widower, and a man of mature years. The very last choice he'd make would be to shackle himself to a difficult, no-longer-young commoner, regardless of her rumored fortune or blue blood. He tolerates your company to deflect the mosquito-cloud of debutantes. If he proves smitten despite all sense to the contrary, I'll convince him to look elsewhere, just as I've convinced the others. Be off with you and your fancies, Lily, though I thank you for amusing me in the middle of an otherwise dull afternoon."

Lily remained standing by the mantel, when she ought to have been bolting for the door. Instead, she smoothed her skirts, offered Walter a curtsey, and marched to the windows. She opened all the curtains as wide as they'd go, then left the room at a dignified pace.

Walter rose to close the curtains—wallpaper, carpet, furnishings, nearly everything of value was eventually damaged by sunlight—but remained by the window, studying the passing scene. Lily's mother had been imprudent in the extreme. Lily's sister had become what was politely termed a handful and more honestly a hoyden.

Lily showed signs of growing difficult as well, though like the pontifications of most annoying people, her viewpoint held a whiff of validity.

Heiresses married. This was for the good of the heiress, her family, and society as a whole. Quiet estates that kept unruly women secured in the countryside charged a lot of money, as much for their unreliable discretion as for their services. Should an accident befall Lily—as so sadly could occur at such facilities—then the courts would once again be sticking their noses into Walter's business.

He stood by the window for a long time, while coaches and foot traffic, a stray cat, and two old beldams holding tiny dogs passed before the house.

The answer to Walter's dilemma came strolling up the walk, swinging his walking stick, hat at a jaunty angle, cravat arranged in a ridiculous knot. Lud, the boy took after his mother, who'd been vain until her dying day.

Walter rang the bell-pull and instructed the footman to send Oscar up straightaway, for the time had come to talk to the boy about the benefits of marrying well.

CHAPTER THIRTEEN

"You're different," Worth said.

The night air was brisk with a hint of rain. Hessian's pace along the walkway was brisk as well, not because of the weather, but because he wanted to get home and make sure Daisy had passed a peaceful evening.

"Jacaranda has set you to interrogating me," Hessian replied. "I'm supposed to oblige you with a recitation of how, for the first time, I'm enjoying London in spring, or some such twaddle."

Worth hung back half a step, refusing, in the manner of irksome younger brothers, to match Hessian's strides. Worth had a devoted wife at home to handle any emergencies in the nursery, and that was irksome too.

"You haven't spent that many springs in London, Hess. You seemed to enjoy the card play tonight."

"The company was agreeable." Though Hessian would have preferred to spend the evening at home, reading to Lily, watching Lily read… kissing Lily.

Making mad, passionate love to her. As satisfying as their initial interlude had been, Hessian had done little since except plan improvements for the next encounter.

"Lily Ferguson has changed too," Worth said, ever so casually.

"With a few notable exceptions, we grow up, Worth." And Lily had done such a fine job of growing up too.

"She hasn't simply matured physically. The Lily I recall was something of a spoiled brat."

Hessian waited at the street corner while a crossing sweeper scooped a fresh pile of horse droppings from the intersection. The smell of manure punctuated more pleasant scents—scythed grass from the park across the street and Worth's delicate French cologne.

"You were something of a rotten boy," Hessian observed, "while I was painfully shy and somewhat priggish."

"Somewhat priggish? You were a hopeless little pattern card of puerile earlishness. Now that you are the earl, you're not half so stuffy."

"Thank you, I think. When are you removing to Trysting?"

A trio of young men, arms linked, beery fumes wafting around them, stepped aside as Hessian crossed the street. He'd never been that carefree, never been that enamored of London's nocturnal blandishments.

He was enamored of Lily Ferguson.

"Jacaranda decides when the household moves," Worth said, "and she says we must remain on hand to provide you moral support."

"Moral support with Daisy? That's very kind of her. I do appreciate it."

"With Lily Ferguson. You and Daisy will muddle along well enough. Have you read the diary?"

Hessian increased his pace. "When would I have had time? I'm too busy being only half priggish, playing cards with your friends, and writing to my wards." He'd asked both of Daisy's brothers to begin a correspondence with her, for purposes of engendering in her an epistolary habit, but also because siblings shared an important bond.

"What was the name of that doll?"

"Worth, how much brandy did you drink?"

"A good quantity. Tresham serves only the best, and it was free. Lily Ferguson's doll ended up in a tree, and you had to climb up and fetch it down."

"The doll's name was Lilith Ann." Hessian recalled the name because a biblical temptress was such an odd choice for a little girl's plaything. "The Patton twins meant to toss it into a mud puddle, but it got caught in a handy tree limb."

Lily had been distraught, all of her girlish hauteur dissolved in loud hysterics. The Patton boys—a pair of imps—had been equally horrified to see the doll stranded.

"That's the only time," Hessian said, "I've heard a female openly admit she wished all males to perdition with a case of dysentery."

Worth tipped his hat to a pair of smiling ladies who probably weren't ladies. "You were concerned that if Lily climbed the tree herself, the boys would peek up her dress."

"I was concerned for my hearing. We missed your turn."

"You missed my turn. I'm walking you home."

Meaning Hessian would have no solitude before gaining his own doorstep. "Why aren't I walking you home?"

"Because Jacaranda has spoken, and I am her slave in all things where some disobliging brother might contradict my story and make me look a fool before my wife. She said to walk you home, ergo, my fate is sealed. Does Lily Ferguson still have a birthmark on the inside of her left elbow? It was shaped like a dove, as best I recall."

Hessian came to a halt. "How the devil should I know, and what the deuce sort of question is that to ask on a public street of your own brother?"

Worth ambled onward. "I couldn't ask you in front of the children, now could I? I can't help but think that I'm missing something where Lily Ferguson is concerned. I have come upon a bit of old gossip concerning a youthful indiscretion of hers, but even that doesn't feel like the evidence I'm seeking."

Hessian resumed walking. "She is still quite youthful, and you might have told me your investigations were bearing fruit."

"Not fruit, not yet, but a few scented breezes. Tresham has recently acquired an auntie-in-law who prides herself on knowing everything about everybody, though she's not a bearer of tales. The lady and I came upon one another walking our dogs in the park the other day and, as fellow admirers of the canine, struck up a conversation."

"I will strike you, if you don't soon get to the point."

"See? That's the unpriggish half of you talking. In any case, Her Grace of Quimbey has noticed you and Miss Ferguson on some occasion or other—playing catch, I think she said—and the duchess wondered if I'd heard the old rumor about Miss Ferguson eloping with her uncle's house steward."

Hessian's steps slowed, for they'd turned the corner onto his street. "I cannot imagine Lily Ferguson being impetuous enough to elope with anybody."

But youthful folly of that magnitude would explain why Walter Leggett kept such a close eye on his niece, why she'd been sent to Switzerland for finishing school, why a somewhat spoiled girl might have matured into a more cautious and self-possessed woman.

"Neither can I," Worth said, "though my recollection of her is that of a young boy who had no use for females of any stripe, other than to torment them."

"At which you excelled."

"Thank Jacaranda for sorting me out."

No light shone from the nursery window, which was a relief and a disappointment. "You have imparted this rumor for a reason. It's old news, and apparently known to very few, if it's true."

Worth plucked a bloom of heartsease from the pot sitting beside the neighbor's mounting block. "That little rumor fuels my conviction that the pieces of Lily Ferguson aren't adding up. Why hasn't she married, Hess? Her mama bagged a ducal spare, meaning Lily is a duke's granddaughter, albeit an Irish duke. She's an heiress, blue-blooded, comely, and a drain on her uncle's finances. She should have become engaged halfway through her first Season. What puzzle pieces are we missing?"

Hessian had missed bedtime in the nursery, for the card party had assembled earlier than most of its kind.

"She may be as yet unwed because the heavenly powers intend her for me," Hessian said. "I will seek Leggett's permission to offer her my addresses next week."

Lily had sent a note that Leggett was much occupied cleaning up some mess created by his son. She would explain further on the occasion of a ride in the park the day after tomorrow.

"I wish you'd wait, Hess. You were always the soul of prudence, the fellow who let nothing sway him from sober deliberation. The very fact that I can't uncover much about Leggett's situation troubles me."

Sober deliberation had little to recommend it, compared to the joys of an impetuous interlude in the conservatory. And yet, Worth had a point: Impetuosity was foreign to Hessian's nature.

With Lily, he was convinced that undue hesitation would cost him the one woman with whom he could be happy.

"I'm not courting Leggett, Worth. I'll marry Lily if she hasn't a penny to her name, and I suspect she feels the same about me."

She'd said little after those shared moments in Hessian's sanctuary, but she'd clung to him desperately just before they'd left the conservatory. Reserved people often expressed with actions what they did not put into words.

"Jacaranda was right, then," Worth said. "You are in love. I wish you much joy of the endeavor, and I'll keep listening for information about Leggett in anticipation of settlement negotiations."

"Listen discreetly, or I'll thrash you."

Worth socked Hessian on the arm. "Love you too." He strolled away, his cane propped against his shoulder.

Hessian paused before his own front door, battling the temptation to keep walking until he was in the Leggett mews. He could toss a few pebbles at Lily's window and recite whispered poetry to the night air, and otherwise...

Make an ass out of himself. He had no idea which window might be Lily's, and tossing pebbles in the dark of night was no way to reliably hit a target in any case.

He nonetheless sat for a moment on his own front steps, pondering the conversation with Worth. Lily was not the woman Hessian would have said that difficult, overindulged little girl should have become. She was far more sensible and likable.

More trustworthy. A boy hadn't dared turn his back on the young Lily Ferguson. She could throw rocks with an accuracy that daunted a young male's fragile consequence.

Hessian rose and dusted himself off, anticipating the joy of peeking in on a sleeping Daisy. His last thought before surrendering his hat, gloves, and walking stick in the foyer was to keep a lookout for that birthmark on the inside of Lily's elbow.

If fate was kind, he might steal a peek at the relevant part of her anatomy in the very near future.

* * *

No fairy tale told Sleeping Beauty what to do with a case of insomnia. The handsome earl—prince, rather—came along and disturbed her slumbers with his kiss, and then what? How did the poor woman return to the blessed oblivion of her dreams?

The best part about sleepwalking through life, about focusing on only the nearest perceived worry, was that Lily hadn't realized how carefully numb she'd become to anything else.

To her own emotions, to her body, to her world.

"It's a lovely morning, isn't it?" she asked the earl.

Hessian Kettering sat his horse as if born to the saddle. He was blessedly oblivious to the depth of havoc he'd wrought in Lily's life, while she could think of little else.

"All mornings have a lovely quality about them," he replied. "Even during the roughest patches of my life, even when I thought I'd made a muddle of everything, mornings still had a sense of hope and possibility."

He brought his horse to a halt and sat quietly. Lily did likewise with her mare. They were nowhere in particular—a leafy patch on a quiet bridle path in Hyde Park, a groom trailing a discreet distance behind—but Grampion was right. Lily had risen lately with a sense of hope and possibility—also, more anxiety than usual.

"Are we having a moment of prayer?" she asked.

"We're having a moment of reflection, for certain geldings have acquired the habit of leaning on the reins, which is a very ungentlemanly behavior indeed."

The ride had begun with a thundering gallop, Grampion's horse was apparently eager for another run, just as Lily was eager to return to that secluded corner of the earl's conservatory.

"He's fit," Lily said. "Unlike my poor mare. One gallop isn't enough for him."

His lordship turned his face upward, as if admiring the arches of a cathedral rather than the plane maples. Sunshine slanted in golden shafts amid the greenery, and sparrows flitted aloft.

"How are you, Lily?"

"How am—?" The question was intimate. A lover's query. "I am lonely for you, every moment we're apart."

That was not a reply Lily would have known how to make even a month ago. Now she couldn't keep such sentiments to herself, and that was a problem.

"As I am lonely for you. Let's move along, before the groom is upon us. My motivation to speak to your uncle has become pressing."

The morning's possibilities and hopes dimmed. "You're returning to the north?"

"No, love. I'm losing my wits. I hope you aren't inclined toward a long engagement."

"My uncle might try to put you off." Had promised to not only put Grampion off, but dissuade him entirely. "He's fond of managing my fortune."

The rest of the tale begged to tumble out: It's not my fortune, you see. It belonged to my mama, then to my half-sister, then probably to King George or my sister's Irish relations, but not to me. Never to the unacknowledged bastard.

"I have the impression Walter Leggett is more fond of managing you."

In that quiet observation, Lily realized why Hessian Kettering's kiss could wake a slumbering princess.

He loved.

His life was not a series of entertainments, as Oscar's was.

He did not spend his energies in bitterness and vengeance, as Mrs. Braithwaite did.

He was not obsessed with getting, spending, and scheming, as Uncle was.

Hessian Kettering cared for those around him. He was devoted to his younger brother, to Daisy, to responsible stewardship of his resources, to even his horse. He paid attention, he was awake, and his sense of focus and investment in those around him was contagious.

"Uncle did not ask to be burdened with a young niece who dealt badly with being orphaned." Walter had spent two years' worth of correspondence reminding Lily of the nobility of his sacrifice. Only after hearing a few muttered asides from Tippy had a more mature Lily suspected Walter's motivation was pure greed without a scintilla of avuncular affection.

"That reminds me," Grampion said. "A rumor regarding your past has come to my attention."

And there went the rest of Lily's hope. Her mare hesitated, as if a sense of doom had penetrated even the limitations of an equine brain.

"Rumors and fortune hunters follow heiresses in equal measure."

They emerged from the trees into a clearing of dew-sparkled grass and sharp morning sun.

"The rumor comes from a reliable, disinterested source who claims that you eloped with your uncle's house steward. You are lovely, intelligent, well-dowered, and of age. I ask myself: Have you remained immune to the addresses of London's most eligible bachelors because you are already married?"

A salvo such as that had been commonplace when Lily had first returned from Switzerland. Somebody would remark a piece of music she had supposedly played exquisitely at some tea dance, and panic would follow, lest Lily be publicly caught out as only half the musician her sister had been.

She'd learned to duck, dodge, prevaricate, dissuade, and otherwise deflect incoming fire, until fewer and fewer cannonballs were lobbed at her decks.

She laughed at Grampion's theory, for laughter was as effective at diffusing such moments as any retort she could manufacture, but her laughter had come one heartbeat late.

"You flatter me, my lord."

Again, he brought his horse to a smooth halt. "I accuse you of living a lie, of deceiving all of polite society, and you laugh."

In other words, he wouldn't desist until he had an answer.

"You accuse me of being nigh irresistible, when in fact, I'm impossible to please—or I was."

"And the house steward?"

This much, Lily could answer honestly. "I know not what became of him, but he and I are not married. His interest was inappropriate, and I was packed off to Switzerland for two years lest he persuade me otherwise."

Uncle had strongly implied that both Annie and her swain had come to bad ends in the same coaching accident, but as in so many other particulars, Lily had dared not ask for details.

"Did this scoundrel break your heart, Lily?"

"No." The truth had never been such a relief. Lily recited a litany Tippy had fashioned for her. "I was young, I was bored, I was not yet old enough to make my come out, and had no mama or auntie to keep me from foolishness. I strongly suspect the gentleman's sole motivation was to get his hands on my settlements."

Hessian used the tip of his riding crop to whisk a fly from his horse's shoulder. "And the man's name?"

This was what came after the warning shot—the destructive volley, intent on wreaking mayhem and inspiring quick surrender. Lily could not afford to surrender, and though she might have heard the house steward's name at some point, she could not recall it now.

"Must we discuss this?"

"Not if it pains you."

"We're wasting a beautiful morning with these trivialities." Though, if Hessian was intent on tracking down the house steward, that was far from trivial. "How is Daisy?"

The horses and the conversation moved on, while the earl grew effusive about letters he'd had from Daisy's brothers. He knew the boys from their summers in the north and pronounced both to be fine young fellows whom Daisy missed more than she admitted.

As the Serpentine came into view and other riders filled the broader thoroughfares, the earl gently halted his gelding for the third time.

"I must speak to your uncle this week, Lily. I can find no reason to keep my interest in you from becoming public. Once I have permission to court you, once we are engaged, we'll have much more latitude, and the fortune hunters will slink off to pursue other heiresses."

Oh, Hessian. "And the widows will pursue other earls?"

"I'm told Wellington himself, despite being married to the sweetheart of his youth, has no artillery sufficient to dissuade that regiment."

"His grace fires only smiles and flirtation in their direction, and he is a duke."

"I am an earl. A paltry prize by comparison, but I would like to be your prize."

Despite Hessian's smile, despite the flattering nature of his objective, Lily felt a sense of doom. Uncle would wave off the only suitor Lily wanted for her own, and another ten years of being the testy, often-tested niece of Walter Leggett would be the best she could hope for.

"Have you ever considered eloping, my lord?"

"No, I have not. When a man of my station elopes for no apparent reason, scandal ensues. The last thing I need now, with Daisy newly added to my household, is scandal."

Well, drat and perdition. "Because of Mrs. Braithwaite?"

The groom drew up ten yards back.

"Because I value your reputation and my own. Because Daisy does not need such drama and talk. Because I am the head of my family, small though it is, and have an unmarried half-sister to consider. As much as I'd love to carry you off and make endless passionate love to you, I cannot justify being that selfish."

Felled by honor. "Then you must speak to Uncle, and if you are to be successful with him, the less said about my fortune the better."

"Lily, I don't give a hearty goddamn for your fortune. When can I see you again?"

This was another symptom of being too preoccupied with present pleasures and not focused enough on practicalities. Lily should have memorized her accepted invitations, the better to coordinate with Hessian.

"I am at a loss," she said. "Perhaps Bronwyn and Daisy might spend another afternoon together?"

A man sauntered in through the park gates fifty yards away, just another pedestrian taking the fine, fresh air, except this fellow had a sizable Alsatian on a leash and was too elegantly turned out to be anything but a lordling.

"My nanny has arrived," Hessian said, turning his gelding in the direction of the park's latest arrival. "But we will use this meddling to our advantage. Have you met my brother, Worth?"

Uncle would be pleased with this development, while Lily was uneasy. "I have not."

"Not since we were children, you mean. Rest assured, Sir Worth is almost harmless now."

Lily had learned that a blunder was best followed by a swift retreat. She'd blundered this morning with Hessian—over her half-sister's elopement, among other things—and because she hadn't withdrawn to regain her composure, her errors were multiplying.

Whereas Hessian was fair, Worth was dark. Hessian was lanky, Worth had a solid muscularity that would be menacing under the right circumstances. He gave Lily a keen appraisal, and that unsettled her as well.

"You must pay a call on my lady wife," Worth said, bowing over Lily's hand. Though she was mounted, and Hessian's brother stood at her stirrup, he was tall enough not to be at a disadvantage on the ground.

"That will suit," Hessian said before Lily could answer. "Perhaps the day after tomorrow?"

Worth stroked a gloved hand over the dog's head. "Two of the clock should see the princess off to her nap. Jacaranda will welcome adult company at that hour."

"Two of the clock," Lily said. "I will look forward to it."

The dog cast her owner a hopeful look, and they were soon on their way.

"I'll call on your uncle tomorrow, then," Hessian said, "and should my schedule take me to Worth's doorstep at two of the clock the day after tomorrow, do try to look surprised."

Tomorrow was much, much too soon. "Uncle might not be in tomorrow."

The groom was walking his horse in a circle, the hoof beats on the cobbles clattering against Lily's composure.

"Then, my dear, I will persist and make an appointment if I must. Are you afraid of your uncle, Lily?"

She should have laughed again, but instead she took up her reins. "Of course not."

"But neither can you trust him to have your best interests at heart. Trust me, then. I do not give up easily."

Hessian extended a hand, though it was always the lady's privilege to offer her hand first. Lily let him take her fingers in his and bow from the saddle. The gesture was courtly, and public, and the groom would doubtless report it to Uncle before Lily's mare was at her hay.

"If you could introduce Uncle to your brother, he might look more favorably on your suit."

Grampion turned loose of Lily's hand. "He wants Worth to make him rich? Hasn't Leggett already a fortune of his own and your fortune to manage as well?"

"I wouldn't know, my lord, but I cannot caution you strongly enough to deal carefully with Uncle Walter. Anticipate dilatory stratagems at least and outright rejection possibly."

"I am forewarned."

Lily took her leave of the earl, wanting nothing so much as to disappear back into the quiet greenery of the park. She instead rode directly home, pondering how she might have better prepared Grampion for the puzzle and problem that was Uncle Walter.

When she reached the mews, Oscar was again sitting on the mounting block, another bottle in his hand. He roused himself enough to assist Lily from the saddle, which confirmed that he'd been out all night. Cigar smoke, sour wine, and sweat perfumed his person.

"Greetings, Cousin," he said, affecting a tipsy bow. "You look very fetching this morning."

Lily's habit was at least five years old. "While you look in need of a bath, a nap, and a shave."

Oscar studied her, while the groom led the mare away. "I'm grieving, or resigning myself to my fate. Your fate too, I suppose."

"Oscar, are you sozzled?"

"Oh yes, a bit, and soon I'll be engaged to be married." He sat once again on the mounting block and urged Lily down beside him.

"Congratulations, I suppose. I hope you at least like your intended."

"I like her quite well, known her all my life. Capital girl with gorgeous settlements."

Oscar was smirking at his wine bottle, while Lily's insides went widdershins. "Do I know this paragon?"

"You see her in the mirror every morning. Uncle has decided we're to be married, though you mustn't let on that I told you. Ceremony won't be until you've celebrated your birthday. I'm finding the notion more appealing by the day."

CHAPTER FOURTEEN

Walter Leggett's town house was spacious, clean, and somehow… off.

Hessian concluded this before he'd handed his hat and walking stick to the butler, a dour soul who said nothing other than, "Good day, my lord," and—when Hessian had passed him a card—"Very good, my lord."

Perhaps the lack of a child in the house made a difference. No little feet pounding overhead, no miniature parasol in the umbrella stand.

Or maybe Hessian was reacting to a lack of flowers. London in spring was gloriously blessed with floral abundance, and yet, not even a sachet of dried lavender hung from the drapery in Leggett's formal parlor.

The parlor itself was generously appointed with upholstered chairs and a velvet sofa in shades of gold and green. The Axminster carpet echoed the same scheme with dashes of rose and cream, while the landscape on the wall was more green with a rosy-tinted sky and cream-colored sheep.

The house struck Hessian as a theater set: Prosperous London Town House. A giggling housemaid with her cap askew would soon enter from stage left, or a footman spouting humorous disrespect for the senior staff from stage right.

And yet, Hessian's business with Walter Leggett was serious indeed.

Would Lily listen to the exchange from behind a door? Would she join them?

"My Lord Grampion, what a pleasure to see you!" Walter Leggett strode into the parlor, hand extended. "I had no occasion to remark it at your recent dinner party, but you are the image—the very image—of your late papa. Let us be seated, and you must tell me how your dear brother goes on and all the news from Cumberland."

At Hessian's dinner party, such effusions would have been overheard by a dozen other guests. This was a performance for the benefit of an audience of one.

"Leggett, how do you do? I had hoped for more time with my guests when last we met, but the evening did not go as planned."

Thank heavens.

Hessian took a seat on the sofa, which, like many sofas, was more ornamental than comfortable. Leggett swept out his tails and appropriated the chair to Hessian's left.

"The dear ladies make a plague of themselves, don't they?" Leggett said. "I am fortunate not to be burdened with a title, or the poor darlings would be climbing my trellises and stealing into my town coach."

What an odd observation from an unremarkable older man. "Speaking of the ladies, will Miss Ferguson be joining us? My Daisy has taken a particular liking to her."

"Lily is very likely still abed, my lord. She's not the type to bestir herself much before noon." Leggett's tone, more than his words, fondly chided such laziness, though during the social season, much of Mayfair slept their mornings away.

"I enjoy hacking out first thing in the day myself," Hessian said. "Will I see you in the park at an early hour?"

Hessian had intended a very different conversation: I esteem Miss Ferguson greatly and would like to pay her my addresses. Simple enough, but not a conversation to undertake without assessing his host's receptiveness either.

Leggett's dissembling—Lily had willingly ridden out early—suggested more reconnaissance was in order.

"My habits are variable," Leggett said. "Does your brother enjoy the park at dawn? You have been conscientious in renewing your acquaintance with your dear papa's friends, but Sir Worth cannot claim the same."

The implied scold was also... off. Sir Worth had been kicking his heels in London for the past decade. Leggett had had thousands of opportunities to pay a call on Hessian's brother if he'd cared to.

"Shall I have you to dinner again?" Hessian said. "Your family and mine, and I'll invite Worth and his lady as well. Informal meals with friends can be among the most enjoyable."

"I have always said as much, and speaking of sustenance, shall I ring for tea?"

"No need." Especially if Lily wasn't to pour out. "My staff frets if I don't consume frequent, prodigious meals. You have a son, don't you?"

Leggett waxed effusive about his charming, dear, good-looking "boy," whom Hessian estimated to be at least twenty-one years of age. Lily had never said anything critical of Oscar Leggett, but neither had she complimented him.

"I have hopes that Oscar might go into business," Leggett said. "He has the friendly manner of the successful solicitor, the common sense of the man of affairs. Your brother is known to employ myriad subordinates, and Oscar might be a fine addition to their number."

"You must broach that topic with Worth, or perhaps Oscar might take that initiative?" For if Worth Kettering rewarded any quality in his employees, it was initiative.

"You're right, of course," Leggett said. "Though I do believe Oscar's focus is in a different direction these days."

What direction could be more compelling for a young man than securing his financial future? "Most young men need a few years to sort themselves out before settling to a profession."

Hessian had spent those years married to a woman he hadn't understood, while Worth had gone forth into the world and earned a fortune.

"Or the young fellows have sense enough to find a lady who can sort them out," Leggett said. "I'm hopeful that Oscar has finally found such a woman right under his very nose, so to speak."

Innuendo wafted around Leggett's smile. The only lady under Oscar's very nose would be...

"He'll take a bride before finding a means of supporting her?"

Leggett's chuckle was rusty and forced. "Younger sons in titled families must find a calling, true enough. The rest of us with means can be more lenient with our offspring. Oscar is my sole heir, and did I not enjoy managing my affairs above all else, I'd be turning the lot of my investments over to him. He'll do better for learning the ways of commerce at another's elbow. Then he can step into my shoes without having been lectured by his papa for years."

A son often learned life's lessons best from anybody other than his father, but Leggett's recitation had the quality of a speech, an oration delivered to convince.

"Some of my fondest memories," Hessian said, "are of riding Grampion's metes and bounds with my father. He knew every tenant, every acre of the land, and every fox in every covert. I saw firsthand the standard I was to aim for, and the example has stood me in good stead."

The cushion beneath Hessian was lumpy to the point of causing discomfort, if the conversation weren't already making him uneasy. The set-piece parlor, the innuendo regarding Oscar's choice of bride, the speechifying about why Oscar wasn't to learn his family's finances from the only person who could instruct him on the matter...

An ill-fitting boot of a social call.

"I'm sure you miss your father very much," Leggett said, "but the aristocracy will regret clinging to the land as its sole source of wealth. Mark me on this, my lord, for I know of what I speak."

"Perhaps young Oscar would benefit from your thoughts on that subject," Hessian said, rising. "I am expected elsewhere, though you may anticipate a dinner invitation from my household to yours in the near future."

Was that relief in Leggett's eyes? Satisfaction?

"If you'd rather not go to the bother of hosting company, Oscar and I could meet you and your brother for dinner at my club," Leggett said. "The ladies find talk of business and politics tedious, just as we fellows find talk of balls and millinery a trial."

"I must disagree," Hessian said as his host escorted him down to the front door. "The company of the ladies, with their poise and graciousness, is preferable to a lot of pontificating men and their stinking cigars. Hosting your family for dinner will be my pleasure."

Provided Lily was among the guests.

Leggett hovered, smiling and chortling, until Hessian was physically out the door.

The entire encounter had been disappointing and disquieting. Was Lily engaged to her cousin?

Was Leggett rolled up?

Hessian turned at the street corner and took himself into the alley that ran between two rows of town houses. A mews sat near one end, along with a carriage house likely shared by several households. The alley was a quiet, shady stretch of cobbles, just like hundreds of other alleys in London. Hessian sauntered along, a gentleman who preferred quieter environs than the main streets, until he'd counted enough back gardens to find himself behind Leggett's town house.

The garden was another theater set—a sundial in the middle, a small patch of overgrown grass between walkways and hedges—but not as well maintained as the rest of Leggett's property.

"Can I help you, sir?"

The question came from a slight fellow in workingman's clothes. He smelled of horse, and his hair needed a trim.

"If I and a few other fellows wanted to toss a note onto the balcony of Mr. Oscar Leggett, or perhaps serenade him with a humorous ballad some night when the rest of his family was out, which window might we assemble beneath?"

The man's smile revealed a total of six teeth. "Mr. Oscar Leggett has that room above the terrace, sir. His pa's to the right, and the young miss is on the left-hand corner. They'd both hear you and your mates, if you chose the wrong evening."

Hessian passed the man a coin. "We'll choose carefully."

The groom returned to the stable, while Hess visually measured the distance from the top of the gazebo to Lily's window. A bow window beneath made the climb reasonably safe, though where was a handy balcony when a fellow needed to turn up swainly by moonlight?

Hessian consulted his watch—he'd promised Daisy a midafternoon picnic if she finished letters to her brothers—and went upon his way.

The meeting with Leggett had not gone as planned, not at all, but Lily would pay a call tomorrow at Worth's, and Hessian would then ascertain if her question about eloping had been idle curiosity or a broad hint.

* * *

"You leave me thinking the worst, Oscar Leggett, the very worst, then take yourself off to sleep the morning away in the stables."

Lily was still angry with him for that, for spending the past two days hiding from her, pretending a megrim, then sneaking out of an evening rather than dispelling the nasty, outlandish implications of their last conversation.

She'd risked confronting him at his midday meal, which for him was an early breakfast.

"If you must scold, at least cease racketing about while you do," Oscar said, pouring himself a cup of coffee. "I was giving you time to reconcile yourself to your good fortune. Honestly, Lily, you could do much worse."

No, she could not. "Why are you awake and dressed before sundown?"

"You informed the stables that you'd need the carriage for a two o'clock call. If we're to be married, we must comport ourselves like a couple, and that means we pay calls together."

That was Walter Leggett's logic, also an excuse to tighten the noose of surveillance Lily had lived with since the age of fourteen.

"I'm going hat shopping."

Oscar slurped his coffee. "Mustn't lie, Lily. That's not what you told the butler."

And the coachman would disclose any and all locations Lily had visited. "I'm going hat shopping after I pay my call."

"Excellent. I adore lounging about among ladies' fripperies, flirting with shop girls, and consulting on purchases. I'm quite good at it."

Lily took the seat at his elbow, when she wanted to toss the coffeepot at his head. "Because you indulge your mistresses."

"One at a time, but of course. Mistresses are an exercise in mutual indulgence."

"Mistresses are a means to contract horrid diseases, waste coin, and act like a fool in public."

Oscar set down his coffee cup and selected a triangle of buttered toast. "If you intend to be that kind of wife, we can live apart once you've presented me with a pair of sons. I don't plan on being difficult about Papa's scheme, Lily, but you clearly do."

Why hadn't she seen this coming? Why hadn't she made plans to run away years ago? A woman at age twenty-one became an adult in all particulars. Lily had less freedom than Daisy, who was closely supervised at every hour.

"Oscar, we are cousins. Surely you agree that cousins should not marry."

"Tell that to King George or his sainted father. Nothing illegal about keeping wealth in the family with an occasional marriage between cousins. Why is there no marmalade for my toast? I always take my toast with marmalade."

A lifetime of listening to Oscar whine for his marmalade was the best Lily faced as his wife.

"And look how His Majesty's marriage turned out," Lily muttered. "I can assure you, there will be no children. You will never know a husband's privileges, Oscar, not with me."

He brushed toast crumbs from his cravat. "You think to keep me from your bed because we are cousins? The church has no objection to such a match, and as to that, I doubt we are anything approaching cousins."

All the worry, resentment, anger, and bewilderment in Lily came to a still point of incredulity. "I beg your pardon?"

"You bear a resemblance both to my cousin Lily and her late mother, but my cousin hated animals of any kind—horses, cats, dogs, birds. Never had a kind word for any species besides her own, and seldom for that one either. You dote on that slug of a mare, sneak treats to that feline hearth rug you call Hannibal, and can't walk past a dog without petting it."

"For God's sake, Oscar, you cannot think… people change. They mature."

"Horses made Lily itch, cats made her sneeze. She was honestly terrified of birds, because some woman at church got a sparrow stuck in her bonnet one Sunday, and the creature ended up dead—the sparrow, that is."

"I am Lily Ferguson, and you are my cousin."

"You are a very good actress, but the Lily Ferguson I knew as a boy was a fiend for the piano. You can barely get out a party piece."

Oh God, oh God, oh God. "Skills grow rusty."

"My cousin couldn't carry a tune in a bucket, which I suspect is why she became so proficient at the keyboard. You sing like a nightingale."

All the years of scrubbing floors at the inn in Derbyshire, all the summers spent hanging linen on the wash line had been leavened by the simple folk tunes that made a workday go more easily.

"I practiced, in Switzerland."

"I do wonder about Switzerland. Perhaps Switzerland is what we're now to call some finishing school in the West Riding, except I've not heard a single rumor to that effect. Nobody suspects, and you've done such a good job of being Lily that I've doubted myself from time to time."

He had no proof, none. So far, all he'd offered was speculation and conjecture.

"I might as well contend that you are not Oscar Leggett. You're some by-blow your mother brought to the marriage because Walter is unable to procreate. You don't resemble him in temperament or looks or… anything."

Oscar's smile was pitying. "Lily, you needn't panic. I do resemble my sire to the extent that I'm capable of exploiting an advantage when it comes my way. We will marry, I will be a decent husband to you, and by degrees, as you provide the grandchildren, I will gain control of Papa's wealth."

"My wealth."

He patted his lips with his serviette. "You're a woman. You can't have wealth. In any case, if Papa proves difficult, I'll simply air my theories regarding your origins and declare the marriage fraudulent."

Lily rose and paced to the far corner of the breakfast parlor, putting as much distance as she could between her and the nightmare munching toast at the table.

"If the marriage is fraudulent, then I go to jail, and Uncle regains control of my fortune."

"Does he? Or does he go to jail with you? You would have been quite young when you undertook to impersonate my cousin. She was seventeen when she disappeared with that Lawrence Delmar fellow, and girls are so impressionable at that age. Helpless, really. Year and year away from legal adulthood. Who knows what promises Uncle made to you, or what threats?"

The silence in the breakfast parlor was punctuated by Oscar slicing his ham, while Lily mentally shrieked at a world gone mad once too often.

At fourteen, she'd chosen Uncle Walter's dubious assistance over certain, repeated rape in the scullery. Other tavern maids had had family to be outraged at their ill treatment, to help them find work elsewhere if the stable boys or guests proved unruly.

Lily had had nobody, and her orphan status had been common knowledge.

"When is the wedding to be?"

"Haven't a clue. I'm to procure a special license, which means some time in the next six months. Your next birthday is significant, I believe, putting control of your fortune into your own hands. If you marry thereafter, your husband acquires that money, or it gets tied up in settlement trusts that I'll manage. If you marry before that date, Uncle will decide the terms of the settlements."

Was Oscar lying? Lily had to assume he was, that the special license was already in hand.

"Uncle will manage any funds I bring to the union. He might have hinted that you will have control, but I promise you—I promise you this on the life of my departed mother—that when you're presented with the documents, they will very prettily accord to him control of every groat and farthing. He will trade on your trust in him as your father, on smoothly ambiguous lies, and on your own lack of acumen with legal language. You cannot trust him, except to operate in his own best interests."

Oscar speared the last bite of ham. "Like papa, like son, eh?" His tone was considering rather than offended. "I will think on this, but while I'm thinking, we will become an item of friendly speculation, Lily. You will drag me about on shopping expeditions. I will grow thoughtful when the other fellows mention holy matrimony. We'll convince the world we're something more than cousins, and all will fall into place."

He rose, came around the table to kiss Lily's cheek, and then left her alone amid the detritus of his meal.

A good two minutes went by before a footman came to clear the table, suggesting that the conversation would not be reported to Uncle.

Oscar wasn't awful. He, like Lily, was trying to make the best of a situation he'd not brought upon himself. For one moment, Lily was tempted to reconcile herself to the future he painted: a marriage of necessity, cordial on the surface, materially comfortable, and honest, in its way.

But then he'd kissed her cheek.

Oscar stank of last night's cigars, hair pomade, and bitter coffee. His lips on Lily's person, his hand on her arm, made her want to vomit. She'd spent years dodging cuffs and kisses at the inn, more than a decade as Uncle Walter's frightened puppet, and now this—marriage to another man who'd use her however he pleased, even intimately.

Her brave pronouncements notwithstanding, Oscar would have every legal right to exercise his marital privileges, and he was not a man who'd forego available pleasure.

Beyond the window, the coach was coming around from the mews to take Lily on her first social call with Oscar in the role of intended. She dreaded to go, and she didn't dare stay home, for it might be her last opportunity to see Hessian Kettering, and she did want to see him again.

Desperately.

* * *

Hessian arrived to Worth's town house at a quarter past the hour, because Daisy had insisted on coming with him. In truth, the child's company was welcome, for he'd have to report to Lily that the interview with Walter Leggett had gone poorly.

Very poorly.

To Hessian's surprise, Oscar Leggett was swilling tea in Jacaranda's parlor, looking as if he and Lily always went about socializing as a pair.

Lily sat beside her cousin, nibbling a biscuit—and avoiding Hessian's gaze.

"Might we take a turn in the garden?" Hessian suggested when Jacaranda had served two cups all around. "I can hear the children making a lovely racket, and mild weather is still a rare treat."

"Capital notion." Oscar Leggett stood and assisted Lily to her feet, while Worth aided his wife.

"I'll get Meda," Worth said. "Are you a dog fancier, Mr. Leggett?"

"Dogs?"

In the space of one syllable, Hessian watched Oscar weigh, measure, and conclude that dog fanciers stood higher in Worth Kettering's esteem than those who had no use for canines.

"I adore a noble hound," Oscar said. "Provided he's a frequently bathed and well-behaved fellow. Man's best friend and all that."

Worth lured Oscar from Lily's side with some taradiddle about finding Meda's leash in the study across the hall, and Hessian affixed himself at Lily's elbow despite Jacaranda's raised eyebrow.

"They will natter on about dogs and hounds and whelping boxes until midsummer's night," Hessian said, leading Lily out onto the terrace. "Talk to me, Lily. Your uncle was very unforthcoming when I called upon him. I did not raise the subject of courtship, and now you look as if you've seen Hamlet's ghost."

Jacaranda had disappeared to instruct some servant or other—and a nursery maid sat on a bench halfway down the garden walk near Daisy and Avery, who chased away pigeons, the better to chalk flowers onto the paving stones.

"Uncle has decided I'm to marry Oscar," Lily said, her gaze on the children. "Oscar is in a state of gleeful anticipation, though I'm to know nothing of my impending nuptial bliss until after my birthday."

Had Lily kicked Hessian in the stomach, she could not have delivered a worse surprise—a worse betrayal.

"You have not objected."

"I have not had time to think, Hessian. I did not foresee this, but it makes perfect sense. Uncle controls the money, and he controls Oscar, and thus... don't look at me like that. I had no notion of this, no inkling, and it qualifies as my worst nightmare short of going to prison for a capital offense. I was too besotted with you to pay proper attention, but I'm soon to turn twenty-eight, and that will change everything, apparently."

The beautiful day, the tidy garden, everything faded behind the dull thud of Hessian's heart against his ribs.

"Will you play me false, Lily? Will you go willingly to the altar because your uncle commands it? What has that bleating stripling to offer you that's preferable to being my countess?"

Lily's eyes confirmed her uncle's scheme was her idea of hell, but of words, she gave Hessian nothing.

"Lily, I had hoped that my feelings for you were reciprocated, else I would never have... I would not have presumed. Then you declare, with no explanation whatsoever, that you will wed another. Help me understand, for I cannot reconcile the woman who yielded so sweetly in my conservatory with the silent, miserable creature in my brother's garden."

"I am so far beyond miserable."

Across the garden, the little girls had gone into whoops of laughter, while the poor pigeons strutted indignantly atop the garden wall. Lily wandered down the walk, and when she came to the first of the chalk drawings, she sat on the paving stones as the children had done and took up a length of chalk.

While Hessian silently lost his mind, Jacaranda reappeared on the terrace with a footman. He bore a tea tray, and every item on the tray was in miniature. The set had clearly come from the nursery, and the girls left off mocking the pigeons to take their tea by the sundial.

Hessian hunkered down as if to admire Lily's sketching, which had resulted in the girls' birds becoming dragons. "Lily? Have you nothing more to say?"

Hessian had more to say, but his tirade was aimed at himself.

Worth had warned him that caution was in order. Bitter experience had taught Hessian to reconnoiter at length where women and matrimony were concerned. Worse, Daisy was growing attached to Lily, and compared to Hessian's consternation, Daisy would be devastated if Lily simply dropped from her life.

Oscar, Worth, and the damned dog came out onto the terrace next, Meda's attention riveted on the children, who were arranging their tea set on a blanket in the grass.

"I cannot say what I need to here with Oscar ready to pounce," Lily murmured as she embellished the wings on the smaller dragon, "but I am sorry Hessian. I'm deeply, deeply sorry. My situation has become... impossible, and that has nothing to do with you."

She'd said she was besotted with him. Hessian clung to that spar of hope in a sea of doubt and outrage.

"Do you want to marry Oscar?"

"Of course not."

Rational thought pushed past the humiliation and confusion in Hessian's mind. Why would a woman of means marry against her will? Why would a woman who'd turned aside many other suitors yield to Hessian what she'd never allowed another?

Those questions plagued him for the remaining thirty minutes of a social call that would never end. He replied to queries when spoken to, he admired the growing parade of chalk drawings. He nearly snatched Daisy up when she threw her arms around Lily's neck and announced that no dragons had come to the nursery since she'd learned to sleep with the curtains open.

Worth cast Hessian odd looks, and the children were very much underfoot. Oscar Leggett was trying to ingratiate himself with Worth's dog, who was making a pest of herself to Lily. Jacaranda sent the occasional glance to the upper windows, where her infant daughter might well be rising from a nap.

"Daisy," Hessian said, "we must soon take our leave. Make your farewells and thank your hostess."

A spate of French between the little girls ensued, for Avery's native tongue was French, and Daisy had apparently yet to figure out that adults could speak the language as well.

"I hope Miss Lily will be my mama," Daisy said, not nearly quietly enough. "And I hope she marries my new papa."

Either Hessian was in the presence of the most socially adept adults in London, or the dog's waving tail, the nursery maid's efforts to tidy up the tea set, and Oscar Leggett's bumbling attempts to present himself as fascinated by the stock exchange meant only Hessian had heard Daisy's confidence.

Avery giggled and confided something about Uncle Worth and Aunt Jacaranda taking more naps than the baby—what a scandalous observation for a small child to make.

Lily had paid attention to the children, though, for her ears were pink, and she was taking inordinate care donning her gloves. She twisted them around her fingers, then both gloves fell to the terrace.

As a young man, Hessian had studied all the flirtations as general studied battle maps. Fans were a popular means of conveying ballroom code, but parasols, gloves, flowers, and other items had been appropriated by lovers seeking to communicate silently.

Twisted gloves meant: Be careful, we are being watched.

Both gloves dropped at once meant: I love you.

And yet, Lily was apparently to wed her goose of a cousin, for no reason Hessian could discern.

He was furious, hurt, and bewildered, but still a gentleman. He picked up Lily's gloves and passed them to her one at a time.

She smoothed them on, thanked him, and looked ready to shatter into a thousand pieces.

Hessian took her arm to escort her through the house, and the throng came with them—the children, the dog, the damned cousin, Worth, and Jacaranda. Hessian used the few moments of sorting through walking sticks, pelisses, and gloves at the front door to study Lily one last time.

He wanted to see devastation in her eyes, and found it, also a wildness he'd never noted before. This version of Lily was hanging on by a thread. She'd asked him once about eloping, and he'd dismissed the question. He couldn't dismiss it now.

Jacaranda passed Hessian Lily's cloak, a light silk wrap of blue that complemented the sprigged muslin of her puffed-sleeve day dress. He tended to the civilities, bowing low over Lily's hand and taking special care with her frogs, while Worth promised Daisy to bring Avery over for tea "soon."

A father learned to prevaricate.

Somebody else had apparently learned to prevaricate.

Hessian watched Lily accept Oscar's escort to the waiting coach in the street.

"You noticed?" Worth murmured.

Hessian nodded. "No birthmark near her elbow."

"Birthmarks can fade."

Jacaranda was tying Daisy's bonnet ribbons, while Hessian's insides were already in a knot.

"Birthmarks can fade," Hessian said, "scars can heal, memories grow unreliable, but I've recalled something else: The young Lily was right-handed. Did you notice when this Lily drew a flower with the chalk on the paving stones?"

"She used her left hand," Worth said.

"She throws a ball with her left hand too—throws it accurately."

Daisy swung Hessian's hand, clearly ready to get back out into the fresh air.

"You whispered something to the lady as you did up her cloak," Worth said. "Oscar was occupied pretending to love my dog, but I noticed."

"One should enjoy the lovely weather while one can. I suggested she unfasten her window tonight."

Worth's brows drew down. Jacaranda laced her arm through her husband's and led him toward the door.

"Thank our guests for coming, Worth."

Worth thanked Daisy effusively and shook Hessian's hand. "If you need anything, Hessian, anything at all…"

He'd needed to hear that he had his brother's unequivocal support, but he also needed answers, and only Lily could provide them.

CHAPTER FIFTEEN

The evening wore on more slowly than a funeral procession, the clock ticking loudly in the family parlor in counterpoint to Miss Fotheringham's snores. Oscar had gone out, of course, while Uncle Walter remained across the room, nose buried in the financial pages.

"Early morning outings have left me fatigued," Lily said, tucking her embroidery into her workbasket. "I believe I'll retire."

The rhythm of Miss Fotheringham's snores hitched, then resumed.

Uncle turned a page. "Good night, ladies."

Meaning Lily was to rouse her companion and escort her upstairs. Miss Fotheringham was by no means elderly, but she had elderly ways, which for the most part, Lily appreciated. A drowsy companion prone to megrims and chills was less of a burden.

The dignified procession up the steps plucked Lily's last nerve, though she parted from her companion on the landing, the same as she had for a thousand other nights. Miss Fotheringham had been an acquaintance of Tippy's, though Lily had never been sure what her companion knew, or what she surmised.

Lily's bed had been turned down, her fire built up, meaning the maids would not disturb her. The first order of business was to unlatch her window, for Hessian's instruction had been clear.

Rather than undress or take down her hair, she went to the wardrobe. Her money was in its little glove box, beneath the satin lining. She poured the lot of it into her oldest reticule. Next, she assembled the least-impressive, sturdiest, most-sensible ensemble she could—brown velvet walking dress, plain brown cloak, a straw hat such as any shop girl might own, gloves darned on the right index finger—

"Might I ask what you're about?"

Lily turned to find Hessian Kettering standing just inside the window she'd opened not five minutes before.

"Hessian." She was across the room without another thought, her arms wrapped around him.

His remained at his sides.

She held him tightly for one more moment, needing the feel of him close, loathing the sense that her embrace was merely tolerated.

"I would greet you as Lily, except I suspect you are not she."

His gaze was once again the distant nobleman, the man easily annoyed with posturing or dithering. Lily stepped back as his words penetrated her whirling mind.

"I am Lily Ferguson."

His gaze flicked to the drab clothing on the bed. "But are you my Lily, or some creature fashioned for your uncle's convenience—if he's your uncle?"

The question was gently put, and yet, Lily sank onto the bed, felled by the disappointment she saw in Hessian's eyes. He remained by the window, probably unwilling to come any nearer to a woman who was a lie.

Protestations suggested themselves, the same ones she'd offered Oscar: You have leaped to conclusions, you speculate, you conjecture from hunches and innuendo.

She barely tolerated Oscar; she loved Hessian Kettering.

"Walter Leggett is my uncle, my mother's brother."

A night breeze caught the curtains. Hessian closed the window and tied the curtains shut. "You are a by-blow?"

Lily seized on the question for the invitation it was. "My mother was newly widowed, not newly widowed enough, and I was conceived. She could not marry the man with whom she'd faltered, so she traveled. I was born in Bern. The first language I learned was German."

Still, Hessian remained in the shadows across the room. "Go on."

He'd be fair, then, hearing her out, or perhaps he was simply appeasing his curiosity. Lily owed him—and only him—an explanation.

"When I was three, Mama found a vicar and his wife in Derbyshire whose discretion she trusted. For the next six years, I was raised as their distant relation. My mother visited when she could and brought my half-sister with her most of the time. I was not unhappy."

Lily got up to pace, and to be nearer to the man she was losing. "My sister treated me as a curiosity. She was more than two years my senior, and though much indulged, she grasped that my circumstances were not as comfortable as hers. Then Mama died."

Oh, how the words hurt. "I'd lived for those visits from Mama, for her letters. I never knew when she was coming, and I never knew what to say to her.

She'd hug me so tightly, then tell me to play with my sister, and I could feel a weight, always, of love, but also frustration, hers and mine. A mother and child should not be parted, but she'd tell me to be good and leave."

Hessian held a square of white linen out to her, at arm's length.

Lily took his handkerchief and dabbed at her cheeks. "I never cry, but then, I never talk about this."

"I lost my mother when I was a youth. I miss her still, and my papa."

"Mama had told me, and Vicar had told me, that I'd be provided for if anything happened to her. Six months after Mama died, Vicar and his wife both succumbed to influenza. They'd not been young, and there I was, nine years old, proficient at French, German, Latin, Holy Scripture, and keeping quiet. Only the charity of the next vicar kept me from the poorhouse."

All over again, the terror of that time struck her, the pitying looks from wealthy congregants who had a coin for the poor box, but no place in their nursery for old Vicar's little niece.

Hessian took her by the wrist and led her to the fire. "This is why Daisy trusts you, because you know the abandonment she's experiencing."

He sat Lily down in the reading chair and took the hassock for his own seat. The air was warmer, the light better, but he made no move to hold her or touch her.

"I know the grief she faces. I wrote to my sister, and I saw the housekeeper post the letter for me. I have guessed that Uncle found me because of that letter. When Annie never replied, I concluded she was ashamed of me, and gave up."

Hessian held his hands out to the fire. "Are you ashamed of yourself?"

Was Lily supposed to say that yes, she was ashamed of the decision she'd made as a frightened fourteen-year-old? Ashamed of being unable to outwit Walter Leggett and a posting inn full of footmen, stable boys, guests, tinkers, coachmen... a horde of masculine dishonor all charging straight for her safety and her virtue?

"What do you want me to say, Hessian? Uncle made it plain that I must choose, and if I was despoiled by some passing university scholar or merchant— which had become a daily possibility—I was no use to Walter. I had one chance to step into my sister's shoes. The alternative was disgrace, penury, disease, and very likely death—for me and for any child I might conceive."

Disappointment settled on Lily, a surprise nearly welcome for the shame it replaced.

Why wasn't Hessian Kettering reeling with outrage at how Walter Leggett had treated a vulnerable poor relation? Why wasn't his almighty lordship appalled that a duke's granddaughter had ended up emptying chamber pots and dodging unwelcome hands?

"Then what happened?"

"Then I died. The chambermaid Lilith Ferguson was taken away from the coaching inn by a wealthy London gentleman. Uncle sent word back to Derbyshire a few months later that I'd taken ill and not survived. The headstrong heiress Lillian Ann Ferguson departed for finishing school in Switzerland."

Hessian checked his pocket watch.

"Am I keeping you from some card party?" Lily asked, for this recitation was making her angry, and Hessian was the only available target. "Is there a debutante who expects you for her supper waltz?"

Her questions met with a fleeting smile. "I am exactly where I planned to be, though the activity on the agenda is not at all what I had envisioned. Is your half-sister dead?"

"I assume so. She did elope with a Mr. Lawrence Delmar, Uncle's house steward. I know not if they married, but Uncle told me their coach overturned in the midst of a storm."

Hessian remained silent for some moments, staring into the fire.

Why did he have to be so attractive? His looks would change little over the years, his hair would fade from blond to wheat to white, his eyebrows might grow more fierce, but he'd weather rather than age.

"How old would she have been when she eloped?"

"Seventeen."

"So your approaching birthday is not your birthday, much less your twenty-eighth birthday?"

"Correct." Though Lily herself had stopped noticing when her true birthday went by, and that added to her anger.

Another silence grew, while the wrongness of Lily's life assailed her. "My birthday is not my birthday. I can barely scrape out a tune at the keyboard, though I love to sing. I have a companion in part to tend to my correspondence, because I cannot match my sister's hand despite years of trying. I cannot use half the cobblers in Mayfair because my left foot is slightly larger than my right, while hers were the opposite. She abhorred pets, while my cat Hannibal is my dearest comfort. Daily, I am confronted with the reality of not being the person I pretend to be."

"You are not her," Hessian said, "so who are you?"

He was watching her now, and Lily had the sense that her answer would decide everything. Whether Hessian remained in her life, whether she went to jail, whether she had a life.

"I had hoped to be Lady Grampion." The first sincere hope Lily had expressed in years.

Hessian rose. "You must know that is an impossibility now."

He was so tall, staring down at Lily. His expression was severe, an angel of judgment. Lily stood, because she would not be looked down upon by any man, least of all one who'd claimed to care for her.

"I have wondered, Hessian, if my tale outrages you on behalf of that fourteen-year-old girl, who was friendless, preyed upon, exhausted, and alone."

"You are no longer fourteen."

He seemed to be puzzling that out for himself as he spoke.

Lily was not puzzled, an unexpected and thoroughly satisfying revelation. "I am no longer fourteen, but finally, I am outraged, and you are free to go."

* * *

Part of Hessian wanted to leap out the window and fly right back to his acres in the north, back to a life of napping in duck blinds and making up the numbers at the neighbors' dinner parties.

The rest of him wished that he and Lily—if that was her name—were in the nearby bed, anticipating their vows, which proved only that his plodding, orderly mind had not grasped the complexity of the upset Lily had dumped in his lap.

"Might I remind you," Hessian said, "if you purport to marry anybody using a name other than the one your mother gave you at birth, the ceremony will be invalid."

Lily subsided into her chair, her indignation dropping away as a sudden shift in the wind leaves even a seventy-four-gunner adrift.

"Invalid?"

"You are not Lily Ferguson."

She drew her feet up under her, something a lady would never do when entertaining a caller. "But I am. I was born Lilith Ann Ferguson. My sister was Lillian Ann Ferguson. We were both named for Mama's favorite aunt, Lilliana. All my life, I have been Lily Ferguson, while my sister went by Annie with me to avoid confusion."

Which relieved Hessian only a little. "On the registry, on the special license, the full, correct name must be used. If I misstate so much as my baronial title, my marriage can be invalidated, provided the right bishop is bribed. The bride's name must also be correct in every detail."

Lily tucked the hem of her dress over her slippers. "I can't marry anybody? Ever?"

"You certainly can't marry that strutting donkey's arse you call a cousin." Much to Hessian's relief.

Lily gazed up at him, though Hessian had the sense she wasn't seeing him or the bedroom where she'd slept for years.

"I can't marry a peer of the realm either," she said. "At any point, Walter could take a notion to have the marriage declared invalid, me sent to jail, and my children declared illegitimate."

Hessian paced over to the window. He'd intended that her children be his children too, more fool he. "I hate messes. I loathe, despise, abhor, detest... This is the mess to end all messes."

Lily worried a nail. "You hate me."

Curled by the fire, she looked young and dispirited. Her bun sagged to one side, and she still clutched Hessian's handkerchief.

"I could never hate you, but this is a muddle." Like Daisy's muddle: Good girls ended up beneath the churchyard; bad girls were sent away.

Lily could not marry him, and she could not remain in Walter Leggett's avaricious grasp.

Hessian took the dress from the bed and rehung it in the wardrobe, along with a plain brown cloak, straw hat, and mended gloves. The smooth white counterpane was a reproach to him, for charging headlong into a courtship despite all sense to the contrary.

He'd hoped to again disport with a woman to whom he was neither engaged nor wed, when in truth, he hadn't even known her true, legal name. What had he been thinking?

Nothing at all, that's what. He hadn't been thinking. He'd been wallowing in wishes and dreams, animal spirits, and selfish pleasures.

"I have seventy-eight pounds," Lily said. "I can make that last a long time. I am conversant in French, German, and Italian, and my Latin, history, and sums are good. I can be a governess or companion. If nobody will have me in those roles, I'm not above honest labor. I've worked in the kitchen, the dairy, the laundry, the stables, and the garden. I've been a chambermaid, scullery maid, and everything in between. I know the New Testament as well as any curate, and I l-like children."

She abruptly bent her head, as if ducking a blow.

Hessian went to her and took her in his arms, despite messes, muddles, and anything resembling rational thought. She'd been worked nearly to death, a household drudge at some busy inn, then taken away from everything and everybody she knew and cast into a scheme not of her making.

At fourteen, Hessian had still considered females an exotic species, of no more import to him than penguins. Females had a natural habitat, a place in the order of creation, but with the exception of one sister, they thrived in environs he did not frequent. That had suited him, for he'd had butterflies to collect and poetry to memorize.

At fourteen, Lily had feared for her virtue and her safety. "I promise you," he said, "you will not be thrust alone into the world again."

She lifted her head from his shoulder, her eyes glittering in the firelight. "I cannot marry you. Walter will learn of it even if we go to Scotland, even if we live in France. You are a peer, and I am a felon."

Hessian scooped her up and sat in the reading chair. Accusations of criminal wrongdoing could turn a muddle into outright pandemonium. He'd taken his turn serving as magistrate and knew of what he dreaded.

"How are you a felon?"

"Walter says that impersonating a dead person to earn their inheritance is fraud, and he's read law."

A man who detested untidiness of any variety excelled at untangling knots and restoring order. Hessian put that part of his brain to work, which was oddly easier when he was holding Lily.

"You are Lily Ferguson. You haven't impersonated anybody. You are Walter Leggett's niece, the daughter of his deceased sister."

"But I'm not the right Lily Ferguson. I'm not Lillian Ann."

"You never said you were. If Walter represented that you were Lillian, he did so out of your hearing. As for earning an inheritance, you've told me you haven't even pin money, and your sister's inheritance has been under Walter's control since her death."

Lily scooted off Hessian's lap to sit on the hassock. "You're saying Walter is committing the fraud? Aren't I an accessory? I've benefitted from his scheme. I'm not emptying chamber pots or scrubbing floors sixteen hours a day."

Starting at the age of nine, after years in a vicarage, for God's perishing sake. "Nor shall you do so again."

Hessian wanted to say more, to assure Lily that he could sort all of this out, but he'd made his last headlong charge where she was concerned. Caution, deliberation, and thorough preparation would be the order of the day henceforth.

Then too, the part of him that had cringed at his reckless courtship of Lily was braced for another quagmire: Did she esteem him honestly, or had she seen him as a way out of Walter Leggett's household?

Something of both? And what if—heaven forefend—she'd already conceived a child?

Hessian's penchant for considering every iota of available information offered him a morsel of comfort: Lily had had at least one opportunity to compromise herself with him—with him and Apollo Belvedere—and she'd not taken advantage. She'd freely admitted Walter Leggett's desire to ingratiate himself with Worth. She'd conveyed this daft scheme to marry her to her cousin at the first opportunity.

Instinct and evidence both prodded Hessian to give Lily the benefit of the doubt. "When is your ostensible birthday?"

"Seventeen days hence."

How to free Lily from her uncle's control without exposing Leggett's scheme to public scrutiny in seventeen short days?

Hessian touched Lily's earlobe, the one that had never been scarred in the first place. "I could elope with you." Though an elopement was scandal on the king's highway and a sure way to provoke all manner of accusations from Leggett. Then too, a trip to Scotland meant hundreds of miles of travel, during which any number of mishaps could occur.

"We can't get a special license?"

"One typically waits up to a week for the license to be prepared. If a license for Miss Lillian Ferguson and a license for Lilith Ferguson are applied for within days, the coincidence is bound to be noted."

Though Lily was perched on the hassock not three feet away, Hessian again sensed she was physically present and mentally elsewhere.

Why hadn't he stayed in Cumberland, where he knew his place and his neighbors, where he'd been the dullest excuse for a widower and resigned to the inevitable approach of middle age? He'd come south mostly out of boredom and to put a stop to Worth's chiding and hinting.

Worth, of course, would chide endlessly over this situation. "Something bothers me," Hessian said.

"I'm no end of bothered. I should have told you the truth sooner, but now that I have told you, it hasn't made anything better. I thought about eloping with you, but that would add intrigue to dishonesty. Then there's Daisy, who must not be made to suffer any more upset. She's just finding her feet again, and more drama would set her back considerably."

Good God, Daisy. "Daisy trusts you."

Lily peered at him. "Am I to apologize for that?"

Hessian made himself think rather than offer some lordly platitude. "Regardless of your proper name, regardless of your dealings with me, you have been genuinely kind to the child and gone out of your way to help her. You have my thanks for that."

The realization steadied him. Lily had taken an interest in Daisy when most other women would have patted Hessian's arm and instructed him to hire more nursery maids. Even the ladies bent on becoming his countess asked about Daisy only in passing.

That Daisy trusted Lily suggested Hessian had been precipitous yielding his heart, but not a complete fool.

"We will not allow this imbroglio to affect Daisy," he said, "but what bothers me is your sister. When did she die?"

"I'm not sure. I was approaching my fifteenth birthday when Uncle came for me. He'd already put the story about that his niece was off to finishing school in Switzerland. He brought Tippy with him, my sister's governess. I'd met her on Mama's last visit. I was so glad to see Tippy again…"

"Is Tippy extant?"

"She lives in Chelsea," Lily said, climbing back into Hessian's lap. "Ephrata Tipton. Uncle keeps an eye on her too."

Despite the utter chaos of the situation, Hessian's body was all too pleased that he was holding Lily, and that would not do. Dear Uncle, conscientious warden that he was, might send a maid by with the evening's last bucket of coal, or Lily's companion might decide to borrow a hair ribbon.

"I cannot think clearly when your hair tickles my chin, madam."

"Good. I haven't been thinking clearly for more than ten years."

An ugly thought emerged from the facts and suppositions in Hessian's head. "Lily, has your uncle mistreated you?"

She scooted around to untie her slippers, while Hessian lectured himself about untoward thoughts and animal spirits.

"I should tell you that no, Uncle has never denied me a meal or laid a hand on me in anger. But he left me at that inn for more than five years. Do you know how an orphaned tavern maid is treated? A girl upon whom anybody can heap a task, whom anybody can slap, pinch, or scold?

"Uncle did that," she went on, setting her slippers aside. "And my mother had assured my foster parents that I'd been provided for. Mama either wrote a provision into her will, or she entrusted my care to Walter. When Walter found me—or bothered to find a use for me—he assured me that I was dependent upon him for every crust of bread. I made my peace with him, faced what awaited me at the inn, or found a handy ditch to die in."

She straightened and began pulling pins from her hair, letting them pile up on Hessian's handkerchief in her lap. "Uncle did that too. Frightened me when I'd already dreaded to fall asleep for fear some stable boy would creep into my cot. Uncle led me to believe my mother had lied about providing for me, had turned her back on me. He told me my sister had never mentioned me and that I didn't exist."

Her hair gave way all at once, a soft mass of fiery curls that fell to her waist. "I exist, Hessian. I'm not sure who I am, or what my future will bring, but I look at Daisy…"

She closed her eyes. "I think of Daisy—I was not much older than she is now when Mama died—and I recall that my uncle, my only possible source of safety, acquired an interest in me solely when he realized that he could control Mama's fortune through me. I am finally more angry than I am afraid."

Hessian brushed her hair back from her shoulder. "You have every right to be enraged with Walter Leggett. The question is, what to do about it. You mentioned the name of your sister's paramour?"

She scooped up the handkerchief and took the pins to her vanity. The firelight turned her hair into a riot of garnet and gold curling down her back.

Hessian gave up lecturing himself.

"Lawrence Delmar, a Scot," Lily said. "Oscar recalled the name. Oscar suspects that I am not the cousin who shared a household with him in childhood. He's prepared to step into Uncle's shoes as the man best situated to wreck my life."

A sliver of resentment lingered in some obscure duck blind among Hessian's emotions. He did not want to be in the business of un-wrecking a woman's life, but… that was hesitation grumbling at him, as if naps were more important than honor.

Whether he and Lily had a future, she deserved to be free of her past and of her uncle.

"Mrs. Braithwaite was here while I was calling on your brother's household." Lily drew her hair over her shoulder and separated it into three skeins. "She left a card and noted an intention on the back to call again soon."

Another complication. Hessian could not simultaneously watch Lily braid her hair and solve the annoyance that was Roberta Braithwaite.

"I will send my man of business to call on her." Worth was prepared to help in any capacity, and he excelled at charming widows.

Lily tied off her braid with a plain black hair ribbon. "According to Mrs. Braithwaite, I'm to wed you, and see that you leave Daisy in her aunt's care posthaste. Your nursery is to be reserved for the offspring I present you with, also posthaste."

"According to your uncle Walter, you're to wed Oscar in a little more than a fortnight." No wonder Lily had at a loss for words earlier in the day.

"Or I can go to jail, possibly to make the acquaintance of an executioner, unless he too expects me to marry him and bear his children." Lily's tone was as colorless as the shadows beyond her window, her glaze bleak as she studied the rope of her braid.

"The law will not hold you to vows spoken under duress."

"The law." Two words that spoke volumes of condemnation. "What has the law done to honor the terms of my mother's will? To stop Walter's mischief, to keep Mrs. Braithwaite from bringing down scandal on you, me, Daisy, and my mother's memory?"

"Valid point." Hessian approached her, though she put him in mind of a cornered hedgehog. Everywhere, spines and bristles, no vulnerabilities exposed.

"If you can't put your trust in the law," Hessian said, "if your relatives have betrayed you, if your resources are inadequate to solve the problems before you, you might consider one last alternative."

Her chin came up. "I promised my Creator and the memories of my mother and sister that a rash act of self-harm would never figure in my plans."

Good God have mercy.

Hessian took her hand. "I'm suggesting… me. I'm suggesting that you trust me."

He kissed her fingers and waited for her answer, though he had no earthly idea, not a hint of a glimmer of a notion, how to proceed if Lily accepted his offer.

* * *

"She's avoiding me." Roberta was as certain of her conclusion as she was sure that Dorie Humplewit was putting on weight. The evidence was incontrovertible. "Lily Ferguson thinks a ducal grandpapa makes her better than anybody else, and that I would not dare expose her family's soiled linen."

Penelope occupied the seat closest to the window, as if having light to read by ever consoled a woman for the damage the sun did to her complexion. Roberta was on her feet, inspecting for the dust about which she'd lectured her housekeeper earlier in the week.

"Perhaps Miss Ferguson was simply out paying calls, ma'am. Yesterday did turn fair as the day progressed."

The words You are sacked! begged to be flung across the parlor.

Penelope was Roberta's third companion in as many years. As finances had become constrained, Roberta had realized that spending a month interviewing candidates for the post of companion meant a month when no salary need be paid. During those companion-free weeks, much sympathy could be earned lamenting the inconstancy of young women in service.

The number of agencies supplying companions was finite, however, and Roberta had already patronized the top three.

"If you knew that I could ruin you with a word, Penelope, would you be larking about Town, trying on bonnets, and gamboling in the park?"

Penelope put down her volume of Wordsworth. She kept that naughty Bryon by her bedside, proof of a wicked streak in her character.

"If you were determined to ruin me, I might be calling on my friends in an effort to gather their support. Marshaling my troops, as it were."

What a vexatious creature, and why, having seen to the dusting, hadn't anybody bothered to polish the brass candlesticks on the mantel?

"Lily Ferguson hasn't any friends. Her uncle fends off the bachelors. Her lack of charm defeats other connections. This must be what Grampion likes about her, for a more dull, humorless fellow I could not imagine, and that is precisely why we must act on Amy Marguerite's behalf."

Roberta had tossed and turned the night away, mentally drafting the letter she'd anonymously send to a half-dozen semi-reputable newspapers. In the morning, she'd taken one look in the vanity mirror, seen the toll Lily Ferguson's stubbornness had taken, and decided that subtle machinations were a waste of time.

The sooner Amy Marguerite took her proper place in Roberta's household, the sooner Grampion's coin would follow.

Then too, Walter Leggett would doubtless pay handsomely to keep his sister's peccadilloes quiet. Grampion would similarly pay to be spared scandal. To blazes with Lily Ferguson, for the nonce. If the idiot woman ever wanted to see her mother's letters, she could jolly well join the list of people from whom Roberta would extract a goodly sum for a goodly number of years.

"We must act?" Penelope asked, clutching Mr. Wordsworth to her chest. "In what regard?"

"Your part is simple. You enjoy reading, you enjoy fresh air. You will become a fixture in the park until such time as you know the schedule upon which Amy Marguerite is let out to play. Nursery maids and governesses cannot function without schedules, and Grampion of all people will insist the child's day be rigidly organized."

Never did a young lady spend more time vapidly gazing out of windows than Penelope Smythe. Perhaps she expected a handsome prince on a white charger to come cantering up the street.

"When I have established Miss Amy Marguerite's schedule, then what?"

Then, Penelope would be sacked and replaced with a governess. "If you see an occasion to win the child's trust, that's all well and good, but your sole objective is to report her schedule to me."

Penelope rose. "It's a fine morning. You'll want me to be off, I take it?"

"The sooner the better. Wear something inconspicuous. You were with me when I called on Grampion, though I doubt he noticed you, meaning no insult. A titled gentleman will pay no mind to a woman who's neither young nor pretty nor well-dowered. You mustn't take it personally."

As if that statement of the obvious required pondering, Penelope stood for a moment by the window.

"I'm sure you are correct, ma'am. I'll be about my assigned task now."

"Take a biscuit or two with you for the girl. Or some bread crusts for the ducks. You needn't abandon your post for the midday meal either. I'll manage without you here."

"Very good, ma'am." Penelope bobbed a curtsey and took her leave.

She'd sit in the park getting freckles by the hour, provided she could take a book along. Roberta would write Penelope a decent character when it came time to let her go, for such a passionless soul was surely deserving of pity, and Roberta was ever kind to the less fortunate.

CHAPTER SIXTEEN

"Where are we off to on this glorious day?" Oscar asked.

Lily had dragged him to the milliner's after yesterday's call on the Kettering household. "My glovemaker, by way of a call on the Countess of Rosecroft."

Hessian had devised this scheme before he'd left Lily the previous evening. She was to pay a call on her ladyship, while Hessian would find a discreet way to approach the earl. Rosecroft and his countess would make formidable go-betweens, because Uncle Walter would not dare restrict Lily's access to them, or theirs to her.

Thank heavens, Hessian had been capable of thinking.

Oscar examined his teeth in the mirror over the sideboard. "Her ladyship is blond, curvaceous, has an unmistakable northern accent? I don't think she cares for me."

"If that's all you noticed about her, then you doubtless failed to impress her. You look fine, Oscar."

He tapped his top hat onto this head, then adjusted the angle. "Fine isn't good enough. I must look my best if I'm to make an impression as your devoted cousin. Sir Worth Kettering was impressed. I certainly made a proper fuss over his stinking dog. I hope Rosecroft hasn't any dogs. Canines are not supposed to be underfoot when one is entertaining callers."

He left off adjusting his hat, his cravat pin, his gloves, and his watch chain to offer Lily his arm.

"Rosecroft's hound is twice the size of Worth Kettering's," Lily said. "The dog is devoted to Bronwyn."

Coach wheels and shod hooves sounded on the cobbles out front, and the butler opened the door.

"Do I devote myself to the child or to the dog?" Oscar asked.

If Hessian could not foil Uncle Walter's schemes, Lily might be sentenced to thirty more years of Oscar's hopeless self-interest.

She took her cousin's arm. "You make much of the dog. Bronwyn, like her parents, does not suffer fools, while Scout's nature is tolerant."

Oscar needed a moment to comprehend the insult, but he smiled as he handed Lily into the coach. "Very clever." He settled beside her on the forward-facing seat, something he would not have done even a week ago. "Is my doting convincing? Papa lurks in his study, peering out of windows at the most inconvenient times."

Uncle's study was the only room in the house to have a view of both the back garden and the front walkway. Lily had noticed this within a week of joining his residence.

"Your doting is convincing. I wish you wouldn't."

He patted her hand, and Lily nearly bolted from the coach. "No need to thank me. I'm not awful, you know."

Yes, you are. "You are also not the husband I'd choose for myself."

"You think I want a tart-tongued woman five years my senior for a bride? That reminds me, what did the Braithwaite creature want? She's called on you twice now in the space of a week. Papa says she was a friend of your mother's, but what sort of friend waits years to pay a condolence call?"

Hessian had warned Lily not to underestimate Oscar—he was his father's son, after all. "If she should call again while I'm out, please do not receive her. She claims to have letters my mother wrote, and I suspect she wants me to pay her for them."

Oscar left off fussing with his sleeve button. "Enterprising of her. Are these scandalous letters? Was your mother propositioning another woman in writing? How naughty."

I shall go mad within the week. "I haven't spoken with Mrs. Braithwaite enough to know the nature of the correspondence, but I will entrust resolution of her concerns to you, should you become my husband."

"That's the spirit," Oscar said, patting Lily's hand again. "Man and wife, wedded and bedded. Shall we pay a call on Mrs. Braithwaite as a couple?"

How long could one coach ride be? "Uncle has warned me not to allow a connection with her. He says she's not good ton."

"Does that mean she's a bit too merry? I fancy a merry widow, though—"

Lily yanked the shade down. "Oscar, you will recall, at all times, in all places, that I am a lady. Your vulgar observations are inappropriate."

He tried for a laugh. Lily ignored him, and at long last, he fell silent. The absence of grating chatter probably meant he was brooding over how to use Mrs. Braithwaite's threats to his own advantage.

"Mrs. Braithwaite expected me to marry the Earl of Grampion," Lily said.

"I was to encourage him to place his ward in Mrs. Braithwaite's household, for the girl is her niece."

"What widow in her right mind would willingly—? Oh, Grampion has money. Of course. Well, you won't be marrying him."

"It's not as if Grampion has offered for me." Though he had, and last night he'd withdrawn his offer, in so many words.

Of all the frustrations and sorrows burdening Lily's heart, that one was the heaviest. Grampion was behaving honorably, aiding a damsel in a mess, but he'd been very plainspoken on the topic of marriage to her.

A peer's marriage must be free of any hint of irregularity. Lily had been spinning ignorant fancies to expect anything else.

"Here we are." Oscar peered out the window at Rosecroft's town house, a modest dwelling on a peaceful side street. His lordship had doubtless chosen the property for two reasons. It was close to the homes of his parents and siblings, and its stables were large and commodious for a Town residence.

"Rosecroft is horse-mad," Lily said as the footman lowered the steps.

"Everybody knows that." Oscar preceded her from the coach and offered her his hand. "They're expecting us?"

"I often call on her ladyship of a weekday afternoon."

"No accounting for taste," Oscar said, putting Lily's hand on his arm. "Let's get this over with. I can use a new pair of gloves, come to think of. I'll put them on your account, shall I?"

Five minutes later, Rosecroft was escorting a bewildered Oscar from the family parlor—"Stronger libation to be had just down the corridor, Leggett"—and her ladyship was closing the door behind the men.

"Lily Ferguson, why on earth would you inflict the company of that strutting noddypoop on yourself, much less on somebody who accounts herself one of your friends?"

"I do apologize," Lily said, "and Oscar isn't... well, he is, but that cannot be helped."

Her ladyship took the place on the sofa next to Lily. "Lily, have you been crying?"

Only half the night. "Of course not."

"I'm a mama. We have instincts about these things. You're in trouble, aren't you?"

"I have been for years." Who on earth had said that? Lily put her hand over her mouth, but nothing would unsay those words. "I beg your pardon. I'm simply... Uncle thinks Oscar and I would suit."

Masculine laughter sounded from down the corridor. Lily wanted to clap her hands over her ears.

"Tell me the rest, Lily. We're friends, and once upon a time, I was in a spot of bother myself. Rosecroft hasn't slept on a bed of eiderdown his whole life either."

Once upon a time… the opening for most self-respecting fairy tales. "If Grampion asks your husband for a private conversation, please indicate to Rosecroft that I'd take it as a favor if he allowed the conversation."

"It's Grampion you'd rather marry, isn't it?" Her ladyship's tone was so kind, so understanding, that Lily's heart broke all over again.

"There's more to it than that, but yes. I'd rather spend the rest of my life doing Grampion's laundry or chopping vegetables in his kitchen than endure five minutes as Oscar's wife, but I'm not sure I have a choice. Uncle is very determined on the matter, and there's a fortune involved, as well as old scandal."

The countess took Lily in her arms. "You poor dear. Your smiling grease spot of an uncle has doubtless helped himself to your money and can't bear for the world to learn of his thievery. Why must people be so venal and greedy?"

Her ladyship's embrace was fierce and unexpected, else Lily might have had some defense against it. Instead, Lily hugged her friend back and tried not to cry.

"I'm tired," Lily said when she'd thoroughly re-wrinkled Hessian's handkerchief. She'd kept the one he'd given her last night and was carrying it as a talisman against despair. "I'm tired of dealing with Uncle, and now Oscar says he and I are to be married after my birthday. I have only seventy-eight pounds, and please stuff a tea cake in my mouth, lest I become a candidate for Bedlam."

Her ladyship held up a plate of cakes. "Take several. They're small, and Rosecroft will be back soon, a one-man biblical plague where baked goods are concerned. What can I do to help, Lily? I can put a coach and team at your disposal, get you to Dover, Portsmouth, or Scotland. Money won't be a problem, and you're welcome to help yourself to my wardrobe, though we're hardly of a size."

Tears threatened all over again. "Thank you, but if I leave England, then there will be fresh scandal, and I can't have that." Then too, leaving England meant never seeing Hessian again.

Her ladyship nibbled on a plain cake. "Grampion probably develops hives at the mention of scandal, and it's Grampion you want."

"You malign his lordship at your peril, Emmaline."

Her ladyship popped the last of her tea cake in her mouth and dusted her palms. "I mean your intended no disrespect. Some men simply have a wide proper streak, my Devlin among them. Those same men can develop a wide improper streak at the most interesting times. You've chosen Grampion, and thus we must see that you aren't shackled to your noddypoop cousin. Has Grampion chosen you?"

Had he unchosen Lily? Stepped back for the nonce? "I don't know."

"Oh dear. Try the chocolate cakes. They are my favorite."

* * *

A muscular arm landed across Hessian's shoulders.

"My commanding officer has dispatched me with special orders. I am to find an opportunity to converse with you privately and nominate myself to serve as your aide-de-camp."

Colonel Lord Rosecroft exuded genial Irish bonhomie, as if he'd had a bit too much of Jonathan Tresham's excellent brandy. Hessian had watched his lordship through a long evening of cards, though, and Rosecroft's drinking habits were abstemious.

His gaze was dead steady, despite the jocularity of his tone.

"Who might your commanding officer be, my lord?"

"My own dear wife, of course. Tresham, thanks for a lovely evening. Until next week." Rosecroft bowed to the company of gentlemen putting on hats and greatcoats, and all but dragged Hessian out the door. "Tresham is doomed, poor sod. A ducal heir with pots of money, and he's not bad-looking."

"Why do we refer to a man contemplating matrimony as doomed? I gather in the right company, the result of speaking the nuptial vows is the opposite of perdition."

Worth and Jacaranda, for example, were besotted. Rosecroft doted on his wife publicly, and she on him.

"Lily Ferguson is in fear of a marriage to her cousin," Rosecroft said. "Which cousin my lady wife will refer to only as The Noddypoop. I gather you are to foil this plot, and I am to assist you."

Worth had begged off this evening, claiming that business had overrun his schedule. Hessian happened to know that the business in question was a teething infant.

"Can you fly, Rosecroft? I'm coming to believe that nothing short of angelic powers will see Lily Ferguson free of her uncle's machinations."

Rosecroft muttered something that sounded Irish and profane.

Tresham had a set of rooms at the Albany, and thus Hessian and his escort had much of Mayfair to cross on foot in the dark. This was fortunate, for Hessian had no idea where to begin his tale.

Lily's tale, in truth.

"Here's what I know," Rosecroft said, "which I gather is the sum of what my wife was able to pry from dear Lily's grasp, even when aided by the formidable truth potion of tea and chocolate cakes: Walter Leggett has bungled management of Lily's fortune. He seeks to keep his penury and ineptitude quiet by marrying Lily to his heir. Lily would rather marry you."

"Which does not mean that she's enamored of me. I'm simply the lesser of several evils." And Hessian couldn't shake the notion that something worse than a mere reversal of fortunes was behind Walter Leggett's scheming.

"Women who spend an hour behind a closed door, sending twice for more cakes, aren't discussing how best to bring about matrimony to the lesser of several evils, Grampion. How can I be of service?"

What a kind, tempting offer.

"You must talk me out of kidnapping Lily Ferguson." Hessian had spent the past two days in thought—his seventeen days were down to fifteen—and no clever plan, no impressive legal maneuver had occurred to him.

Though every obstacle, risk, and impediment had.

"Why talk you out of it? By the time the grandchildren show up, an elopement would make for a good tale and add a dash of derring-do to the family legends. Lily's of age, and so, my friend, are you."

This was not the advice Worth would have handed out. "For me to abscond with the lady opens the door for Walter Leggett to further mishandle her funds. We'll be years prying any coin from his grasp, if any coin yet remains."

This reasoning was a factor, because Hessian yet held out hope that Lily—Lilith, his Lily—was entitled to some funds from her mother's estate.

"You don't care half a rotten fig about the money."

"Lily might, but you're right. I also have responsibility for three small children, as you know. Scandal attached to my name is an opening for their aunt, Roberta Braithwaite, to snatch the youngest child, Daisy, from my control."

"You're an earl," Rosecroft scoffed. "The aunt won't get a hearing from any court of competent jurisdiction for several years, and by then, the child will be all but grown and quite attached to her dear guardian."

True, as far as it went. "Your Bronwyn will make her bow in about ten years."

"Go on."

"When Bronwyn was conceived, you'd have been mucking about in Spain, chasing the French across the mountains, and trying not to die of dysentery."

"Your point?"

Gone was the cheerful companion who'd while away an evening stroll in good company. In his place was a growling former soldier ready to make a good showing with his fists.

"You are not Bronwyn's father, and whatever the legal arrangements, whatever the truth of her patrimony, you are already worried about the reception she'll receive when she makes her come out ten years from now. She's an unusual girl with an unusual provenance. Even with an army of ducal relations behind her, she'll face a challenge."

Rosecroft marched along in silence until they came to the next corner. "The widow would not prevail in court, but you're right: She could make Daisy's life difficult. Eloping with Lily might, possibly, devolve to Daisy's discredit. Maybe."

"I cannot gamble with that child's happiness on a maybe, and Lily would not want me to."

"You still haven't told me how I can help."

They passed a brothel on St. James's, the scent of hashish wafting on the night air. Lily might have ended up in such an establishment, but for her uncle's intervention. That thought alone kept Hessian from cleaning his dueling pistols.

"Please assure me that this conversation will be held in strictest confidence, Rosecroft."

"I will overlook the slight to my honor, because you're in love, which equates to being half-daft in the newly smitten."

If this was love, this endless anxiety, this constant muddle and heartache, Hessian would rather have a toothache, a megrim, and a touch of the Jericho jig.

"I will convey to you a story," he said, "of a family well situated but not titled…" He sketched Lily's past, her mother's indiscretion, the early years of limited contact, the death of the foster parents, and the years in service at the coaching inn. "And Lily was retrieved from the coaching inn, because the legitimate sister eloped at the age of seventeen with a house steward. She reportedly died in a coaching accident on the way to Scotland with her intended."

Rosecroft paused to sniff at a precocious rose growing from a pot beneath the porch light of an otherwise darkened town house. "That is a prodigiously convenient coaching accident."

"Convenient for Walter Leggett, who has lied to Lily often and convincingly. Who has kept Lily nearly under guard, who has monitored everything from her correspondence, to her social habits, to which bachelors she stands up with for the supper waltz."

"My brother needs to water his roses," Rosecroft said, snapping off the blossom and tucking it into his lapel. "You think the sister is alive."

"Have you fashioned a will, Rosecroft?"

"Of course."

"And is one provision that your daughter inherits her portion upon the sooner of a certain birthday or her lawful marriage?"

Rosecroft resumed walking. "At seventeen, a woman cannot lawfully marry over her guardian's objection."

"She can in Scotland."

"Hence your comment about needing the ability to fly. If the sister is alive and kicking her heels in the Borders, she can sue Walter for mishandling her fortune."

"And that brings us back to scandal and to Lily being left with nothing, assuming the older sister is alive and assuming I can find her and produce evidence of her existence in two weeks."

"I can see why the ladies went through three plates of tea cakes. What will you do?"

Scotland was three-hundred-fifty miles away by awful roads, and even if Lily's sister had married over the anvil at Gretna Green, Hessian had no way of knowing if the happy couple had settled in Scotland or darkest Peru.

"You ask what I'll do," Hessian said. "At first, I cast caution to the wind with Lily, and now all I see are bad options. One hardly knows what to do."

"I live three streets that direction and serve a fine nightcap."

"Thank you, but I must decline, for some course of action must be settled on, and I do my best thinking in solitude. I have too much supposition and not enough facts." All the logic in the world still required some basic facts to reason from.

"Much like being a parent," Rosecroft said. "You do the best you can and hope divine providence weighs in favor of your children. The offer of a nightcap stands."

"Perhaps another time. Please keep a close eye on Lily for me, and if you can spare Bronwyn for an occasional outing to the park, Daisy and I would be most appreciative."

"And about this other?" Rosecroft waved a gloved hand that encompassed stolen fortunes, elopement, an illegitimate daughter, and at least nineteen other scandals.

"I will begin with a trip to Chelsea tomorrow and then pay a call on the Duchess of Quimbey. I'll confer with my brother thereafter and then start packing for a trip to the north."

"So you do have some notion of how to go on?" Rosecroft asked as the bells of St. Paul's tolled in the distance. "A strategy?"

"I have a hunch, and a fortnight to prevent disaster, scandal, and heartbreak."

"Best of luck, Grampion, and you will most assuredly need it."

* * *

Lily came awake when a cool breeze wafted across her cheeks—and there he was, standing in the shadows by her bedroom window.

"Hessian."

"You should be in bed, madam."

Had he hoped to find her in bed? The mantel clock said Lily had slept for only a few minutes, and yet, exhaustion had molded her to the deep cushions of the reading chair.

"I was thinking," she said. "I must have nodded off. How are you?"

He looked tired and serious, also a bit wicked. His attire was dark, not even a white neckcloth relieving the black, no signet ring on his finger, no pin winking from the folds of his neckcloth.

"I am... Is the door locked?"

"Yes." Lily had started taking that precaution as a result of Oscar's gleeful hand-patting. When in his cups, he might attempt to anticipate vows Lily would never willingly speak.

Hessian took the hassock, rather than open his arms to Lily or draw her to her feet. "Ephrata Tipton appears to have departed from Chelsea, at least temporarily."

The hollowness Lily had carried in the pit of her stomach since learning of her mother's death years ago opened up wider. "Where would she go?" Please let her be safe. And then: Why would she leave me?

"On her wedding journey, as it happens."

Anxiety receded—it did not vanish, for not all wedding journeys were happy—and yet, Lily was also aware of a touch of envy.

"Good for her. I hope he's worthy of her."

"He's a retired Navy captain who frequently visits friends at the royal hospital. He and Miss Tipton struck up an acquaintance nearly a year ago. I have his name and direction, though the cottage in Chelsea has yet to be vacated."

Lily had to touch Hessian, even if he merely tolerated the overture. She leaned forward enough to run a hand through his hair.

"You have learned much, and yet, you don't appear pleased with yourself. I am pleased to see you."

His gaze brushed over her. "I am pleased to see you as well. I engaged in a subterfuge."

"You would abhor subterfuge." Did he abhor her?

"My opinion on the matter has grown complicated. We learn the classic works of drama because they are art, a form of great literature. We play charades at every house party to pass the time in harmless diversion. We tell tall tales over a pint in the pub... I told the innkeeper that my sister-in-law was a former charge of Miss Tipton's, and I'd offered to look in on the old dear."

"And now, having told a harmless fabrication, you feel like a confidence trickster?" What did that make Lily, who was fraud wearing a ballgown—or a nightgown.

Hessian's smile was crooked as he tucked Lily's lap robe over her feet. "I feel clever, which is very bad of me. The innkeeper volunteered that I sounded as if I'd grown up in the Borders and bided there still. Perhaps I lived near my brother in Birdwell-on-Huckleburn?"

That smile... that smile was not among the smiles Lily had seen on Hessian to date. It brought out the resemblance to his brother, Worth, and went well with the dark clothing.

"What has Birdwell-on-Anywhere to do with Tippy?"

"The innkeeper was showing off, flourishing his eye for detail. Somebody has been writing regularly to Miss Tipton from Birdwell-on-Huckleburn. I grew up in Cumberland and have occasion to know that Birdwell is a market town not far from Dumfries. Her Grace of Quimbey confirmed that Lawrence Delmar had been a braw, bonnie Scot and that he and Walter Leggett quarreled loudly on the eve of your sister's elopement."

Hessian's recitation provoked such a degree of upset, Lily put a hand over his mouth. "A moment, please. Somebody has been writing regularly to Tippy from Scotland?"

He took her hand, his grip warm. "Mrs. Lawrence Delmar. She is among Miss Tipton's most faithful correspondents. She writes every other month, has no need to cross her letters, and seals them with a family crest."

Hessian was trying to convey information—facts, implications, conclusions. Lily could not make her mind work to grasp any of it.

"My sister is alive, and Tippy never told me?" Lily wanted to shout, to throw things, to climb out the window and dash headlong for Birdwell-on-Deception. "I don't know whether to be… but Annie is alive—she was always Annie to me—and surely that is a miracle. I refuse to cry, because this is good news. It must be."

"And yet," Hessian said, "you are dealt another blow to learn you've been subjected to yet another falsehood. I'm sorry, Lily."

She did not want his apology, because he hadn't wronged her by bringing this truth to light. "Hold me, for the love of God, please hold me."

He plucked her from the chair and carried her to the bed. Lily had turned the sheets back to warm and scooted under the covers, while Hessian tugged off his boots.

"Get in here," Lily said, untying her dressing gown and flinging it to the foot of the bed. "Get in here and tell me everything you know, Hessian Kettering. I will not engage in strong hysterics, despite the temptation, but neither can I promise you a ladylike vocabulary."

He draped his coat and waistcoat over the back of the reading chair and drew the window curtains closed before coming to the bed.

He stood for a moment, gazing down at Lily as she lay on her side, willing him to join her.

The mattress dipped, and he was drawing the covers up over them both. "We must conclude your sister is alive and thriving, Lily. She doesn't need to skimp on paper to the extent of crossing her letters. She uses a family crest to seal correspondence. She has the leisure to write regularly, and in all the years she's been corresponding with Miss Tipton, her direction hasn't changed. She's not haring about after a man who can't hold a job, not fleeing the law, or using an alias."

"You are trying to reassure me."

Hessian tucked an arm under Lily's neck and drew her along his side. "Is it working?"

His sane, sensible conclusions would sink in after he'd left. What calmed Lily was his nearness. "Some. What did Her Grace of Quimbey have to add?"

Hessian had a way of holding Lily that was at once snug and easy. The bed was immediately warm with him in it, and despite all the clothing—far too much clothing—the fit of his body to Lily's was comfortable.

Also comforting.

"Her Grace explained London to me. I seldom use my Town residence and haven't paid much attention to domestic details. Most neighborhoods use the same dairy, the same bakeshop, the same laundresses and tinkers. The dairy maids, night soil men, crossing sweepers—they all share news and gossip, and they carry it from one back entrance to another, one stable to another."

"You did not know this?" If there was any pleasure associated with working at a coaching inn, it was the sense of having all the news from every corner of the realm. A crop failure in Dorset, a spectacular barn fire in East Anglia, a great fair in Yorkshire—the coaching inns heard about everything in first-person accounts.

"I did not grasp the extent of a wealthy widow's news sources, and for years before her present union, the duchess was widowed."

Lily untied Hessian's neckcloth and drew it off. "How is this relevant?"

The linen smelled of him, of soap and cedar, and faintly of starch. She tossed it in the direction of the reading chair.

"Her Grace of Quimbey keeps journals and thus was able to regale me with astonishing details. Lawrence Delmar was an exceedingly handsome, friendly fellow. The ladies all noticed him, from the maids, to the laundresses, to the occasional visitor paying a call on Walter. Delmar lived in and served as much as a man of business as a house steward. For a young man, he had a lot of responsibility, but he also rose to whatever challenge Walter Leggett threw at him."

Next, Lily opened the buttons at the top of Hessian's shirt. "Uncle speaks well of those with ambition, until they're wealthy. Then they become encroaching mushrooms."

"Lily, if you persist..."

She kissed him. "One can't be comfortable in a bed when fully clothed. Finish your story."

Hessian held her so her face was pressed to his shoulder. "How am I to think logically when you are removing my clothing?"

He let her go, and Lily subsided against him. Had he kept his hands to himself in aid of self-restraint? That would be very like Hessian Kettering.

"Delmar and Walter had a spectacular falling-out," he went on. "The shouting could be heard throughout the house, though such a disagreement was unprecedented in their relationship. Nobody knows if the subject was permission to court your sister, a financial matter, or something else entirely. The next morning, Delmar was gone, and your sister was missing as well. Nobody saw them leave, and Walter was soon putting it about that his niece was off to a fine finishing school in Switzerland."

"And Uncle has never had a house steward or man of business since," Lily said. "Not that I know of, nor has he permitted Oscar to learn much about the finances."

"Your hair... Do you use French soap? I can't place the fragrance."

Hessian sniffed right above Lily's ear, and beneath the cozy covers, she shivered. "I buy it from a shop in Chelsea. If my sister is kicking her heels in Scotland, Uncle is probably that much more desperate to get her money out of the trust accounts and into his own hands."

Next came more of a nuzzle than a sniff.

"If Walter knows your sister is alive and well. Maybe she served him a portion of his own recipe and dissembled about her demise, the better to be left in peace."

Quiet stretched, with only the crackling of the fire to mark the moment. Lily tried to think—tried to parse how Hessian's discoveries would impact Walter's behavior—and was foiled by a welter of sensations.

Hessian's fingers, casually stroking her arm. The beat of his heart beneath her cheek. The sheer, shameless relief of being close to him.

"I should be packing for Scotland," Lily said. "I don't want to move."

Hessian shifted to peer down at her. "You cannot in any way let your uncle know what you've learned, Lily. For the next two weeks, he controls the money, but it's in trust for you, your sister, your ducal relations, somebody. If he has you followed to Scotland and learns that the real heiress is alive, what will he do? Look at the lengths he's gone to with you. Two years in an exclusive finishing school, an elaborate charade, significant expense, this farcical notion of marrying you to Oscar."

"You're saying Uncle is desperate."

Hessian brushed her hair back from her brow. "Only a desperate man would risk deceiving ducal in-laws for years on end, much less defrauding them of settlements that in all likelihood should have reverted to their hands."

"But if my sister—"

He kissed her, barely a peck on the lips. "I will go to Scotland. I'll investigate your sister's circumstances, if indeed Mrs. Delmar is your sister. You must stay here and carry off one last deception, Lily. You have always done your uncle's bidding, however much you might grumble. You must for two more weeks be that resentful but submissive niece and give me time to untangle this mess."

They would be the longest two weeks of her life. "I'd rather go myself," Lily said, winnowing her fingers through Hessian's hair. "If my sister is alive, I want to hear her explanation. I want to see her. I want to know what she can tell me about who my father is."

Hessian dropped his forehead to Lily's. "If you attempted the journey to Scotland, the instant your uncle caught up to you—there being very few wellborn redheaded young ladies traveling the Great North Road at speed— he would claim you've taken leave of your senses and apply to become your guardian. I beg you, don't give him that opportunity."

Recent threats from Walter suggested he would enact even that plan.

"Be careful," Lily said, holding Hessian tightly. "Please, be very, very careful."

He wrapped his arms around her, Lily shifted, and as if the room had been shaken by thunder, she realized that despite all the information Hessian had conveyed, despite the clear thinking he was capable of, he had also convincingly dissembled for the second time in one day.

Hessian had been a dutiful reporter, he was prepared to gallop forth on his next assignment, and his affections thus far had been bestowed reluctantly.

And yet, he was aroused. He was utterly, absolutely, wonderfully aroused.

CHAPTER SEVENTEEN

Hessian buried his face against Lily's shoulder and buried a coach-load of self-reproach as well.

He'd had such worthy ambitions for his day: interview the former governess, speak with the duchess, report to Lily, and formulate the next step in a plan to see her freed from Walter Leggett's schemes.

Items notably missing from that agenda had included:

Playacting to cozen confidential information from an unsuspecting innkeeper.

Peering into kitchen windows and climbing through same to inspect the governess's personal abode.

Perching like London's most unlikely gargoyle outside Lily's window and watching her drift off to sleep before the fire.

Climbing into bed with Lily for any reason, even to comfort her amid upheaval that would have sent a woman of lesser fortitude into strong hysterics.

Making love with Lily.

Hessian had tried to stand fast against the need to hold her, touch her, kiss her. Without even trying, Lily had blasted through his best intentions, and here he was, hard as any standing stone decorating the Cumbrian countryside.

"Lily, this isn't wise."

She stroked his hair. "It's much too late for wisdom, Hessian. Wisdom would have prevented my mother from risking my conception—and my father, whoever he might be. Wisdom would have put somebody trustworthy in charge of Mama's money rather than my varlet of an uncle. Wisdom would have seen me raised somewhere other than a coaching inn and never let my sister be lost to me. We must make our own wisdom now."

Her illogic was beguiling, her touch was irresistible. Hessian allowed himself a protracted kiss that started off tender and ended up incendiary.

Bad idea. Glorious, bad idea. "When I come back from Scotland, we can discuss—"

Lily resumed kissing him, bringing up the topics of desire, pleasure, and present joys rather than distant negotiations or headlong journeys. She had a firm grasp of the subject matter and a firmer grasp of Hessian himself.

"I want you naked, Hessian, and I want you badly."

As an accomplished horseman, Hessian knew of two strategies for dealing with a runaway mount. The first, learned early in a horseman's career, instructed the rider to use main strength to pull the horse's head around to the rider's knee, to force the beast to travel in smaller and smaller circles, which necessarily resulted in a reduction in speed—or in a series of vigorous bucks aided by the physics of a curve taken at a gallop.

The second strategy was one Hessian had come upon on his own: allow the creature to run free. Revel in the privilege of being one with an equine glorying in its natural spirits and pray God the footing was sound. Exhaustion usually brought the horse back under control soon enough, without a fruitless and often dangerous battle waged by the rider.

Hessian also theorized—hoped, more like—that knowing the occasional wild dash was permitted allowed a spirited animal to better tolerate domestication. Horse after horse had proved his theory worthy.

Hessian was not a horse, but the compulsion to dash headlong, despite all caution to the contrary, pounded through his veins.

He extricated himself from Lily's arms and sat back. Her gaze held reproach and disappointment... until he untied the bow in the center of her nightgown's décolletage. Then she smiled, and the considerable animal spirits lurking in Hessian's soul sprang into a joyous gallop.

"This is not wise," he said. "But for us, now, I cannot think it wrong."

He pulled his shirt over his head, and Lily's smile became all the encouragement he needed to shed his breeches and help her out of her nightgown. She beheld him as if he were her every passionate fantasy brought to life, and then she beckoned.

Hessian straddled her, his eyes closed lest the sight of her unclothed send his best intentions straight into the ditch. She brushed her hand over his chest, stroking the fine hair more than his skin. The effect was maddening, until her hand drifted lower and lower still.

"The last time," she said, "I didn't get to see you. I like this better."

Hessian loved this—loved the gloss of her fingers over his cock, his stones, every part of him that knew nothing of plans, schedules, or calendars, and everything of wild pleasure.

"I like it all," he said. "I like your every touch, your sighs, your kisses, your passion. I like your silences and your tart tongue. I like—I like that rather a lot."

She'd sleeved him with her grip and begun a slow stroking.

Then, "I like that rather too much. My turn to play, Lily."

She was gracious in victory, letting him put his hands and mouth to her breasts, until she was an undulating sea of desire beneath him.

Hessian had been faithful to his wife, but he'd not been a saint before or since his first marriage. Nothing in his experience prepared him for the enchantment that intimacies with Lily wove. The experience was profoundly physical—and pleasurable—but also an encounter of the heart. Pleasing Lily was not only a matter of consideration, but also the measure of his own satisfaction.

"Hessian Kettering, you have toyed with me long enough."

Not nearly. He braced himself above her nonetheless, because the hour was late, and morning would arrive all too soon.

"That feels…" Lily's sigh was the sweetest benediction. "You feel marvelous."

Her body eased around him in glorious welcome, and then thought was impossible. All was pleasure, stretched between clamoring desire and a lover's determination to deliver his lady more satisfaction than one mortal woman could endure.

Hessian succeeded—barely—for Lily had apparently been intent on a reciprocal goal. She lashed her legs around his flanks and counterpointed his thrusts until Hessian's control began to slip.

Lily unraveled beneath him, and Hessian withdrew even as his own satisfaction overtook him. He shuddered his release against her belly, heaving as if he'd been run to ebullient exhaustion.

Which he had. He drifted into the drowsy aftermath, heedless of tomorrow's challenges, heedless of anything save the soft rise and fall of Lily's breasts against his chest. Her legs fell to his sides, flesh caressing flesh in yet more sweetness.

"I cannot let you go, Hessian." She sounded dazed and disgruntled.

"At present, I can barely move."

Lily smacked his bum—gently—which helped him pull together the scattered parts of his mind. Some brave, determined soul needed to leave the bed and locate a damp flannel. Hessian nominated himself, for Lily could not move until he peeled himself away from her.

In fact, she did not move even when he was standing beside the bed, the damp flannel in his hand. The picture she made—naked, tousled, replete—sent naughty thoughts coursing through him, when he should not have been able to sustain a naughty thought for the next week at least.

"You withdrew," she said, stroking his hair as he swabbed at her belly.

"I nearly couldn't." Nearly hadn't. "And withdrawing is not a guarantee of anything."

"So why do it?"

"Because we are not married." Weren't even engaged. "Any reduction in the likelihood of conception should be encouraged."

Logic was trickling back into Hessian's brain, and he resented it for the irritant it had become: The preferred approach to preventing conception was to keep one's breeches buttoned.

"You'll come back." Lily spoke with assurance, and yet, her eyes held a question.

"I will return from Scotland, but that's not enough, Lily. I must return with enough proof of Walter's scheme to pry his fingers from your fortune and your future. By traveling north, I leave you to face a significant risk, for we have no guarantee Walter will wait another two weeks to see you wed to Oscar."

Lily studied the cloth in Hessian's hand, then flipped the covers up. "But that ceremony will not be valid."

Hessian took the flannel behind the privacy screen rinsed it thoroughly, and wrung it far more tightly than the occasion warranted.

He came back to the bed and sat at Lily's hip. "The ceremony will not be valid, but you must go through with it, lest Walter become suspicious that you are intent on exposing his malfeasance. And following a wedding, Oscar will expect a wedding night."

The idea made Hessian ill, but to deny the possibility was to deny Lily time to plot against that fate.

She sat, back braced against the headboard, knees drawn up, covers tucked high. "Oscar would not survive such a wedding night, and then I'd be a felon in truth."

"That's one option," Hessian said. "Not one I can recommend."

Lily studied him, though the fire was dying and not much light remained. "You've been thinking about this."

"I've been fretting about it." Endlessly. "I have a few ideas."

Lily scooted over, Hessian climbed in beside her, and they talked far into the night about ways to keep Lily safe, while Hessian was hundreds of miles away, searching for a means to set her free. He made love with her once more—withdrawing again—and then slipped out into the waning night after promising her that come fire, flood, plague, or pirates, he'd return to London.

And to her.

* * *

"I never suspected you of a devious streak," Worth Kettering said. "You were always the fellow who insisted on citing the rules, even when we played cricket or got up a team for crew. You arrive on time, you never overstay your welcome. You reply to all correspondence within a week and pay your tithe to the penny, no matter how poor your harvest."

Worth would also have said that Hessian was a firm believer in a good night's sleep, and yet, his lordship looked far from rested in the dawn's early light.

"What rule do I break by trading traveling coaches with you?" Hessian replied as the grooms loaded a trunk onto the back of the vehicle.

Jacaranda might have asked such a question. "The rule that says I'm the brother who has all the mad adventures, takes stupid risks, and rackets about the realm on short notice."

Hessian accepted a leather satchel from the butler, who returned to the house after sparing Worth a nod. The only activity in the alley was from Hessian's household, a quiet, purposeful procession of servants and goods from mews to house and back again.

"Walter Leggett spies," Hessian said, rummaging in the satchel. "He watches Lily, her old governess, his own son, and he's probably watching you and me, or he soon will be. Send my coach out to Trysting to fetch Yolanda, as I indicated on the schedule, and I will be much in your debt. The damned thing isn't in here. Kendall, a moment."

The footman scampered around from the back of the vehicle, leaving his compatriot to finish securing the trunk. "My lord?"

Footmen were to come in matched sets in the best households, and Kendall's complexion would not match that of any other servant in Hessian's employ. Worth noted this as another inconsistency between the man Hessian had become and the rather dull fellow Worth had decided he must be. The Earl of Grampion ought to observe society's unwritten rules as well as those printed in the manuals of the sporting associations.

"I forgot a handwritten volume," Hessian said to Kendall, "a journal, in the drawer of my bedside table. The book is marked with a year embossed on the cover and spine. Might you retrieve it for me?"

"Of course, my lord." Kendall was off at a trot, while Hessian tossed the satchel into the traveling coach.

"About that schedule," Worth said. "Will I have to hire Oscar Leggett in truth? From what I've observed, he hasn't a thought for anything except getting drunk, chasing opera dancers, and getting into arrears at his club."

"Such a waste of good tailoring would benefit enormously from seeing how hard you work," Hessian said, flipping open a gold pocket watch then eyeing the gray sky. "You will look after Lily? Communicate regularly with Rosecroft? Look in on my staff?"

Another footman charged across the alley bearing a picnic basket that was stashed inside the coach.

"You think I work hard?"

"Incessantly, would be closer to the mark," Hessian said, tucking his watch away. "I don't suppose you've come across any more clues regarding Leggett's finances?"

Worth took Hessian by the arm and led him a dozen steps from the coach. "He hasn't a single marker out at any club I know of, not one. Nobody can recall seeing him at a charity do for the past two years, not even in the company of his niece. He attends social dinners, but he's yet to host any this year."

"Is he growing eccentric?"

Kendall reappeared from the house, Lady Evers's journal in his hand. He remained by the coach, a respectful distance away.

"Leggett's behavior is growing eccentric." Which was bad news for all concerned when a fortune had likely gone missing. "What's in that box?"

Another parcel had been affixed to the back of the coach, this one sizable, but with one side of wire mesh rather than wood.

"Pigeons. Rosecroft has kindly lent me two. They'll cover the distance from Dumfries to London in less than a day, if the weather's fair. Kendall, my thanks."

Who was this man? Hessian had thought through details Worth would never have considered, had minions running in six directions, and was attempting a journey in two weeks that Worth would not have tried to complete in a month.

The footman passed over the journal, which Hessian stashed into a pocket of his greatcoat.

"Will there be anything else, my lord?"

Kendall was a young man, tall and lean, as footmen were supposed to be. After tearing into the house, climbing three flights of stairs, and tearing back to the mews, he wasn't out of breath.

"You miss her, don't you?" Hessian said. "You miss your Jenny."

Kendall's expression went from polite inquiry, to astonished, to blank. "Grampion is my home, my lord. London is... not home."

As best Worth recalled, there was a scullery maid named Jenny at the family seat.

"I have yet to take my leave of my ward," Hessian said. "If you can pack a bag and be on the box in fifteen minutes, you may accompany me. The journey will be brutal, but we'll stop at Grampion, however briefly. You will bide there when I return to London."

Never had a footman smiled as broadly, bowed as quickly, or leaped a garden gate as handily.

"How did you know he was pining for his lady?" Worth asked, not that a footman was supposed to have a lady.

"Because I'm pining for mine," Hessian said, "and I haven't even left Town. And here is my other lady."

The nursery maid had carried a sleepy Daisy down to the mews. The child was in her nightgown and swaddled in a blanket. Her braid was all but undone and her expression cross.

"I want to go with you," Daisy said as Hessian took her from her nursemaid and perched the girl on his hip. "I want to go home."

Worth took himself around to the back of the coach, rather than watch a small child wake up an entire neighborhood with an early morning tantrum.

"I wish I didn't have to leave you," Hessian said. "I will miss at least eight outings to the park, four visits with Miss Bronwyn, three visits to a certain toy shop with your Auntie Jacaranda. Your Uncle Worth will get to feed ducks with you, take you for an ice or two at Gunter's Tea Shop, and take you up before him in the park. I will miss all of this, and so much more. You will write to me, won't you?"

The question bespoke genuine regret to be parting—from a child who'd turned the household upside down.

"Will you write back?" Daisy asked.

"I will, though I'll probably return before my epistles reach you. You must do me one special favor while I'm gone, Daisy."

"I'll be good."

"You are always as good as you know how to be," Hessian said. "You must keep an eye out for our Miss Lily. If you see her in the park, you will offer her cheerful company. If you run into her at the toy shop, you should ask for her to aid your selection. She has very few friends, and you are special to her."

This was part of Hessian's plan to ensure Lily Ferguson had frequent opportunities to send for aid or to inform others of her uncle's mischief. Worth was to keep a coach in readiness to take the lady to Dover—bags packed, coin on hand—until Hessian returned.

He'd thought of everything—and of everyone—and Worth hated that his brother was making this journey without him.

"Do you promise, cross your heart, that you will come back?" Daisy asked.

"I promise, cross my heart, that I will come back," Hessian said, coming around the rear of the coach. "You must promise me that you'll not have so much fun at Uncle Worth's that you disdain to rejoin my household."

Daisy squeezed Hessian tightly around the neck. "Uncle Worth is nice, but you're my..." Little brows drew down.

Hessian kissed her forehead. "Precisely, I am yours to keep, forever. Worth, take the best care of my Daisy. No stuffing her with sweets or choosing a pony for her so she'll like you better."

Worth took the child from his brother. "Not even one pony?" Because that was what he must say to keep himself from bursting into tears.

The footman Kendall made another graceful leap over the garden gate, a tied bundle in his hand. "I'm ready, my lord!"

"So one observes," Hessian said. "Up you go."

The coach rocked as Kendall climbed up to the box, and the horses, knowing well what a boarding passenger presaged, shifted in the traces.

"Worth," Hessian said, pulling on his gloves, "you will take as good care of my Daisy as you would of your own dear child. If you must buy her a pony, it shall be the handsomest, sweetest, best-behaved pony in the realm. Do I make myself clear?"

For the first time in years, yes. The real Hessian Kettering was coming clear to his own brother. Greater love hath no man, than he who will cede to another the pleasure of buying a girl her first pony.

"I understand completely, your lordship. Daisy, shall we wave the coach on its way?"

She rested her head against Worth's shoulder. "He promised. He can go now. I will name my pony Grampion."

Hessian brushed a kiss to the child's cheek, smacked Worth on the arm, and climbed into the coach. "That is the best name a pony could ever have," he said, peering down through the window. "My love stays with you, Daisy. Remind Uncle Worth to open the bedroom curtains at night."

He blew the child a kiss—when did Hessian start blowing anybody kisses?—and the groom raised the steps and closed the door.

Worth retreated a few feet, the coachman gave the command to walk on, and the coach rolled down the alley at a sedate—unremarkable—pace.

"I miss him," Daisy said. "Will he really come back?"

Don't cheer her up, Hessian had said. Admit that her sadness is appropriate and then distract her from it. Had Hessian's own grief and sadness taught him that strategy?

"He will absolutely come back, or you and I and Auntie Jacaranda will collect your friend Miss Lily and trot up to Scotland to fetch him home." As plans went, that was a pale sketch compared to the field orders, lists, maps, and calendars Hessian had put together on very short notice.

No matter. Worth's plan was sincere and sound, and he had two weeks to talk his wife into it.

"Would you like some breakfast?" he asked. "I could use a serving of toast and chocolate."

"I'm supposed to make you take me to look at ponies," Daisy said. "This will cheer you up. His lordship said."

The coach turned onto the street at the end of the alley.

Godspeed, Brother. "One never shops for ponies on an empty stomach or in one's nightgown. Are you packed for your visit with me and Aunt Jacaranda?"

"Do you still miss him? I still miss him."

"Yes, Daisy. I still miss him." And will every minute for the next two weeks. Doubtless, only Lily Ferguson is missing him more.

CHAPTER EIGHTEEN

Hessian's schedule was rooted in common sense: Lily was to walk in the park before noon, when Oscar would still be abed. If the weather was foul, she would alternate outings to Gunter's or the toy shop at the same hour, and on Sundays, she'd contrive to visit with Jacaranda after services at St. George's. If all else failed, she could ride in the park at dawn and be assured of crossing paths with the Earl of Rosecroft.

Every day, she'd have at least one opportunity to communicate with an ally, or to flee Walter Leggett's household temporarily—or permanently. Worth Kettering had a coach in readiness to take her to Dover should desperate measures be called for.

In the past week, Lily had been to services once, the park three times, the tea shop twice, and the toy shop once.

She was once again taking the air in the park, a maid trailing behind. The maid alone would not have sufficed as a chaperone, but Jacaranda Kettering waited on a bench not thirty yards away.

She was a striking woman, statuesque and sturdy. "You are punctual," she said as Lily took a seat on the same bench. "A commendable trait."

"Uncle expects it of me." Along with perfect manners and unfailing obedience.

Jacaranda's gaze turned to her husband, who had taken the baby for a stroll along a path fronting the Serpentine.

"You expect punctuality of yourself," she said. "How are you?"

Hessian had asked Lily that same question, once upon a time. From Jacaranda, the query was leave to recite a report, not an invitation for Lily to unburden herself.

"The earl's calendar helps," Lily said, something of a revelation. "I usually resent being told what to do, where to go, when to dress for what outing, but this is my agenda, not my uncle's. When I rise in the morning, I'm focused on an objective of my own. I am not some gormless private in the military, waiting to be told on which battlefield I'll dodge bullets."

Jacaranda opened a parasol, a frilly, lacy business that had to have been a gift from her husband.

"I enjoyed the same aspect of being a housekeeper," she said. "I was in command of a staff and of myself. I decided when to set the maids to beating the rugs, when to send them off to gossip and pick berries. I didn't sit about embroidering for hours on end, waiting for some neighbor to call or one of my brothers to drag me along on his flirtations."

Jacaranda had seven brothers. Lily could not fathom such a wealth of family, though by reputation, the Dorning brothers got up to a deal of flirtation, which would—

"You were a housekeeper?"

The prim, rather intimidating lady smiled and became a different person— mischievous, charming, even friendly.

"I was the housekeeper at Trysting for five years and made a proper job of it. I still regularly inspect the kitchen and larder. Worth doesn't dare object."

"But you're the daughter of an earl. Why on earth would you go into service?"

Worth was now sharing a bench with a slender, blond young woman who'd been reading a book. She was smiling now, while Worth held the baby against his shoulder. Jacaranda looked amused rather than annoyed that her husband would be flirting in the park.

"I didn't regard honorable work as anything to be ashamed of," Jacaranda said. "My brothers were utterly out of control, and I was all but drudging for them. I told them if I had to work that hard, for so little appreciation, I'd at least have a half day off and a salary for my efforts. They thought I was bluffing."

Farther down the path, Worth was holding his daughter above his head, making the infant laugh. The woman with the book was smiling, as everybody must when in the company of a happy baby.

"You think I should have remained at the coaching inn," Lily said. "The work was honest, as you say. I earned a wage." A pittance, plus any number of kicks, slaps, and scolds, with the occasional burn, pinch, or splinter for variety.

Jacaranda slowly twirled her parasol, which in the language of flirtation meant, Be careful—we are watched. She probably knew that, as did her husband.

"Scrubbing floors at a coaching inn is no place for a lady's daughter," Jacaranda said. "My papa was an earl. Can you imagine my daughter scrubbing floors at some coaching inn?"

The infant was once again propped against her father's shoulder. She peered in Lily's direction, a world of innocence in her gaze.

Lily's chest ached when she beheld the baby slurping on a tiny fist. The little mite was utterly safe in her father's arms. She'd never scrub a floor, carry a chamber pot, or go weeks without proper rest unless she jolly well pleased to.

"The men began to notice me," Lily said. "I wasn't safe at the inn, or I'd probably still be there."

"While I went into service because the men who should have noticed me failed to. We do what we must, and yet, you're once again in a situation where you're not safe. Had you not spent those years at the inn, you'd probably have been married to your cousin long since."

Worth rose, bowed to the lady, and tucked the baby against his shoulder. He went off on some circuit of the surrounds from which he'd doubtless be able to see Lily and Jacaranda at all times, while the young woman returned to her reading.

Jacaranda implied that years of incessant menial labor had imbued Lily with some measure of independence, of... consequence.

"I don't dare cross my uncle," Lily said. "I might lie awake, plotting foul crimes against him, but I attend the dinner parties and balls he chooses, I wear the fashions he approves of."

"Minor concessions," Jacaranda said, rising. "Letting him think he has the upper hand. When it comes to major decisions, your uncle has tread carefully. Witness, you are not yet married to Oscar, or to any other toady of your uncle's choosing."

Lily got to her feet as well, hoping Jacaranda was correct. "Grampion is not offering for me. He is being all that is kind, but matrimony is not under discussion between us."

Hessian had been much more than kind, but he'd also made certain Lily did not regard him as a fiancé. Not at present.

"Well, that's as it should be," Jacaranda said, twining her arm through Lily's. "You deserve some wooing, and Hessian needs to know his addresses are welcome."

"Should he return from Scotland, I will offer him an emphatic welcome," Lily said. "Why do you suppose that young woman has been in the park every time you and I have walked here over the past week?"

Jacaranda's reply was forestalled by Avery and Daisy bounding up from the water's edge some yards away.

"We're out of corn," Daisy bellowed. "The ducks ate it all up."

"The ducks and the geese and the swans," Avery added. "When can we feed them again?"

"We mustn't feed them too much," Lily said. "They'll grow too stout to float."

Avery began to chatter in French about learning to swim the previous summer at Trysting, and the water had been cold as ice and many, many, many feet deep, as deep as the ocean…

"That lady paid a call on the earl," Daisy said, frowning in the direction of the dedicated reader. "She came with the other lady."

"Were you spying?" Avery had lowered her voice, envious rather than scolding.

"I was manning the crow's nest."

"Which other lady?" Jacaranda asked.

Lily knew which other lady. The only woman to call on Hessian since he'd taken up residence in Mayfair.

Daisy grinned. "The one with the"—she held her hands open about a foot from her skinny little chest—"and the hat that looked like a blue chicken roosting on a Viking ship, except it wasn't a chicken."

"A peacock," Lily said. "A very attractive bird, though only the male has the fantastic plumage. Shall we find our escort?"

For she abruptly felt the need to locate Worth and ensure he hadn't been kidnapped by brigands or a certain greedy widow.

Jacaranda, with no evidence of hurry at all, organized the little girls and the nursery maid, Lily's maid, and Lily herself in a sedate parade back to the coaches waiting along the street. Worth was soon at their side, handing the baby to her mother.

"The young lady," Lily said, keeping her voice down, "the one with the book who's been in the park during every outing we've made for the past week. Daisy saw her in company with Mrs. Braithwaite when she called on the earl."

"I was manning the crow's nest," Daisy said, taking Lily's hand. "I wasn't spying."

Worth tossed the child into the coach, stealing a kiss to her cheek that set her to giggling. "I noticed her as well, hence I presumed to share her bench and strike up a conversation."

"I should join you for an ice," Lily said, "and you should hand me up into your coach straightaway."

"Excellent suggestion."

Worth waved off Lily's coach, and her servants and companion along with it. He climbed into the coach with the ladies, taking the backward-facing seat and putting Daisy on his lap.

"We're off to Gunter's," he announced. He thumped on the roof of the coach once, meaning the horses were to proceed at a walk.

"We went to Gunter's on Monday," Avery said.

"We can go again," Daisy countered.

The children bickered for the short distance to Berkeley Square, while Lily wanted to scream, and Jacaranda and Worth exchanged unreadable looks. The nursemaid chivvied the children into the sweet shop and Worth put a hand on

Lily's arm before she could follow them from the coach.

"The question becomes, is Mrs. Braithwaite's companion in the park to spy on you, or to spy on Daisy?" he mused.

"Both," Lily replied. "But to what purpose? You've heard nothing from Grampion?" Though he would have barely arrived in Scotland, traveling at a dead gallop.

"Not a word," Worth said. "Though you should know, Lily, that Oscar Leggett has applied for a special license, and barring the unforeseen, it should be ready within the next week."

* * *

There was good news, of a sort: Once Hessian arrived in Scotland, Lawrence Delmar's household wasn't difficult to find. Getting there, however, had taken six grueling, bone-rattling, exhausting days. If Hessian was to collect Mrs. Delmar in time for her to celebrate her birthday in London, he'd have to start the journey south in the next day or two.

All the while praying for decent weather, sound horses, the continued good health of his coachman and grooms, nothing untoward befalling Lily in London, and an absence of highwaymen.

"There it is," said the groom, who'd been hired at the Birdwell livery. "Bide Cottage."

Like many cottages in Britain, Mr. Delmar's abode was commodious. Whitewashed stone rose to three stories across a seven-window façade. Two-story wings spread on either side of the central structure, and the whole sat on a rise handsomely landscaped and terraced. The driveway was circular, with a small stone fountain in the middle and a pair of short, bushy palm trees flanking the front steps.

If Lillian Ann Ferguson Delmar was the lady of this house, she'd done quite well for herself.

"I don't know how long I'll be," Hessian said to the groom. "Let the horses blow, then set them to walking the drive at intervals."

"Aye, milord. The Delmars are friendly people. Not too high in the instep, as you English would say." The groom was older, and his accent proclaimed him a native son of the area. He tugged his cap and unwrapped the reins from the brake.

Hessian had no plan for this part of the expedition. He'd simply knock on the door, explain to the lady of the house that her sister had need of her. In aid of that sister's circumstances, Hessian was prepared to commit housebreaking, theft, kidnapping, riot, affray, and mayhem.

As plans went, it was somewhat lacking for well-thought-out details.

Hessian was admitted by a housekeeper into a spotless foyer, then shown to a sunny parlor sporting a deal of green-and-blue plaid upholstery. Mullioned windows made a pattern on a similarly plaid carpet, and a bouquet of bright yellow gorse—surely the prickliest of shrubs—sat on a spinet.

"Himself will be along directly," the housekeeper said, bobbing a curtsey and leaving Hessian in solitude.

A sketch hung above the piano, of a woman who had something of Lily about the nose and chin. She was young, her expression both coy and pert. The artist had signed the work, "Lady Nadine Leggett on the eve of her presentation." The year and initials had been tucked into the lower right corner.

"She was very pretty."

This observation was made by a dark-haired man of about Hessian's age. He was an inch or two shorter and lean. Even four words were enough to reveal his burr.

"Mr. Delmar." Hessian offered his host a bow. "Hessian, Earl of Grampion, at your service. My thanks for welcoming a stranger into your home."

Shrewd blue eyes measured Hessian over a genial smile. "You're our neighbor down in Cumberland. I've bought sheep from you, or from your factors, and I suspect you've purchased a bull or two from me. Shall we have a seat?"

Hessian had driven past acres of lush pastures, where shaggy dark Galloway cattle had grazed in significant numbers.

"My errand is somewhat delicate," Hessian said, remaining on his feet. "I've come to make off with your wife." Yes, he had just said that. "I'm sorry. That came out badly. I've gone perilously short of sleep." His boots had gone short of several polishings, his greatcoat had been left in the gig for reasons, and his cravat was nothing short of disgraceful.

He was short of sleep, short of plans, short of sanity, and unbearably short of Lily.

Delmar took a seat by a hearth swept clean of ashes, though the scent of peat smoke perfumed the parlor.

"I thought kidnapping womenfolk from across the border went out of fashion before our grandpapas' time, but you're welcome to try. Mrs. Delmar can be contrary and lively when certain moods are upon her. Shall I ring for tea?"

This was not a man who rattled or took offense easily. Some of the dreadful tension Hessian had carried for nearly four hundred miles eased.

"A pot of tea would be appreciated." Hessian took a matching chair, grateful for something to sit on that neither jostled nor rocked. "In the normal course, I'd maunder on about the weather or your fine pastures and gradually wander around to admiring that sketch above the piano. I take it that's your wife's mother?"

"'Tis. I never had the pleasure. Her ladyship died before my bride and I spoke our vows."

Delmar had the Scottish ability to hold a silence, while Hessian felt an un-English temptation to rant, wave his arms, and shout.

"Did you know Mrs. Delmar has a younger half-sister?"

Delmar swore in Gaelic, something about bull pizzles and the English always bringing trouble behind a polite smile.

"Do I take that for an affirmative?"

"Ye do, not a happy one. We keep in touch with an old friend, who tells us that my sister-in-law is thriving, in great good health, and wanting for nothing."

"If you refer to Ephrata Tipton, her reports are inaccurate, though I suspect her editorializing is well-intended. Lily is in good health, but she wants very much for freedom from Walter Leggett's schemes."

Another oath, this one referring to greedy, black-hearted, conscienceless bastards.

"I cannot claim to be fluent in the Erse, Mr. Delmar, but I did grow up in Cumberland and have studied a number of languages besides English."

"I will call Walter Leggett a black-hearted, conscienceless bastard to his smiling face," Delmar said. "My wife will call him worse than that. A greedier man I never met, nor one less grateful for all the privileges of his station. Which brings us to the interesting question: What is your role, my lord? Are you married to my sister-in-law? A suitor, perhaps?"

"I'm the man who will bring her some long-overdue answers." And Hessian was Lily's lover, for now.

"A hopeful, then. The English must do everything their own way, I suppose. Mrs. Delmar has gone into the village with my sister. They claim they're visiting the shops, but we have a bakery that makes scones no mortal man or woman should resist. If we're lucky, Cook will put a few on the tray for us."

The tray Delmar hadn't ordered, but which nonetheless showed up in the very next moment. The offerings were enough to make Hessian's belly rumble and his spirits rise. Aromatic China black tea brewed to full strength, scones, butter, biscuits, peeled oranges, and that particularly Scottish confection, tablet.

Hessian made himself eat, because he was famished, and because Delmar, for all his geniality, was not to be underestimated.

Then too, the scones were luscious.

"What do you know of Walter Leggett?" Delmar asked as Hessian finished his third cup of tea.

"Not enough. He socializes selectively, and I suspect our paths would never have crossed but for two things. First, he and my father were friends and I sought to respect that connection when I took up residence in London earlier this year. Second, my brother is something of a commercial genius, and Leggett seeks to take advantage of Worth's expertise. What's interesting about Leggett otherwise is how little we've learned of him."

"He's canny," Delmar said, "or he was when I knew him. I learned a lot from him. My great-uncle left me a tidy sum, but said that working for a man like Leggett would teach me how to turn one coin into three. Leggett doesn't gossip, gamble, or chase skirts. Doesn't entertain lavishly, doesn't call attention to himself in any way."

"So he was secretive even before he decided to substitute one niece for another?"

Delmar dusted his hands over the tea tray, peered into his empty cup, set it back on the tray, then folded his serviette just so.

Hessian munched a scone and held his peace.

"I've suspected that's what Leggett was about," Delmar said. "I don't bother with the London papers. What good would they do me when Leggett all but hides? We mind our own business, and Leggett has been content to do likewise. Now there's an English earl on our doorstep, looking like a death's head on a mop stick, and I can only conclude—"

The door opened, and a pretty redhead filled the frame. Hessian couldn't see much resemblance to Lily. This woman was average height, where Lily was petite. Both women had red hair, though this lady's was lighter than Lily's.

Hessian desperately hoped he was not in the company of Lily's sister, because whatever else was true of the lady, she was in no condition to travel the distance to London. By Hessian's admittedly inexpert estimation, the poor woman was about fourteen months gone with child.

* * *

"As regular as the summer mail coach," Roberta said, taking the scissors to the very edge of her cutwork. "Did I not say so? Nursery maids and governesses are creatures of habit and routine, and thus Amy Marguerite is marched out to the park rain or shine at precisely the same time three days each week. The poor dear must feel like a convict."

Penelope's nose remained buried in her book. "Not rain or shine, ma'am. Since this dreadful rain began, I've seen no sign of the child."

For three days, the skies had visited upon London the dreariest mizzling damp. During those three days, Roberta had plotted and planned and even gone so far as to buy a used doll in one of the charity shops.

Roberta was practicing a new cutwork pattern on an old letter from Dorie Humplewit. She opened the paper and found she'd cut too few diamonds into the center of each panel of her hexagon.

"Have you befriended Amy Marguerite yet?" Roberta asked. "Will she recognize you?"

Penelope lay a length of embroidered silk between the pages of her book. "I've told you, the child is well guarded. She often has another little girl with her, a nursery maid, a footman, her aunt, the physically Sir Worth, Miss Ferguson, and the London public attending her every visit to the park. If I snatch her bodily, I am a kidnapper, and even for you, Mrs. Braithwaite, I will not take that risk."

Independence was such a disagreeable quality in a servant. Roberta took up another old letter, cut it into a circle, and folded it into sixths.

"Let me be very plainspoken, Penelope. If you do not contrive to coax the child from the park—I would never condone kidnapping—then you will soon find yourself again enjoying the company of your aged parents and nineteen brothers. Amy Marguerite belongs with me, and if you must tempt her to pay a call on her aunt with candy, kittens, or promises of a puppy, then do so."

Penelope rose and picked up her book. "I'd best locate some sweets, then. This rain cannot go on forever."

Roberta snipped away. "Belinda was partial to dolls. There's one in the spare room. Perhaps you could embroider a new dress for it."

Anything to pry the infernal books from Penelope's hands. Anything to get Amy Marguerite where Grampion would have to take Roberta's situation seriously.

"I can find some scraps to make into a doll's dress, but ma'am, I beg you to reconsider this scheme. Amy Marguerite dwells in the home of a peer. Her uncle has the ear of the sovereign and has married into another titled family. Her playmates include an earl's daughter, and that earl is related to half the titles in Mayfair on his father's side."

"That is the very point," Roberta retorted, stabbing the air with her little scissors. "I am but a helpless widow arrayed against the powerful and privileged. If helplessness is all that's left to me, I'll use it to shame Grampion into doing his duty."

The courts wouldn't see it that way—Grampion had that blasted will on his side—but Grampion would never let his ward become the subject of a lawsuit.

"Did you mean to cut up that letter, ma'am?"

"It's merely so much old gossip—oh, blast." The letter was one Roberta's late husband had penned to her from Ireland, the last trip he'd taken before he'd died. Seeing the snippets of paper all over the table, Roberta was irrationally annoyed with her late husband, her late sister, the Earl of Grampion, and Penelope. "I'll frame it and start a new fashion for preserving the letters of the departed."

"I'm sure it will look lovely, but I cannot kidnap your niece right out from under Miss Ferguson's nose, ma'am. Sir Worth is nothing if not protective."

"You mistake the matter," Roberta said, taking one more tiny snip at Sir Hilary's letter. "Lily Ferguson is finding every opportunity to ingratiate herself with the Kettering family. She hopes that Grampion will resume his outings to the park, and thus she can further her acquaintance with the earl. Lady Nadine Leggett's daughter is not stupid nor she is attached to a noisy, difficult child."

Though if Grampion was no longer taking Amy Marguerite to the park personally, Lily Ferguson's ambitions in that regard were doomed.

"If you say so, ma'am." Penelope bobbed a curtsey and left, her French grammar clutched in her hand. What she was doing with a French grammar,

Roberta did not know.

Developing airs above her station, no doubt.

* * *

"This time next week, we'll be man and wife." Oscar twirled his walking stick, clearly in charity with the world. Lily wanted to wallop him over the head with the nearest heavy object.

The rain came down in a steady drizzle as she and Oscar waited beneath the port cochere for the town coach.

"Have you and Uncle finished negotiating my settlements?" she asked. "I do hope you've notified the Fergusons, lest they take you to court over the whole business."

Oscar's twirling stick clipped his hat brim and cocked the hat down over one eye. He righted his hat and tucked the walking stick under his arm like a baton.

"Papa has everything in hand. You and I will be man and wife, all legal and binding, before the Fergusons catch wind of the nuptials. Ireland is the other side of civilization, you know, especially the west of Ireland. You'll likely be with child before you hear from your father's family, and then it will be congratulations on finally finding a fellow willing to shackle himself to you."

Doubtless, Uncle had concocted that taradiddle, but then, for the past ten years, the Fergusons hadn't been much in evidence that Lily could see.

Oscar breathed on the handle of his walking stick and used the sleeve of his coat to polish the silver. The handle was fashioned into the shape of a bowsprit or mermaid, her hair and long tail forming part of the grip, her head and breasts the rest.

Her naked breasts.

"Oscar, that is not a decent article to take with you to a toy shop."

"Nonsense. Mermaids are fanciful creatures from fairy tales, and children love fairy tales."

The coach pulled up, the horse's iron shoes striking sharply against the cobbles. Lily climbed in, ready to beat Oscar with his own walking stick if he so much as touched her hems while assisting her into the coach.

This was what marriage to him would be like, a constant struggle for the last word, for dignity and reason over selfish fancies. And that would be the daylight portion of the undertaking. He'd tried her lock last night—or somebody had.

Lily had slept with her window half open, ready to bolt from the house if need be to avoid Oscar's attentions.

They arrived at the toy shop, and Oscar commenced flirting with one of the shop girls. Lily pretended to examine the storybooks, but she was coming to know the inventory, and children's tales didn't take long to read.

If Rosecroft was on the premises, he wasn't about to approach Lily while Oscar stood guard.

"Perhaps we might interest you in some of our newer items?" the shop owner said. She held a girl's fan, small, painted with a colorful rendering of a rainbow. She closed the fan, tapped it against her lips, and laughed. "I loved dressing up as a child. Perhaps you did too?"

The woman had white hair in a neat bun, kind eyes, and a grandmotherly air. She was also regarding Lily very steadily as she touched the fan to her lips.

Tapping the mouth with a fan meant: I wish to speak with you.

Lily took the fan and half closed it, shielding the lower portion of her face: We are being watched.

"Dressing up as a fine lady never much appealed to me," Lily said, "but even a small child can appreciate a fan on a warm day."

"Maybe travel books are more to your taste?" the owner asked, drawing Lily away from Oscar's discussion of toy guns and aiming for small targets.

"I do enjoy reading," Lily said as the owner thrust a book into her hands.

"I particularly like the story that begins on page fifty-one. So full of inspiration for young ladies in difficult circumstances."

She moved away, leaving Lily with the book. In the margin on page fifty-one, somebody had scrawled a few words in light pencil: G heading south. Complications. Delay WL's plans at all costs. R.

Lily read the message three times and turned the page just as Oscar came up on her elbow. "Should I purchase your morning gift from among this inventory?" He snatched the book from her. "Travel stories? Perhaps you'd like a wedding journey?"

Lily took the book back and set it on a shelf between a stuffed bear and a stuffed horse. Rosecroft's message had said to delay at all costs.

"I'm more concerned with where the happy couple will live," Lily said. "What have you and Uncle decided?"

"Decided?" Oscar had lowered his voice, as if Lily had brought up a great scandal.

"Let's discuss this in the coach." Lily prayed the shop owner was eavesdropping as she tallied a purchase for another customer. "I can come back tomorrow morning to browse at greater length if the weather is too dreary to begin my day riding in the park."

"Your infernal racketing about will stop when we're married." Oscar tipped his hat to the shop girl and held the door for Lily.

So polite while others were watching, and so intent on ruining Lily's future.

"What do you expect me to do all day, Oscar? Sit about embroidering your initials onto my handkerchiefs?"

"Heavens, no. You'll be too busy embroidering them on mine." He handed her into the coach, smiling as if he'd made a joke.

Lily settled on the bench and pulled the shade down. "Oscar, please tell me you've at least read the settlements before you speak your vows. I do have paternal family, and they will expect that much of you if you're determined to keep them from seeing to my welfare. What do the agreements say about my pin money, for example?"

Oscar had taken the place beside Lily, and again, she allowed it. Make small concessions, Jacaranda had said.

"Why do you need pin money?" Oscar asked. "Papa pays all of your bills."

"As my husband, that responsibility will fall exclusively to you. I'm also curious about where we'll live and how many servants you expect us to have."

He raised the shade on his side of the coach and peered out the window. "We'll live with Papa, of course. Lovely house, discreet staff. Excellent address."

"All very true. Uncle does have a lovely house, a discreet staff, and an excellent address."

The coach pulled into the street, while Oscar left off gawking to scowl at her. "What is that supposed to mean?"

"This coach is Uncle's." And while the exterior of the coach was beautifully maintained, the velvet on the interior was growing worn.

"And?"

"And the clothes I wear were bought with his money, designed with his fashion preferences in mind. The menus are prepared for him. The flowers on our table are chosen to suit his whims, when we have flowers." Which was never, lately.

"What do I care for a lot of wilting posies? I'll be a husband, and that has certain benefits."

Good God, could he think of nothing else? "You will have certain responsibilities too, Oscar. Under English law, you are responsible for your wife's well-being. You must keep her fed, clothed, housed, and cared for. You, not your father. If he tosses us out the day after the wedding, how will you meet those obligations, much less pay your own bills? I can prevail on my friends to get me to my ducal relations in Ireland, but who will take you in?"

Oscar shined his mermaid's breasts again. "I have friends, but Papa will never cast me out. This whole conversation is ridiculous."

Wasn't it just? "Oscar, a university-educated, married man who has no grasp of the financial arrangements surrounding his nuptials is the embodiment of ridiculous. You have the ability to keep my fortune in the Leggett family and keep the Fergusons from nosing about in Uncle's business. If I marry anybody else, Uncle doesn't get what he wants. Make him give you what you want and what you deserve for speaking vows with a woman you do not love."

Oscar patted her knee, and Lily nearly jumped out of the coach. "I don't hate you, and I do esteem the notion of a wedding night in the very near future. You've given me something to think about."

"Think long and hard, Oscar. Refuse to speak the vows unless your future is settled along with my own. You're giving up a lot to accommodate the father who hasn't seen fit to share the smallest of his business endeavors with you."

Oscar used the handle of his walking stick to hook Lily's chin and turn her face to his. Even the warmth of his residual body heat against her cheek made her flesh crawl.

"Try to come between my father and me, and you'll regret it, Lily. I know what you're about, hoping to put off the inevitable. I'll read the settlements, and I'll make sure my own interests are protected. Your safest course is to align yourself with me. I'm prepared to be a fair, decent husband, provided you don't give me any trouble."

As Walter Leggett had been a fair, decent uncle—keeping Lily all but a prisoner to his ambitions.

"Read the settlements. After the wedding it will be too late to bargain, and you know it."

"What I know is that I've recently come into seventy-eight pounds in winnings at the hazard table. While you've been trying to curry favor with friends in the park, I've been bestirring myself to enjoy my mornings at home."

The coach clip-clopped along through the damp streets. Oscar gave Lily's knee another slow pat, and she bore it. Small concessions, insignificant gestures.

Seventy-eight pounds she'd spent years accumulating—gone.

The privacy of her bedchamber—violated.

Thank the kind powers, Rosecroft had confirmed that Hessian was already on his way back to London, for Lily was running out of time.

CHAPTER NINETEEN

"What do you mean, she's lame?" Lily stroked her mare's nose, while Uncle's head groom stared at a spot beyond Lily's left shoulder.

"Came upon her of a sudden this morning, miss. Sometimes the horses like to have a lie-down in the straw, then they sleep funny and wake up offish."

A rural coaching inn often owned hundreds of horses, and Lily had never heard of an equine going lame while resting in its stall.

"Let's see if she walks out of it," Lily said, reaching for the latch on the stall door. "She's a slug, but a generally sound slug."

A large, callused hand with dirty fingernails landed atop Lily's sleeve and was quickly withdrawn.

"Best not, miss. You can make it worse, get her all excited about an outing. Then she might never come right."

This was balderdash, and after a fortnight of fretting, worrying, and putting up with Oscar, Lily felt a compulsion to get away from Walter Leggett's household.

"Then saddle me another mount," Lily said. "The sun is out for the first time in days, and I'm determined to start my morning on a quiet bridle path."

The groom stood very tall, and such was Lily's own lack of stature that even he had several inches of height on her.

"Sorry, miss. We have only the one mare trained to carry a rider sidesaddle."

"Then hitch up the phaeton." Rosecroft would find her, though the wheeled traffic used different paths than the equestrians.

"Young Mr. Leggett said he'd be needing the phaeton this morning."

Tomorrow, Lily would celebrate her sister's twenty-eighth birthday, though Lily had heard nothing about a wedding ceremony. Perhaps Oscar had heeded her warnings earlier in the week and actually read the settlement documents.

Lily dearly hoped Oscar had aggravated his papa with demands for independent funds, and that thwarting Lily's plans for the day was a retaliatory display of Uncle Walter's petty tyranny.

How had she put up with ten years of this nonsense? "Young Mr. Leggett is never out of the house before noon unless he's accompanying me on a call. I can assure you I have not sought his escort for my morning ride."

"Miss, please don't ask it of me. I'll lose my post and have not even a character to show for it."

Doubtless the poor man was telling the truth. "My mare had best be sound tomorrow. Use every poultice, lineament, and salve you have, but bring her sound."

The groom's relief was pathetic, which warned Lily that trouble was afoot—more trouble than usual. No matter. She had a plan, and that plan so far had kept her sane. Today, she'd take the air in the park on foot. By tomorrow, Hessian should be back, certainly by the day after.

Lily informed her companion that they'd be enjoying the footpaths in Hyde Park. The result was several minutes of muttered protests—megrims, rheumatism, an impending catarrh, a sore ankle—followed by grudging capitulation provided Lily put off this misguided outing until later in the morning.

"One hour," Lily said. "That's time enough to break your fast and change into a walking dress."

Though Miss Fotheringham invariably took a tray for her morning meal rather than brave Uncle Walter's charming company in the breakfast parlor.

Lily hoped to avoid her uncle as well, so she changed out of her riding habit and chose a walking dress Uncle had said made her look pale. She took some care with her hair, for Uncle preferred she wear it in a simple bun.

Please, God, let the sun continue to shine.

Please let Hessian be safe.

Please let Oscar be set upon by brigands at the earliest opportunity.

Lily took a moment to inspect herself in her bedroom mirror. "I look different." She looked... like herself. Not like Annie's impersonator, not like a rabbit of a woman who could hear the pack in full cry on the very next hill.

"Hessian will come for me, and all will be well." Let him come soon.

Lily had the breakfast parlor to herself, which was fortunate. In her present mood, she was tempted to start an argument with Uncle Walter, to tell him she expected to read any settlement agreements herself—not that he'd admitted his scheme to see her married to Oscar—and would send a copy to her Irish relations before signing anything.

Uncle would have an apoplexy at that declaration, and Oscar would whine endlessly. Perhaps Jacaranda had been right: Years of menial work in a coaching inn had given Lily the fortitude to handle her present situation.

"Ah, there you are." Uncle Walter beamed at her from the doorway of the breakfast parlor.

Lily set down her fresh cup of tea untasted. "Good morning, Uncle."

He seemed to expect her to say more—apologize for breathing, perhaps?—but she remained silent. She added extra butter to her toast, then a layer of jam.

"I'd like a word with you," Uncle said. "In the family parlor."

Lily saluted with her toast. "As soon as I've done justice to Cook's offerings." Because nothing Uncle had to say was worth a moment's hurry on Lily's part.

His smile was smug. "Suit yourself. I'll await you in the parlor."

The lame horse who wasn't lame, a hale companion unwilling to take a short stroll, and now, Uncle Walter smiling and telling Lily to suit herself.

Hessian, I need you. I need you desperately.

* * *

"You're too late." Worth handed Hessian a brandy, then poured a measure for himself.

"How can I be too late? I've been gone exactly fourteen days, and Lily's ostensible birthday isn't until tomorrow."

Fatigue weighed on Hessian like a shroud, but he'd done the impossible—traveled hundreds of miles in mere days, despite endless rain, lame horses, a coachman complaining of a putrid sore throat, a lovesick footman, two encounters with highwaymen—which had been settled to the satisfaction of Hessian and his coaching pistols—and other factors too numerous and frustrating for human endurance.

Worth took his drink to the window and stared out at a foggy London night. "I'm sorry, Hess. The ceremony was today at Walter Leggett's home, and a special license means the location was permissible."

Hessian could not afford the luxury of cursing, but made himself tarry in Worth's study for a few more moments. "You're sure?"

"Lily did what she could. She insisted on reading the agreements word for word, then she insisted on sending for Rosecroft and his lady to stand up with her. The wedding breakfast included only family, the clergyman, and the Earl and Countess of Rosecroft. I'm sorry, Hessian. We tried. We followed your plan to the letter, and it was a good plan."

"Not good enough, if Lily has been married to her cousin." Though Hessian himself had tried to warn her of that possibility.

Damn the rain, the roads, and damn Walter Leggett to the blackest pit.

"The hour grows late," Worth said, stroking the hound sitting at his side. "I'll bring Daisy home to you tomorrow. She would not allow me to buy her a pony. She said that was for you to do, because you'd know the best one for her."

"I'll be somewhat occupied first thing in the morning," Hessian said, setting his untouched drink on the sideboard. "If you could divert Daisy with another outing to the park and a stroll past Tattersalls, I'd be obliged. I'll meet you thereafter."

"You have to be exhausted," Worth said, turning away from the darkness. "And you haven't told me what transpired in Scotland. There are also a few developments you should be aware of regarding Roberta Braithwaite, whose companion I had occasion to meet. Let me put you up here for the night, and—"

Hessian marched for the door. "Roberta Braithwaite is the least of my concerns. I'll explain everything tomorrow. Meet me in the park with Daisy, and I'll be eternally in your debt."

"Where in the hell are you going at this hour? The law frowns on wife-stealing, Hessian."

"Bugger the bedamned law."

"You are an earl," Worth retorted. "A peer of the realm and my only brother. You cannot bugger the law. Buggery is illegal. Housebreaking is illegal. Coming between a man and his lawfully wedded wife is very illegal, also stupid and bound to get you called out. Hessian, for God's sake—"

Hessian was already out the door and barreling down the front steps. "Meet me in the park. If I'm not there, tell Daisy I love her and please buy her a perfect damned pony."

* * *

Hessian, I need you.

Lily had dithered and dawdled and delayed from the moment she'd spied an unfamiliar clergyman alighting from his gig outside the breakfast parlor window, to the moment when Uncle had explained to her—in patient detail—that her time was up.

She either meekly participated in a wedding ceremony with Oscar and signed the appropriate documents, or she'd be immured behind high walls in the countryside from whence she'd sprung.

"I got rid of your sister," Uncle had said. "I can get rid of you too."

That pronouncement had settled Lily's nerves, oddly enough. Hessian had told her how to proceed, so she'd signed the agreements slowly and carefully. When Uncle had towed her by the wrist across the corridor into the library, she'd found a beaming clergyman and a fidgety Oscar waiting.

Lily had put on a show, demanding that they wait for Lady Rosecroft, whom Lily claimed had "agreed" to stand up with her. Uncle had silently fumed at this subterfuge, while the clergyman had apparently been unwilling to offend a countess, and the countess had conveniently taken a good while to appear.

Her ladyship had also brought her earl along with her, but neither Uncle nor Oscar allowed Rosecroft within ten feet of Lily.

I got rid of your sister. Would Uncle get rid of the earl? Of Lily herself?

She spoke her vows slowly. She sipped her wine at the wedding breakfast slowly. Rosecroft had kept his distance, engaging the clergyman in a discussion of coaching horses, but her ladyship had whispered to Lily in parting that her door was open to Lily at any hour, no matter what.

Lily had taken the longest bath in the history of bathing, and as darkness had fallen, she'd locked her door and wedged a chair beneath it, then packed a few items of clothing into a bundle. She tossed the bundle from her window, though she didn't dare sneak across the garden while light still shone from the library below.

Hessian, where are you?

A soft tap on her door was followed by Oscar's singsong voice. "Lily? Darling wife?" He jiggled the handle. "Have you fallen asleep?"

"Give me a moment." She moved the chair so she could retrieve one last item to stuff into the pocket of her cloak. The slim packet of letters from her mother was hidden in the bottom of a hatbox that was kept on the top shelf of her wardrobe. Oscar could keep his purloined seventy-eight pounds, as long as Lily had Mama's letters.

She'd no sooner retrieved the letters and was carrying the chair back to the door when it swung open.

"You spend your wedding night moving furniture," Oscar said, stashing some sort of metal pick into the pocket of his dressing gown. "Interesting. Why are you still dressed?"

Because I will leap out that window rather than endure the conjugal act with you. "I'm nervous."

"You're reluctant," Oscar said, closing and locking the door. "That's to be expected, but for God's sake, Lily. You aren't an ignorant fifteen-year-old. Sooner or later, a wedding night befalls all women of means. If you don't give me any trouble, I'll be as considerate as I can. Get your clothes off and get in the bed."

She had never been an ignorant fifteen-year-old. "Your notions of consideration leave me less than impressed, Oscar."

He unbelted his dressing gown, revealing a voluminous nightshirt—thank heavens.

"I know what I'm about when it comes to bedsport, and you know nothing. You have no choice but to trust me on this. And if you think non-consummation will get you out of this marriage, you are sadly in error. Papa says that's not the law, in any case. Why aren't you undressing?"

He'd taken off his slippers, and the sight of his pale, bare feet made real to Lily that he was in her bedroom, expecting to exercise conjugal rights because Lily had no choice.

She did have a choice. Maybe at fourteen, she hadn't had a choice, maybe not at nineteen, maybe not at twenty-two, but now, she did have a choice. Lily gathered up her cloak as if to return it to the wardrobe and, at the last instant, tossed it through the window and braced herself to climb over the sill.

Oscar, alas, looked up from unbuttoning his nightshirt at the wrong moment and was across the room in four strides. He was stronger than he looked and had six hands to go with his four arms.

"Are you daft? For God's sake, cease your damned—" He fell silent while Lily struggled on.

She would not do this, could not do this. If she had to face incarceration in an asylum or in Newgate itself, she would never, ever—

"I have a choice, damn you," she panted, tromping hard on Oscar's bare foot. "I am not your chattel, I am not your wife."

He howled, but his grip on her grew only tighter. "You spoke vows, you agreed, you knew jolly well exactly what—damn you!"

She'd resorted to the serving maid's best weapon, a knee to the stones, but she hadn't been able to get good purchase, and her blow had gone wide of the mark.

Oscar picked Lily up and made as if to hurl her onto the bed, when the window banged open, and a cold voice cut through Oscar's cursing.

"Leggett, if you do not unhand that woman this instant, I will blow your head off and enjoy doing it."

A pistol cocked—the sweetest sound Lily had ever heard, after Hessian Kettering promising doom in the nick of time.

* * *

One thought stayed the temptation to hurl Oscar Leggett out the window head first: Hessian had been in time to prevent the worst from befalling Lily.

Not too late. By a handful of minutes, not too late.

Leggett turned loose of Lily as if she'd sprouted snakes for hair. "She's unharmed. She nearly killed me, but she's unharmed."

"Lily?"

"I'm well enough."

"You will soon be in much better spirits, as will I. Leggett get on the bed." Hessian waved the pistol, which was very bad of him when the deuced thing wasn't loaded. Bad of him, and... fun. "Lily, we will need several silk scarves. Shall you hold the pistol while I bind your cousin, or would you prefer to tie him up?"

She withdrew three colorful scarves from the bottom of her clothes press. "I'll take the gun, lest I fashion a noose for yonder noddypoop by accident."

Leggett moaned, then showed a modicum of sense by remaining passive as Hessian bound him snugly hand and foot, and used the last scarf to gag him as well.

"The staff won't dare intrude on a wedding night," Hessian said, giving the bindings a final tug. "Though I suspect there was no wedding."

"I spoke vows," Lily said in the same tones she would have admitted to finding horse manure stuck to her boots. "Uncle promised me a dire fate if I refused."

"Then we have proof of coercion, should we need to reference it in the annulment proceedings. Rosecroft chatted up the parson and got his direction, also the amount of the bribe your uncle paid the man to perform an irregular ceremony. More on that topic later. We must away, Lily."

On the bed, Leggett squealed.

"You will be captive for one night," Lily said, "certain of rescue in the morning. Imagine what it felt like for me to be a captive for years, Oscar. No safety, no privacy, no allies, no respect from the people who should have been my refuge."

Oscar closed his eyes and turned his face away.

Lily stood for a moment by the bed, as if she'd say more. Hessian touched her shoulder. She took one final look about the room.

"Take me away from here, my lord. I never want to see this place again."

Hessian boosted her over the windowsill, then silently closed the window and got Lily down to the garden. Her bundle and cloak were where he'd stashed them on a bench, a fat marmalade cat sitting atop the lot.

"Hannibal." Lily conveyed a wealth of affection and regret in the beast's name. "You have been my friend."

"Then he comes with us," Hessian said, passing Lily her cat. The dratted creature weighed a ton and started up a mighty purring as Lily took him in her arms. "We can send for your personal effects later."

He draped Lily's cloak about her shoulders, gathered up her bundle, and led the way to the coach waiting for them in the mews. When he'd handed Lily up and taken the place beside her, Hessian put an arm around her.

She rested her head on his shoulder, the cat purred, and finally, Hessian Kettering was home.

* * *

"There's a proper breakfast waiting downstairs," the maid said, "but you aren't to go down unless you please to, miss. His lordship's orders."

She set a tray on the counterpane, the aromas of toast and bacon bringing Lily more fully awake.

"Is his lordship breaking his fast at table?" Lily lifted the lid of the teapot, and fragrant steam wafted up. No reusing the leaves in this household, no serving Lily on the chipped every day plates, no forgetting to bring her a tray in the morning until she realized that breakfast with Uncle was the only breakfast she'd get.

She had so much to be angry about, and so much to be grateful for.

"His lordship is yet abed," the maid said, pushing back the window curtains. "Traveling to Scotland and back has nigh worn him out. We're to wake him on the hour, and later today Miss Daisy will be back with us again."

The chambermaid was a solid woman with an honest face and a kind smile. She also sounded as if she'd been raised in the north.

"You're from the staff at Grampion Hall?"

"That I am," she replied, peering into a vase of irises. "Cumbrian to my bones. Shall I come back to help you dress?"

This good cheer from the staff, neither presuming nor patronizing, was another revelation. "I have only the one—" A pretty blue day dress had been laid out over a chair. "Is that for me?"

"Aye. His lordship thought you might want a change from yesterday's outfit."

"I never want to see the dress I wore here again. You may have it to do with as you please." And didn't that feel marvelous, to give away something of value? For too many years, Lily had been denied even the pleasure of consigning her old clothing to the maids.

"I am waking up." Though, when would she see Hessian? He'd been silent on the ride over from Uncle's town house and parted from Lily with a kiss to her forehead outside her bedroom door. She'd been turned over to the care of the housekeeper, who'd soon had her tucked up in an enormous fluffy bed.

An enormous, fluffy, lonely bed.

The maid took a whiff of the irises. "It's a lovely day, miss. The bell-pull is in the dressing closet, and if you need anything, I'm Hanford. I'll wish you good day."

She bobbed a curtsey and left, closing the door silently.

Lily sipped strong, hot tea and mentally enumerated differences: no sense of being spied on, nobody resenting the need to bring her a bucket of coal, no waking up in a bedroom that would never see morning sunshine, no dreading to leave the limited sanctuary of her chamber, no peeking out the window in hopes of seeing Uncle headed off to his club. No listening—always listening—for his voice or his footsteps.

But no Hessian either, though he doubtless deserved days of rest.

Lily made herself eat a leisurely breakfast, dressed—the bodice buttoned up the front—and did her hair. The vanity was equipped with brushes, combs, a hand mirror, and hairpins, and the slippers Lily found with the dress fit her as if made for her.

A tap on her door suggested she was dawdling, though for very different reasons than she'd dawdled for the past ten years.

"Come in."

Hessian opened the door, and left it open, taking only two steps into Lily's room. "Good morning." He looked tired and impossibly dear, also delectable in his morning attire.

Lily remained at the vanity. "My lord. I owe you enormous thanks."

"At the risk of disagreeing with a lady, that is utter balderdash. You had to go through a ceremony with the noddypoop, as Lady Rosecroft calls him. How did your name appear on the license, Lily?"

Flirtation, this was not. "As my sister's name. Is she…?" Lily rose and stood immediately before Hessian. He's said nothing of Annie the previous night, and Lily hadn't had the courage to ask. "Tell me the truth, please. Is she dead?"

"Not unless she expired between last evening and this morning. I left her and her spouse at a hotel off Grosvenor Square, where they insisted on staying rather than crowd me here. I do believe they were trying to leave us privacy, or prepare themselves for a difficult encounter with you. I've arranged for you to bide with Lady Rosecroft after today."

The old Lily, the Lily who feared to call attention to herself or risk her uncle's disapproval, would have thanked Hessian again.

"Am I not welcome here?"

"You are very welcome, but circumstances…" Hessian cradled Lily's cheek against his palm. "If I were to close this door, you'd be on that bed in the next half minute. I'm a peer of the realm and, more to the point, a gentleman. Your good name must be protected, now more than ever, and certain topics must be resolved between us. We're to meet your sister in the park in about an hour."

Meet your sister… They were wonderful words, also unsettling. "Stay with me, Hessian. Don't abandon me to her company, please. Annie is my sister, but there's much I don't understand."

He dropped his hand. "I was more intent on getting her to London than sorting out ancient history. Then too, her husband is formidably protective. I think you'll like Mr. Delmar."

Hessian liked him. Lily took heart from that. She also took a kiss for herself.

"For courage," she said. "Where is our dear Daisy? I have delighted in watching her blossom, though she missed you terribly and made certain all and sundry knew it." I missed you terribly too.

Hessian tucked his hands behind his back. "We will rendezvous with her in the park as well, after you and your sister have had a chance to renew your acquaintance. Mrs. Delmar chose that dress for you."

"This is hers?"

"No. She said you'd spent too long wearing her shoes, and you should never be made to wear her dresses. She's almost as fierce as you are."

Lily crossed the room, the better to keep her hands to herself. "Then why leave me to Uncle's tender mercies for years on end? Why not come back to London, claim her fortune, and claim me as family?"

Why had Hessian had to fetch Annie the length of the realm? Why hadn't she at least written? Why hadn't Tippy said anything, ever?

Hessian abandoned his post by the door and joined Lily near the window. "Worth and I didn't speak to each other for years. We had our reasons and would probably make the same mistakes again, given the same circumstances. I hope you and your sister can go forward without estrangement. I also hope that between the two of you, you can hold Walter Leggett accountable for stealing a fortune."

These words were comforting, but only comforting. Hessian was being gentlemanly again, damn him.

"Is the money all gone?" Though in truth Lily cared more about ten years spent fearing exposure, fearing Uncle's wrath, fearing prison.

"Likely not, but Leggett has much to answer for. Shall we share a pot of tea before we leave?"

"I'd rather share the bed."

Hessian's smile was fleeting, a will-o'-the-wisp of yearning and passionate memories. "If you choose to again join me in a bed, Lily Ferguson, you will do so after being put in full possession of the facts regarding your situation and my own, and in possession of whatever wealth is rightfully yours. Do you suppose anybody has freed Oscar yet?"

"I hope not. I hope he waits until Domesday for rescue. Am I married to him?"

"The marriage is not valid, by virtue of duress and by virtue of the license being inaccurate. At best, the noddypoop might have attempted to form a bigamous union with your sister, which is both felonious and invalid."

Lily accepted Hessian's arm, for if she dragged him to the bed, they'd miss their appointment in the park—they'd miss all their appointments for the next month.

"I said my vows before witnesses, Hessian."

"True, but Rosecroft also reports that the clergyman made no effort to speak with you privately, despite the irregularity of the circumstances. At no point were those present asked if they knew of an impediment to the union. Worth hasn't much contact with the ecclesiastical courts, but he knows the Bishop of London. If you are married today, you won't be by this time next week."

In the middle of the corridor, Lily stopped and wrapped her arms around Hessian. "I was so frightened."

Slowly, his arms came around her. "You're safe, Lily. You're safe at last."

She went a little to pieces, because she had needed for somebody to say those words to her, somebody she could trust. Hessian led her to an alcove and sat with her on a small sofa, his arm around her, his scent soothing her frayed nerves.

"I'm furious, Hessian."

"You have every right to be."

She was also, in a corner of her heart, still afraid. Hessian had said that when she knew her own circumstances—and his—then she might again join him in a bed. Was he keeping secrets, and if so, were they the kinds of secrets that could prevent Lily from marrying him?

CHAPTER TWENTY

All manner of inanities occurred to Hessian as he escorted Lily to the secluded clearing where he'd arranged to meet the Delmars.

Don't be nervous.

Promise me you'll listen.

I have a daughter.

I love you.

None of that would help Lily get through this encounter with Mrs. Delmar.

"You're very quiet," Lily said as they emerged into a patch of sunlit grass.

"I'm very grateful to be done with my journey and have it successfully concluded." To have known you and loved you. He seated Lily on the bench , took the place beside her, and consulted his watch. "We're early."

"You like to be early."

How pretty she looked in a new dress, and how kissable. "I like to be punctual." They had more than ten minutes to spare, which was an eternity to a man in love. "That's not entirely true. Sometimes, I'd like to throw dear Papa's watch into the middens. My grandfather's watch, actually."

He should move farther down the bench. They were more or less in public and would soon have company.

Lily slipped her hand into his, and Hessian damned all gloves to the bottom of the Serpentine.

"What is it you're not telling me, Hessian?"

That I'll love you until the day I die, that if you don't choose me of your own free will—

Somebody was whistling Ae Fond Kiss, which was one of the most mournful parting songs Hessian had ever had the displeasure to learn.

"They're coming," Lily said, gripping Hessian's hand more tightly. "You promised, Hessian. Don't abandon me now."

"As if I could." He rose and drew Lily to her feet. "Your sister is more nervous than you are, and for good reason. She owes you, Lily. Don't forget that. I owe you too."

Lily had time to send him one baffled look before Hessian arranged her hand on his arm and arranged his features into that expression Worth referred to as His Bored-ship.

Delmar and his lady trundled into the clearing and came to a stop. Mrs. Delmar appeared to shrink against her husband—the self-same husband who had dismissed his own sister's lying-in as an excuse for putting off this journey. He whispered something into Mrs. Delmar's ear.

She squared her shoulders and held out a hand. "I have missed you so, Lilith. I have missed you and missed you."

Lily curtseyed. "I thought you were dead."

Hessian could feel the upset welling in her, feel the fury. "Lily, may I make known to you your brother-in-law, Lawrence Delmar. Delmar, Miss Lily Ferguson, as she has come to be known. Perhaps the ladies would like to have a seat?"

"Fine idea," Delmar said. "Fine, fine idea. Lovely morning, isn't it?"

Nobody answered him. The women subsided onto the bench, gazes fixed on each other. Mrs. Delmar was an inch or two taller than Lily, her figure fuller. Her hair was the same shade as Lily's, her eyes the same gentian blue. She was the plainer of the two, for all her dress was the more fashionable, her bonnet the fancier.

And yet, the sisters inclined toward each other at the same angle, drew back at the same time, and both said, "Well..." at the same instant.

Hessian ached for them, and clearly Delmar was at a loss as well. Where to begin? "Perhaps Mrs. Delmar might explain her supposed death in a carriage accident."

"Start there," Lily said. "And don't think to spare a detail. I would have given anything—anything—to have known my sister was alive and well."

Mrs. Delmar exchanged a glance with her husband, which Hessian translated easily: This is hard/I have faith in you.

"Uncle was a tyrant," Mrs. Delmar began. "I was still in the schoolroom, and he had ideas for which spotty heir or gouty old ruralizing earl I should marry."

Mr. Delmar cleared his throat. Hessian examined the canopy of lush foliage above rather than point out that the Kettering family had no propensity for gout, and the present titleholder was not old.

"Uncle is still a tyrant," Lily said, "and he all but married me to Oscar just yesterday. You at least had the Ferguson relations taking a hand in your affairs, while I… I had my cat."

"The Fergusons? They were so angry with Mama for turning the head of their darling baby boy, they took no interest in me at all. I gather the present duke is a decent fellow, but I only met him the once, when he was traveling down from university. He's your father, you know. The present duke, that is."

Lily reached up blindly, and Hessian took her hand. Damn the proprieties and damn the present duke.

"He has no idea you exist," Mrs. Delmar went on. "The affair was doomed. A man, even a duke, cannot marry his brother's widow. He eventually married some marquess's sister, but as far as he's concerned, his brother's line has died out—brother, sister-in-law, and daughter."

Lily sat for a moment with her eyes closed. When she opened them, she released Hessian's hand. "Does Uncle Walter know who my father is?"

"I doubt even Walter would have perpetrated his scheme had he known you're a duke's by-blow, and rest assured, substituting you for me was all Uncle's idea. Mama wanted to tell the Fergusons about you, or at least tell your papa, but Walter talked her into waiting—babies sometimes don't live very long—and then you became harder and harder to explain."

"I intend to be very hard to explain," Lily said. "But perhaps this is why we look so similar. We are maternal half-sisters as well as paternal cousins."

Mrs. Delmar set her reticule on her lap. "Are we enemies, Lily?"

Hessian gave Lily's shoulder a squeeze.

"We are not friends," Lily said. "You kept yourself from me. Now I learn that you kept my father as well. That was badly done of you, Annie."

Mrs. Delmar blinked hard at her lap. "You are the only person to call me that, now that Mama is gone."

Lily's expression remained impassive. "Tell me about your death."

"I nearly did die," Mrs. Delmar said. "Uncle and Lawrence had a terrible difference of opinion, and when Lawrence told me he was returning to Scotland, I begged him to take me with him. I could see what Uncle had in store for me, and I suspected he was frittering away my fortune."

Delmar cleared his throat. "Leggett and I argued about that. He directed me to misappropriate some funds from the trust accounts, and I refused. Our disagreement was conducted at ungentlemanly volume, and Leggett threatened to have me arrested for stealing."

A breeze stirred the trees such that a beam of sunlight danced across Lily's face, making her look very young.

And very brave. Hessian fell in love with her for about the fourth time that morning.

"Tippy mentioned something recently," Lily said, "about Mama being constantly criticized growing up, and Uncle able to do no wrong. He apparently played fast and free with Mama's money, tossed out threats of criminal prosecution in several directions, and generally comported himself like a brat overdue for a spanking."

"He certainly threatened Tippy," Mrs. Delmar said. "Threatened to cut her off without a penny, threatened to lay the whole ruse with you at her feet."

Lily sat quite tall. "Not a ruse, Annie. An elaborate and fraudulent deception, in which I gather you were complicit."

"When I learned of it," Mrs. Delmar said, "which was more than two years after my arrival in Scotland, I remained silent. I'm sorry for it, and I hope someday you can forgive me."

* * *

This is not what I want.

The thought ran through Lily's mind like a Greek chorus, counterpointing the action in a drama Lily wished were over.

I don't want a father—much less a ducal father—who is ignorant of my existence.

I don't want a sister who left me to make shift with a lying, manipulative bully of an uncle.

I don't want to forgive anybody—except myself. I assuredly want to forgive myself.

"Perhaps," Hessian said, "if you explain the circumstances in Scotland, Mrs. Delmar, Lily will be better able to understand your motivations."

Thank God for Hessian Kettering and for his ability to keep the peace when Lily didn't know whether to weep, shout, or leave the scene in high dudgeon.

Except, this was the bucolic splendor of Hyde Park, one of the few places she felt safe and happy. Bedamned to any sister who thought Lily would yield this ground without having heard the whole, miserable truth.

"When Lawrence left London," Annie began, "he begged me to stay behind, to make a good match, to patch up my differences with Uncle Walter. I could not do it. I could not put up with Uncle's schemes to marry me off, his constant innuendo about Mama. I made Lawrence take me with him. We could not afford to go by post, so we ended up on a public stage."

At seventeen, Lily's sister had been able to choose her future. Lily was bitterly resentful—also glad for her sister.

"Public stages are notoriously prone to overbalancing," Lily said. They carried as many passengers as they could cram inside, on the roof, and clinging to the boot, and half the time, the coachman was drunk.

"Ours got into a spectacular crash," Annie said. "One elderly woman did not survive her injuries. I broke my arm, sprained my ankle, and took a blow to the head. I was not expected to recover. Lawrence had been riding on the roof and was able to jump clear."

Hessian's hand on Lily's shoulder was an anchor to the present moment, but she recalled all too well the silent tension at the coaching inn when a stage was late, then later still. The roads were miserable, accidents frequent, and tragedy not uncommon.

"But you did not die," Lily said. "I am glad you did not die." She could concede that much, could concede it was better to know the truth, to have a sibling alive and well.

"I healed slowly, with frequent headaches, and I have never been able to recall the accident itself. As I lay in my bed, day after day, I thought about what going back to London would mean. I had no idea Uncle would inveigle you into impersonating me, Lily. No idea at all.

"All I knew was that Uncle had made Mama and me miserable. He'd assured me you were well provided for, but refused to tell me where you were. I don't think Tippy knew either, not then. I could go back to London to my supposed fortune, my excellent birth, my doting Uncle, or I could have Lawrence. I chose Lawrence."

"And we," Mr. Delmar said, "chose to deceive Leggett. I had a cousin post a letter from France informing Leggett that his niece had died as a result of injuries sustained in a coaching accident, nothing more. We knew the Ferguson fortune would remain in his hands, but we honestly thought it would become yours, Lily."

"I never wanted a fortune," Lily said. "I still don't want a fortune." Though Mama had said Lily would be provided for. Had she told Annie that her younger sister would be taken care of?

"And I never wanted you to take my place," Annie said. "Was it awful?"

Clearly, Lily was supposed to offer her sister a soothing lie. "Yes, life with Uncle Walter was awful. I wanted for nothing in a material sense, but I had no privacy. I was afraid all the time, for myself, for Tippy. I had no independence and few friends, nobody I could trust with the truth. He made your life hell, Annie. Imagine the havoc he wrought with mine."

Annie scowled, her expression reminiscent of Lily's mama. "That's what Uncle does. He cuts you off from anybody who might give you a good opinion of yourself, frightens you, and then pretends he was just joking. When I learned that you were being paraded around London in my place, I'd already presented Lawrence with our oldest boy. Tippy assured me you were managing, and I hoped you might make the good match Uncle was always trying to arrange for me."

"To Oscar the noddypoop?"

They shared a smile, and Lily felt a spark of hope.

"If I might ask," Hessian interjected, "how did you learn Lily had taken your place?"

Excellent question. Lily also wanted to know why her own sister hadn't done anything to re-establish contact.

"Tippy was my governess," Annie said, "my rock, when Mama died and thereafter. Lawrence didn't think it fair to let her believe I was dead. He wrote to her sister in Chelsea, and two years later, when you had made your bow, Lily, Tippy began writing back. She was in a difficult position."

"More difficult than I was?" Lily retorted. "Tippy had a snug cottage she could have sold, a tidy sum earning interest, and no obligation to Walter Leggett. I was fourteen years old, Annie. Fourteen, not a friend in the world, holes in both boots, and the stable boys were drawing lots to see which one would despoil me. Uncle offered me pretty frocks, lessons in French, and a come out. Not until he'd shipped me off to Switzerland did he make it plain all of this largesse was conditioned upon my learning to impersonate you."

Squirrels chattered overhead, and from beyond the hedges came the sounds of laughing children and a honking goose. Hessian had been right to choose this place rather than some parlor or garden Lily didn't own.

"I am sorry, Lily," Annie said. "I am so very sorry, but I wasn't much older than you when I married Lawrence. I'm not proud of the decisions I made when I was seventeen, though I'd do the same again if it meant I could have these past ten years with Lawrence in Scotland. I hope you'll give me the rest of our lives to put matters right between us."

Seventeen for a pampered London heiress wasn't much older than fourteen, and Annie had been much closer to Mama than Lily had been.

"I must think on this," Lily said. "I am angry with you, though I don't want to be. I have wished…"

Hessian took her hand without her having to ask.

"I have wished," she went on softly, "that I was dead, that Uncle was dead. I have also wished that you were alive, Annie, and of all my wishes, I'm glad that one came true."

The realization gave Lily some peace, and Hessian's hand, offered freely and before others, gave her strength.

"And yet," Annie said, "I never questioned Tippy's reports when she claimed you were thriving, even though I knew Walter Leggett better than anybody. I am your only family worth the name, and I'm not worth the name."

Lily rose, keeping Hessian's hand in hers. "Not so, Annie. We share an uncle and a cousin, both of whom have played us false. I'm told I'll be biding with the Countess of Rosecroft for the nonce. Perhaps you might pay a call on me there later this week?"

Delmar helped his wife to her feet, and Annie seemed to need his support.

"You don't want to be seen in public with me," she said. "I understand."

"No, you do not," Lily said. "Uncle thinks you dead, and if you and I should be seen together, our resemblance is striking. Walter Leggett must not have any warning that his plans have come to an even sorrier pass than he knows. He has disrespected Mama's memory, her in-laws, both of her daughters, and her legacy. We were young, without resources, and did the best we could, but Walter Leggett has no excuse."

"That is generous of you," Annie replied. "Also the truth. Mama's inheritance was sizable, and if Walter has frittered the lot of it away, he's the next thing to a thief, as well as a bully and a charlatan."

She looked like she was about to cry, as did Delmar. Hessian looked as if he wanted to call out both Noddypoop the Elder and Noddypoop the Younger.

What a fine man was Hessian Kettering.

"We won't let Uncle get away with this," Lily said, hugging her sister. "He's had everything his way, no matter the cost to anybody else, and somebody must hold him accountable."

The embrace was careful and brief, but it was a start. Lily watched Annie go, wanting to call her back for another hug, and also relieved the initial encounter was over.

But what to do about Walter? Perhaps Hessian had a few ideas. He was ever one for developing sound and detailed strategies.

* * *

"That went well," Lily said.

It hadn't gone awfully. Hessian had managed to keep foul oaths behind his teeth, for example. "You were kind," Hessian replied. "You have much to consider." Too much to consider, which was why he wasn't on bended knee importuning Lily for her hand. "There's more, Lily."

"If you tell me I have a brother... but I do have a brother. His Grace of Clarendon doubtless has an heir or three. More family who know nothing of my existence."

She turned and wrapped her arms around Hessian, and he indulged in the need to hold her too, despite their relatively public location. Lily had been so composed, so fierce, with her sister, even as she'd withstood one revelation after another.

"Whether your paternal family continues to be kept in ignorance is up to you," Hessian said, stealing a kiss to Lily's cheek. "Though Clarendon's offspring are cousins to your sister, and thus have a connection to you regardless of who you decide to be."

Lily peered up at him, and Hessian could see mental gears turning. She drew away and wandered toward the path.

"You seem to think I have a choice. If I admit that I'm Lilith, Uncle can have me arrested for fraud. If I don't admit that I'm Lilith, he'll likely have me arrested anyway. He'll be the injured party, taken in by his sister's scheming by-blow, and that's assuming you can get that farce of a wedding annulled, and then there's the small matter of Mama's fortune having gone missing, and if I lay eyes on Oscar again, I will do him a violent injury, which would mean assault charges, and—"

Hessian grasped her by the wrist, lest she work herself into a temper. "Your Uncle Walter is in no position to make demands, Lily. On the way north, I was thrown much into the company of my footman, Kendall."

"He's the African?"

"And a canny young fellow, also very much in love. I have Worth making discreet inquiries, but I suspect dear Uncle Walter has tried to make a fortune off enslavement of others like Kendall."

The puzzle pieces fit neatly, particularly when Hessian added tidbits of remembered gossip to hunches and suppositions.

"Enslaving others is illegal," Lily said, sinking on to a bench. "Please tell me... but then, Uncle Walter is no respecter of the law. We know this. I hope he lost every farthing, if that was his idea of how to manage funds."

"He couldn't touch the Ferguson portion of the trusts," Hessian said, taking the place beside her, "but I suspect he put every penny he could steal into his illegal businesses, and there's some indication he was also involved in smuggling. This explains why Oscar knows nothing of his father's enterprises, why even Worth hears nothing of Walter's investments. I should have put the facts together sooner, but I was distracted."

In love qualified as distracted.

Lily gazed out across the park's verdure, while Hessian resisted the urge to take her hand.

"The Fergusons will ruin Walter," she said. "They won't care about the scandal, and I won't stop them. Lord, I'm half Irish."

This was why Hessian must bide his time. Lily was coping with too much change, too much upset, for him to ask her for the rest of her life now. He hadn't a notion how or when or where to propose again. He knew only that now was not the time.

"You are Lily," Hessian said. "You are the same person who befriended my Daisy, the person whom the Countess of Rosecroft had best not interrogate too closely." The woman I love.

"Daisy," Lily said, her smile softening. "She will be quite the handful in no time. She missed you awfully, Hessian. I did too."

Hessian hugged that admission to his heart and glanced about, for a patient suitor need not be a suitor entirely deprived of kisses. He led Lily behind a massive oak, and she seemed to sense his intent, when a scream pierced the air.

"That's Daisy," Lily said. "I'm sure that's our Daisy."

She lifted her skirts and took off down the path, Hessian racing beside her.

* * *

The scene Lily found a hundred yards up the path made her blood boil as all the recent revelations had not.

Mrs. Braithwaite had Daisy by the arm, while Worth Kettering stood two yards away, Jacaranda at his side. The widow looked ready to arch her back and hiss, while Daisy's expression was purely frightened.

No. No, this would not happen. "Turn loose of our Daisy," Lily said, striding up to Mrs. Braithwaite. "Turn loose of her this instant, or I will see you scorned from here to the Hebrides."

"How dare you?" Mrs. Braithwaite sneered. "Of all people, you well know where scorn will be directed if this child is kept from me any longer."

"Of all people?" Lily countered, stepping closer. "I've the blood of a duke flowing in my veins, a fortune to command, not one but two earls and a baronet who regard my welfare as a serious matter. Do your worst, madam, but let Daisy go lest I do mine."

Lily was aware of Hessian standing to the left and one step back. He'd intervene if Mrs. Braithwaite took complete leave of her senses, but only then.

Brilliant man.

"Your ducal family might like to know of a by-blow rusticating in the Midlands," Mrs. Braithwaite countered. "They might like to know that a woman whom they accepted as a daughter-in-law lifted her—"

Lily relied on the simplest maneuver known to the most inexperienced tavern maid. She peeled Mrs. Braithwaite's smallest finger from Daisy's wrist and wrenched back, hard.

Daisy was free, the widow was yelping, and Lily was barely getting started.

"Do you know what it's like to be a child, alone in the world, frightened for your very life, when adults think only to exploit you? Do you know what it's like to be so exhausted at the age of nine that you fall asleep on your feet and are punished for it? Do you know what it's like to have no hope, no joy, no affection for years on end? I will be damned if I'll let you threaten Daisy with such a fate."

Mrs. Braithwaite's gaze slewed around, for this was London on a fine spring day, and a crowd was gathering. "I know what I know, Miss Ferguson. Don't expect me to remain silent."

Hessian took Daisy up on his hip. "Do as you please, Mrs. Braithwaite, though I'd urge you to wait for a call from my brother before you undertake another rash act."

The widow stomped off, the crowd parting for her.

Worth came up on Lily's right, Jacaranda beside him. "Her companion warned me she'd try something like this."

Jacaranda watched Mrs. Braithwaite marching for the park gates. "Flirting again, Worth?"

"Gathering intelligence. I offered Miss Smythe a hundred pounds to put Daisy's interests ahead of Mrs. Braithwaite's. The young lady was all too happy to take that offer. I believe she'd like to open a millinery shop and has caught the eye of a young tailor who'd be a perfect partner in that enterprise."

"Well done," Hessian said. "And Lily, very well done. I hadn't grasped how to manage Mrs. Braithwaite—gentlemanly manners can be such a burden when one longs to throttle a woman in public—but you've given me some wonderful ideas."

Lily remained between the two brothers, knowing full well that their conversation was intended to give her time to calm her nerves.

"I wanted to push her down and bloody her nose," Lily said. And that was wonderful. To have felt a sense of injustice and been able to act upon it. To have sent at least one conniving toad packing with a few unvarnished truths.

"I'm glad you made her go away," Daisy echoed. "She was not nice."

Lily found the nerve to look Hessian in the eye. She anticipated distaste for a public spectacle, or for a spectacular lapse in manners. Patience maybe, if she was lucky, or even amusement.

She found great, beaming approval.

Hessian kissed Daisy's cheek, though Lily sensed the gesture was for her.

"You have the right of it, Daisy," he said. "The widow was not nice. Our Lily, however, like the true lady she is, would have none of that. What say we all go for an ice? I've been told that in my absence, Gunter's has set aside a table for the exclusive use of the Kettering family."

Hessian took Lily's hand—again in public, this time before his family—and restored her sense of balance and her hope. Mrs. Braithwaite could start talk, Uncle Walter could bring criminal charges, Oscar could contest the annulment, and the ducal Fergusons might be scandalized fourteen times over, but Hessian would be by her side.

And Lily by his.

CHAPTER TWENTY-ONE

"Your annulment," Worth said, tossing a sealed document onto the desk. "You may thank the Earl and Countess of Rosecroft, who both provided information regarding the suddenness of the ceremony, the bride's obvious reluctance, and the celebrant's utter failure to establish her consent. Their recollections match up in every detail with Lily's version of events."

"Because Lily's version is the truth." Hessian examined the document, reading it word for word and checking the date twice. "I'll want copies. Can Leggett contest this?"

Worth snorted and leaned back in his chair. "How many ways do you want to ruin him? He can make a fuss, but the facts speak for themselves. To reveal the defect in the license is to reveal Leggett's own criminal wrongdoing where Lily is concerned. He's better off leaving the annulment at lack of consent. He can blame that on a misunderstanding or his unruly son."

Hessian wanted to ruin Walter Leggett as many ways as a man could be ruined. Lily, abetted by her sister, had come up with a plan that met with Hessian's heartiest approval.

"And how will Leggett account for the money gone missing from the trust accounts?" For he'd lost nearly every penny, thanks to the diligent efforts of the Royal Navy.

Careful investigation over the past week had revealed that, indeed, Leggett had invested heavily in various forbidden trades. While the war with France had been in progress, risk had been low for Leggett and men of his ilk. Peacetime had resulted in more resources devoted to enforcing the laws at sea, and more risk for those intent on eluding justice.

"I'll be curious to hear his explanation for funds gone missing," Worth said.

"If an explanation he has."

"Your guests have arrived," Hessian said as the Leggett town coach rolled up on the street below. "The first order of business for you is to prevent violence."

"You think they'd be that stupid? We're bigger, stronger, and faster than either noddy—Leggett Senior or Junior."

"I'd be that angry. Lily counseled restraint, but I have spent the past week being restrained when I wanted to call out the pair of them."

Worth rose from behind his desk, shrugged into his coat, and assumed the air of a man of serious business.

"Rosecroft and I have already agreed we'd make a fine pair of seconds. Lady Rosecroft volunteered to bring the medical kit."

Her ladyship would do it too. Such were the friends Lily had made despite all effort to the contrary on Leggett's part.

Worth managed the meeting, by arrangement. Hessian remained mostly silent, while Walter Leggett strutted, huffed, and gradually grew quiet, then silent. Hessian's only possible contributions—"Damn you to hell," or, "Name your seconds"—would not have added much to the conversation.

"If you insist the vows were spoken under duress," Walter said, "you can have the marriage set aside. Few females know their own minds, I'll grant you that. Still, Lily is family, and I expect you to return her to my care."

Worth sat back, collecting the evidence of annulment. "My lord, what say you?"

Hessian checked his watch. "I say I have never met a greater pair of scheming ne'er-do-wells. The woman in your care is not Lillian Ann Ferguson. That good lady departed for parts north more than a decade ago, intent on becoming the lawfully wedded wife of one Lawrence Delmar. Mr. Delmar well recalls your plan to defraud Lady Nadine's daughters of their inheritance."

Hessian tugged the bell-pull. Oscar had gone pale, while Walter rose and glowered down his nose.

"I have never heard such a preposterous tale. My niece is very much alive, and I have paid dearly for Lily's upbringing. I admit she has become a trifle unbalanced. Her mother was never very steady, and this story fits exactly with what I'd expect from a young lady whose mental condition is rapidly deteriorating."

Worth pinched the bridge of his nose. "Sit, Leggett," he said gently. "Nobody alleged that you've a dead niece. Nobody but you, that is."

"Perhaps we've heard enough," Oscar said, popping to his feet. "Lily and I had a misunderstanding, plain enough. I wish her the best, and Father and I will just be going."

"You haven't heard nearly enough," Hessian said. "Did you know your father has been profiting from the illegal enslavement of others, Oscar? From smuggling and trafficking in contraband goods? Or trying to profit? Every groat he could steal from his nieces—note the plural—has been invested in out-lawed trade. Your own inheritance from your sainted mama was similarly squandered."

Oscar sank back into his chair. "I don't have an inherit—? Papa?"

"You were a minor," Walter snapped. "Managing the funds for you was my duty, just as managing funds for that spoiled, ungrateful, undeserving, lying, little—"

The door had opened quietly, and Mrs. Delmar stood in the doorway. "You were saying, Uncle?"

Oscar mopped his brow with a handkerchief. "Oh God. That's Lily. That's the Lily who's my cousin. She looks a deuced lot like the other Lily. I think I shall be sick."

Delmar ushered his wife into the room, seating himself between Mrs. Delmar and her uncle.

"Leggett," Delmar said. "Greetings, from Scotland. And yes, this marriage was and is legal. Had I any idea the chicanery you were capable of, I'd have eloped with my dear bride that much sooner. You look a bit peaked. Felons tend to have the loveliest complexions. Years without seeing any sunlight has at least that benefit."

Leggett braced his hands on the back of his chair. "You can't prove any of this nonsense."

"Have a seat," Hessian said, when he would rather have smacked a glove across Leggett's arrogant face, "while I regale you with proof. Roberta Braithwaite has letters from Lady Nadine confirming the conception and healthy birth of a second daughter more than a year after the death of Lady Nadine's husband."

Actually, Hessian had those letters now, and had been glad to pay handsomely for their possession.

"The present vicar of a certain Derbyshire parish," he went on, "has signed an affidavit confirming that one Lilith Ferguson was in the care of his predecessor and sent to work at the age of nine at a specific inn in the same town. Mrs. Delmar has a birthmark on the inside of her elbow that exactly matches the birthmark Lillian Ann Ferguson still bore at the age of seventeen."

Leggett more or less fell into his chair.

Alas for Leggett, Hessian was not finished. "The innkeeper confirmed the girl's employment and description, and further confirmed that her uncle, one Walter Leggett, took her away at the age of fourteen. Said uncle was good enough to sign the guest registry in a very legible hand, and his signature is dated. Ephrata Tipton, now the wife of Captain John Spisak, has contributed extensively to the narrative as well. Shall I continue, Leggett?"

"Papa, we need to go," Oscar croaked. "We need to leave and pack, for this is ruin. A few years on the Continent and we might return, but Grampion is an earl. Lily is friends with a countess. We need to leave."

And now came the best part, the part Lily had devised with her sister's consent.

Hessian forbade himself to smile, though Worth was looking quite smug. "You, Oscar," Hessian said, "may take yourself to darkest Peru, but your papa faces a different fate."

Finally, Leggett had nothing to say. Hessian wished Lily could see him in that moment, afraid and ashamed, held accountable at last. No false smile lit his features, no sly self-satisfaction lurked in his eyes.

"There's money," Leggett said. "The Fergusons have funds that would go to Nadine's daughter upon her marriage or her twenty-eighth birthday, whichever shall first occur. The sum is handsome, and nobody need do without because I made a few unfortunate investments."

Mrs. Delmar snorted. Oscar half rose and sat back down.

"You will do without," Hessian said. "You will do without your freedom. We've seen Lady Nadine's will, Leggett, and her estate was left to her offspring living at the time of her death, share and share alike. She was purposely vague so that both of her daughters would inherit. You lied to the judges in Chancery—under oath, of course—the better to further your schemes."

Leggett's shoulders sagged. He'd aged ten years in the past quarter hour, but his purgatory was just beginning.

"Do you know, Leggett," Hessian mused, "what it's like to have no hope, no joy, no affection for years on end? To hold on to your honor as best you can regardless, to be as decent under the circumstances as you can be, despite all the injustice visited upon you?"

Leggett was staring at the carpet. Oscar was simply gazing into space.

"Mrs. Braithwaite," Hessian said, "had the letters from Nadine proving the existence of two daughters. Her silence on the matter comes at a price, one only you can pay. You will propose to Roberta Braithwaite in good faith, marry her in a legal and binding ceremony. You will become responsible for her welfare and her expenses, and you had best not displease her. She is no longer in possession of the letters, but she has a fine memory for a slight."

"I'm to be… married?" Walter said.

Laughter welled, but Hessian contained himself. A gentleman never ridiculed another's misfortune, even when that misfortune was the most exquisite justice.

"You are to be married," Hessian said, "and may God have mercy on your soul."

Leggett was silent for a long time, regarding the documents on Worth's desk before he pushed to his feet. "Come along, Oscar. We're finished here."

They were finished in every sense, almost.

"One final item," Worth said. "Miss Lily Ferguson is missing the sum of seventy-eight pounds, which was taken from her by her cousin Oscar. She wishes him the joy of his thievery and hopes he'll use that money to learn a trade or seek his fortune abroad, for it's the last money he'll ever see, save for what he can earn with his own efforts."

Oscar remained in his seat. "But I've already spent twenty pounds. Celebrating my upcoming nuptials with the fellows."

"Do hush," Worth said, "before you become more pathetic than you already are. I'll see you out. Now."

Leggett shoved Oscar on the shoulder. "Come along, boy, and prepare to meet your new mama-in-law."

Worth escorted them from the room.

Hessian pulled out his grandfather's watch, but it was no good—no damned good at all. He tossed the watch in the air and caught it. He was still laughing uproariously when Worth returned with Lily, a tray of glasses, and a bottle of champagne.

* * *

"I'm told the bride was radiant," Lily said, though Lady Rosecroft had actually used the word gloating. Walter Leggett's bride had been gloating and resplendent in a new gown edged in cloth of gold.

"One hopes the groom was overwhelmed by his good fortune," Hessian replied, joining Lily on the park bench. "A pity Oscar could not attend."

Oscar, in a gesture that Lily had found oddly hopeful, had returned twenty-nine pounds to her, with a promissory note for the remaining forty-nine pounds. He'd taken ship for Stockholm, where a friend had found him a clerk's position in a counting house.

"The real pity is that Daisy wants nothing to do with her aunt," Lily said. "Could this day be any more gorgeous?"

Hessian was looking gorgeous, all dapper and lordly, though he'd forgotten to wear his pocket watch.

"In point of fact, yes, this day could be more gorgeous."

Spring was at her finest, the sunshine benevolent, the park's trees in full leaf, birds flitting about in the greenery overhead. Daisy and Bronwyn were casting corn to the ducks. Worth and Jacaranda, Andromeda at their side, occupied a bench in the shade, the baby cradled in Worth's arms.

"I don't see how this day could be improved upon," Lily said. "Your family is with you, my situation has been resolved, and all is well." Except all was not quite well. Annie and her husband had returned to Scotland the week before, and Lily already missed her sister, already watched the post for letters from the north.

And biding as Lady Rosecroft's guest was no sort of plan for Lily's future.

"It's about family that I wanted to speak with you." Hessian's gaze was on Daisy, who was trying to lure the ducks within petting range. Bronwyn's corn had long since been snapped up, while Daisy was parceling hers out to ducks brave enough to come near.

"You disagree with my decision to approach my father," Lily said. "I think he has a right to know the truth." Soon, not yet.

Worth, as Lily's man of business, waited for her direction regarding Mama's estate, half of which Walter had been unable to touch. Annie, who'd never known material want, insisted that Lily decide what was to be done with any money and with the Fergusons.

"As it happens," Hessian said, "I agree with you where His Grace of Clarendon is concerned. Rosecroft's papa has a passing acquaintance with your father. He reports that Clarendon is an amiable, pragmatic fellow, liked and respected by all who know him. When the time is right, I'm sure he'll welcome you on any terms you choose."

Daisy crouched before the boldest duck, and Lily wanted to tell her to step back. Ducks could pinch awfully and were amazingly fast where food was concerned.

"She'll be fine," Hessian said. "She has my affinity for animals."

Something in his voice made Lily regard him more closely. "You miss Cumberland. You and Daisy are both longing for the north."

Hessian dug his fingers into his watch pocket. "I keep forgetting I gave the dratted watch to Worth. I do miss home, and Daisy is torn between wanting to see her brothers and loving her new friends. A father hardly knows what to do."

The rest of the beautiful spring day faded, leaving one very dear man beside Lily on the bench. "Daisy is your daughter?"

He nodded. "Her mama was desperate for more children, and I was handy. It's all in her ladyship's diary. Both her guilt for having prevailed upon me—though I hardly resisted—and the great joy she took in being Daisy's mama. Now the joy is mine, though I wish…"

Daisy laid down a bit of corn, and as the duck nibbled its treat, she touched gentle fingers to the top of its head.

"Were you in love with her mother, Hessian?" Would he always be in love with a memory? Was that why he'd not proposed to Lily again?

"I was not," he said. "I was lonely, she was determined, and then I was having relations with another man's wife. I am ashamed of that, but I could never be ashamed of Daisy. I want you to know that. I want to be as forthcoming about my past as you've been about yours. You deserve to know the man I am, not the man I want you to think I am."

Lily took his hand, for parsing out Hessian's philosophical flights was always easier when she touched him.

"Lord Evers gave you guardianship of all of his children. I'd say your transgression, if a transgression it was, has been forgiven. We make mistakes, Hessian, we choose poorly sometimes. With time and love, we come right. I hope my father sees it thus when I explain why I agreed to Uncle Walter's scheme. If Papa chooses to be judgmental, then I'll have some pointed questions for him about my conception."

Hessian withdrew a piece of paper from his pocket. "You are so fierce, and I love you so much."

Lily leaned against him, his words a greater blessing even than the sunshine and the gift of his trust.

"I love you, Hessian Kettering. I'm sure you have four other names, at least, but the names don't matter so much, do they?"

As far as society was concerned, the woman on the bench with Hessian was Lily Ferguson, only daughter of the former Lady Nadine Leggett. The Fergusons would learn otherwise, Worth would handle disbursement of any inherited funds discreetly, and neither Lily nor Annie would provide any explanations to the contrary. On that, Lily and her sister had agreed easily, and to blazes with what anybody else thought.

Hessian gestured with the paper. "The name on this special license is your true, honest name, Lily. If you agree to marry me, the ceremony will be legal and binding. Before I could ask that of you, I also wanted you to know exactly who I am, and that Daisy is very dear to me. The boys are older, they won't be underfoot as much, but my daughter..." He paused, blinked, and put the paper away. "My daughter will always be a part of my household."

He'd been right—the day had just grown more glorious than Lily had imagined possible. "You'll tell Daisy the truth?"

"Her mother, in her journal, said I might, when the time is right. Will you have me, Lily? Will you have me and Daisy? I tramp about with my fowling piece by the hour and never manage to bring down any game. I nap in duck blinds, or I used to. I go for mad gallops and pretend the horse got the bit between his teeth."

Burden after burden rolled away from Lily's heart. The burden of an uncertain future and a difficult past, the burden of loneliness, the burden of secrets, the burden of loving and not knowing what to do about it.

"I want to be married here, Hessian, in this park, and soon."

"To me?"

"Of course to you. Only to you, always to you. I want our wedding to be as public and joyous as my past was private and miserable. I want everybody here when we speak our vows—the little girls, your family, the ducks, the dogs. Everybody, even Hannibal. Let there be no mistaking the fact of our union or that the Earl of Grampion, despite marrying an heiress, has found himself a great, passionate, romantic love match."

Hessian kissed her, a chaste, lingering, smiling brush of lips, but still—a public kiss in a public park, with children, ducks, dogs, and family looking on. Lily was so pleased she kissed him back, rather thoroughly.

Very thoroughly.

The wedding took place the next week, with the Earl of Rosecroft escorting

Lily to the service, and Worth and his lady standing up with the bride and groom. Daisy, Bronwyn, Avery, Andromeda, and Scout stood as witnesses as well, and Hannibal looked on from Lady Rosecroft's lap. When Daisy sprinkled corn all about, the ducks came to join the ceremony, and the situation grew quite messy, also hilarious.

Grampion was beaming as he spoke his vows, Lily recited hers between fits of laughter, and every single guest of every species was smiling too.

And Lord and Lady Grampion lived happily, if not always quietly, calmly, or tidily, ever after.

To my dear Readers,

I hope you enjoyed Hessian and Lily's story, and yes, there will be more True Gentlemen to come. Jacaranda's many brothers are in my crosshairs, as is Mr. Jonathan Tresham—Yikes, did I just get the eyebrow raised at me!

While we're waiting for those stories to come out, I thought you might like to read an excerpt from Too Scot to Handle, the s
econd book in the Windham Bride series, which hits the shelves July 2017. I got to write another braw, bonnie Scottish hero in Lord Colin MacHugh, and Miss Anwen Windham is more than a match for him. There are urchins and wastrel lordlings, and of course, Percival and Esther stick the ducal oar in too. Do I have the most fun job in the world or what?

In September, I'm teaming up with writin' buddy Theresa Romain to publish a novella duet, The Duke's Bridle Path, which features a pair of stories set deep in the Regency countryside. Legend says the first person you kiss beneath the full moon on the Duke's Bridle's Path will be your one true love. The authors say, "Down, fellas. It's not going to be that easy…." Heroes, heroines, horses, and happily ever afters… mostly in that order. Excerpt below, and I hope you like it!

The third Windham Bride story, No Other Duke Will Do, comes out in November, and in October, I'm also teaming up with Carolyn Jewel, Miranda Neville, and Shana Galen for a novella anthology: How to Find a Duke in Ten Days. Haven't we all been asking that very question?

If you'd like to stay current with my new releases and sales, you can follow me on Bookbub , sign up for my newsletter, or connect on Facebook or Twitter.

Bookbub: Bookbub.com/search/authors?search=Grace%20burrowes
Newsletter:GraceBurrowes.com/contact/
Facebook: Facebook.com/Grace-Burrowes-115039058572197/
Twitter: @GraceBurrowes

For information on these or any other books, visit http://graceburrowes.com

Happy reading!
Grace Burrowes

Read on for an excerpt from Too Scot to Handle!

Too Scot to Handle

Anwen Windham and Lord Colin MacHugh meet for a dawn ride in Hyde Park, and Anwen's hat has unfortunately goes missing. Diligent searching behind the hedges reveals something other than a lady's missing millinery...

Nothing penetrated Anwen Windham's awareness except pleasure.

Pleasure, to be kissed by a man who wasn't in a hurry, half-drunk, or pleased with himself for appropriating liberties from a woman taken unaware by his boldness.

Pleasure, to kiss Lord Colin back. To do more than stand still, enduring the fumblings of a misguided fortune hunter who hoped a display of his bumbling charms would result in a lifetime of security.

Pleasure, to feel lovely bodily stirrings as the sun rose, the birds sang, and the morning reverberated with the potential of a new, wonderful day.

And beneath those delightful, if predictable pleasures, yet more joy, unique to Anwen.

Lord Colin had bluntly pronounced her slight stature an advantage in the saddle—how marvelous!—and what a novel perspective. He'd listened to her maundering on about the boys at the orphanage. Listened and discussed the problem rather than pontificating about not troubling her pretty head, and he'd offered solutions.

He'd taken care that this kiss be private, and thus unhurried.

Anwen liked the unhurried part exceedingly. Lord Colin held her not as if she were frail and fragile, but as if she were too precious to let go. His arms were secure about her, and he'd tucked in close enough that she could revel in his contours—broad chest, flat belly, and hard, hard thighs, such as an accomplished equestrian would have.

Soft lips, though. Gentle, entreating, teasing...

Anwen teased him back, getting a taste of peppermint for her boldness, and then a taste of him.

"Great day in the morning," he whispered, right at her ear. "I won't be able to sit my horse if you do that again with your tongue."

She did it again, and again, until the kiss involved his leg insinuated among the folds and froths of her riding habit, her fingers toying with the hair at his nape, and her heart, beating faster than it had at the conclusion of their race.

"Ye must cease, wee Anwen," Lord Colin said, resting his cheek against her temple. "We must cease, or I'll have to cast myself into yonder water for the sake of my sanity."

"I'm a good swimmer," Anwen said, peering up at him. "I'd fish you out." She contemplated dragging a sopping Lord Colin from the Serpentine, his clothes plastered to his body....

He kissed her cheek. "Such a look you're giving me. If ye'd slap me, I'd take it as a mercy."

"I'd rather kiss you again." And again and again and again. Anwen's enthusiasm for that undertaking roared through her like a wild fire, bringing light, heat, and energy to every corner of her being.

"You are a bonfire in disguise," he said, smoothing a hand over her hair. "An ambush of a woman, and you have all of polite society thinking you're the quiet one." He studied her, his hair sticking up on one side. "Am I the only man who knows better, Anwen?"

She smoothed his hair down, delighting in its texture. Red hair had a mind of its own, and by the dawn's light, his hair was very red.

"No, you are not the only one who knows better," she replied, which had him looking off across the water, his gaze determined.

"I'm no' the dallyin' kind," he said, taking Anwen's hand and kissing it. "I was a soldier, and I'm fond of the ladies, but this is...you mustn't toy with me."

Everlasting celestial trumpets. "You think I could toy with you?"

"When you smile like that, you could break hearts, Miss Anwen Windham. A man wouldn't see it coming, but then you'd swan off in a cloud of grace and dignity, and too late, he'd realize what he'd missed. He wouldn't want to admit how foolish he'd been, but in his heart, he'd know: I should ne'er have let her get away. I should have done anything to stay by her side."

I am a bonfire in disguise. "You are not the only one who knows my secret. I know better now too, Colin." She went up on her toes and kissed him. "It's our secret."

Order your copy of Too Scot To Handle!

And read on for an excerpt from His Grace for the Win, a novella by
Grace Burrowes in

The Duke's Bridle Path...

On some stone tablet Moses had probably left up on Mount Sinai—stone
tablets were deuced heavy—the hand of God had written, "Thou shallt not hug
a duke, nor shall dukes indulge in any spontaneous hugging either."

The consequence for this trespass was so well understood that nobody—
not dear Ada, not Lord Ramsdale in his cups, not Philippe's mistresses, back
when he'd had bothered to keep mistresses—had dared transgress on Philippe's
person once the title had befallen him.

Harriet Talbot dared. She alone failed to heed that stone tablet, ever, and
thus with her, Philippe was free to pretend the rules didn't apply to him.

She was a fierce hugger, wrapping him in a long, tight embrace that conveyed
welcome, reproach for his absence, protectiveness, and—as a postscript noted
by Philippe's unruly male nature—a surprising abundance of curves.

Harriet was unselfconscious about those curves, which was to be expected
when she and Philippe had known each other for more than twenty years.

"You do not approve of Lord Dudley," Philippe said. "Did he insult one of
your horses?"

"He'll ruin one my horses," Harriet replied, taking a seat on the saddle
room's sofa.

Philippe didn't have to ask permission to sit in her company, she didn't ring
for tea in a frantic haste—there being no bell pulls in horse barns, thank the
heavenly intercessors—nor tug her décolletage down with all the discretion of
a fishmonger hawking a load of haddock.

"Then why sell Dudley the beast in the first place?" Philippe did not
particularly care about the horse, but Harriet did. She cared about horses to the
exclusion of all else, or so Philippe sometimes thought.

He'd never seen her hug a horse, though.

"I will sell my darling Utopia," Harriet said, "because his lordship has coin
and needed a mount for a lady, and Papa has horses to sell and needs that coin."

Never had the Creator fashioned a more average female than Harry Talbot.
She was medium height, brown-haired, blue-eyed, a touch on the sturdy side,
and without significant airs or graces. She did not, to Philippe's knowledge,
sing beautifully, excel at the pianoforte, paint lovely watercolors, or embroider
wonderfully.

She smelled of horses, told the truth, and hugged him on sight, and to
perdition with beautiful, excellent, lovely, and wonderful.

"Do you have reason to believe the lady who will ride the horse is incompetent in the saddle?" Philippe asked.

"I have no idea, but his lordship is a terrible rider. All force and power, no thought for the horse, no sense of how to manage his own weight. He rides by shouting orders at the horse and demanding blind obedience."

Women criticized faithless lovers with less bitterness than Harriet expressed toward Dudley's riding.

"He might return the horse," Philippe said. "He might pass the horse on to the lady after all."

"I live in hope," Harry said, sounding anything but hopeful. "How are you?"

To anybody else, Philippe could have offered platitudes about the joys of the Berkshire countryside at harvest, the pleasure of rural quiet after London's madness.

This was Harriet. "Coming home at this time of year is both sad and difficult, but here is where I must be. At least I get to see you."

"Papa will invite you to dinner."

This was a warning of some sort. "And I will accept."

"You need not. Papa will understand."

Philippe hated that Harriet would understand. "I'll even bring along Lord Ramsdale, because you are one of few people who can coax him to smile."

"The earl is a very agreeable gentleman." Harriet affected a pious tone, at odds with the laughter in her gaze.

"The earl is a trial to anybody of refined sensibilities. How is your father?"

They chatted comfortably, until the wheels of Lord Dudley's phaeton crunched on the gravel drive beyond the saddle room's windows, and the snap of his whip punctuated the early afternoon quiet.

The sound caused Harriet to close her eyes and bunch her habit in her fists. "If his lordship isn't careful, some obliging horse will send him into a ditch headfirst."

"He's also prone to dueling and drinking," Philippe said. "But put him from your thoughts for the nonce, and take me to see your papa."

"Of course," Harriet said, popping to her feet. She never minced, swanned, or sashayed. She marched about, intent on goals and tasks, and had no time for a man's assistance.

And yet, some assistance was apparently needed. The roses growing next to the porch were long overdue for pruning, the mirror above the sideboard in the manor's foyer was dusty, the carpets showing wear. Harriet's habit was at least four years out of fashion, but then, Harriet had never paid fashion any heed.

Philippe was shocked to see how much Jackson Talbot had aged in little over a year. Talbot still had the lean height of a steeplechase jockey, his grip was strong, and his voice boomed. Not until Harriet had withdrawn to see about the evening meal did Philippe notice the cane Talbot had hooked over the arm of his chair.

"You're good to look in on us," Talbot said. "Good to look in on me."

"I'm paying a call on a pair of people whose company I honestly enjoy," Philippe said. "Harriet looks to be thriving."

She looked… she looked like Harriet. Busy, healthy, pretty if a man took the time to notice, and dear. That dearness was more precious than Philippe wanted to admit. He'd come home because duty required it of him, but seeing Harriet made the trial endurable.

"Harriet is doing the work of three men," Talbot said, "and she thinks because my eyesight is going that I don't notice. I notice, damn the girl, but she doesn't listen any better than her mother did."

That was another difference. Talbot's eyes, always startlingly blue against his weathered features, had faded, the left more than the right. Talbot held his head at a slight angle, and his desk had been moved closer to the window.

"Women are prone to worrying," Philippe said.

"Now that is an eternal verity, sir. Harriet will fret over that mare, for example, though Lord Dudley's no more ham-handed than many of his ilk. Will you have time to join us for dinner before you must away back to London?"

"Of course. I've brought Ramsdale along, lest he fall foul of the matchmakers while my back is turned."

"Man knows how to sit a horse, meaning no disrespect."

This birching of Philippe's conscience was as predictable as Harriet's outdated fashions, but far less endearing. "Talbot, don't start."

"Hah. You may play the duke on any other stage, but I know what it costs you to eschew the saddle. You were a natural, just like your brother. You'd pick it back up in no time."

"All my brother's natural talent didn't keep him from falling to his death, did it?" The silence became awkward, then bitter, then guilty. "I'm sorry, Talbot. I know you mean well. I'll be going, and if you send an invitation over to the Hall, expect me to be on better behavior when I accept it. I can't vouch for Ramsdale's deportment, but Harriet seems to enjoy keeping him in line."

Perhaps Harriet was sweet on Ramsdale. She liked big, dumb beasts. Ramsdale might have agreed to this frolic in the countryside because he was interested in Talbot's daughter.

Ramsdale was devious like that, very good at keeping his own counsel—and he rode like demon.

"No need to get in all in a lather," Talbot said. "Young people are idiots. My Dora always said so. Let's say dinner on Tuesday."

He braced his hands on the blotter as if to push to his feet, and that too, was a change.

Not for the better. "No need to get up," Philippe said. "Bargaining with Dudley was doubtless tiring. I'll see myself out."

"Until Tuesday," Talbot said, settling back into his chair. "And do bring along the earl. He's the only man I know who can make Harriet blush."

Talbot shuffled a stack of papers as if putting them in date order, while Philippe took himself back to the front door. A sense of betrayal followed him, of having found a childhood haven collapsing in on itself. He'd always been happy in the Talbot household, had always felt like himself, not like the ducal spare, and then—heaven help him—the heir.

Harriet emerged from the corridor that led to the kitchen, a riding crop in her hand. "You're going already?"

Was she relieved, disappointed, or neither? "I have orders to return on Tuesday evening with Ramsdale in tow. Where are you off to?"

"I have another pair of two-year-olds to work in hand. I'll walk you out."

Philippe retrieved his hat from the sideboard. "You train them yourself?" When had this started?

"The lads have enough to do, and Lord Dudley's visit put us behind. The horses like routine, and I like the horses."

She pulled driving gloves out of her pocket, and eyed the horse waiting for her in the arena as Philippe walked with her down the drive. Already, she was assessing the beast's mood, taking in details of his grooming.

Philippe hadn't seen Harriet for more than year, had scanned every letter from Ada for details regarding the Talbots, and had missed Harriet more than was comfortable.

She paused with him by the gate to the arena. "You walked over?"

"Of course. Most of the distance is along the bridle path, and Berkshire has no prettier walk."

"Well, then, have a pleasant ramble home. I'll look forward to seeing you on Tuesday."

She was eager to get back to work, clearly. Eager to spend the next hour marching around in the sand, her side pressed to the sweaty flank of a pea-brained, flatulent horse.

Of whom, Philippe was unreasonably jealous.

The least Philippe could do was give Harriet something to think about between now and Tuesday besides horses. He leaned close, pressed a kiss to her cheek, and lingered long enough to whisper.

"Until next we meet, don't work too hard." Up close, she smelled not of horse, but of roses, and surprise.

Her gloved hand went to her cheek. "Until Tuesday, Your Grace."

Now here was a cheering bit of news: Ramsdale was not the only fellow who could make Harriet Talbot blush. Philippe offered a bow and a tip of his hat, and went jaunting on his way.

Order your copy of The Duke's Bridle Path

Made in the USA
Middletown, DE
19 May 2021